COME ARMAGEDDON

Also by Anne Perry and available from Headline

Tathea
The One Thing More

The Willian Monk series
The Face of a Stranger
A Dangerous Mourning
Defend and Betray
A Sudden Fearful Death
Sins of the Wolf
Cain His Brother
Weighed in the Balance
The Silent Cry
Whited Sepulchres
The Twisted Root
Slaves and Obsession
A Funeral in Blue

The Inspector Pitt series
Bedford Square
Half Moon Street
The Whitechapel Conspiracy

COME ARMAGEDDON

Anne Perry

HEADLINE

First published in Great Britain in 2001 by
HEADLINE BOOK PUBLISHING

10 9 8 7 6 5 4 3 2 1

British Library Cataloguing in Publication Data

Perry, Anne
    Come armageddon
    1.Fantasy fiction
    I.Title
    823.9'14[F]

ISBN 0 7472 6940 8

Typeset by
Letterpart Limited, Reigate, Surrey

Printed and bound in Great Britain by
Clays Ltd, St Ives plc

HEADLINE BOOK PUBLISHING
A division of Hodder Headline
338 Euston Road
LONDON NW1 3BH

www.headline.co.uk
www.hodderheadline.com

To all those who helped with ideas, time given, and above all love
and belief:

My mother
Meg Davis
Don Maass
Meg MacDonald
Elder Alexander Morrison
Elizabeth Sweeney
Ken Weir
My brother, for the title

Thank you all.

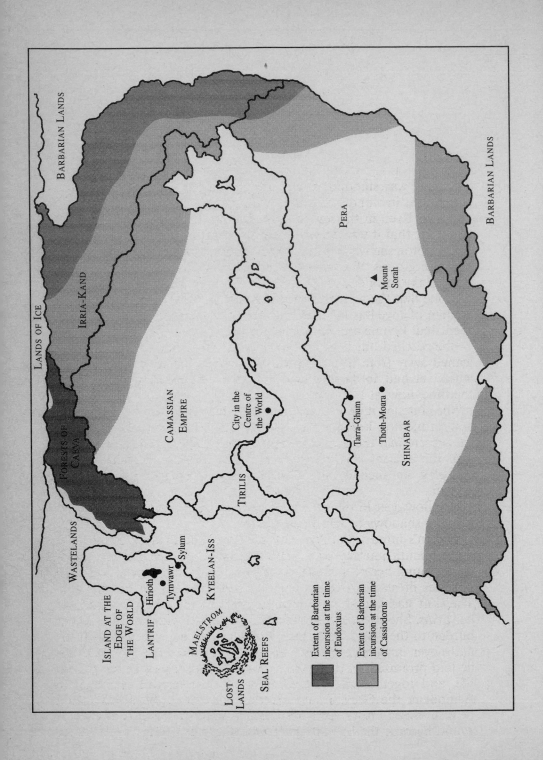

Prologue

The staff was standing alone, upright on the forest floor. Tathea stared at it in wonder and then with a sharp prickle of excitement and awe. Even in the muted light through the canopy of trees she could see that it was carved down the shaft in tiny hieroglyphs.

On tiptoe she walked over to look more closely. They were in six separate groups. She tried to read the first, but it made no sense, nor did the second, nor the third. It was only when she came to the last one that the words were as clear as fire in the mind: 'when the woman of love has kneeled in the ashes and taken up My burden, then shall I come and receive My own.'

She reached out her hand to take the staff, and as she did so it leaned away from her, southwards, towards the edge of the forest where she had not been able to pass in five hundred years. Was this the time, now, at last?

She clutched it and started to walk, shivering a little. She had an appointment to keep, not just for herself but for every living thing, the present and the past. She stepped over the gnarled roots twisted into the ancient soil. Urgency impelled her. She started to run, climbing an incline and slithering down, splashing through a stream.

A fallow deer lifted its head at her approach and then sprang off into the shadows of hazel and birch.

Tathea's mind was filled with memory. She could see the place on the soul's journey where she and Ishrafeli had parted as if it were around her now, the dark slope down to the water's edge, the glimmer of starlight over the sea and Sardonaris on the horizon. The skiff had lain at its moorings ready. She had had the Book in her arms. She had expected Ishrafeli to return with her to carry its burden to the world, and instead he had told her the one truth she had never imagined. He was an angel. His time was not yet. But he had promised that one day he would come and take his mortal life, and together they would fight the last terrible war against Asmodeus, the Great Enemy. If they won, then the world would be resurrected into a glory and a joy beyond the heart to dream. It would become the habitation of God for time everlasting, and for

1

all those who in their testing had loved Him with undivided heart.

And if they lost, then Asmodeus would make it the seat of dominion to rule and ruin all other worlds he could reach, spreading an ever-widening misery until the light faded across the universe and darkness owned them.

Tathea was running faster now, brushing past whipping branches and over stones and ruts, her feet soundless on the dark earth. Briars reached out and tore at her clothes and she ignored them. Old prophecies thundered through her mind. In her memory she was back in the desert of Shinabar again, the hot sand abrading her skin, the light dazzling, and Iszamber's voice telling her that in the final war, when nations plunged into violence and desolation, still the Island at the Edge of the World would stand, because here the light of faith would never be entirely quenched.

It was here that the warriors would be nurtured who would fight Armageddon. One king would unite the warring tribes long enough for the truth to be taught again. The Book would be unsealed and the old glories of the light of God would harrow men's souls, and fire such faith in them as would rekindle the stars.

And at the very last, Asmodeus would be able to walk the earth, and she must take the keys of the world from him before God could renew all things into eternity.

Another clearing opened in front of her, larger than the last, but here there was no sunlight on the grass. She hesitated and looked up. The sky was dark with scudding clouds, and a cold wind whipped the tops of the trees. She felt its breath on her skin like ice. She was glad to reach the far side where the stinging edge was broken.

Tathea was on a path now, and the trees were less dense. There were elders, white with flowers, dizzying scent; ash and wild cherry.

The first hailstones struck so viciously it seemed as if the pellets of ice must leave bruises on her flesh. Stumbling, teeth clenched, she ran on, half blinded. Whatever the storm, she must not stop. Everything depended upon her being there in time.

Thunder rumbled around the skirts of heaven, then, without warning, cracked above her with ear-shattering sound. Flights of birds shot out of the trees, whirling up against the sullen sky and small animals fled for cover, huddling under logs and stones in terror.

Lightning forked down. A tree exploded in a sheet of fire. It swayed for a breathless moment, then crashed down across the path in front of her, trailing gaudy ribbons of flame which caught other branches and blazed up, roaring, crackling, spreading wide.

She stopped abruptly, scrambling to keep her balance. She could not retrace her steps. She would have to force her way through the undergrowth to go round it.

The wind was harder, rising to a high, shrill whine in the upper branches, whipping them back and forth as it changed direction, snapping them off and catching them whirling up in the air.

Tathea wanted to find any lee side of a bank where she could crouch down and protect herself. There were plenty of places. She knew the forest, its heart and its nature. She loved its great trees, its slender saplings, and every creature in it. It had fed and sheltered her for five centuries. If she turned back, maybe this terrible destruction would end. Perhaps there was another way? She stood motionless, her hand clenched on the staff.

When she tried to pull it back, it would not move. It would yield only southward, drawing her on.

She stumbled over fallen branches across the path. Ahead of her the trees thinned, white wood showing in great wounds where the storm had ripped branches away.

Now she was at the path's end. Beyond was open land. She hesitated, afraid. The moment had come. If she could walk beyond the last tree, then the forest no longer held her. It truly was the beginning.

The sky was purple-dark, heavy-bellied with hail. Behind her she heard the scream of the wind and the crash as another tree was rent from the earth. Lightning flared, and ahead she saw the figure of a woman coming towards her, floundering as if heavy-laden and near exhaustion.

The moment of indecision passed. The woman was in need. Tathea went towards her swiftly, away from the forest edge, free from its hold. There was no sense of surprise, no barrier. The storm, the piercing cold, the rage in the sky, told her that the earth itself knew the waiting was ended.

She reached the woman and in the livid, fading light saw why she had moved so awkwardly. She was heavy with child, and close to the time of birth. Her clothes were torn, stained with mud and blood and the dark smears of burning. Smoke streaked her face, and her eyes were grief-hollowed.

Tathea clasped her, taking some of her weight. The woman was shuddering with exhaustion. Her clothes wrapped around her thighs, the long, wet skirts tangling every movement.

'Gently! Gently!' Tathea urged her. 'There's no one behind you.'

But the woman struggled on towards the outlying trees. 'I must reach Hirioth,' she gasped, fighting to keep her balance as pain shot through her and she stumbled, almost dragging Tathea down with her.

'You can't,' Tathea told her more clearly, forcing her to stop. 'Your time is come. I'll look after you. I know a little of birth.' She remembered, with the old, heart-consuming ache, her own child,

3

and the moment of drenching horror when she had discovered his small, blood-soaked body, the night of the coup in Shinabar. The tightening of the throat, the pain through the body was always the same.

But there was no time for the past.

The woman had a strange and subtle face with a beauty unlike any other.

'Who are you?' she said in little more than a whisper as another spasm grasped her.

'Tathea,' she answered. 'But you must rest. The rain has stopped, and you will be dry under the trees here.'

The woman stared at her, her eyes wide with wonder.

'Come!' Tathea urged, pulling at her arm.

'Tathea?' The word was spoken with awe, as if there were magic in the sound of it.

'Yes. Please come! You have not long.'

The woman's eyes clouded. 'I know,' she said softly. 'I shall not live to raise my child, not even to hold him in my arms.' Again the spasm took her and she sank to her knees, holding herself, rocking back and forth.

'Yes, you will!' Tathea kneeled beside her, clasping her as she fought to control herself. 'It will seem terrible, but it will pass.'

'No . . .' The word came between clenched teeth. 'I have come too far, my strength is gone. But I had to . . . to reach Hirioth. Now I know why.' She let out a cry and gripped Tathea's hand so hard it was as if she could transfer her own pain.

Tathea held on to her. A great feeling flooded through her that the woman was right and a stupid and futile denial would comfort no one.

'Sardo . . .' The woman continued after a moment. 'Sardo gave his life to help me escape the city. He loved me, and he knew the child . . .' Again she had to stop to give herself over to the pain. 'Will you tell him about us?' she asked after a few more moments. 'My name is Mairin. I am sister to Aelfrith, Earl of the Eastern Shore. My husband was Sardo . . .' She gulped and her eyes filled with tears. Perhaps it was only hours since he had died.

Tathea held her closer, feeling the pain reach through her, aware of Mairin's failing strength, the violent beating of her heart. She ached for her that she would hold her child for no more than a few moments before she would have to trust him to a stranger to guard and protect his life, to nurture him, teach him, and above all to love him as she would have.

Tathea knew that this child was to be the king who would unite the Island, so no more women would have to flee ruined cities because of war with neighbouring tribes or pirate raids from the

4

Sea Isles. He was the one who would create a golden age before the great and final war. The violence in the shattered forest had told her that, and her freedom at last to leave its bounds, to walk beyond its keeping and into the world.

Though her strength was ebbing fast, Mairin spoke of her youth, and how she had met Sardo, and how they had loved each other. Then her body convulsed and the moment of birth came. There was no more time left.

An hour later Tathea stood in the fading glory of the evening light with the baby in her arms, wrapped in pieces of Mairin's robe.

Mairin had held him herself for a few moments, touched his face, and named him Sadokhar. Now she lay in her final peace, her blood-stained gown her winding sheet, and Tathea could do nothing for her but pull some of the broken branches to cover her, and think how she would care for her son.

She had only just taken the first steps towards the distant village, when she saw the man coming up the rise, his black hair blown by the wind. He was slender, strong, and he moved with unusual grace as though his feet barely touched the ground.

For a moment Tathea's heart knocked with a familiarity so sharp it pierced her with a physical pain.

He was close to her now and she could see his face, the broad brow and chiselled features, the blazing blue eyes.

Of course she knew him. Her soul had known him since before the creation of the world. He was the Great Enemy, Asmodeus himself, walking the earth like a man.

He stopped in front of her and looked at the child in her arms.

'Sadokhar,' he said softly, as if he knew him already.

Tathea held the baby so closely he seemed almost part of her. Asmodeus could not harm him physically, and yet she could smell her own fear. Why had he torn up the forest, breaking and wounding it, if not to prevent her reaching Mairin in time, and saving the child?

Asmodeus was smiling. 'Sadokhar,' he repeated with infinite satisfaction. He held up his left hand and in it was a bunch of keys, heavy and dull-gleaming black.

She stared at them, transfixed.

'The keys of this world,' he told her. 'The power and the dominion of it.' He leaned a little forward. 'It is mine! And neither you nor that child will take it from me – nor Ishrafeli, when he comes.'

Her lips were dry, her heart pounding. 'If God wills it, we can do anything,' she said huskily.

' "Can"'? The word was a challenge, a cry of derision. 'Maybe you can . . . but you won't!' He looked at the child again. 'He won't!

5

You remember nothing, but I have known each of you since the foundation of heaven.' He held up the keys again. 'The earth is mine!' Then he turned on his heel and strode away.

She heard his laughter, thin and hard like a knife blade into the flesh, and a moment later she was alone in the wind and the sunset, and the child began to cry.

Legs shaking, Tathea walked away from the vast prison and shelter that was Hirioth, and into the world.

Chapter One

Tathea looked at Sadokhar beside her, then at Sardriel and Ardesir opposite. All the tables in the Great Hall were crowded with the scores of warriors and advisers who served the castle and city. The torches in the hall burned low, casting shadows on the coffered ceiling and sending a golden glow on to the bronze of half-empty bowls of fruit and the curves of wine glasses. The sounds of laughter and conversation filled the air. The embers of the fire faded and the dogs stirred hopefully, looking for scraps.

It had been twenty-eight years since Tathea had left Hirioth, bringing with her only the staff and the golden Book of the word of God. Sadokhar was a grown man and he had accomplished all that she had promised Mairin he would, and all that she had dreamed for him herself. Some of it had been savage – war and reprisal. She still shivered at the memory of Cunaglass's rebellion and how Sadokhar had hunted him down and, in his rage at the needless ruin and death he had caused, the betrayal of those who had trusted him, had slashed off his head with a sword, and painted his name across the fortress walls with his hair dipped in his own blood. If Sadokhar regretted it he had never said so.

But the Island at the Edge of the World was united at last after two centuries of strife. For nearly ten years there had been peace. The old and the young walked in the open without fear. No one was hungry or sick and went uncared for. Justice was swift, but anyone might plead their cause before the King and be heard.

This beautiful city of Tyrn Vawr had been built, and artists and poets, philosophers and dreamers, architects and musicians lived here, dined and talked far into the night in Sadokhar's hall. The learning and the wit of the world found their way here at one time or another.

Four years ago had come Sardriel, Lord of the Lost Lands, to pledge peace with the King of the Island. Sadokhar had liked him immediately, drawn to the love of truth in him. Tathea had watched his quiet face, with its high cheekbones and cool, intelligent eyes, and seen the passion in the curve of his mouth. She felt in him a strength of the spirit and a fire in the mind, and she grew increasingly sure that he was one of the warriors foretold in the dim days of her waiting, who would come in the evening of time to fight the last great war.

Sadokhar had read the first hieroglyph on the staff when they were still in Hirioth, as she had known he would – 'when the man of courage enters and leaves where I am not'. He had looked at her, his grey eyes puzzled, aware only of mystery. Many times since he had asked her to explain, but finally he had understood that it was something that could be grasped only when the knowledge was already in the heart.

One quiet evening a year after Sardriel had come, when Tathea had glimpsed the patience in him and the swift, secret moments of loneliness as well as the brilliance of mind, she had shown the staff to him. He had taken it in his hands, turning it over, marvelling at the workmanship of it, and he had read the third inscription – 'when the man of truth hungers for a lie, and casts it to the deep'.

He had said nothing. He was older than Sadokhar had been, less impetuous, and she did not need to tell him that only time and battle could teach him to understand it. Now that battle was already darkening the horizon.

From that time onward he had returned to Tyrn Vawr every few months, leaving the stewardship of the Lost Lands with his cousin and ally.

A year after Sardriel had read the inscription, Ardesir had come from Shinabar, and before that from the southern deserts of Pera. When Sadokhar, in his wilder youth, had for a space rejected the high calling he felt Tathea had placed upon him, they had quarrelled, and she had left him on the Eastern Shore with his mother's people. She had gone back to the centre of the world alone, and then on to Shinabar. It was then she had met the younger Ardesir, still afire with ideas, a man of laughter and imagination, an architect who held visions of building palaces, arches and towers of the mind as well as of stone. He sought in the perfection of form and purpose a meaning that could be held in a single grasp. They had been friends, savouring together the subtlety and laughter of Shinabari art, the long desert evenings, the smell of the night wind off the endless sands, sweet wine and bitter herbs, the intricacy of the old ways.

Then she had returned to the Island, knowing that she must try again with Sadokhar. The lesser part would never be enough for the hunger in his soul, no matter how it glittered before him now.

He had stood before her a little abashed, uncertain how to acknowledge the change in himself, and yet his eyes were shining with joy to see her. He had asked softly for another chance, but she

8

knew that he would have wrested it from her had she not given it willingly. They knew each other so well!

Then years later, when the Island was at peace and its fame spread wide, Ardesir had come to Tyrn Vawr and found the perfect field for the arts he had perfected since.

It was Sadokhar who insisted Tathea show Ardesir the staff.

'I can't read it!' he had said with confusion. 'Can anyone?'

Tathea had felt a plunge of disappointment. But before she could answer, he had looked at it again. 'Except this one!' he went on. ' "When the man of faith embraces terror to himself"'! What does that mean?' Then his face had paled and his voice dropped to a whisper. 'Why can I read that, and not the others?'

'Because that one is for you,' Sadokhar had answered. 'As the first is for me, the third for Sardriel, and the last for Tathea.'

'And the others?' Ardesir had asked.

'We don't know . . . not yet, but we will.'

'When?'

'Before the final war with the Great Adversary.'

'Before its beginning?' he had asked. 'Or before its end?'

'I don't know,' Tathea had said, barely above a whisper.

Now they were still waiting for the last two warriors, but Tathea felt the urgency grow within her that time was brief.

She looked from one to the other of them as they sat talking now, Sadokhar telling a story, his face animated, on the edge of laughter, Sardriel listening, his lips curved in a slow smile. He knew he was being teased and the acceptance in it, the knowledge of his rational scepticism was part of the joke.

'I feel we have little time left,' Tathea said aloud.

Sadokhar stopped his tale and looked at her with sudden gravity.

'We have two of the inscriptions still unread,' Ardesir reminded, but apologetically, his face tender. 'And Ishrafeli has not yet come.'

It was the one thing Tathea could not ignore or reason away. It was the single, bright certainty she had clung to all the long centuries. Awake or asleep she had waited for him.

'He has not come to us,' she said quietly, 'but we don't know that he is not alive somewhere.'

'There are other things,' Sardriel said reasonably, his voice soft so that those at the further end of the great table would not hear him. 'It grows dark, certainly. Every new word from the east brings more news of the barbarians attacking, but the great empires still stand. Asmodeus does not yet walk the earth again, and most of all, we cannot open the Book.' His eyes were steady, not wavering from hers.

'I know, but it will be soon. We must prepare.' She turned to Sadokhar. 'You said Kor-Assh of the River covenanted with you to come to Tyrn Vawr. When?'

'Lantrif is not an easy land,' he answered, his eyes careful and bright. 'He cannot leave until he has made all provision for its peace in his absence. But we have yet to speak with Ulfin of Kharkheryll also. Knowing all you have taught me of the Flamen belief, I am sure he will be with us. They above all others love the earth. How could they not join in the last war to save it from Asmodeus?'

'If he comes then we will be five, and if Kor-Assh does also, then all six,' Ardesir agreed, turning a little in his chair towards Tathea. 'But that is not Ishrafeli, nor does it open the Book. Without that we don't have the knowledge of God; we understand only a shadow of the truth and it won't be enough! We dare not start until we have every weapon and every shield!'

He leaned across the table, his elbow against the empty pewter bowl where the sweetmeats had been. His face was pale. 'We fight not only envy, ignorance and evil in the world, but the forces of hell and beyond from places unimaginable. We will be tested to the end of all we have.' He looked at each of them. 'Don't go into the last conflict as if it were something we cannot lose. We can! All eternity depends upon us. Every step must be with prayer, and certainty that we are obeying God, not our own impulse.'

What he said was true, and yet it did not dispel the conviction inside her that the Enemy was closer. It was not faith like Ardesir's, reason like Sardriel's, nor courage like Sadokhar's, it was memory in the soul of wars lost in the distance of time, the touch of darkness closer than the skin.

Sadokhar leaned back in his seat, resting his elbows on the arms of his chair, watching Tathea. 'We need more news of Camassia, and of Shinabar. Are they preparing for war? Are they even aware that the threat is real? Or do they imagine it is no more than the sporadic troubles they have had for centuries, and it will all die down again as it has in the past? There are travellers among us, especially one old man who has recently come from the City in the Centre of the World. Shall I send for him?' It was a courtesy that he asked; he needed permission of no one.

'Yes,' Tathea said immediately, not certain what she expected to hear. She had loved the City long ago. Its golden stones, its teeming streets and cypress-crowned hills had been her home in the days of the height of the Empire. It had sheltered her when her own land had cast her out. 'Yes, send for him.'

'Bring the traveller Eudoxius,' Sadokhar ordered.

The page he had addressed bowed and went to obey.

Within minutes an old man walked the length of the hall from the bottom table. His head was high but his body gaunt and round-shouldered, his features battered by wind and sun. Only as he was feet away was the humour clear in his faded eyes, and the bitterness about his lips.

'Sit with us and take wine,' Sadokhar directed him, indicating one of the vacant high-backed chairs opposite.

'Sire . . .' The old man obeyed, but he did not incline his head. He was a citizen of the world and he was bowing to no Island king.

'Tell us of your travels,' Sadokhar continued. 'What news do you bring of the world?' He was courteous, but there was no mistaking the command in his voice.

'You have fed me well,' Eudoxius replied. 'And given me shelter. What would you hear?'

'The truth!' Sadokhar snapped. 'When I want tales I will send for a bard and have them to music!'

Eudoxius' weary eyes opened a little wider, there was an instant's black laughter in his face, and then it was gone again. 'Shinabar is rotten to the core,' he said very quietly. 'They deal in bribery and lies as other men deal in bread. No man knows what another is doing. Camassia still has a coating of civilisation, and a kind of spurious vitality that is thin as the colour wash on the walls of a tomb.' He glanced at Ardesir's dark, desert face. 'Painted scenes of the dead, for the comfort of the living, who know as surely as sunrise tomorrow that they too will one day inhabit those same mansions of oblivion. The barbarians of the flesh are at the borders, pressing closer with every season, but the barbarians of the heart are already there.'

Tathea looked at Sadokhar and saw the shadow cross his features, the merest tightening of the lips as if the words had touched an old understanding inside him, memories of things she had taught him long ago. It was another shard of prophecy fallen into place.

'Is that new, sir?' Sardriel asked Eudoxius gravely. His courtesy never wavered – he would have considered that a gross weakness, a betrayal of the inner self – but neither did he stay his hand in pursuing reason to the end. To have done that would be to insult both speaker and listener. 'Or are you merely referring to the nature of mankind, perhaps darkened by your own exile?' he pressed. 'Forgive me, but I perceive that you are much travelled, and yet you bear no embassy nor do you carry the goods of trade. You are past the years of being a soldier and your bearing suggests you serve no master, and yet you have the marks of both hunger and ill-use.'

'You observe well,' Eudoxius said without self-pity, but there was a bitterness in him. 'But my path is self-chosen. I have no desire to live in Camassia any longer.' He looked beyond the few dark plums left in the burnished dish in front of him. His voice lowered a little.

11

'What I saw in Camassia was not honest greed, as in the long past, it was evil pretending to be good.' He twisted the stem of the glass goblet in his fingers, the light red through the wine. 'The Emperor is weak. He loves the glory and the praise of men, and in his eagerness to satisfy the crowds he has forgotten any beliefs of his own. He appoints his friends to power, and accounts it loyalty to protect them at any cost.'

'In what way?' Sadokhar asked sharply.

Eudoxius shrugged. 'He does not stop corruption or incompetence if the perpetrators are his friends,' he replied. 'No one admits fault any more. There is little honour left.' He looked from one to the other of them, his expression suddenly darker and openly edged with fear. 'Irria-Kand lies directly on our northern borders right from the far east across to the forests of the west. It is not a united empire but a series of city fortresses, and already half of it has fallen to the barbarians sweeping in from the lands on the rim beyond.'

No one interrupted him. Sardriel sat motionless. Ardesir was tight-lipped. Sadokhar leaned a little further forward, his attention total. This was military news of the gravest kind, and he had been too long a soldier, left too many good men on bloody fields, to weigh lightly a word of it.

'The Emperor has been told,' Eudoxius continued, watching Sadokhar's face. 'Word comes almost weekly, but he chooses to disbelieve it. He says our armies have never been beaten and it is treason even to think they could be now. But they are untrained for anything but garrison duty, and parades. They have never seen war. If Irria-Kand falls and the barbarians reach the great forests of Caeva to the west, they will find nothing there for them, and they will turn south into Camassia. Who wouldn't? The whole land lies in front of them, all but unprotected! Hundreds of miles of wheat and vines, orchards and woodlands there for the taking, all the way to the City in the Centre of the World, and the sea.'

No one had interrupted him. One of the dogs stirred briefly by the embers of the fire.

'Leadership requires that your first debt is to the demands of honour,' Eudoxius continued. 'If you are not prepared to do that, if you must be praised at all costs, then step back and leave the crown to someone who will.'

His eyes did not leave Sadokhar's. He did not see the sorrow in Ardesir's eyes, nor the flash of pity in Sardriel's. 'We overlook faults we should not, because we are too afraid of invasion to admit that it could happen.' He waved away a servant with a bowl of honey cakes. His voice was thick with anger he no longer tried to conceal. 'The barbarians will cross the borders one day. We shall be conquered and all the beauty and sophistication, the buildings, the art and the inventions of a thousand years will be lost under the tide. But perhaps we will drown ourselves in our own filth before that, and when the savages come they will find only more savages, no better than themselves . . . merely different.' Then he smiled suddenly, but there were tears swimming in his eyes. 'Only I will not live to see it.'

A coldness filled Tathea, as if she had swallowed ice. Could that be what Armageddon was – not consuming war at all, but the corrupted heart eaten away, until when the barbarians came in the end, there was nothing for them to conquer but decay? Was the end not violence at all, but a living rot?

Then what were all their preparations of wisdom, self-discipline and the arts of strategy worth? The Book of God could not be opened, but Tathea remembered much of it and had written it out again, disconnected, precept by precept, but still a light to the soul. At every step they had prayed in humility, and retraced each mistake and sought to mend it.

For a decade Sadokhar had ruled so that there was a surplus of food, and safety from violence or need. There had been space for thought and to learn, to take months apart from daily tasks in order to enrich the soul. He, Sardriel and Ardesir had argued and discussed, explored the natures of good and evil. They had ridden together, built, known failure and success, quarrelled, tested each other and forgiven. There had been experiences which had winnowed the wheat from the chaff, refined the compassion and the integrity. Each had in one manner or another walked an inner path which had learned his courage of the soul, and found it enough.

They knew who they were, not only in this mortal life, but from eternity to eternity, children of God on the wild and dangerous journey home. Each had committed himself irrevocably to the conflict and forged his covenants with heaven.

The servants moved around Tathea, fetching and carrying. Light winked on polished metal and glass. The sound of chatter came dimly and she barely heard it.

Where was the war? What weapon was there to strike an enemy which was a nameless horde a thousand miles away?

She looked at Eudoxius sitting opposite her, and saw the torch-light shine through his thin hair, and the marks of age on his skin. Once he had been as young as Sadokhar, in the prime of his strength. Now he was already too tired to fight.

For all their passion and courage, even purity of mind so they could face any evil, Asmodeus had the ultimate weapon against which there was no defence – time. He needed only to wait.

The room swam around Tathea in a haze of flame and shadow, golden reflections on pewter and shining wood. The familiar faces blurred. Voices were a sea of sound like waves on a shingle beach, and over them all she heard laughter, cruel and soft, not in the ears but in the heart. She knew his voice. He had cursed her before, and promised he would never forget the injury she had inflicted on him, once, long ago, nor forgive it.

'Tathea . . .'

It was a sound almost without meaning.

'Tathea!' Now there was anxiety in it.

She blinked and forced the room into focus again.

Sadokhar was staring at her, his grey eyes clouded.

Should she say that all was well? He would know she was lying, he always had, even as a child. Habit forced her to smile back at him; put off the moment. 'I'm sorry,' she apologised. 'I was thinking of what Eudoxius said of Camassia.' She turned to the old man. 'Is Shinabar like that also?'

He bit his lip, equivocated. 'I have not been there lately, my lady. They have barbarians on the southern borders, but then they always had.' He shook his head. 'In half a millennium they've not been conquered, not since Ta-Thea returned with the Book. Perhaps the fear of it hasn't given anyone the power to abuse, as it has with us.'

Sardriel leaned back in his chair. His expression gave nothing away, but Tathea knew him well enough to be aware of his contempt for evasion.

'Do you know if they are mobilising armies?' Ardesir asked, frowning and pushing his hair back unconsciously with his fingers.

Eudoxius shook his head. 'No more so than usual. The army is a good career, especially if you have no land.' He smiled fleetingly. 'There is always a kind of comfort in having someone else tell you what is right and wrong. It saves all the energy of thought, and the blame for any decision that turns out badly.'

Tathea did not argue. She had seen the reality of war herself and knew that even a battle won is terrible beyond the imagination to conceive. And she had no certainty what kind of war they were facing now. Surely it would be more consuming than even the clashing of gigantic armies, tens of thousands wounded or dead? It would be weapons of the spirit as well, the blinding and maiming of souls.

Eudoxius was given leave to depart. The torches guttered against the sunset-coloured walls. Others departed also, friends and guests, among them the eleven Knights of the Western Shore who had kept the faith whole since Drusus and Merdic five hundred years ago. Finally there were only Ardesir, Sardriel, Sadokhar and Tathea left.

Sadokhar was looking at her, his gaze unwavering. The flickering lights picked out the fine lines of his face, with its strong nose and broad mouth. She felt the strength in him, the purpose that through all the horror of battle and the grief of personal loss had become fixed. Nothing in him now rebelled against the weight of his task and the hideous certainty of it. He was quick-tempered, arrogant at times, but never a coward. He faced any enemy no matter how powerful, and any truth, the bitter with the sweet. A warmth filled her, and sudden tears sprang to her eyes. She remembered Asmodeus walking away from her on the edge of Hirioth the night Sadokhar was born. She saw again the swagger in his stride, and heard, with a chill of the flesh, his laughter. Now she understood it.

'Eudoxius believes he will not live to see the barbarians conquer Camassia,' she said quietly. 'We've thought of defence against all kinds of weapons Asmodeus might use against us, and prepared to face them – but we have no shield against time.' Her voice was raw with the edge of despair. 'We might be here with sword in hand and hearts ready for a war which never comes. He knows we cannot wait.'

They stared at her, horror dawning slowly in each of them as they grasped the terrible meaning of what she said.

'There must be a way!' Sadokhar protested, his voice thick with defiance. 'We are meant to fight! God has chosen us for it and we are covenanted! It's years since you've tried to open the Book. Try it again!'

She rose from her chair, the room swimming around her.

'And if you succeed?' Ardesir whispered. 'What then? Armageddon?' There was faith in his voice, and fear also. He was not blind to what it meant.

She did not answer, but turned and led the way out of the hall, through an antechamber and up the wide, curving stairs to the upper chambers. They followed her in silence, hearts pounding.

She unlocked the doors to her apartments and went in. They followed, Sardriel closing the doors after them. Inside was full of warm, golden colours, deeper now in candlelight, shadows like burned earth. She crossed the floor to the far wall and the alcove, and with a key from around her neck opened a heavy cupboard door and lifted out an object about a foot square, and wrapped in a blue silk cloak. All three watched her as she carried it across and laid it on a small table.

Sadokhar moved one of the candlesticks closer, the flame wavering with the trembling of his hand. He did not take his eyes from the blue silk cloak. The Book inside it had come from Tathea's journey of the soul to the world before this, where God and devil had fought face to face for the future of man.

Again he was in awe of her. Her familiar face he had seen in a thousand moods, her marvellous, fierce, dark eyes which knew they had seen heaven, and forgotten it . . . except in sudden agonising and sublime moments, and partaken something of hell also, and the memory of its shadow lay across her.

She reached forward and her fingers lifted the fold of the silk and pulled it back. It fell easily, slipping on its own smooth surface.

Sadokhar held his breath, his heart hammering.

The gleam of the beaten gold shone, chrysolite burned like diamonds, catching the milk-white purity of pearls.

Then he heard Tathea give a long, shuddering sigh – not wonder but, strangely, fear – and he saw them the moment after she did, resting on the gleaming gold: long, black keys, as dense as night and yet subtly iridescent, casting no shadow. He heard Sardriel draw in his breath.

Tathea's face was stiff, eyes blank with fear as if she could not believe what she saw. Her hands were rigid and she began to shake.

Her fear flooded into Sadokhar as if he were still a child at her skirts and his life depended upon hers.

'What are they?' Ardesir said hoarsely, panic in his voice.

'Keys to what?' Sadokhar whispered.

For a moment it seemed she could not reply. Her throat convulsed, choking. Her skin was white, no blood in it. She started to move backwards.

'To what?' Sadokhar shouted, stepping forward, although he had no idea what he meant to do.

Tathea staggered a little, losing her balance.

He caught her in his arms. There seemed no weight to her, her body was weak and so thin he could feel her bones through the fabric of her gown. He looked at her in horror, his skin prickling and cold with sweat. The face he saw was old, withered and all but fleshless, the eyes blind, the hair lank and blasted with white.

'No . . .' A long, moaning cry of denial broke from him. The woman he held was alive, but only in the beating of her heart. The spirit was gone, the courage and the strength that had carried her through five hundred years was shrivelled away, her mind wasted in senility.

Ardesir stood as if paralysed, unable to believe.

Sardriel bent forward as if he would help, then stopped, not knowing what to do.

Sadokhar held Tathea gently, his arms locked, body aching. He began to rock her back and forth, as if she were a troubled child. He wanted to say something. But what could bring her back and undo the horror of the last few moments? What would make it as it had been?

16

He held her more closely, feeling her body almost weightless, as if she were slipping away, even in his arms. Her breath rasped in her throat, struggling to fill her lungs.

'Don't,' he said hoarsely. 'We'll fight . . . We'll make the war happen, I promise!' It was a cry of desperation. He had no idea how, no plan. 'We'll win! We've got to . . . It is what we were born for.' That was not true either. It was what he was born for, not she. But he could not do it without her. 'Tathea! Come back!' he cried. 'We can't win alone! We don't even know what it is! Help us! We don't understand it!'

He moved to try to make her more comfortable, and knocked his leg against the table. The candlestick swayed, spilling golden lights and shadows across the gleaming surface of the Book. He knew that inside it was the word of God to His children, the promises of the light and glory of eternity. It could not be wrong! Those who believed in it had to win. However long the struggle or how hard or high the climb, in the end there had to be that heaven which was the soul's dream, the passion, the love beyond all others.

'Tathea!'

But she did not answer, even with the slightest movement.

Sadokhar looked up and saw Ardesir's face ash-pale, and knew the fear in him as if he could taste it in his own mouth. Ardesir's body was rigid and it was seconds before he spoke.

'Asmodeus has never defeated her before,' he said gently, forcing his voice to be steady, even warm although it trembled a little. 'He won't now – not with us here too.' He put his slender hand on Sadokhar's shoulder. 'We'll keep vigil, and pray. Our faith will be strong enough . . . but it is a bitter test.'

Sadokhar felt a tiny seed of calm within himself. He rose to his feet and carried Tathea through to her bedroom and laid her on the bed. Ardesir and Sardriel followed and they all kneeled beside her, each asking in his own words for the help of God to restore Tathea as she had been, and give them the power to fight in His cause.

But as the night deepened she did not move, nor did she as dawn came, and sunrise.

'You must go and wash and eat,' Sardriel said quietly as the light broadened across the room, showing their faces gaunt with weariness and shock. 'Sit in the judgement hall as usual, speak to people, receive visitors.'

Sadokhar's body clenched in denial, but he knew Sardriel was right. This was the first blow against them, and already he was prepared to let the world see it had drawn blood. He stood up slowly. 'Yes . . . of course. I'll return when I can. Send word to me if there is any change.'

Sardriel and Ardesir both nodded silently. Sardriel went with

17

Sadokhar as far as the outer chamber. For a moment it looked as if he were about to say something more, some word of hope or grief, the emotion was in his eyes, then it was concealed again, and he merely said goodbye.

The day passed in duties performed with half the attention, and the night in vigil, with snatches of sleep. The second dawn brought no change but a deeper bending together of resolve, a few words of faith, brief because there was too little to say.

From the moment the darkness closed over Tathea, she was sucked from all she loved into a place of isolation and chaos. She knew with terrible certainty who it was she faced. His presence was around her more surely than the whirling rubble in the air or the choking clouds of dust.

'They will fail without you!' he said from behind her, his voice as intimate as a touch to the skin. 'The people will return to their old ways. The faith you taught them was only skin-deep. Come the first cold winds withering their prosperity and they'll go back to their old superstitions. I can send stones to drown their coasts, blight on their crops, rains to flood their valleys. Rock their comfort, make them afraid and you'll see the truth of their mettle.'

There was nowhere for her to set her feet. She was drifting.

'Some will, but there will be more who won't,' she argued. 'Destroy things and they'll rebuild. Afflict them and they'll find courage to fight back. They'll close ranks against you!'

He laughed, a wild, hollow sound like the breaking of ice.

'They'll turn on each other, every one for himself! Fear will kill all the seeds you've planted, it will strip away the thin paint of virtue and show the heart of self beneath. Even those you think you know, Tathea! Kor-Assh will never come to Tyrn Vawr. He will dither and hesitate for ever, always finding yet one more excuse to wait in Lantrif, outside the battle, until it overtakes him and it is too late.'

Still he was behind her, but she could feel his breath on her cheek.

'And Ardesir will grow more and more afraid, until at last his terror overcomes him and he runs away. He is afraid – you know that! You have seen it in him – the cold, sick gripping of the stomach when pain is there in front of him, real pain, horror, failure.'

'He'll overcome it,' she whispered, not even sure if her voice was strong enough for him to hear. 'Everybody with intelligence and imagination knows fear. It's what you do with it that matters.'

'And Sardriel will retreat further and further from the pain of feeling,' he went on. 'Until in the end he feels nothing at all – no

18

love, no pity, no laughter, no hope. He will become a brain without a heart.'

'No he won't! There's no point in being alive if you can't feel! The purpose of being is to have joy! He knows that!'

'He knows you said it!' he jeered. 'Words, and where are you now? Silent and cold in a bed! They watch over you and hope and pray – but for how long?'

'Until I return!' she cried, swinging round to face him, the blood pounding in her body till she shook with the force of it.

He stood there proud and terrible, familiar as eternity. A smile curved his lips. 'And even Sadokhar – especially Sadokhar – will fail. His courage will turn to savagery, his justice to vengeance on those he thinks betray him – which they all will, in the end. He will cease to be king and become tyrant, drowning in the blood of his own people.'

She refused to believe it, she could not! She stared at him, defending the only way left, by attacking. 'And what about Ishrafeli?' she demanded. 'You couldn't beat him before. You shook the earth and you blotted out the stars, but you couldn't kill the love in him! You can't quench the light in any of us unless we let you – and we won't. I won't!'

His eyes narrowed to slits of fire. 'Oh yes, you will! Your human imagination cannot begin to think what I will do to them. Time is mine, Tathea. They will grow old and die, waiting for a war they will never fight and their souls will wither inside them. In the end the earth will be mine, and everything in it, every bird and beast, every tree and blade of grass. And you will see it, exhausted, bitter and alone, to the last twilight!'

Tathea's eyes opened wide. She was lying on her own bed and Sadokhar was kneeling beside her, tears on his face. Beyond him Ardesir was smiling, so widely he was almost laughing, and Sardriel's lips moved in a silent prayer, his eyes bright.

Sadokhar held her gently and she sat up, feeling the strength returning, her hair black again where it fell forward over her shoulder.

She saw the golden Book on the small table by the wall, the dark keys still on its face.

Sadokhar turned to follow her gaze. 'What are they?' His hand tightened over her arm so she could not have reached for them even if she would.

'Asmodeus' keys to this world,' she answered, her voice coming between dry lips. 'He showed them to me the night you were born.'

He understood. She did not need to put it all into mundane words for him. He would die. Ardesir and Sardriel would die, and

Kor-Assh also, if he came. Even Tathea herself could wither with doubt. She too was vulnerable if her faith slipped from her . . . and for the first time in his life he realised that it could. He had seen the weakness in her soul as well as the glory, the burden of time – when she had fought and waited alone, shoring up her strength for the day of the last battle, always clinging to the faith that they would win.

Today she had been swayed by doubt that perhaps they would not. Asmodeus would stay his hand, and without war the end would be not a cataclysmic battle in which they could be victorious, but a long watch until one morning they saw the emptiness of it all, and realised they were alone, and there was no prize to win or lose, only the slow descent into oblivion. The whole journey had been purposeless. They had endured all the agony and the sacrifice and the hope so Asmodeus could mock them. And through them, God Himself!

'There is a way!' he said with more strength than he thought he had. 'I don't know what, but I'll find it.'

'The keys . . .' Ardesir said softly. He knew the prophecy, as they all did: Tathea must take the keys of this world from Asmodeus himself.

'No!' Sardriel reached out his hand, but he was too late. Ardesir stretched forward and grasped them, and as his fingers touched the leaden metal it shimmered and dissolved, all except one key which slithered to the floor without a sound.

Ardesir closed his eyes, blind for a moment with despair.

Sardriel stood rock-still.

Sadokhar bent and reached for the solitary key on the floor, and felt its metal on his flesh. He closed his hand over it, and it remained, solid as the key to the castle gates. It was not Asmodeus' key to the world, it was something else, and as he kneeled there a wild and terrible thought filled his mind, memory of a door in the ruined city of Sylum, a wraith-like man he had seen there, and an idea so fearful he could not speak it aloud.

Tathea saw him and lunged forward, grasping his arm, but she was too weak to hold him. Sardriel caught her as she swayed, holding her steady, unwittingly shielding her with his own body as Sadokhar slipped out of the door, and the instant after, she heard the heavy lock turn and knew they were shut in.

Chapter Two

Sadokhar stopped only long enough to dress for the journey, then he went to the stables, saddled his horse and rode out into the night. The city was asleep. The clatter of hoofs on stone was the only sound that disturbed the darkness. He was long used to battles with the sword and he knew his own skill, but this was different, unknown and unguessable, a war of the spirit, and he knew the weakness within himself, the possibility of failure. It had been years ago, he had been little more than a boy, when he had met the bear in the forest, before he and Tathea had left Hirioth for the Eastern Shore. It had stood before him in the glade, a giant woken from sleep, and he had frozen with terror, incapable of fighting or running.

It was Tathea who had rescued him, seizing his arm and scrambling, half lifting him up the great oak tree until at last the beast grew bored and shambled away. But Sadokhar had never forgotten that faced with the unknown, he could fail.

Now he rode through the night past the guards at the city gates, and out on to the moonlit road eastward. Last night had taught him many things. Deep in his heart with an immovable ache was the knowledge that Tathea was vulnerable. Perhaps she was not immortal as he had always assumed, not incapable of any wound but that to the soul. Her body and her will could be broken. Armageddon must not wait.

Kor-Assh had not yet come. They had sent no embassy north to Ulfin, but last night had also taught Sadokhar that the last words of the prophecy meant exactly what it said. Before Tathea could take the keys from Asmodeus, he must walk the earth himself. They must be taken from his hand, not some vision of them grasped so easily from where he had placed them on the Book. That had been a threat, a gesture of his power. Sadokhar should have known it. Asmodeus would never have left them could they be stolen so simply.

And yet Sadokhar had the one key that was not of this world, but of another, far more terrible, and if he used it then he could seek out Asmodeus, face him, and goad him into bringing the legions of hell to begin the final war.

He rode hard all night, following the old Imperial road from the Heartlands to the sea, as he and Tathea had done when he first left Hirioth with her.

He passed villages and towns and saw the glow of torches in windows, the thousand peaceful homes filled with laughter and pain, passion and triviality, each one seeking untold dreams. He felt an ache of love for everything they were, and could be. The night wind was soft on his cheek, carrying the scent of herbs and trodden grass, and the vast distances of the night. Far away, water gleamed under the moon like the polished surface of a mirror.

He lifted his face towards it and felt his heart tighten inside him. He could never love the beauty of it enough. He had loved Hirioth with its ancient trees, its beasts, its millions of whispering leaves. He had loved the great bare mountains of the Wastelands arching up to the wind-driven clouds. Above all he had loved the storm-racked, surf-booming beauty of the Eastern Shore with its endless skies and pale, rib-streaked sands.

If it really were hell which lay beyond the portal in Sylum, then he might never see the world again with its familiar, precious and terrible wonder. He would be somewhere else . . . Alone? And if not, with whom? Spirits of those who had denied God and everything He had made and loved? Even to imagine it was unbearable.

He stared at the silver light across the arch of heaven, and the sleeping earth beneath.

If he did not go, if he stayed here, loving it, and Armageddon came at another time, when he, Ardesir and Sardriel were dead and Tathea left alone and weakened by doubt and the waiting, the crushing disappointment, then Asmodeus might win . . . No, more than that – he would win!

There was no decision to make. But if he gave himself time to think of all it meant then his courage might fail him. Now that he had seen the choices clearly he had no escape. It was not his mission to fight Armageddon as he had believed all his life, but to provoke it. That was the great and terrible service he could do the world he loved so fiercely. It would demand from him the ultimate sacrifice.

He turned his horse and started to ride down again towards the sea. It was time to stop thinking and just do it; give fear no room.

It had been sunset when side by side he and Tathea had first breasted this rise and seen the ruins of the great city below them, flushed with the colours of the dying day.

He remembered his indrawn breath of amazement even now, twenty years after. At their backs the west had burned in a sea of

22

gold, shards of fire stretching across a scalding sun, feathered clouds like the vast underside of some world-folding wing hung, closing in the sky.

In front of them the pillared streets had been lent an illusion of beauty. It did not matter that the columns supported the empty air. The black scars of smoke melted into indigo, no more than shadows on the ochre, peach and rose of the crumbling walls. They had been too far away to see the wreckage of pavements, or that the green was not the gentle order of gardens but the thick riot of thrusting weeds. Thistle heads were amethyst lamps in the sunset; ivy and bindweed strangled the last of the unbroken columns and loaded the arches with clinging weights of vine.

He had seen the tears on Tathea's face, not understanding then that those shattered glories were the wreckage of a nation she had known and loved.

They had gone down into it in silence together. He remembered a moth fluttering lazily past his cheek on silken shadow wings. The colours had deepened, turned to the violet of night. They had chosen not to sleep in the ruins, but rather in a hollow in the summer grass near the top of the cliffs.

Now in the dawn light he gazed at the crumbling mortar, the cracks where the scarlet lichen and the velvet-soft, creeping mosses covered the marble and the limestone. Tendrils pushed up through the ancient floors, lifting the tiny coloured mosaic pieces a hair's breadth a day, until they lay like so many bright, random pebbles on a shore.

Here was the forum and the great state buildings. Sadokhar stared around him at the rows of columns, the flights of steps, the arches. There to the left were the military headquarters, the courts of justice and the libraries, the embassies of foreign princes . . .

He did not hear the soft footfall behind him, no more than the rustle of night wind in the weeds. It was the voice that jerked him back with a stab of fear.

'There's little here except ghosts and rubble,' it said. 'But perhaps if you listen at twilight you will hear the echoes of a hundred thousand marching feet that have trodden the battlefields of the world.'

Sadokhar swivelled and stared at the man before him. He could see little but the dim orb of his head and the outline of his robes. He was even thinner than he had been twenty years ago, almost wraith-like, and his feet made no sound whatever on the pavement.

'Orocyno?' Sadokhar whispered, his heart pounding.

Orocyno peered at him in the broadening light. 'I remember you,' he said softly, his voice like a sigh in the wind. 'You came here before, with the woman.'

'You told me you were the last priest of the Light Bearers.'

'So I am.' There was the suggestion of a smile on his lips, of pride in him.

Sadokhar looked around at the decaying stones. 'There's no one here.'

'Oh, there are people!' Orocyno assured him. 'Not here, not now – but one day.'

'When?'

The smile was certain, secretive. 'The future . . . the past. Time is not what you think. But I cannot tell you – it is forbidden.'

'The gateway—'

Orocyno shivered, moving back a step as if Sadokhar had threatened him in some way. 'You can't use it! I found it and it is mine alone.'

'Into the past . . .' Sadokhar said gently. 'Into time.'

Orocyno nodded, the widening light silver on the folds of his cloak, as if it were formed of mist. The dry skin of his cheek seemed almost translucent.

'One door?' Sadokhar asked.

Orocyno shook his head. 'Two.' His voice was barely a sigh. 'I have not the key to the door beyond, nor do I want it.'

'I have it. Open the first for me, and I will open the second myself.'

'I can't!' Orocyno took another step back, fear making him waver like an image on ruffled water. 'Every time I use the portal it weakens it!'

'But you do use it!' This time Sadokhar stepped towards him.

Orocyno shuddered violently. 'I can't help it! It pulls me! I fight – but I lose. I swear I won't, but always one day or another, I go through.' He drew in his breath.

Sadokhar closed his hand over the black key in his pocket. 'Take me.'

'I can't!'

'Yes you can – and you will.'

Orocyno shrank away.

'You want to be part of the Light Bearers?' Sadokhar challenged him. 'Do you want to be remembered in the history of the worlds as the last and the greatest of them?'

Orocyno's eyes shone as if the fire of the dawn had been lit inside him. The sky was brimming with light spreading a path of silver shivering across the sea. 'What must I do?' His breath sighed from him in words barely audible.

'Open the first door for me,' Sadokhar answered.

'It will weaken the portal!' Orocyno said again.

'I know. Do it.'

His head high, Orocyno turned towards the light and seemed almost to float across the pavement floor between the thistles, and Sadokhar followed him. Whatever Armageddon was, and he did not know, it was better to be beaten than to have died without ever facing the Enemy and fighting with all the energy of his soul.

It was over an hour after the door was locked that Sardriel and Ardesir managed to open it, and Tathea rode after Sadokhar.

She knew evil as he never had, right from the night over five hundred years ago when she had awoken to find her child dead and the palace in Shinabar overrun. That had been prompted by Tiyo-Mah, her mother-in-law, who had purchased the murder of her son and her grandson in order to keep her own power.

Tathea had been exiled, and years later returned as Isarch herself, but she had had no vengeance on Tiyo-Mah. She remembered with a chill, even here safe on the Island, how she had gone to the ancient palace in Thoth-Moara to face the old woman, and found her there with the golden dwarf, and the room filled with the suffocating spirits of the dead, unrepentant and unforgiven. She had taken armed men with her, but Tiyo-Mah had gone down into the underground chambers, and there, in the treasure store-house, had turned and walked into the wall . . . and through it.

The golden dwarf had said she had gone into time, and would one day return for her own vengeance on Tathea, who had deposed her, not once but twice. He had taught her the arts of necromancy, a raiser of the spirits of the merciless dead, those who had looked upon the light, and chosen the darkness.

Had Tiyo-Mah gone through the portal in Thoth-Moara to bring back her terrible army? Was that what lay beyond it – not time, but hell?

And in Sylum, what had the wraithlike Orocyno found through his gateway? Eternity, or simply the past with its angels and demons, its good and ill?

She had seen Sadokhar pick up the key from the floor and she knew he had taken it to open the doors of hell and let it loose in the world – to force Asmodeus' hand in the beginning of Armageddon.

She had no need to think. She took the way eastwards towards the ruins of Sylum, and the portal Sadokhar knew.

It was dawn as she found the fork in the road and followed it across the soft hillside, down the incline, then over the last rise, and saw the city ahead of her as the light streamed on to the silent, weed-strewn pavements.

Her eyes searched for sight of Sadokhar. Could she be too late already? The wind moved between the pillars with a sigh, stirring the honeysuckle that twined corrosive fingers deeper into the marble columns carved to honour battles long since forgotten. In the evening it would send a web of fragrance into the air as sweet as wine. Now it was scentless in the cold sunrise.

Her eyes sought for movement. Surely at least Orocyno would be here?

But it was twenty years since she and Sadokhar had first seen him. Perhaps he was dead?

She was ashamed for the thrill of hope that surged up inside her. If he were no longer here, then Sadokhar would not find the door. Or if he did, it would take time. How long had Orocyno been here before he had stumbled on its secret? Decades?

She started to move down the hill swiftly in the broadening light, travelling easily. She was almost at the first outlying villa, its walls crumbling outwards, thistles spearing through the courtyard stones, fountain filled with dust, when she saw Sadokhar's dark figure fifty yards to her left, and below her, in the sunken amphitheatre. He was walking slowly, head high and stiff. His fists were clenched at his sides. She knew as if she could feel it within herself how the fear choked him.

She dismounted, looped the horse's rein over the remains of a pillar, and started forward.

There was a movement to her left, little more than the shifting of a shadow across the stones. She turned, staring. She could barely make out the shape, the figure so insubstantial it could have been a curtain blowing in the wind, without flesh or bones inside it . . . except for the head. There was no hair, only a gleaming skull with deep-socketed eyes and fleshless lips: Orocyno, the priest who had found a deadly secret, and used it until it consumed him.

Sadokhar was closer to her than he was. She could call out to stop him. She drew in her breath and the cry was half strangled in her throat. Orocyno made no sign of hearing her.

But Sadokhar turned, staring directly at her.

'Sadokhar!' The word was a whisper swallowed in the wind. The sun was above the horizon now, a rose-clear light over the shattered stones.

He stared at her, waiting. The question was in his face – was she going to stop him? Was that what he wanted? To be relieved at the last moment from his terrible mission?

And what if she did not? Had he come trusting she would follow? If she now let him do this irrevocable thing, would he understand? Or would the child in him feel betrayed?

She knew the fear in him as if he had spoken it aloud. Failure! It was the unknown beyond the doorway, the monsters of soul.

Her voice choked, and yet she found the words. 'You won't fail,' she said with certainty. 'You know yourself this time.'

26

His eyes lingered on hers for a moment, then he turned and started to walk forwards again. Ahead of him Orocyno moved soundlessly over the stone steps as if his feet did not touch them.

Tathea watched and did not speak. She must not take the choice from him.

Orocyno was at the bottom of the steps. He cast no shadow. The sun poured into the amphitheatre like fire filling a bowl. It caught Sadokhar's robe and edged it with flame. The dust at his feet was gold.

Sadokhar stopped. He did not turn to Tathea again. She watched his face, the angle of his body, and the wraith of Orocyno yielding.

She felt the warmth of the sun on her face and the grief freezing her heart as Sadokhar and Orocyno turned and walked together to a great archway carved with laurels and lilies, and passed into its shadows.

She waited. The sky was blue overhead. The birds still sang. The air smelled sweet and dry.

Orocyno came back. The wind blew his robes and there was nothing inside them. He was alone. Sadokhar did not return.

Tathea stood still for long minutes, as if waiting could somehow change what would happen. Would he find Asmodeus and lure him into starting the great and final war, or might he simply be lost in hell for ever? To lose him to that would be the end of laughter and peace in the heart, and a kind of love which was torn out of her as if from her own body.

Then she heard it, far away, beyond the stones of the portal, a thin, raucous screaming, a fury of voices that had once been human, as if for an instant the door of hell had opened.

Sadokhar walked slowly through the archway in Sylum, staring around him at the carved stone. It was cracked in places where ivies had eaten it away, dark-stained with the rain of centuries. Ahead of him he could see a higher dome curving upwards. The floor was smoother, protected under a still unbroken roof and the years had not marred it so deeply.

Orocyno took a silver key from a pocket in his robe and fitted it into the lock of a great, coffered door, its panels rubbed satin-smooth. It swung open and Orocyno stepped through. Sadokhar followed and came into a long chamber.

The air was warm and a little dusty. It smelled very old. The wall beside him now was archaic sandstone carved with signs, and painted with terracotta and white, little pictures of figures like sticks. For a moment he thought he heard voices to his left, as if he were close to a vast room filled with a babble of sound. He saw massed people in rich and muted colours, bright sunlight through glass, then it dissolved. Orocyno was drawn towards it, his step quickening until the distance swallowed him and Sadokhar was alone.

In front of him was another door, darker, heavier than the first, its surface mirroring changing images as if some grotesque parody of life were playing out in front of it, and yet there was no one there but Sadokhar, and he stood motionless, the black key in his hand.

The lock was plain, unscarred as if it had never been turned. The decision was made. There was nothing to wait for. Fumbling only a little he put the key into the hole and turned it. It moved without the slightest effort, the door swinging open at a touch.

There was light in front of him – flat, white light, unlike the sun. There was something in its lifeless glare which made his step falter. The air was still warm, and he was not touching the stone, yet inside he was chilled. There was no sound at all. Even his own feet were utterly silent. They hardly seemed to carry his weight on the smooth tiles.

He stood in the harsh glare of shadowless light. He raised his head, putting up his hand to shelter his eyes, but there was no sun, only a white sky stretching to the horizon without change.

Ahead of him the land sloped away, dry and sterile. As far as his eyes could see there were outcrops of rock in the rubble and dust, and piles of broken stones as if they had once been buildings. The air was motionless, clammy on the skin and it had a peculiar, stale odour as if it had been long closed in a dead space.

He could see no trees, no plants, not even any driftwood or bones. It was as if nothing had ever lived here. There were no footprints of beasts of any kind, no birds, not even insects.

At least half the rocks seemed cut and piled by art, long ruined now and holding not even memory of beauty. But there had once been life here, human life, at least. And human life did not survive without herbs, trees, grasses of the field.

Where should he look for Asmodeus? He could be anywhere! There was nothing to indicate in which direction even to begin.

Sadokhar glanced back at the portal and for a moment an infinite yearning filled him. He choked it back, put stones against the door to wedge it open, and started to walk, not with purpose so much as to give himself the illusion that he still had some mastery of himself. He was not here in a wasted sacrifice, although the fear of that had already entered his soul.

He had been moving only a short while – the shattered columns and the portal were still visible – when he heard a great shout, as if a thousand throats were roaring some tremendous cheer, but it was wordless, a senseless exultation.

28

He started to run, floundering in the dust, sending up clouds which clung to him, choking his breath, clinging in his nose and throat. He tried to sweep it away with his arms and staggered against an outcrop of rock, tearing his skin and feeling the sweat sting.

After a moment he started to climb a little through the defile in the rock, and had gone forty or fifty yards when suddenly the passage widened out. Ahead of him in a sunken amphitheatre stood a mass of beings, men and women crowded together so tightly their arms and legs seemed almost tangled. All their faces were lifted as one towards a single figure who stood high on a natural platform on the rock jutting out above them, only feet away from Sadokhar. She was an ancient woman, scrawny and almost bald, her black hair pulled tight across her high skull. Her nose was prominent, like the beak of some gigantic bird of prey, and her narrow shoulders were hunched like wings.

'I will lead you to be great again!' she told them. Her voice had no power, no timbre, yet it carried in the motionless air as if she had whispered in the ear of each one of them. 'Take the courage of your wrongs and I will give you revenge upon those who have injured you!' she cried. 'Think of all that you could have had, all that was justly yours!'

Again the roar went up and she lifted her arms as if she would ride the wave of sound as a vulture would ascend on the currents of the air.

She began again, whipping up their anger, their sense of self-pity and blame, their passion for vengeance to collect payment for every slight, every defect and failure of life. Again and again they returned the great cry of adoration for her.

Sadokhar knew who she was. The certainty of it crystallised within him with edges that cut his mind. This was Tiyo-Mah, Tathea's enemy from the birth of time to the end of it. She was promising these unpardoned dead some prize on the earth she could never give them. Unless she had foreknowledge that one day someone would open the portal? Perhaps time had no meaning here, and whenever he had come through he would have found the same thing happening?

The wave of sound filled the amphitheatre again, buoying up the old woman as if it physically carried her. With a smile of triumph on her mouth, soft like perished silk, at last she turned away, and in facing back from the platform she saw Sadokhar.

Her surprise was unmistakable, though she masked it as soon as she could.

She walked through the cleft in the rock towards him, still just within sight of the mass of her followers, like a pale sea behind her.

29

'So you are going to lead them back into the world?' Sadokhar said quietly.

'Fool!' she spat under her breath. 'No one leaves hell till the world ends . . . and perhaps not then. But there is a doorway into the past and I can take them one by one. It is enough for their dreams.' She was staring at him, amazement growing in her eyes and a shadow that looked like fear.

'The past?' he said derisively. 'Is that all?'

Now the amazement was certainty. Her lips parted in a smile of infinite cruelty. 'Sadokhar! So you are dead! You failed! Five hundred years in the waiting, and after all that you are dead – and you fought no Armageddon!' She started to laugh, a dry, hideous sound gurgling in her throat, incomparably coarse.

'No, I'm not dead,' he said very clearly. 'I came here through the portal – as you did. Except I chose it. No one drove me here.'

Tiyo-Mah's face flickered briefly with rage at the memory of Tathea's victory long ago, but Sadokhar had seen the place to taunt her.

He put a little swagger into his stance. 'There is no Armageddon, nor will there be,' he said. 'Tathea is too strong. Asmodeus won't win this world – in my lifetime or any other. There is peace in the Island at the Edge of the World, just as Iszamber foretold. The light still burns there, and it always will. We have wine and fruit, timber and grain, silk, precious gems of the earth. Travellers sit at our tables from all over the world and listen to her wisdom.'

'So you have left all of that to come here?' Tiyo-Mah said with grating disbelief.

'I've come to find Asmodeus,' he replied, smiling.

Her hairless eyebrows shot up. 'Asmodeus!' Then she started to laugh, this time wild and hysterical, soaring upward out of control, ricocheting from the narrow walls of the cleft. It was a maniacal sound, and yet unmistakably human in this lifeless landscape.

Then abruptly she stopped. 'Asmodeus isn't here, you fool! Erebus is his place – not this!' She jabbed a long, crooked finger at the dust around her. Then she started to laugh again, but there was only malicious pleasure in it, quiet, back in her control. Her eyes never left his face.

He knew she spoke the truth and his whole wild plan crumbled. The key to hell had gained him nothing!

What could he salvage? What was there left to do? He stared at the fearful woman in front of him. Surely there was evil enough in her to lead the forces of destruction, and then Asmodeus would have to follow? He could hardly allow her either victory, or defeat!

'I'm sure you'll do as well,' he lied. He looked beyond her to the throng of people still waiting for her to return. 'Keep your promise to them. What is Queen of Hell worth, compared with leader of an army on earth? And how long will you keep them, with nothing to offer? Have they loyalty?' Now he was jeering and he saw the flare of anger in Tiyo-Mah as she recognised it.

'You serve Tathea,' she said softly now, her shoulders hunched, her head forward like an animal's preparing to leap. 'Why would you want me to enter the world?'

He knew she would ask. He must offer her something she could not resist, bait to catch an angel of the Pit. 'If Asmodeus will not come while she is alive, then you must,' he replied. His heart shivered with fear. 'Offer him Tathea, broken, defeated in her strength, and all her warriors with her! He will make you his consort in eternity. You will have won the right.'

'Liar!' she said between her clenched teeth, but her eyes shone. 'You will die, but she never will! Do you think I don't know that? She is as old as I am, all but a few years.' She held up one rope-veined arm, the flesh hanging loose, jerking fingers to display her contempt for the moments of time the difference represented.

Now he taunted her back, blue eyes wide. 'A few years? Her face is smooth, her hair thick and black. She walks upright, dances, rides, wields a sword as well as any man. She has laughter and life and friends she loves. And when she does leave the earth, it will not be for this!' He too flicked his hand to indicate the arid waste around them.

Tiyo-Mah's face suffused with dark blood and her body began to tremble with a rage and hunger that devoured her like a fever. The sweat glistened on the bald dome of her forehead and through the thin strands of hair over her skull.

'You think you can beat me?' she screamed. 'Fool! Imbecile! You know nothing. I'll destroy everyone she loves, one by one, and she'll watch, and her soul will bleed.'

Sadokhar knew he had succeeded, and he was washed over with fear. She was more terrible than anything Tathea had told him of, more than the imagination of nightmare could have created, because she was real. The remnants of humanity were unmistakable in her, calling out like the most hideous, and totally familiar in himself. Had he been less sickened he might have backed away; as it was he stood motionless, not in courage or defiance, but paralysis.

Then Tiyo-Mah turned and stalked back to the rock outcrop on which he had first seen her. The crowd broke into another crescendo of applause, and she raised her arms to them, letting the noise thunder around her until it finally subsided and the crowd stood waiting, faces uplifted.

'The time is come!' she cried out. 'We are ready and the portal to the world is open. Asmodeus is not yet come, so I will lead you against the world and we shall win, and then present him with the prize!'

They began to cheer again, this time a rhythmic chanting of her name, mounting into a climax of sound that was almost unbearable.

As Tiyo-Mah lowered her arms the ground on which the people stood began to shift and heave as five craters appeared, hollowed out beneath their feet and they slithered and fell, howling, into the depths.

As they struggled they began to twine around one another, fighting helplessly, first arms and then legs, writhing together, contorting, backs arched, mouths gaping in silent screaming as if they were compelled against their will. In hideous battle like a pit of snakes, they melted into one another.

A stench arose of open sores, of rotting, pustulant flesh. Intestines belched forth, slimed over with black blood.

Sadokhar gagged and sank to his knees, overcome with nausea, but he could not drag his eyes from the sight in case one of the monstrosities should come towards him.

Eventually no more than five huge men stood on the sand, their muscles still swelling and shrinking as the separate entities fought for freedom from the imprisoning flesh, and were trapped. The agony was unimaginable.

Tiyo-Mah stared at them with a slow smile spreading across her face, then she lifted her head back and uttered a long, thin wail which filled the arena and rose to the flat sky above. It seemed to hang in the air long after it had ceased as if the enclosing silence remembered it.

Then at each of the entrances to the arena four figures appeared, all mounted on beasts, one at each gateway. They were the Lords of Sin. Even Tiyo-Mah shivered at the sight of them, but she did not retreat.

'The portal to the world is open,' she said, not loudly, but her voice seemed cradled and magnified by the rock. 'We can go through into the days and nights, into the colour, into the sounds and visions of the flesh.'

There seemed an endless wait. Then one of the four figures came forward leading a white mule dressed in colourless trappings, and stopped in front of Tiyo-Mah. He was tall and slender, dressed as a legionary of the old Camassian Empire, and his face was serene, perfect featured, his skin smooth as sunrise. Only his eyes were brilliant with desire. His name was Ulciber.

'Give me a body,' he said softly. 'Let me taste the wine and the peaches, let me feel the ground under my feet or the wind on my face.'

Tiyo-Mah hesitated.

32

He turned away as if to go.

'Possess mine,' she said hoarsely. 'For a day!'

He stopped. 'A day?' he said, still with his back to her.

'A day each year!' she amended, holding out her hand.

He touched it incredulously. 'For ever?' he breathed.

'We shall win!' she said with scalding conviction, snatching her hand back. 'Then we shall have all worlds!'

His shoulders relaxed and he turned back to her smiling, and offered her the mule. She mounted it, hauling herself unaided into the saddle and turning the creature's head so she led the procession away from Sadokhar, towards the portal.

He slithered in sudden haste as he moved from his place in the rock cleft, back over the jagged stones and ran through the dust the way he had come, breathless, the sweat streaming on his skin.

The horsemen seemed oblivious of him. He half crouched behind a pile of broken boulders. Not one of the riders glanced to right or left, but followed Tiyo-Mah on to the smooth surface like ancient paving before the arch of the portal. Never once did he see her turn to ascertain their obedience. Her face was lit with a terrible appetite as if her heart already tasted the vengeance she had waited for for half a millennium.

The second one in the outlandish procession was a dwarf, squat and broad, dressed in a glittering coat of diamond-shaped panes, yellow as gold, shimmering even in this heatless light. His eyes were agate-coloured, with pupils like a goat's, and he seemed to be so immensely heavy that the sway-backed creature that carried him staggered, its feet sinking deep into the dust and leaving three-clawed footprints behind.

After him came the man who had struck the bargain with Tiyo-Mah. He rode a blue-roan horse, almost iridescent, like the sheen on rotted flesh, bruised dark. Watching motionlessly, Sadokhar felt as if at a touch it might fall away, corrupted to the core. The breath strangled in his lungs. There was not enough air to fill them.

The fourth was a huge man with mighty shoulders, bold eyes and thick lips. His hair curled richly from his brow. He wore chain armour and carried a long sword, unsheathed and stained with blood. The horse he rode was red as fire and vivid as destruction. Its hoofs left charred imprints even in the sterile dust.

Sadokhar knew them all from Tathea's words in his youth. The golden dwarf was Azrub, Lord of Delusion; the ageless soldier, Ulciber, the Corrupter of Souls; terror was the realm of Cassiodorus, his rage recalled from the journey of the spirit. Tathea had not seen him in life, but his parting words of hate had never left her.

Then came the five creatures from the vast throng which had

33

filled the amphitheatre, their faces indistinguishable as they still melted into one another, forming and reforming in a legion of tangled spirits. One turned for an instant, and Sadokhar saw with skin-crawling horror the eyes, terrible with the warring of souls and the knowledge that they were locked for eternity in an embrace of destruction.

They were those who had lived with cruelty, filth and lies, unrepentant after death. Even in the presence of light and the gift of redemption, they had chosen their darkness. They pressed forward now through the gateway into the world again, to become Lords of the Undead.

Last of all came a rider on a black horse. He was clothed in black, a ragged cloak hanging like torn wings from his shoulders, his hair a night shadow over his head. His face was broad-nosed and thin-lipped, and the end of all hope was in his eyes. He left no trace on the arid landscape, as if it were his own and it held him so familiar it did not feel his passing.

This was he whom Tathea had faced and beaten off on the battlefield of the Western Shore, but now he was renewed, the last and strongest of all the Lords of Sin, Yaltabaoth, who held the power of despair.

One by one they passed under the archway and disappeared until only Yaltabaoth was left.

Sadokhar felt the black key in his pocket and his hand closed over it. He must wait until they were all through.

Yaltabaoth hesitated and turned. He looked directly at Sadokhar and his thin lips parted in a smile. He lifted his hand and in it was a key. He held it up.

Sadokhar tightened his own hand – it was empty.

Yaltabaoth tossed his key into the air and it vanished, then he swivelled in the saddle and rode through the archway and was gone, leaving Sadokhar alone in the rubble.

Chapter Three

Tathea waited in the ruins of Sylum till the sun rose with a glory of light, splashing warm radiance over the stones and picking out the vines in clarity, leaf by leaf. She stood sheltered behind a vine-coloured pillar, watching where Sadokhar had gone.

Then the stillness was broken by the emergence of an extraordinary figure from the archway. In spite of the centuries, Tathea knew her immediately. It was Tiyo-Mah, riding a white mule, its trappings scarlet and gold, and behind her came the Lords of Delusion, Corruption, Terror and Despair. After them, on foot, shambled four creatures unlike any she had seen before, muscles bulging beneath purple-black skin scarred and pitted, as if from innumerable pustules burst and healed over years. One was bull-necked, another lantern-jawed, a third rodent-like, thin, sharp-nosed. They trooped behind as Tiyo-Mah turned south towards the sea.

Alone, and cold in spite of the sun, Tathea crept down to the archway and under its shadow. She searched its crumbling stones, and those of the next arch, and the next, but there was no door, nothing but more rubble and broken columns, shattered pillars and mosaics of long ago.

At last, as the sun was high and bright, she mounted her horse and rode fast back to Tyrn Vawr, to tell Sardriel and Ardesir that Armageddon had begun.

She reached the courtyard of the castle and slid from her horse. Knowing what she did, she felt as if now it should all have been hideously different, a darkness in the very air. And yet the flowers still bloomed in the sun and two guards stopped mid-laughter as they saw her and snapped to attention.

'Find Ardesir and Lord Sardriel!' she shouted, gasping for breath. She turned to her horse, looking for a groom to care for it. It stood head down, foam-flanked. 'Where is everyone?'

A page appeared and she gave him orders to take the animal, and before he was gone Sardriel came down the steps from the main door, a quill still in his hand, his face pale.

'He went to Sylum.' Tathea cut the silence. 'He found the doorway to hell.'

Ardesir came from the other door and stood at her elbow.

She clenched her hands and stood motionless, forcing herself to breathe deeply, to keep her voice steady. 'He went through, and I waited. It was nearly an hour, then Tiyo-Mah came out.' She described the procession she had seen, and what she knew of them.

'And Sadokhar?' Sardriel whispered.

She shook her head minutely. 'No. I . . . I looked in the arch. There was no doorway left. I don't know how to find it.'

Ardesir opened his mouth to speak but he could find no words adequate. She could see behind his eyes his imagination racing. He knew all the subtle, ancient legends of darkness. The possibilities of evil were boundless. He was struggling to understand how she could have allowed it to happen.

Tathea looked away from him to Sardriel, and saw in his dark eyes pity, and a flash of grief which caught at her heart. Then it was concealed as if it had never been, and he nodded very slightly.

'It was a terrible price to pay,' he said quietly. 'And I don't know how we shall win the battle without him.'

How could he be so certain, and so resigned? The unblemished light of his mind was a sublime asset to their forces, but still she longed for some human vulnerability like her own, an instant's crying against the loss. Was the pain in him only an illusion, imagined from her own wound? She looked back at him, knowing her anger was in her face and wanting him to see it.

'We must get him back!' Ardesir protested. 'There must be a way!' He turned to Tathea, his eyes brilliant with pleading.

'I don't know what it is. We can only pray,' she answered. 'Search and pray.'

Sardriel reached out his hand as if he would touch her, then let it fall.

Tathea turned again to Ardesir. 'Tiyo-Mah went towards the sea. She will take a ship for Shinabar. That is the seat of her ancient power, and the country she will find easiest to corrupt. You must follow her and learn what she means to do. Watch her, listen and send word back.'

He nodded. He required no further explanation, and if he was afraid he masked it in his steady gaze.

Sardriel was waiting.

'The barbarians have already taken at least half of Irria-Kand. When they reach the forest, if not before, they will turn south into Camassia.' She reminded them of what Eudoxius had told them. 'Knowingly or not, they are allies of the last darkness. Take from the Treasury and sail to Caeva. Find their mercenary armies, and those from the Sea Isles, and buy them to fight in Irria-Kand. If we can hold the barbarians there, perhaps make some kind of truce,

36

even temporary, it may be enough to shore up the borders of Camassia. Perhaps fear of war will cleanse them as peace could not.' She knew what she was asking of him. It was two thousand miles away across the far edge of the known world, vast plains swept by storms, tinder-dry in summer, snow-bound in winter. But the eastern flanks of Camassia were the vulnerable rim of civilisation. They could not choose their theatre of war.

'How much of the Treasury?' was all Sardriel asked, but his face was pale and stiff, and she understood the ache that was within him.

'You will need all we can spare,' she replied. 'Take two-thirds of it. We will manage with what is left. We have wheat and timber, and there will still be trade for a while.' She saw the question in his eyes. 'There are two of us yet to find,' she said softly. 'I will send for Kor-Assh and Ulfin. And if they cannot read the staff, I will look further. Whoever they are, the last two will come.'

'Of course,' Ardesir agreed quickly, holding out his hand.

She clasped it for a moment, warm and strong, and then let go.

'I shall take a dozen men, to safeguard the money,' Sardriel said. 'We shall leave at dawn tomorrow. I will send word as I can, but if you hear nothing, keep faith that I am fighting and shall not surrender. It may be that no one will pass from Irria-Kand westwards to carry news.' He held out his hand and she took it also, just for a moment. Farewells were understood. There was no time for lingering.

Tathea wept long and deep that night, and sleep came only with exhaustion. She rose knowing that Ardesir and Sardriel had left and she alone still waited in Tyrn Vawr. That day, and the next, and the next, she busied herself with the tasks of government that Sadokhar would have done were he here, consulting with Ythiel and the other ten Knights of the Western Shore, especially about the defence of the Island, when the time came. But each time she heard a footstep on the stair that sounded even faintly like his, she started with a wild hope that somehow he could have returned, only for it to fade, and leave her crushed.

Looking out of the windows she saw a figure in the distance who walked with the same ease he had, or bent his head in such a way, and the wound of Sadokhar's loss was raw. The loneliness without him was a void which threatened to swallow everything, and she had no belief that time would heal it.

Then word arrived that Kor-Assh of the River was coming, and Tathea prepared to meet him as if Sadokhar were still with them, and might return any day. Rooms were made ready for him and the court dined in the Great Hall as always. But there were fewer visitors from other regions than usual, as if the whole city held its breath, waiting for something to happen which would explain everything, and make it right. They had lived so long in peace that fear was a small thing, not truly believed. A hundred people still sat at the tables and laughed and ate, passed the meat and the wine and told tall stories to each other.

Tathea did not take Sadokhar's seat. It remained empty, but she sat alone a little distance from any others, even Ythiel and the Knights of the Western Shore.

They were halfway through the meal when there was a sudden ceasing of conversation at the far end of the hall as the doors opened and a man came in, followed by six others, but he alone came forward to the head table. He was dressed in a travelling cloak, dusty from the road, and he walked with grace, even though he must have come far and been tired. He was of more than average height, slender and strong. His hair and eyes were dark, the balance of his features spoke of both passion and strength so intense they had burned away the lesser quirks of character. It was difficult to tell his age, but he was not young. There was experience in the lines around his mouth, and time had left its imprint on him.

Tathea felt herself swept dizzy by a wave of memory so powerful it was as if the rest of the hall and all the people in it faded from her awareness and she saw only the one man as he walked the length of the floor towards her. She knew him! Images melted into one another in her mind, gone too quickly to hold. She saw a man half turn towards her, hatred in blazing blue eyes, intimately as if something filthy had touched her soul. Asmodeus!

But this man's eyes were dark, and as he stopped in front of her, there was only the slightest flicker of recognition in him – there for an instant, then vanished, as if he himself had been confused by it and dismissed it as untrue.

She wanted to speak – she ought to from courtesy if nothing else – but all she could do was stare at him.

It was Ythiel of the Knights of the Western Shore who spoke for her.

'Welcome to Tyrn Vawr,' he said gravely, politely. 'Will you dine with us, or would you prefer to rest and eat alone?' He did not ask the man's name. Whoever he was, the hospitality would have been the same.

'I am Kor-Assh of the River,' the man said with the slightest inclination of his head. 'I have come to keep my covenant with Sadokhar, and all who stand with him.' His eyes flickered to the empty seat, but he said nothing of it. Perhaps word had already spread that Sadokhar was gone.

'Welcome, Kor-Assh,' Ythiel replied, indicating a place at the table.

Kor-Assh accepted, casting aside his cloak, which was immediately taken by a page. Food and wine were brought for him.

At last Tathea spoke. 'Welcome to Tyrn Vawr. I hope your journey was pleasant and we have cared for your men and your animals.' They seemed meaningless words, mere politeness.

Kor-Assh replied with wry, throwaway humour, thanking her for her care and assuring her that the hospitality was excellent.

Tathea sat still, the voices around the table beating in her ears, drowning out the sounds of crockery, laughter, distant conversation, the footsteps of the serving men. A dog snored gently on the floor, knowing it was too early to expect titbits.

'. . . my error,' Kor-Assh was saying ruefully to another of the Knights. 'The innkeeper mistook me for a travelling trader and sat me in with half a dozen merchants from Dinath-Aurer. I never want to smell uncured leather again, as long as I live!'

There was more laughter.

Tathea watched Kor-Assh as he spoke. His voice seemed to wash around her almost like a familiar touch to the skin, awakening emotions that scoured the very core of her being. She knew him; in some way deeper than life, she had always known him. Certainty flooded her soul like light over the sea that this was the time of Armageddon, because although Kor-Assh did not know it himself, it was not in his eyes nor his words, but he was Ishrafeli. He had come as he had said he would, more than five centuries ago on the lake shore, to take his mortal life and fight beside her until the world was won or lost.

A servant passed by with a dish laden with sweetmeats and fruit. Another poured more wine.

Someone was asking about Lantrif. He knew it only by repute, and the tales of its strange history intrigued him. It was the western boundary of the world, and its people were different from all other Islanders, older and subtler, their origins obscured by legend.

'No one knows who was there before the Silver Lords,' Kor-Assh answered with a slight shrug. 'Some stories say they were the first children of the gods who were punished for their arrogance by being made mortal.' He smiled. 'A mistaken belief, to my mind.'

Tathea was startled. Surely Ishrafeli could not have been so changed from the man she had known that, even for an instant, he could have countenanced such an absurdity? Of course, once born into the flesh, no one remembers their spirit life before. If they did it would be no proving of their souls. Walking with knowledge, only a fool chooses the darkness, whereas having nothing but faith and one's own agonising discovery of good and ill, choosing the light is an exact measure in the scales of eternity.

The Knight too was startled. It showed in a slight widening of his eyes, no more. 'There are those among your people who consider it a possibility?' His voice was almost level.

Kor-Assh's smile widened, making his face oddly more vulnerable. He picked up a handful of bright strawberries. 'I've met those who certainly behave as if they thought that they, more than most men, were descended from gods,' he replied. 'But that was not what I meant. The mistake I referred to was the notion that mortality was a punishment. Surely the passion of it, for good or ill, and the fact that it is so precious yet can so easily be wasted, is a blessing?'

Tathea felt her heart hammering in her throat. This was a glimpse of the Ishrafeli she half recalled.

The Knight leaned forward, his face alight. 'What other legends are there, more likely to be rooted in fact? Or is that possibly some tale of rebellion coloured into a story more worth the telling?'

Kor-Assh regarded him with a flash of interest. 'I suppose it could be! I always supposed it was just the same arrogance lending itself a shadow of legitimacy. But whoever they were, conquerors, rebels, or voyagers from another shore, the Silver Lords were ruthless in the beginning, and their descendants still guard their secrets.' He bit into the strawberries, then went on to describe the Silver Lords' hereditary power, some of the great battles they had led, and the resistance against the Camassian conquest half a millennium ago.

Tathea listened. He had been her teacher and her guide on that journey they had shared in the past. He had known the truth towards which she only stumbled. Now, as she sat here in this crowded hall, with the gold of the torchlight sending shadows across the deep coffering of the ceiling, she knew the truth, and Ishrafeli did not. It seemed he had not even a vision of who he was or how unimaginably great the task that lay ahead of him. He had heard of the Book from Sadokhar; he had no possible imagination that it was he himself who had led her to it in the beginning, he who had fought the beasts of good and evil on the shores of eternity so she might escape Asmodeus' rage and bring the Book to the world. Or that it was his hand which had sealed it at the last, and left her here to guard it until one came who was worthy to open it again.

Could it be her task to teach him?

They were still talking, easily, with interest, as new friends do, discovering each other's thoughts, asking for facts, but listening to the heart behind the answers.

'Of course, the Camassians tried to take Lantrif,' Kor-Assh was saying. There was both laughter and regret in his face – she did not understand why – and there was an element like pity, as if he knew of something sadder and deeper than the surface facts. 'They

40

formed a secret army of spies and saboteurs, the Brotherhood of the Chain,' he went on. 'It worked brilliantly. The Camassians tried to occupy us, but even the military might and precision of the Empire was not strong enough to withstand the Brotherhood. No one knew who they were. They recognised each other by secret signs, and their oaths were stronger than death.'

'But you pity them!' Tathea broke in. She had to know why. It mattered intensely. He had Ishrafeli's face, and voice, even remembered shreds of his humour, but had he his heart? She kept her hands locked together under the table, where no one could see them shaking.

Kor-Assh looked at her. In a moment too small to measure there was something in his eyes, an uncertainty, a question, as if an echo crossed his memory also, but vanished before he heard its meaning.

He blinked. 'Did I say that? I don't know why I did.'

Ythiel looked at Tathea curiously. Of course he could have no idea what was clamouring in her mind, drowning out everything else. They had known each other since he had come south from the Western Shore. They had spoken of loyalties, terrors and dreams, and yet the love at the centre of her heart she had not shared even with Sadokhar.

'No,' she answered Kor-Assh. 'I just thought I heard it in your voice.'

He looked down, a touch of colour faint in his cheeks. 'I don't know why anyone should pity the Brotherhood of the Chain,' he said quietly. 'They have power and safety, belief in themselves and in their cause.' He looked up at her quickly. 'And yet you are right. I hadn't realised it, but I do feel a . . . a pity for them.' The surprise was in his face, a shadow on his brow, a tenderness in his mouth.

'Why?' Tathea pressed.

Could he answer her? He remembered nothing of their journey, of the love or the loss, but surely even without it, he was the same inside himself, his ability to feel, his striving to understand? But who was anyone, without the knowledge of all that they have been up to that moment? Yet there was experience in his face, mistakes understood, fear conquered, laughter and understanding as before.

She remembered all that Ishrafeli had been, the beauty of his heart, with an ache that tore her open. Would he ever become that man again, fulfil all that was his? And if he did, learning step by step as he must, would he love her as he had before? Or would it be different? Perhaps he would love someone else, or no one with that wholeness ever again?

'Why?' she demanded, staring at his face. 'Why do you pity the Brotherhood of the Chain?'

He blinked.

41

A page approached with a dish of baked pastries, and sensing something larger than hunger of the flesh, turned away again, his feet almost soundless on the floor.

'Because they lost the light,' Kor-Assh replied at last. 'Somehow the means became the end in itself, and the true end was forgotten.'

The warmth broke open inside Tathea. She smiled at him with a radiance that fascinated him, and frightened him because he had no understanding of its cause. He met her gaze uncertainly, then looked away, turning to Ythiel instead.

Tathea did not speak again. The page returned with the food, and the meal continued until it was time to retire.

Tathea did not sleep, and in the morning she was tired and restless, unable to direct her mind to anything.

She stared into the glass, and saw the same face look back at her as had done the day she had entered Hirioth to give the Book back, five centuries before. Time had marked her heart, but not her flesh. The dark eyes held the same intelligence, the same hunger of the will. The mouth betrayed the same passion, and the same startling power to be hurt.

Only Sadokhar had known her long enough to question it. To Sardriel and Ardesir it was only a handful of years. Why should she change in that while?

She rose and began on small tasks she had taken over since Sadokhar left, but she could not keep her attention to them. They had always spoken of Armageddon as if it would be open, something cataclysmic, violent and obvious. But why should it? Asmodeus was the father of deception, the begetter of lies. Surely now, of all times, he would deceive? He could lead them to fear what was ugly but harmless, and send them running into the arms of a sweet and terrible corrosion of the soul, a last death from which there was no resurrection. How would they know? What could unmask the face of the enemy and show them his reality?

Ardesir had a passion of faith which climbed heights others only dreamed of. But his imagination also showed him what terror to fear. Sardriel had an incorruptible love of truth, an integrity which had never been broken. Sadokhar had had the courage which met the ultimate test in life – she dared not think what hell might do to him now.

What would Ishrafeli bring? She did not yet know. She must speak with him, tell him Sadokhar was gone and Tiyo-Mah and the creations of damnation were in the world.

But what if Kor-Assh, still with no knowledge of who he was, felt relieved from his promise? What if he quailed at the thought of an other-than-human enemy? She did not even know how much

Sadokhar had told him of the war to come, because they had all thought then that it would be an attack they could see, and for which there was a defence, whether it succeeded or not. At least it would be plain against whom they fought.

But above and beyond that, she must show him the staff and see if he could read it, and if he did, what it said.

She sent him a message requesting him to speak with her, and an hour later they met in the courtyard. He regarded her steadily and with courtesy, but she was sharply aware that for him they were strangers, allied by a cause, but no more.

'I know you were expecting to see Sadokhar,' she began after they were seated. 'I shall tell you where he has gone, but first I must tell you why.'

Then gravely Tathea explained how they had realised that Asmodeus had the weapon of time against which there was no defence; she saw more than horror in Kor-Assh's eyes as he understood. There was a flicker as if some memory or deeper understanding stirred, but vanished before he grasped it. The temptation to speak to him, to try to tell him what it was, to demand he remember by repeating it over and over, was so strong she was dizzy with the effort of self-control. She longed to stretch across the space between them and touch his hand, even when her mind was telling her it was both ridiculous and intrusive. It would offend him, and embarrass them both.

She was aware he was waiting for her to continue. How much should she tell him? He was Ishrafeli! Did he remember anything, or was it all gone in the life of Kor-Assh, a man Sadokhar had trusted but of whom she knew nothing?

'In the ruins of Sylum there is a man,' she said cautiously, 'growing thinner and wearier with the years, as he yields to the temptation to use a terrible discovery he has made. There is a doorway into time among what is left of the oldest buildings there.' She saw the shadow in Kor-Assh's face, but he did not stop her. 'Through it he has gone again and again back to the great days of the Empire,' she went on. 'Each time he has done so he has weakened both the doorway and himself. He was gaunt when Sadokhar and I first met him, twenty years ago. Now he is a hollow man. The wind blows his robes as if about a skeleton whose bones will shimmer and bend like reeds in water.'

Kor-Assh could keep his peace no longer. 'He told you it was a doorway into the past?'

'Into time,' Tathea corrected. 'He chose the past, or it was given him. Long ago I knew someone else who used such a doorway, and that was into both the past and the future.' She took a deep breath. 'She was the most evil woman I know. She learned the art of

43

raising the spirits of the dead who have seen both light and darkness, and chosen the darkness.'

Kor-Assh's eyes widened, but he did not argue.

She tried to read him and failed.

'Did Sadokhar know of this woman?' he asked.

'Yes.'

His face paled. 'And he chose . . . to test the doorway of hell?' His voice was hushed.

'Yes,' she answered. 'The other doorway was in Shinabar, in Thoth-Moara, in the most ancient quarter. There are things there that are more fearful than most of us even . . .' She tailed off, not sure how to continue.

'The Silver Lords of Lantrif believe in sorcery,' Kor-Assh said in the silence, 'and in the creatures of the Pit, and beyond. In the days of their power the Seneschal of the Seven-Sided Tower was said to have raised hell-kites, and the Lamia, half woman, half fish, who lures men to their drowning.' He frowned, the small smile touching his mouth, a little self-mocking. 'I know there are powers beyond our most hectic dreams, both for good and for evil. If Sadokhar went through that doorway in Sylum, to provoke the Great Enemy, then he loved the world more than it deserves . . .' His voice trembled. He struggled to mask some of the emotion in his face. It stood naked and vulnerable for an instant, before he could conceal it.

'We must all be loved more than we deserve,' Tathea said softly, tears swimming in her eyes, the ache inside her endless, 'or else we will not survive.' She rose, turning away from him, and heard the slight sound of his shoes on the stone as he took a step after her.

'I have a staff I must show you.' Her voice trembled. 'You may be able to read the hieroglyphs on it.'

'Hieroglyphs?' He caught up with her as she crossed the sunlight towards the big door of the castle, studded with brass. She heard the doubt in his voice.

'Yes,' she said, not willing to give any more explanation.

Kor-Assh pushed the door and held it for her, then followed across the wide, marble-flagged entrance hall and up the stairs to the rooms that faced over the inner court. The sunlight poured in, warming the walls and casting back the colour, shining on the polished wood of the floor.

Tathea went to the curtain that concealed the staff and took it out, holding it for him. Her hand was steady, but her fingers were so stiff he had to pull it gently for her to let go.

She watched as he studied the carved figures one line after another. He frowned and looked up at her, his dark eyes puzzled. 'I can read only a little of it,' he said with sharp disappointment. 'This part here . . .'

The answer shivered through her like fire.

'What does it say?'

' "When the man of wisdom has spoken the name of all things",' he answered. 'It doesn't make sense alone, and I can't read the rest.'

She held out her hands, but she did not need to take the staff from him to read the final inscription. ' "When the woman of love has kneeled in the ashes and taken up My burden, then shall I come and receive My own",' she finished. 'That leaves only one line unread . . . one more warrior to find.' She closed her hand on the staff, and his remained, fingers inches from hers.

'Do you know who he is?' he asked.

'I believe it may be Ulfin of the Flamens, but I am not certain. I can't be until he has read the last inscription.'

'And if he does? Or someone else does?'

'We can't afford to wait,' she answered. 'Ardesir has followed Tiyo-Mah to Shinabar, and Sardriel has taken two-thirds of the Treasury to buy mercenaries so we can fight the barbarians on the eastern rim, perhaps hold them long enough for Camassia to find its heart again, and its courage.'

'Barbarians . . .' Kor-Assh said the word slowly, tasting its ugliness, and looking slowly around the soft colour of the walls, the perfect proportions of beauty. The hurt of its spoiling was plain in his face.

Tathea followed his eyes, and realised with chill that the soldiers storming in, trampling it, scarring the wood and stone, would be like a personal violation. Did millions of people the earth wide love their homes like this? Was war the ruin of loveliness, the spoiling of places where people had created peace and learned reverence for work, love, the treasures of mind and of form?

And the answer was immediately in her mind. No. It was not physical. It was corruption of the soul Asmodeus wanted.

'The barbarians are only part of Armageddon,' she said suddenly. 'Perhaps the catalyst. They may be worse than before, but they are human. They can hurt us, even kill us, shatter our homes and pillage our land, but they cannot touch who we really are, and I very much doubt they would even understand such an idea.'

'Then what are we to do?' Kor-Assh said levelly. His eyes never left hers. He was searching for her meaning far deeper than the words between them. She could almost see his memory fighting to recall something frightening and precious beyond all else, which eluded him.

Should she try to tell him? Was that what he was asking, but would not put into words? Was that not what everyone yearns to know above anything – who am I?

'Kor-Assh . . .' she began. How odd that name sounded on her lips, when her heart was saying 'Ishrafeli!'

His look answered her, waiting.

Surely that was her mission now, to teach him the enormity of who he was? His courage was ready for the unknown, but he had no conception of what it would be, or what it could cost him. And yet he was ready to enter battle with Asmodeus himself.

He was still waiting for her to speak.

In the silence she heard footsteps along the passage. Outside, below the window, someone laughed.

'Our greatest battle is of the spirit. All men can wield a sword,' she answered at last. 'We must do far more than that. We must recognise the true face of the enemy, because it may not be what we expect. We must walk so passionately and so wholly in the light that we cannot be misled or deceived with lies no matter how subtle or how sweet.'

She was watching his face. 'We must find the sixth warrior, and prepare the Island against attack whether it is from outside, or from within, or both. Above all, we must seek the mind of God, so we never pick up an evil weapon, even to defend the good. Sardriel has a love of the truth, a wholeness of heart that is greater than any man's I have known. He will face heaven or hell, and not turn from it. That is his weapon.' She breathed in and out slowly, trying to still the emotion in her. 'Ardesir has a power to endure, never to give up or allow failure or disillusion to break his faith. His spirit never wearies of trying. That is his. I used to think Sadokhar . . .' her throat constricted at mention of his name, '. . . would fight beside us . . . lead us . . . but now I know his path was the greater sacrifice.' She saw the admiration shine in his eyes, and knew she had no need to say more.

'And yours?' he whispered.

'I am not certain. I brought the Book in the beginning. Perhaps mine is done until the end.'

'Who opens the Book again?' he asked. 'Is it not you?'

'I don't know. I thought it would be Sadokhar.'

'And what of me?' His voice trembled. 'What mission have I?' He looked at the staff still in her hands. 'What does it mean to name all things?'

She saw the hunger and the dreams in his eyes. His whole being burned for some calling of equal beauty with those she had described for others.

'It is not given me to know.' Her voice cracked as she spoke. 'First you must do what Sadokhar would have – reaffirm the allegiance of all the Island Lords, and warn them what is to come. Keep patience for the rest. You will know it when you need to.'

'Will it—' he began, then stopped.

She knew what he wanted to say – would it be as great? Would it ask of him all he could give?

'Yes,' she answered his thought. 'And more.'

'You . . . know?' He was asking her more than that, leading towards the bond that lay between them, feeling it without knowing what it was.

'Yes,' she answered.

He put out his hand, his fingers gentle on her arm, warm through the fabric of her tabard. Then suddenly he withdrew it as if it had been a guilty gesture. He stepped back. His eyes met hers only for a moment, then he looked away.

She felt a rejection so sharp it was as if he had closed a door just as she had put her hand to it, slamming it, locking her out. She almost heard the bolts slide in her mind. It was absurd to have the tears prick her eyes. To him they were strangers, barely met. Certainly they were united by a common cause, but that was no kind of familiarity, not yet even friendship, let alone love. You could not demand love, you could not even earn it. It was freely given, a grace never deserved, only burning the heart with gratitude and lifting the soul on wings.

She must never remind him that once they had loved, on the soul's first journey, with pure passion of the spirit, awaiting completeness here in the fullness of this world with its flesh, its pain and its glory. To do so would be to reduce to words a memory that had been the meaning of her life, and to him would be an embarrassment, the intrusion of a stranger into the intimacies of the heart.

She turned away also, so he would not read her face or see the uncontrolled tears spill over her cheeks. It took all her strength to keep her voice from choking.

'I pray I shall be equal to it,' he said gravely.

'Of course you will be equal to it!' she rejoined. 'Do you think God mocks any one of us by asking what He knows we do not have?' It was herself she was telling. God would not ask her to bear a pain beyond her either. She must believe that. 'Don't look to know what you are not yet ready to understand. You must have faith!'

'Yes . . . yes, of course,' he answered, hurt, his voice low and a little rough. Then she looked up and saw a shadow in his face, different, touched with shame.

She did not understand.

'It is hard to know what is right,' he said softly, the words drawn out of him. 'Lantrif is an uneasy land. I have done all I can to leave peace behind me, but I don't know how long it will last. I am not Lord by birth, but by marriage. My wife has poor health . . .'

Tathea did not hear the rest of what he said. The words were senseless sounds beating around her ears while her heart shrivelled inside her. It was incomprehensible, and hideously clear. Why had she imagined he could not be married? But she had assumed it as if it were a destiny to which she had a right.

He was still talking, his voice quiet and clear. He was telling her of his wife's suffering, and how she needed his support. Tathea had grasped none of it. It could have been in a foreign tongue. There was only one meaning in it all that touched her, and that was too bitter to absorb. It was amazing that the room was still filled with sun and her heart still drove the blood through her body.

'But I will fight the Enemy wherever God wills it,' he said, watching her face, seeing the change in her and not understanding what had wrought it. 'I gave Sadokhar my word, and I repeat it to you. As long as I do not betray my own people to tyranny and civil war, I will do whatever you ask me.'

Her lips were dry. 'Yes . . . I . . . I know you will.' She tried to swallow but her throat was too tight. 'We shall prepare to go north . . . and . . . and see if we can ally Ulfin to our cause. Perhaps he is the last warrior.' She should care that he was, it should matter intensely, and now it meant almost nothing.

'I shall be ready.' He hesitated only a moment, finding nothing else to say, then he turned and walked to the door and went out, closing it softly behind him.

As soon as he was out of earshot Tathea went to her rooms, flung herself on to the bed and wept as she had not done in years. She wept for loneliness, for grief too great and too certain, for loss of Sadokhar and for fear of all that was to come which she could not see.

Chapter Four

Ardesir stood on the deck of the ship as the bow cut through the blue water towards Shinabar. The great lighthouse of Tarra-Ghum was clear in the distance, a white needle against the cobalt of the sky. But he would have to travel inland to Thoth-Moara, that is where Tiyo-Mah would be, at the heart of power. He remembered it so clearly that in his mind he could already smell the bitter herbs in the wind off the desert and feel the scorching heat and the prickle of the ever-moving sand on his skin.

How would he find Tiyo-Mah? Tathea had described her, and surely there could not be two like her? Would she have the Lords of the Undead with her, or would they remain in hiding until she had established her power?

Ardesir still had friends in Thoth-Moara and he knew the city. It was not so long since he had left, but whom could he trust with a weight such as this?

He thought back, memories crowding his mind.

Thoth-Moara was so like his home in Pera to the east, and yet the differences were sharp. The enamelled domes of Pera had a unique grace, the blue and green walls inlaid with tiles, the sudden flashes of gold in the sun. Columns were slender, some twisted or spiralled, not like the massive buttresses of Shinabar. They were more fanciful. Sudden oddities surprised the wanderer, a spark of humour graced a tower, or an eccentricity made one laugh aloud.

In those days he had been young and dreamed of creating something so beautiful men would marvel at it, and he would give it to one special woman, and she would love him because of it. So he had gone to Shinabar, the heart and source of all subtlety and ancient half-rhythms, colours that faded one to another, and yet never died, and they knew the arts of falling water that cooled the air.

He had learned even more than he hoped – tricks of wit and grace, embellishments of loveliness – but most profoundly the true connections between purpose and beauty, exactly how to use each material to its utmost advantage.

He had never been afraid of ideas, however strange or enormous.

49

His intellectual courage was boundless. It was his soaring mind, the limitless flight of his dreams that had won him Tathea's regard when they had first met a decade earlier. And that regard was more precious to him than he ever admitted, even now.

From her he had learned a concept of love that transcended anything he had thought of before, something that encompassed the earth itself, and everything that had being upon it. As they had walked the narrow streets of the ancient quarter, or ridden the silent desert and shared laughter and pain, talked of good and evil, and what was written in the Book, the passion to fight in the last great war was born in him.

As the ship drew closer to the shore the harbour was plain to the sight. Ardesir recognised the large wharfs and warehouses in which were stored the goods of the world. Great triremes lay at anchor; barges and skiffs moved easily over the smooth, inner waters, dark blue under the brilliant sky. At a glance it all seemed just as it had been when he left to follow Tathea to the Island, and offer his zeal and his honour in the cause. But now, as the ship swung round the outer wall and slowed, he could see the shabbiness of the stone, the broken edges, the faded colours where once they had been bright. One of the largest wharfs was unusable, its piers too badly eroded to be safe.

He was struck with a sudden grief. This land had sheltered him and taught him, and it had once been great. It was like returning to visit a beautiful woman one had loved, and finding her raddled and strangely vulgar. For an instant he wished he could have avoided coming.

Then he heard voices shouting across the water in the familiar Shinabari tongue with its subtlety and music, and he understood why it had to be here that Tiyo-Mah began to build her power before she could spread it across the world. These were the people she knew; the shell of empire was still here, the wisdom and artifice that could be corrupted by her knowledge.

Ardesir disembarked, feeling the familiar heat scorch his arms and face, beating back from the stones and, even here by the water's edge, the ever-present prickle of sand shifting and whispering in the wind off the desert.

He must find a caravan going inland to Thoth-Moara. No one willingly travelled the desert alone. Unless you were native to it, it was safer to join the merchants and traders who moved with up to fifty horses at a time, thirty of them pack animals laden with goods. There was no time to waste. Tiyo-Mah would not have lingered; neither must he.

The caravan masters still met where they always had, in the shade of the great covered market, and he saw three before he even had to enquire for them. It was customary to bargain and it was expected. He approached the first. One must not look too eager. He strolled casually, as if it were of little importance to him whether he went or stayed.

The master was a lean man, but with blunt features, not the hawk nose and hooded eyes of the desert princes.

'Leaving soon?' Ardesir asked conversationally.

'Depends,' the master replied, looking him up and down with calculating eyes.

Ardesir gazed upwards as if judging the weather, then back at the master again. The heat shimmered around him, pressing on his skin. He did not need to speak his thought.

'It's good enough,' the master said guardedly. 'In a hurry?'

'Not at all,' Ardesir denied. 'I'll go when you're ready or unless you have no places left?' He smiled, knowing the man would not be here, were he not still open to business.

'You wish passage to Thoth-Moara?' the master asked, freeing his hand from his robes ready to take the money.

'I think so . . .' Ardesir still wished to sound indifferent.

'Eleven pieces of silver,' the master replied.

Ardesir was surprised. It was dearer than it used to be.

The man must have seen his expression. 'Dangerous days,' he explained, shaking his head. 'Have to have outriders, well armed. It all costs money.'

'Against whom?'

The master's black eyebrows rose. 'Barbarians, of course. Where have you come from?'

'The Island at the Edge of the World,' Ardesir replied, then the instant he had said it, with some pride, he knew it was a mistake, but it was too late to take it back.

The caravan master's eyes flickered and a secret, smug satisfaction touched his lips. 'Then you can hardly be expected to understand our problems. You dealt with your pirates. I hear it is very easy there now. You have had a decade or more of peace, isn't that right?'

It was pointless to argue. It was known everywhere. 'Yes. But I thought this far north you'd hardly be troubled?' He made a question of it.

The master pursed his lips. 'Only because we are always careful. Personally, I've never lost a traveller.' His hand stayed extended for the money. 'Not to sandstorm or thirst either . . . or heatstroke. Bad risk that, for those not used to the desert.' His eyes were hard as stone. 'Needs a skilled master to make sure he doesn't lose anyone, no matter what. A man would die in hours . . . alone.' He smiled suddenly, but the threat was as real as the curved and jewelled knife at his belt.

51

Ardesir glanced past him to the other caravan masters waiting.

'We all know it,' the one in front of him warned softly. 'You won't find anyone to say differently.'

It was true. Ardesir understood it with a sick certainty. They were all watching him. If anyone wanted to get across the desert to Thoth-Moara, or anywhere else, they would pay for protection from barbarians a thousand miles away, or the risk of being lost and left behind, denied water, or whatever kind of murder one wished to call it. But they would pay.

He took out the eleven pieces of silver and passed them across.

'Better be safe,' the caravan master said silkily. 'Another couple of pieces, and we'll look after you specially. Plenty of water.' His smile widened, showing his teeth.

There was no escape. Ardesir must be in Thoth-Moara. What were two pieces of silver, or even yielding to corruption, although it burned him like acid, compared with failing to learn what they needed to know?

He gave it, struggling to hide his rage and contempt.

The master took it with satisfaction. 'We'll start out tonight, at sundown. Good travelling to you . . . safe travelling!'

Ardesir did not reply.

The beauty of the desert night swept away his anger, and riding what was admittedly an extremely good horse, alone in the darkness with the silence, the milky dazzle of the stars across the summer sky, the enormity of creation in its infinite value, dwarfed everything else. A million corrupt men could not darken the ultimate light. He turned his face upward, and his soul ached with prayer. He would fight anything at all to preserve this, and be worthy to remain a part of it.

As soon as they reached Thoth-Moara Ardesir left the caravan, and went in a roundabout way into the ancient quarter of the city. He even went to the exact corner where he had first met Tathea. He remembered it so clearly. There had been such sadness in her it had startled him. Of course now he knew why. It was for Sadokhar, who had at that time refused his high calling, with the sacrifice it would ask of him.

Ardesir found a catch in his throat as he thought how little Sadokhar had understood then! He had seen only the giving up of the sweet, domestic comfort he had hungered for, instead of the lonely path of leadership.

But Tathea had seen him choosing mere decency, instead of the greatness possible for him, and it tore at her heart.

And she must surely also have thought of Tiyo-Mah, who had lived in the ancient palace with its high carved doors. And with the mention of Tiyo-Mah had to come the grief of loss for her child, murdered in the coup. Surely she could never have thought of the dowager Empress without also thinking of Habi, and remembering the night of his death?

If the creatures of the Pit were here with Tiyo-Mah now, then this heart of evil would be their first place of refuge, as it had been her last before she was driven out.

Ardesir stood in the heat of the shadowed, airless pavement and stared up at the towering mass of the palace, basalt polished till it shone. How long had it nestled here, cellars deep into the bowels of the earth? Two thousand years, three thousand? What sins had been committed in its chambers?

He must watch Tiyo-Mah, learn her strategy and then create one of his own. He stood motionless on the hot stones, the heat choking him, his skin covered in sweat.

Then at last he turned away. He should find lodgings until he could judge whom to trust and to burden with his mission, and some kind of work to explain his presence in the city. Names and faces filled his mind, but judgement must be perfect. There was no room for even the slightest mistake.

In Erebus, that region of air and shadow that is neither the world nor hell, but something eternal between the two, Asmodeus paced back and forth. The fury was dark bile inside him as he thought how Tiyo-Mah had disobeyed his command. Not yet, he had told her. It was not time! A few more years and the warriors Tathea had forged would wither. Age would rack their bones and the waiting would dull their hearts. The end would be only death, and the knowledge that all their preparation was for nothing. Asmodeus had the one weapon she could not fight – time. Even Tathea would weaken in the end. It had begun to happen already. She was vulnerable. She loved Sadokhar; through his failure she had nearly been destroyed.

And now he had taken everything into his own hands, broken all the laws and gone through the portal! How could anyone have foreseen that outrageous sacrifice? How could Tathea have allowed it? She knew what he was going to do – and she had let him do it!

And Tiyo-Mah, arrogant, self-willed, cruel, ever-hungry Tiyo-Mah, had gone into the world, taking the Lords of the Undead with her. Only Yaltabaoth had seized back the key to prevent Sadokhar himself returning!

But they were all of no importance. Asmodeus slashed the dark air with his left hand in a furious gesture, dismissing them from thought. They were only the souls of the damned. They were his already. He would deal with them in his own time. As it was, they were condemned for ever to be locked in one body with others of their overriding sin, never to be free of them, never to have privacy or rest, or even command of their own limbs. The never-ceasing voices and wills of others would be quarrelling within them, pulling, tearing, making every gesture a labour, and silence loud with dissension. They no longer possessed an individual existence or the power so much as to pick up an object or take a step without the agreement of others.

How Tiyo-Mah would hate that! Not even the workings of her innermost body would be secret any more. There would be no rest, not ever, not while the stars burned in their courses or the galaxies wheeled in splendour through the night.

That is what he would do to her, when this was over. Even if she were part of the victory, still she must be made to suffer for her disobedience.

But not yet . . . she might be useful. This rebellion, like all others, could be turned until it was an advantage.

Asmodeus stared across the darkening chasms of his prison in the air, clouded, shadowed, encompassed by the void, his right hand clenched on the keys of the world, and considered the others who had awoken his wrath. They too must be punished. He had known them since the birth of time. Like himself, they had chosen the plan which was not God's, nor their elder Brother's, and they had never had forms of flesh. They were of the spirit, and only by act of will could appear to have body, but no resurrection awaited them.

His lip curled as he pictured Azrub, the golden dwarf who had perfected the art of delusion. He could read men's hearts and understand what it was they desired, good or evil, and he could create from those dreams the semblance of reality to the last touch and smell, until they believed they possessed it. What man can resist the desire of his soul and take the bitter reality instead?

Yes, Azrub was a superb tool, Asmodeus knew that, even as he was revolted by him. It was not the dwarf's yellow eyes or his pale, fluttering hands, or the weight of him that repelled, it was the licking of his lips, the appetite that raged inside him. His lust fed on the dreams of others, and his toying with them satisfied his hunger. Without it something in him starved. Asmodeus thought of that with relish. Azrub would suffer an unsatisfied lust which would consume him, eating away his inside. That is how he would be punished!

And how, Asmodeus thought, would he use Cassiodorus, the Lord of Terror? There was nothing to be gained by merely allowing him to rampage through the world with violence. That would destroy physical things, maybe kill a few hundred or a few thousand. But it would not corrupt any souls, and Armageddon was not about death, it was about that part of man which never dies, the inner, immortal core. God could raise as many dead bodies to live for ever as there are stars in the heavens, but He cannot make one soul better than it chooses to be.

No, Cassiodorus was a weapon to keep until the time was right, and terror could be used to purpose.

That was true of all of them! It was even true of Asmodeus himself. He dare not walk the earth too soon and risk being seen by men. If he made the smallest gesture he showed his hand. His greatest weapon now was the very fact that people did not believe in him. 'Devil! What devil? There is no devil!' Likewise 'There is no God!' Grant one, and you grant the other.

Asmodeus must bide his time, wait until Tiyo-Mah had ripened the field for him and the harvest was ready.

In the meantime, how would he punish Cassiodorus for his disobedience? Set him in a world where everything was already smashed to fragments, and there was no one left to terrify. Then he too would starve.

And Ulciber, the beautiful, ever-youthful Ulciber, who desired above all to have a body of flesh which could be resurrected and live for ever. Ulciber, who understood the heart of human weakness so well because he was so nearly human himself! Ulciber was the first and easiest to use, as he always had been. He would begin with the suggestion, the word in the heart, the small voice that tells you what you want to hear. He had the art to make evil seem good, even necessary. He would reap many souls down and the harvest would be rich.

But in the end, of course, he must be punished as well. Asmodeus stared over the moving darkness into the void, and savoured the thought in his mind. He would set him among those already so corrupt they could sink no lower. He would become idle and hungry, robbed of use. Then what would he have to feed on, what left to destroy?

Lastly Asmodeus thought of Yaltabaoth, Lord of Despair, and his own limbs grew cold and his bones ached. Azrub could not deceive him, he knew all truth. Cassiodorus could not frighten him, he was master of chaos himself, and not even Ulciber could taste the knowledge of corruption he possessed.

But in Asmodeus there was a fierce, white-hot belief that he would win, come Armageddon, and when he did, the earth would be his to have and hold for eternity! It would be his star from which to spread out in endless power and dominion. Millions of worlds would be his. His glory would never end.

When he won!

Yaltabaoth's was the one power which might touch him. He had fought this battle from the daybreak of eternity. He had always believed he would win! But the wing of despair brushing the heart was a wound to which even he was not invulnerable.

He would not use Yaltabaoth yet. Not for a long time. The world was far from despair. Of course, there had always been individuals, and there would be now. But not Tathea, not her warriors forged in the peace of the Island, and the rich knowledge she still kept from the days when she could open the Book!

Yaltabaoth could truly work only when Asmodeus had already sown the seeds and the harvest was ripe. He would reap in the last remaining souls, the ones nothing else could touch.

But how to punish him for his arrogant disobedience in returning to the world now, before he was commanded? That was something Asmodeus did not yet know. But he would find a way. Yaltabaoth would have his weakness. Everyone did!

The wind raced hollow and dark across the emptiness, and he paced the ramparts, his mind filled with visions of the day he would have them all in his hand. Perhaps it was only a disobedience that they had begun so soon, not a disaster. He should have no fear of Tathea, or anyone she could persuade to follow her. She was human, full of doubt and terror, like anyone else. After all, she was cut of the same cloth as himself, a sister from the first morning of creation. She too could be tempted by beauty, by praise, by the knowledge that she was loved, and needed! She also was afraid of failure, of loneliness, of pain. She believed, but she could be darkened by despair, the fear of loss, of being betrayed, that those she loved were not equal to the call – as, of course, they were not! None of them was. They would all turn to ease and cheap glory in the end. He knew that!

But more than doubt in others, she could be made to doubt herself! She could be weakened to nothing by the fear that she was not good enough, not strong enough, and above all, not loved enough! That was the final cut to the soul – the knowledge she would have to face in the end – no one would love her enough to light the stars across the darkness of the last defeat.

This was his world! He would keep it! He had the keys, and he would use them. His hand clenched and he held them up, smiling. He would not lose – not this time! And it was this time that decided eternity.

Ardesir moved cautiously, but one friend from the past of whom he was certain was a writer and fellow architect named Min-Obal. He proved easy to find, since he now worked in the Isarch's palace, and one or two discreet enquiries, made as if from idle politeness, ascertained where he now lived.

56

Within five days of his arrival in Thoth-Moara, Ardesir was lodging with his old friend, sitting one evening in the quiet inner courtyard of Min-Obal's house watching the water shimmer over the walls of the upper pool and slide almost without sound into the outer pool where the lilies lent their perfume to the fading sunlight.

At first they both spoke only of the pleasure of seeing each other after such a long absence, recounting all that had befallen them between then and now, laughing at quicksilver Shinabari jokes. But the shadows in Min-Obal's dark, curious face made it easy to move to the wider things that hovered on the edge of the consciousness all the time.

'It's worse, even in the last few days,' Min-Obal said with an edge of surprise in his voice. He shrugged very slightly. 'I suppose the barbarians have been growing stronger for years and it's been so gradual we've hardly noticed it. Border raids have been one of life's hardships for generations. But just this morning I heard that an old woman, a widow from the southern desert, arrived in the city a day or two ago, and she says that it is far more serious than even the worst reports have said.'

Ardesir heard the edge of fear in his friend's voice, carefully disguised. He was a good man and not easily disturbed. He knew the rumours of politics well.

'An old woman?' Ardesir said with a tiny shiver even in the still heat of the evening. 'What kind of an old woman? What does she look like?'

Min-Obal was startled. 'Look like?'

'Yes. Have you seen her? Do you know anyone who has?'

'I've heard she is small and gaunt, and her hair is thin enough to see her scalp through it. What has that to do with the news of the barbarians?'

'I don't know,' Ardesir confessed. He was uncertain how much truth to tell even Min-Obal. And yet if he trusted no one, he might still learn information, but far more slowly and perhaps too late to be of use. But more than that, without allies, what measures could he take to fight against her?

Min-Obal was watching him, knowing he was weighing how much to trust him.

Ardesir chose courage above the careful voice of sense within himself. He could not tell anyone the truth – he had no facts, no proof to make it believable – but he must come as close to it as he could.

'She is a woman of immense evil,' he replied, looking at Min-Obal intently. 'She will use any means she can to gain power. I followed her here from the Island. I know more of her than I can tell you yet.'

There was neither doubt nor belief in Min-Obal's face. 'She says the barbarians are far more numerous than we supposed, and are massing for a serious attack, to drive inwards even as far as Thoth-Moara one day,' he said levelly. 'There are indications that that is true.'

'Perhaps,' Ardesir conceded. Deliberately he lightened his tone. 'But I need to find work. I have a certain amount of money, but it will not last for ever, and my days of being a hungry student of the arts are a memory I don't wish to resurrect!'

Min-Obal smiled, making himself relax also. 'There is not a great deal of building at the moment, especially of the quality you would be interested in, but I shall enquire. They are talking of a courthouse towards the northern sector of the city.' Then his look darkened. 'The city has changed even in the short time you've been gone. There's more corruption, and it's deeper, even in places you don't expect to find it. There is not much which can't be bought, if you have the price and know where to offer it. And you can lose things – jobs, commissions, even horses – without ever knowing why, although you can guess. But it's wiser not to.'

Ardesir was saddened, but he knew he should not be surprised. Eudoxius had said as much of Camassia, why not of Shinabar also?

'I would rather be in the centre of the city,' he said, not referring to the corruption but meeting Min-Obal's eyes ruefully. He could not afford to be far from Tiyo-Mah. He plunged on. 'Is there nothing in the palace?'

Min-Obal looked surprised only for an instant. 'Not at your level of skill,' he answered. 'Clerk of restoration works. That is half the money you could earn.' He smiled. 'And a quarter what you are worth.'

'Can you get it for me, even if I have to pay?'

Min-Obal was puzzled, but he did not argue. 'I think so. Are you certain?'

'Yes . . . yes, absolutely. Please?'

Ardesir began work in the palace the day he was given the news by Min-Obal. It mattered not in the slightest whether he earned little or much, but he had to be careful not to raise suspicion by being seen to be too eager to accept such a comparatively lowly office. There were those who remembered not only his skills but his ambition, and would find indifference to advancement impossible to believe. Therefore he allowed remarks as to his one day designing a new palace to go by with a smile and no demur.

Every other day more news came in of barbarian raids on the desert oases of the south, and each time the atrocities recounted were more hideous. People were killed needlessly and their bodies left in the sand. Women were mutilated. The tales of horror grew and spread a fire of terror in the city.

Within weeks panic was in the air and it was then that Ardesir saw Tiyo-Mah for the first time. The Isarch, a man in mid-life, already running to sallowness and slack flesh around the paunch, was asking particularly for someone to advise him how to deal the barbarians a blow that would crush them and send them back into the wilderness. His generals had grown complacent, unused to war in generations; the army was a parade-ground force who had never faced the privations of a desert campaign, let alone actual blood-shed, and he had lost patience and temper with their excuses. The courtiers were pedlars of favour, influence and money, and they hated each other more than they perceived any danger beyond the confines of the city which had nourished and divided them for centuries. They answered with flattery and blame, and evaded the issue.

That was when Tiyo-Mah came forward. Ardesir saw her. She was as Min-Obal had said, a small woman, narrow-shouldered and bent with age, her hair scraped back over the dome of her head. She wore a dark green tabard, almost black, embroidered with turquoise and gold, the ancient royal colours of Shinabar and before the modern taste for purples, aping the Camassian Empire.

She came quietly, a widow from the south, bringing news of yet more devastation, and yet reaffirming her belief in victory in a time of common bereavement. She did not kneel before the Isarch, but her age excused her that, and he seemed blind to the power in her black eyes and her cruel, beaked face. To him she was no more than marred with age and loss, and he received her with courtesy, because he wished to hear the news himself, even if he dreaded it.

Ardesir stood in the place he had been granted for such audi-ences, beside other minor palace officials who swelled the ranks of courtiers without taking more important men from duties that mattered.

'We grieve for your loss,' the Isarch said in answer to her account of a village massacre in which she had supposedly seen five members of her family put to the sword.

She kept her eyes down, but her body shuddered. 'We must defeat them, Majesty, before they destroy all our southern cities, and move on to Thoth-Moara itself,' she said urgently. 'But of course you are doing that! No doubt you are preparing even now to levy greater taxes so that your armies can be increased, and better weapons forged for them.' The faintest smile touched the corners of her soft, perished lips. 'And you will already be seeking new generals who are more experienced in war . . . not easy in a land

59

which has enjoyed centuries of peace. Perhaps an old woman who knows the barbarian can offer her loyalty in the form of advice to her lord?' She did not wait for his answer. 'There are men of my tribe who are scarred and hardened by experience of such wars. They know the ways of the desert, and they hunger for the place and the means to serve their country and find their revenge at one time.'

There was a slight murmur around the chamber as fear rustled through like a wind, then, as the Isarch raised his hand, hushed to silence.

Very slowly Tiyo-Mah lifted her head.

The Isarch paled. His hands gripped the ends of the armrests in his golden seat.

'You speak well,' he said, his voice hoarse. 'We must all be avenged for our losses. We must drive the barbarian back into oblivion with a lesson he shall not forget, nor his children's children. I am doing all that you say. But if you know such men of experience, send them to me!'

'At once, Majesty,' she replied. Her voice was dry like the breaking of old wood, but it carried to every corner of the huge chamber. 'Then every man, woman and child of the Shinabari people will be safe again, once the might of the army stirs and you stretch forth your sword to strike the enemies of your people.'

There was a whisper of approval from the courtiers, and those still awaiting audience. But Ardesir saw that most of them were looking not at the Isarch slumped in his high seat with its gold panels, but at the old woman who stood on the tessellated floor in front of and below him, bent, haggard with age, and less than half his weight, but with a passion of will that all but drowned him.

She withdrew, to send messages back south across the desert. The Isarch refused any further petitions and retired to his rooms.

Every day the news grew worse. Fear mounted. Tiyo-Mah's name was repeated more often. Word came of her courage, her will to fight, her belief in victory.

Within ten days she was given rooms in the palace and Ardesir saw her almost every day, carrying messages, relaying orders, giving advice which the Isarch never refused, while everyone waited for the generals from the south whom she had promised.

A sense of purpose settled over the city. Panic subsided. Taxes were doubled and no one complained. Then they were tripled, and the few dissenting voices were quickly silenced.

Men with money invested it in great foundries to make swords and armour. Tanneries sold leather to cobblers who made boots for the army. Fabric was woven and stitched for military tunics and tabards. Carpenters and wheelwrights built chariots. Grain,

60

dried dates, honey, salt and water flasks were sold to army quartermasters.

Extra money was paid to those who worked longer hours. Profits soared. The Isarch was praised, but there were few who did not know it was Tiyo-Mah's advice he took, her voice which goaded him, her will he finally dared not displease.

Then the first of Tiyo-Mah's new generals arrived at the army camps to the west of the city. Word spread like fire of his brilliance, his ruthlessness. Overnight the discipline of the army changed.

Every week more men were drafted and the army swelled to vast proportions. Battalions were sent south into the desert and news returned of terrible fighting on the caravan trails, in the oases and around the outlying towns. Notices of the dead were posted in the city every third or fourth day. A sense of the reality of war came at last with the knowledge of soldiers who would not return, fathers, brothers, and sons lost for ever.

But Thoth-Moara prospered. Every able-bodied man found all the work he could do. The only poverty was among those who were old or sick in mind or body, those crippled by the hurts of life, simple of mind or wounded of spirit.

For a little while they were ignored, then gradually they were seen as a drain on a society fighting for survival. As summer faded and winter approached the mood became more than an intolerance for perceived idleness. Thoughts were expressed that the precious substance of the nation should not be used to sustain those who purchased nothing. It became illegal to give to beggars, regardless of whatever misfortune had driven them to such recourse. Idleness was a sin, and to foster it, or aid and abet it became a crime. Those who indulged in it were punished with confiscation of their goods, with hard labour, and if persisted in, eventually with execution as traitors to the common good.

All this required monitoring, controlling, and even acts of force when necessary. A secret police was the most efficient answer, and when Tiyo-Mah put it to the Isarch, he understood and grasped it.

The army became vast, and for the first time in centuries it was a machine of war. New captains were appointed from the desert, men of a very different mettle from those Shinabari who had postured at its head in time of peace. The ability to stand straight, behave with panache, and look good in a dress uniform were of no value. Men who were cunning and tireless, and ruthless not only with the enemy but with their own subordinates as well, were needed now.

The name of Tiyo-Mah's general was on every tongue, with respect, hope of victory at last.

But when finally he came from the camp into Thoth-Moara the

61

name was whispered with awe and a shudder. When Ardesir saw him, walking with a slightly rolling gait in one of the palace corridors, he knew why.

Mabeluz heard Ardesir stop behind him and he turned. Only part of his face was visible because he wore a black silk mask over most of it, but his skin was purplish-black and covered with lumps and pustules. The muscles of his neck seemed to be constantly moving, but involuntarily, without reason. His small eyes were without whites, like an animal's, and filled with such malignity that Ardesir felt the strength go from him and he stood motionless, staring back.

'Who are you?' Mabeluz demanded. His voice was hoarse as if his throat hurt to use it, and it had no timbre.

'Ardesir, sir,' Ardesir replied. 'Clerk of works to ... to the palace.' He nearly said to the Isarch, then realised that this man of all of them knew that the Isarch was Tiyo-Mah's puppet.

'Why are you following me?' Mabeluz glared at him. 'Do you want to be a soldier, eh? You don't look fit for it, tiptoeing around the corridors like a servant!' It was an insult, almost an accusation. His neck twisted and his shoulders hunched. He seemed to have some nervous tic in his scalp, the bristles of his hair moved, and it was hard to drag one's eyes from their hideous fascination.

Now Ardesir understood with horror who this creature was. Tathea had described the six who had followed Tiyo-Mah through the portal. This thing was one of them.

What should he say? He was in the presence of hell walking the earth. His throat was dry and his mind in chaos. But Mabeluz demanded an answer, he was not a nightmare but intensely real. Ardesir could not only see him and hear his breathing, he could smell a strange sourness in the still air of the palace corridor in spite of the cool stones of the floor and the water rippling over the fountain edge a dozen yards away.

He swallowed again and felt his throat constrict. Please God, give him an answer. 'I want to serve my country in any way I can,' he replied, careful to avoid using the Isarch's name. 'Whether it is here, or anywhere else.'

Mabeluz grunted. It displeased him, because almost everything did, but he could find no fault with it. 'You should do well in the police!' he said viciously. 'You have the face for it.' And he turned on his heel and resumed his odd, slightly rolling gait to the end of the corridor and turned the corner out of sight.

Ardesir was left shivering and covered with sweat. Suddenly the evil had assumed a new reality. Tiyo-Mah, for all her skill and her evil, was human. This creature might have been once, but he was not now.

That evening, in the quiet of their own courtyard, Ardesir sought Min-Obal. He moved beyond the fountain where the sound of the water would mask any speech from being overheard in the house, or the street beyond. He had become accustomed to the knowledge that there were listeners everywhere, and potential betrayal.

There was no time to lead up to his purpose gently.

'I saw the new supreme general of the armies today,' he said as soon as Min-Obal had sat on the edge of the pool. Now was the time for the truth.

Min-Obal's face darkened. 'So did I. He looks scarcely human. I didn't think even the vilest of the barbarians from beyond the last oasis looked like that!' He spoke with a wry smile, but it did not hide his understanding of something beyond ordinary evil, or his fear of it. 'God knows what lies behind the mask, if it is worse than what we can see!'

'Only because God knows everything,' Ardesir replied, matching his tone. 'But I think the devil is more likely to be acquainted with it.'

Min-Obal became suddenly very still, his eyes intense, as if he recognised a moment of new truth. There was no sound in the courtyard but the soft slithering of water down the walls of the upper pool into the lower. The perfume of lilies filled the air, and of bitter herbs blowing in from the desert on the sunset wind.

'The devil?' Min-Obal said with a lift in his voice, even though it was no more than a whisper.

'Asmodeus,' Ardesir answered. 'The Great Enemy, who would wage the final war of the world, and destroy the souls of every living thing, and then take it for his own.' He watched Min-Obal's face for incredulity, but he did not see it.

'You believe there is such a being?' Min-Obal asked, but his eyes betrayed that he accepted it already. Something within him understood.

'This is the final war,' Ardesir said urgently, 'in the last victory of good or evil.' He watched Min-Obal's face. 'It was prophesied in the Book which Ta-Thea brought over five hundred years ago.'

Min-Obal's eyes widened.

'She still lives, in the Island at the Edge of the World,' Ardesir went on.

Min-Obal watched him gravely, belief deepening every moment. 'Asmodeus?' he repeated.

'There has to be opposition in all things,' Ardesir said. 'Without the extremes of choice, there is no freedom, and without the freedom to be anything at all, what are we? Pygmies of the soul. There are no limits to good or evil. Heaven's door was always open, if we would climb to it – but now is the beginning of the end, and hell's door is open too. Mabeluz is one of the creatures who has come through it.'

'And Tiyo-Mah?' Min-Obal whispered.

'A human soul in the last corruption,' Ardesir answered. He wondered if Min-Obal was ready for the truth of that, and of Tathea. Perhaps not yet. 'Such a one has unique powers, because all humans are children of God, and that which could have been good and chose evil is always blacker than that which never possessed that possibility. The depth of the fall is the measure of the sin.'

Min-Obal looked at the water gently stirring around the lily leaves and the tiny flies hovering on gilded wings above it. 'What can we do against them? There must be something! Where is the power of good?'

'Within us.'

'Can we win?' Min-Obal looked up, fear and hope struggling in his eyes.

'Yes! But only if we give everything we have, and more than we believe we do . . .'

'Then we must strike at Tiyo-Mah.' Min-Obal's face was pale as he said it, and he did not try to mask his horror.

Ardesir closed his eyes for a second. 'I know. But first we must find her weakness – if she has one – and we must believe that she does. Watch her, for need, fear, pain, hunger, any vulnerability at all. I will too. But be careful! Don't ask questions, trust no one else, especially the Isarch.'

Min-Obal gave a short, bitter laugh. 'I haven't trusted the Isarch in years! And watch for his son, Bol-Ferrat, as well. The boy has neither mercy nor loyalty. He would be a natural leader of the secret police if he were older. Give him five years, and he'll have the job.'

Ardesir turned down his mouth in acknowledgement of an ugly truth.

Days passed into weeks. More news came of losses to the army, around the southernmost oases. Fearful atrocities were committed against civilians: women were raped and disembowelled, men castrated. Hundreds of men were dead and thousands wounded. Gains were small, savage and greeted with jubilation.

However, neither Ardesir nor Min-Obal saw the slightest weakness in Tiyo-Mah. She grew from power to power. After four months in Thoth-Moara she no longer even pretended to defer to the Isarch. The palace staff had realised within weeks the extraordinary force of will that drove her, and that the Isarch was a weak creature compared with her. Now even the crowds in the streets knew that she was their hope of salvation from an enemy who grew more dreadful with each passing day. Terror gripped them and soared beyond any form of reason. Even the lists of missing and dead posted at regular intervals did not dampen their ardour and willingness to sacrifice anything and everything to the cause of war.

Tiyo-Mah herself took time from her duties to speak with the new widows and orphans of the men lost. Ardesir was present one bright winter day when at last the air was cool even in the city near the palace, and he saw her walk out under the palms towards the bent and grieving women, some holding small, bewildered children by the hands.

As Tiyo-Mah emerged into the sunlight again Ardesir saw her face clearly. It was the first time he had stood so close to her in two or three weeks. He was startled how haggard she looked. Her hair was even thinner and it seemed to drag across her skull, pulling the skin tight, but even so, it could not smooth out the hollows around her eyes, nor conceal the shadowed, almost bruised-seeming skin. She looked bloodless, as if she had not eaten or slept in days. Her mouth was soft and sunken over her teeth. Her hands, clawlike, grasped her ebony stick, and she seemed to need its support as she walked unsteadily over towards the first widow awaiting her. If Ardesir had not known who she was, he would have admired her courage in attempting to come out here to offer sympathy to those so recently bereaved. He could even have imagined her to be showing a profound pity. It was plain in the faces of others watching her that that was what they felt. A swell of emotion greeted her, a reverence.

Tiyo-Mah reached the first woman and stopped, looking up into her face. She murmured a few words, inaudible to Ardesir at this distance, and stretched her skeletal hand to touch the woman's face, still wet with tears.

She moved on to the next, and the next, speaking to each one, touching them, and then touching her own face as if she could absorb their grief and share its burden.

It was not until she had spoken to them all and was returning to the palace that she passed Ardesir within half a dozen paces. He saw her face with a shock as if lightning had struck him, tingling sharp and burning his mind. She was no longer gaunt and drained, her flesh did not look dark nor paper-thin. The strength was back in her, the blood, the passion of will. She was too clever to have altered the way her back was bent or how she leaned on her stick, but the power vibrated in her, her eyes were bright and hard, and her mouth was firm with all the old cruelty again. She had been rejuvenated.

He tried to keep the elation, the wild hope out of his voice when he told Min-Obal. It must be confirmed. It was only an idea.

'Watch next time she comforts the bereaved,' he said quietly when they were alone. 'Look at her before, and after. See exactly what she does, and tell me.'

Min-Obal started to ask why, then stopped himself. He must have seen the urgency in Ardesir. His own face quickened with hope, and he said no more.

It was three weeks before they were certain. Then they met in the courtyard by the pool again, after dark when the night wind was chill off the winter desert and the stars blazed so low in the sky they seemed almost within reach of an upstretched arm.

'I'm certain,' Min-Obal whispered. 'I've seen the same thing every time. She comes out almost on the point of exhaustion. She speaks to them, touches them, and then returns with her strength renewed.'

'Does she always touch them?' Ardesir pressed.

'Yes.'

'Always their faces?'

'Yes, and then her own.'

Ardesir leaned forward. 'Whether they weep or not?'

'No – they always weep, but she doesn't touch them all.' Min-Obal hesitated but Ardesir could not read his face in the dark. 'She only touched those who wept for grief. I've seen her with those who wept for self-pity, or rage at loss. She spoke to them but did not touch. It is grief, only grief which feeds her.'

Ardesir hesitated, but the certainty grew inside him.

'What is there to wait for?' Min-Obal asked. 'It is worse every day. The whole city is changing, there is fear everywhere, people suspect one another. There are fewer and fewer who would not betray someone else to save themselves. Nobody knows who the secret police are. The old and the sick are starving and no one dares help them. Once we used to nurture the simple or the troubled and count it a mark of honour. Now we deliberately destroy them. Our fear of the barbarian is consuming our humanity and we ourselves are becoming a kind of barbarian of the soul.'

'You are right,' Ardesir conceded. 'There is nothing to wait for.' He felt the fear flutter inside him. 'We know her vulnerability. We must use it. We must deprive her of the tears of grief.'

'How? Have you thought yet?'

Ardesir had barely the vestige of an idea, and he was not yet ready to own even that. 'No . . .'

'I have,' Min-Obal said quickly. 'They are new widows every time – by definition they have to be. They are strangers to her.'

Ardesir swallowed hard. 'How does that help?' He almost knew what Min-Obal would say, and for all his hate of Tiyo-Mah and his knowledge of what she was, he dreaded the moment of commitment. He needed a little longer to prepare himself.

'If we give her women who can weep on command, actresses whose tears are real, but sprung from skill, not grief, they will not feed her,' Min-Obal answered.

Ardesir was flooded with relief, and shame for it. 'It won't work! She is strengthened almost immediately. She'll know they are not widows.'

'Then we must arrange a time when she cannot ask for more,' Min-Obal replied. 'It must be immediately before a big audience with armourers, the Isarch, anything for which there would be no sensible excuse. After all, she cannot tell anyone she needs the tears for her own survival!'

'No . . . but it can hardly stop her seeking more people, nor from destroying the actresses in her rage,' Ardesir pointed out.

'If it is all done in front of a huge audience – courtiers, ambassadors from Camassia and Pera, even the bankers from Tirilis – then she cannot risk being seen to show any vulnerability at all.'

'But how long can we keep her from more grief? How long must she be starved before it kills her?' Even as he framed the question, Ardesir knew Min-Obal would have the answer, just as he had it himself.

'She has never gone longer than three days,' Min-Obal replied. 'At the rate of change in her that we've both seen, five would be enough. What we need is to have others within the household who can take her to her room, tell her that someone with deep grief wants to see her, so she will stay, and then lock her in.'

Fear ran through Ardesir like cold water drenching him. It was a moment before he could find his voice. 'Even one mistake . . . would be fatal.'

'I know. But will doing nothing not also be fatal?' Min-Obal asked.

'Yes. We must be certain. Who else can we trust?' It was a rhetorical question. Both he and Min-Obal had been seeking and testing, watching, judging over the past months. They knew the answer already. There were about a dozen men and women they were certain of, who would risk their lives, even against the kind of death Tiyo-Mah would exact in vengeance. Now was proof that all those hours had been well spent. Ardesir answered his own question, reeling off their names before Min-Obal could reply. 'We must warn them of the risk,' he finished, cringing inside at the knowledge of what they faced.

Min-Obal was already naming the men who would keep Tiyo-Mah

67

occupied with officials she could not afford to deny, and the actress who would find others of her skill, and the captain of the guard who would lock and bolt Tiyo-Mah's door. This was his city, his people. He had already weighed it in his mind.

Ardesir could do no more than agree, praying in silence for success, or if not, at least for survival of those brave enough to offer their lives in such a venture.

The first step worked superbly, with the rhythm of a perfectly conducted ensemble of musical players, each striking his note at the moment, singly or together.

Tiyo-Mah gave her regular audience to the most lately bereaved. The real widows were received by a senior palace official, the actresses stood in the courtyard under the trees, hands lowered in respect, their faces wet with tears, and murmured their thanks as the old woman touched them.

She departed as gaunt and weak as she had come, her brow furrowed with confusion but her anger concealed. Min-Obal himself offered her his arm and she needed it to support her return.

'You must be tired, my lady,' he said softly to her. 'So much grief for you to comfort. I hesitate to ask anything further of you, but I know you have given more to the war than anyone else, even the Isarch or the generals.'

'What is it?' she said roughly, staring ahead of her as she leaned on him as they climbed the steps.

'A man who has lost all his sons, four young men of unquestioning courage and devotion . . .' He did not wish to say too much and raise suspicion. Invention was always best kept to a minimum.

She murmured something almost inaudible. He felt her weight deadening his arm. Hope surged up inside him. Was this all victory required – planning, care and the nerve to carry it out?

He guided her inside. She seemed willing to go towards her own chambers. He passed under the great archways and along the corridors with their painted walls. Bol-Ferrat, the Isarch's son, was lounging in one of the ante chambers, his youthful face creased in lines of discontent. He hated Tiyo-Mah because he was frightened of her, and he saw her eating away his father's power, and so eventually his own. He would like to have been insolent, but even in her weakened state, he dared not. He straightened up and unfolded his arms.

Min-Obal and Tiyo-Mah passed him in silence. Min-Obal knew the boy would be staring at them, possibly pulling a face at the old woman's retreating back, but she was too weak to turn and catch him.

'Fetch the man who lost his sons,' she ordered as they reached

68

her quarters and the guard stood to attention. She did not notice the captain himself was there, nor that the soldiers were not the usual ones; her attention was on Min-Obal.

'Are you certain you have the patience to see him, my lady?' he asked, savouring the moment, but dropping his voice with concern.

She too played the part. 'I am tired. All this grief, this loss. But the war is for our survival! He has given his sons for his country. Of course bring him to me, but quickly, so I can rest.' Her black eyes were filmed over, as if she were growing blind, and the gaunt flesh of her face sagged.

Min-Obal felt a twinge of pity. She had once been human. Could Ardesir be mistaken? Mabeluz was certainly a creature of hell, but could Tiyo-Mah be no more than a magnificently brave old woman, fired by her own losses, and the leader the nation needed against the barbarian, who was certainly real enough? Was it pity, or sheer strength of will which renewed her?

Then to lock her in would do no harm.

'Yes, my lady,' he said obediently. 'Rest yourself for a moment, and I shall bring him to you.'

The captain of the guard opened the door for her and she went in without glancing at him. He closed it and pulled the bar across soundlessly. He looked at Min-Obal, then Min-Obal turned and left.

From the courtyard Ardesir had watched them, his heart pounding, his mouth dry. He had followed a few minutes after, in time to see Bol-Ferrat glaring at the back of the old woman with hatred in his face.

Ardesir had gone on and up the stairs to the old woman's rooms. He'd felt a surge of relief as he'd seen the guard standing at ease at the door and had met his eyes. The guard had nodded very slightly.

When Ardesir returned two hours later and found Min-Obal also there, it was a totally different scene. The guard was pale, a sheen of sweat on his face in the reflected light from the high windows, and Tiyo-Mah's voice was audible through the door, hoarse, rattling like death in her throat.

'Let me out! Fool! If I die in here, what do you imagine will happen to you?'

The guard gave no answer. He looked beseechingly at Ardesir, then Min-Obal.

'No!' Ardesir barely mouthed the word.

There was silence for several minutes, then they heard a faint scratching on the inside of the door, as if fingernails were drawn along it, someone straining for the handle but too weak to reach it.

Tiyo-Mah's voice came again, dry as dust. 'If I die Mabeluz will avenge me. He will destroy your body in agony, and take your soul to hell! He can do it – think of his face, his eyes, and know that I am not threatening in vain! Let me out!'

The guard was shivering, biting his lip.

'No,' Min-Obal repeated. Then, looking at the barred door, and the guard's face: 'If we let her out now, she'll kill us anyway,' he added. 'She would never forgive us for making her beg. Keep the door barred. Say nothing. Don't answer her. It won't be long. She sounds weaker by the moment.'

But they remained there, afraid to leave the guard alone in case somehow she reached his fear or his compassion, and gradually Tiyo-Mah's voice grew weaker. The threats were more vicious – she described the tortures of hell, the agonies of the mind which never die – but now only some of her words penetrated the weight of the door, and they heard no movement any more.

It was hot in the passage. The air seemed motionless in spite of the watered wall only yards away with its glistening surface and the lilies in the green pool below.

'Go and make sure Mabeluz is occupied,' Min-Obal said after another hour. 'I have made provision, but I would be better assured if you checked that all is well.'

Ardesir nodded and turned to leave, glad of an honourable reason to escape the enclosing prison of the corridor, its airlessness and the knowledge of what lay behind the barred door, waiting to die.

But he had gone only as far as the main hallway at the bottom of the stairs when he saw the Isarch's son, Bol-Ferrat, again.

The boy looked at him, at the stair behind him, then, as if he had suddenly perceived a wonderful idea, he turned and moved swiftly along a side passage which appeared to lead only to storerooms. But in his time as clerk of works Ardesir had learned it actually led to the entrance of a series of passages within the walls.

He went after the boy. He had never either liked or trusted him. He had seen a cruel streak which made it easy to believe that he could be anciently descended from Tiyo-Mah. There were characteristics in him which leaped the five hundred years, and the thought of it sent Ardesir along the same passages with a sense of urgency.

He could not see Bol-Ferrat ahead of him, but there was only one place he could be going, and Ardesir knew the way, at least in theory. He had never actually followed it.

He found the entrance and opened it without difficulty. It was dark inside, but not as stale as he had expected. He certainly was not the only person to be using it! He closed the doorway behind him and felt his way along softly, keeping one hand to the wall to

70

guide him. Bol-Ferrat must be somewhere ahead. He listened but he could hear nothing, no footsteps, no breathing.

He lost track of time and of direction after he had turned half a dozen corners, and the passage itself had curved and gone up a slight incline. He tripped and fell to his knees when he came to a flight of steps upward, but the air was still fresh. And then ahead of him he saw light coming from a vent high in the wall to the left. But it was not the end of the passage. It forked. There was no indication which way Bol-Ferrat had gone. Ardesir chose the left. He was wrong. It led to the Council Chamber. He knew that as soon as he opened the entrance an inch wide. He closed it again, retraced his steps and went to the right.

Ten minutes later he heard the sound of weeping, and a thin shaft of light showed him Bol-Ferrat crouching before a hole in the wall, big enough to see through, no more. His shoulders shook and he seemed to be trying to deny something.

'No!' he gasped. 'No, no, no!' But he believed it, his voice was strained with grief. 'I won't let it happen! There's got to be something left!'

Then a long, thin finger came infinitely slowly through the hole and touched his cheek, and withdrew again. Then as he watched, paralysed, the finger came again, hard and swift, pointed nail like a dagger straight to the eye and the brain. There was a long-drawn-out, high and terrible scream. For a hideous minute Bol-Ferrat hung pinned to the wall, kicking. Then he stopped and slithered off to lie crumpled on the ground. The long, scarlet finger withdrew, leaving a rim of blood in the hole.

Ardesir knew they had lost. The boy had gone to spy on the old woman, to see if she was really as weak as she seemed, and she had seen him, and told him something which had hurt him so badly he had wept. Ardesir would never know what it was, but he could guess. There was little Bol-Ferrat held dear except his heritage, but some spark of decency in him loved that, and the ruin of it awoke a real grief in him. He was still young enough to cry. Then she had taken her vengeance on him, because he had seen her extremity.

Clumsy and half blind with despair, Ardesir stumbled back along the passage, and in his drenching horror became lost, his mind too numbed with dread of what would happen to all those brave enough to have dared the conspiracy. There was no time to weep, but he felt grief sufficient to have fed Tiyo-Mah into eternity, could she have touched him.

He was too late to warn and no one could help. Tiyo-Mah's strength was renewed tenfold. She had the power to force the door herself, and her vengeance was hideous and immediate. Before Ardesir could find his way out of the passages, Min-Obal and the captain of the guard had been arrested, and all those on duty, who had obviously complied, and those who had arranged for the changes in routine.

Naturally there was no trial. Tiyo-Mah could not afford to have their crime understood. They knew her weakness. She must take steps to guard against it for ever afterwards. Perhaps when there was enough grief in the world she would not need to. She might even grow stronger, used enough to the world not to need constant sustenance. But she could not let anyone know how close they had come to defeating her.

The conspirators were charged with treason in their absence and before sundown they were put to death in the ancient way of the Isarchs of the first age, a thousand years before Tiyo-Mah's time.

Min-Obal was tortured, as were they all, but they spoke no one else's name. Certainly Ardesir's did not pass their lips.

They were then taken to the place of public execution, laid on the ground with their arms tied to stakes, and their mouths were wedged open and hot sand poured down their throats until they suffocated to death.

Ardesir was the only one who escaped, by the accident of having followed Bol-Ferrat into the passages and becoming lost so that he was nowhere in sight when Tiyo-Mah burst out.

But he knew his discovery was only a matter of time. He had lodged with Min-Obal. If it was not already known, it would be within a day or two, perhaps even by morning. And he was not master enough to hide the grief and the guilt which consumed him in a pain almost unbearable. His failure was total. Had it cost his own life that would at least have been just, but he was alive and unhurt in body. He had sacrificed some of the finest people he knew, and a dear friend who had believed in him. Now there was nothing for him to do but effect his own escape, because the war continued. The cause was greater than any one man's pain or loss, any man's guilt or desire to redeem his failure, or indeed have concern for himself at all.

He left before sunrise to cross the desert towards Tarra-Ghum and the sea.

He had been there a week, trying to find a ship westward to the Island when he overheard a group of sailors talking excitedly about the profit to be had in taking Tiyo-Mah and her embassy across the sea to the City in the Centre of the World, where she was going, apparently, to incite the Emperor of Camassia to ally with her in one vast empire to save the world from the barbarian.

Of course Camassia would be a junior partner in this! But she could hardly tell them that! They would find it out in time, afterwards, when the barbarian was conquered and the world was at peace again.

They laughed.

Ardesir stood on the quayside, the sun glittering sharp as knives off the bright water, and felt the salt wind on his face as if it had blown off the ice.

Chapter Five

Sardriel began his journey from the Eastern Shore of the Island where Sadokhar had spent the latter part of his youth, where he had learned obedience and comradeship, skill and loyalty, and eventually obedience. Its bright, turbulent waters haunted his dreams, and as the ship pulled away Sardriel's mind was filled with memories of their plans for this war, and how differently it had come to pass. Yet if Sadokhar could make this sacrifice into the most hideous unknown man could imagine, then to lead mercenaries east to the uncharted steppes of Irria-Kand was a small thing, and he would do it with a whole heart. It was only nature and the barbarian he was going to face. It was mortal, a thing of the body, no worse.

The voyage to Caeva was short. They were only two days sailing with a hard wind behind them, and then a third following the deepest fjord inland between heavily forested shores where the trees came right down to the water's edge.

Sardriel put ashore, leaving the treasure in the ship, and alone set out to follow the wide road inland. There was no point in taking men with him. He was going to meet the leader of an army.

Just over two miles from the shore the way ended in a clearing where he saw the hall of Almerid.

He was accosted almost immediately by sentries dressed in leather armour studded with iron. The breastplates were scarred and bloodstained from use, and the soldiers stood easily, unafraid of one lone man emerging from the trees, wearing a green jacket and cloak, and carrying only a dagger.

Sardriel introduced himself and they recognised a client for their services, welcoming him inside the great hall with joviality.

He stared around with interest. The hall was built of split tree trunks, smooth and polished, and the wooden floor gleamed warm with the mellow tones of gold and red. Fires blazed at both ends, filling the air with the sharp smell of smoke, and beside them were seats covered with the soft, shaggy skins of bears and wolves.

He had little time to look further, but he saw no art to compare with that of Tyrn Vawr, or the Lost Lands. These were men whose

75

lives were spent elsewhere. This place was for luxury, for physical ease between the long, hard months of battle. Booty might be sold, or even given away, but the luxuries of the imagination held little worth for them. Perhaps creating a place of beauty, things to love, was something they dared not think of.

Standing in the middle of the hall, stared at with curiosity by threescore men, ale mugs in hand, and at least half as many women, Sardriel was acutely aware of the trees hemming them around on every side, whispering, moving, towering to the sky with clouds racing past their speared crowns, and the silent carpet of needles on the floor beneath. It stretched hundreds of miles, covering the land to the borders of the plains of Irria-Kand. The pathways were not easy to find, nor the rivers to ford. He would be dependent upon these men, not only for victory, but for life itself.

Almerid rose from his seat at the head of the high table and sauntered down the length of the open floor till he stopped in front of Sardriel. He was stocky, broad-chested and heavy-shouldered. His hair was dark, and chopped rather than cut, but the first impression was of the power of his mind rather than his body. His eyes were watchful and clever, afraid of nothing. His face, criss-crossed with scars, was hard with years of self-discipline. The knowledge of command was in the air around him before he moved or spoke.

Sardriel stood squarely facing him, his head high. 'I am Sardriel, Lord of the Lost Lands,' he said levelly. 'I come from the Island at the Edge of the World to purchase your services in war. I have the wealth of the Treasury at my disposal.'

Almerid pursed his lips. 'You carry nothing,' he observed. There was a gleam in his eye, it might have been humour.

'Of course not,' Sardriel answered, smiling very slightly. 'I would not want to waste it – for either of us – should I have failed to reach here safely.'

Almerid relaxed a little. He saw ahead of him the challenge and the entertainment of a good bargain.

And so it proved. They offered, argued and counteroffered for two days, each knowing that ultimately they would find terms acceptable to both. It was not the quest nor the payment that mattered, it was a testing of will and intelligence between them, a measure of nerve, of agility of mind, of temperament and above all of strength of purpose.

They walked in the forest by day, Almerid grinning as they stood alone under trees that towered to a leaden sky, the men's feet silent on fallen needles centuries deep.

'Gets cold,' Almerid said on the first day, looking around, knowing Sardriel had lost all sense of direction, as he had intended

76

him to. 'The bears sleep in the winter, but the wolves don't.'

'Then I imagine you don't either,' Sardriel replied wryly. As long as no bargain was made he was safe and they both knew it, but Almerid was enjoying himself. Every added skill, everything for which Sardriel was dependent upon him could be an extra expense.

'Only with one eye closed!' Almerid acknowledged. He walked over to a small, scruffy-looking sapling and picked a handful of dark berries. He stuffed them into his mouth, then picked more and offered them to Sardriel. It was a tacit way of pointing out that he knew what was edible, and Sardriel did not. The berries were surprisingly sweet.

In the evenings the hall was filled with laughter and the sounds of eating and drinking. Cider flowed freely and was extremely powerful, as Sardriel learned to his cost the first morning. He felt as if the horns and drums of the previous night were still sounding in his head.

Almerid was immensely amused, but he quickly realised he could not pull such a trick twice. He showed a good-natured contempt for a man who could not hold his ale, but Sardriel was thereafter abstemious and his host did not refer to the subject again.

He tried offering Sardriel one of the best-looking women, but smartly withdrew the offer when he saw the anticipation of pleasure in the woman's eyes, and this time left Sardriel the laughter, even if it was silent, and well concealed.

In the end they reached an agreement in which both were satisfied. A messenger was sent with a letter bearing Sardriel's seal in order that the first two-thirds of the treasure might be brought. The final third awaited their successful return.

It took seventeen days for the army to assemble, so huge a force was it. Of course the mercenaries' reward was not only the huge treasure Sardriel had brought from Tyrn Vawr, but also all the booty they could take from the barbarian they conquered in the course of war.

Sardriel watched with growing awe as the bands of soldiers arrived, although he hid it behind an impassive face. Some came only a dozen at a time, others nearly fifty strong, but all were weather-burned, though by sun, wind or ice he could not tell. And all wore armour slashed by sword, pitted by arrows and spears, and stained by long-shed blood. They were every kind and colouring of man: yellow-haired, black-haired, bearded and clean-shaven, short and tall, lean and heavy. But all had in common a curious, confident way of moving, a slight roll to the step, and a wariness, as if forever ready to attack the instant of threat.

They asked neither food nor shelter, only the terms of payment. They did not even seem greatly concerned as to who the enemy

77

might be, nor where they would have to travel to find him. War was their trade, and if the price was right all else was only the ordinary risks and chances of life. Sardriel never heard the justice of the cause questioned. Either it was assumed, or they did not care.

On the eighteenth day just short of fifty thousand armed men, with horses and wagons of supplies, moved out on the long trek east. They went five hundred at a time, and it took them until the twentieth day before the final battalion entered into the forest, walking upright, swords at their sides, broad-bladed knives at their waists, helmets and armour glistening in the last of the sun.

Sardriel felt a moment's awe, wondering what force he had unleashed. How would its skill and precision decimate the primitive barbarian and change the balance of the world? And when the barbarian was crushed, perhaps even destroyed, what would Asmodeus do next?

Then another more corroding thought entered his mind. If they exterminated the barbarians as a race, was that perhaps a sin great enough to have played into Asmodeus' hands? Could it be his purpose to lure them into such an act, barbarous of soul, using their higher civilisation to meet a threat with infinitely greater force than was necessary to protect themselves, and thus commit a greater evil?

But it was far too late to prevent it now, or even to curb it. Sardriel could do nothing but set out with the rearguard and begin the long march eastwards, hoping his own strength and endurance would equal theirs and his battle skills match those of the barbarians.

For nearly sixty days they marched relentlessly from shortly after dawn until just before nightfall. The forest did not change character: mile after mile it stretched in perpetual, whispering green shadows, centuries of fallen needles making the floor silent even to the footfall of tens of thousands of men weaving their way through its density.

Sardriel walked beside Almerid or close behind him, learning from his skills at survival. He, like the men, knew where to find the roots and berries to eat and could trap small or large animals and use every portion of them.

They spoke little, travelling widespread across twenty miles or more, so as to be able to forage over a greater terrain. They went single file because of the closeness of the trees, and saved their strength.

But sometimes over the low campfires at night, sufficient only to cook their meat, baked rather than roasted in the open, Almerid allowed his curiosity to surface.

'What does the King of the Island at the Edge of the World owe to the Irria-Kanders that he spends his Treasury to defend them?'

he said, picking at the last of a rib-bone and throwing it away over his shoulder. It landed soundlessly on the needles behind him. 'You don't trade with them. There are no roads through this forest, and no sea lanes around it.'

'We owe nothing to the Irria-Kanders,' Sardriel admitted. 'But their enemies are our enemies, and are moving west as never before.'

Almerid raised scarred eyebrows, giving his face an exaggerated quizzical look in the under-lit glow of the embers. 'Leave it alone, and we might beat them for you,' he said sceptically. 'Then you could keep your treasure! Not that I'm not happy to have it, of course!'

Sardriel leaned back, relaxing in the warmth. He was learning to become accustomed to roots. He tried not to remember fish and crusty bread, and apples. 'Of course!' he agreed with a smile, although he still saw doubt in Almerid's eyes. He was not sure how much he should trust him, or even how much he would understand, but it was not in him to prevaricate. 'When barbarism threatens to overtake the world, where do you stand against it? When it has conquered everything else and reaches your own door?'

Sudden appreciation flared in Almerid's dark eyes. For a moment he sat perfectly still, looking back at Sardriel.

'Too late,' he said succinctly. It might have been a military answer rather than a moral one, but he perceived the crux of it. Then he grinned. 'On the other hand, Irria-Kand is a little early, don't you think? All the plains could fall, the barbarians aren't likely to come through the forest to find Caeva, let alone the Island. They've never seen the sea, still less sailed on it!'

'How long would it take them to learn?' Sardriel asked, more for the argument than because it mattered. He wanted Almerid's respect; he did not seek or expect his understanding. He would not tell him of the dark Lords who walked the earth and stirred the armies of destruction for the final war, and that at the head of the barbarian hordes they might find not an untutored man of the wilderness, but a creature loosed from hell.

Almerid shrugged. 'It won't happen,' he said with confidence. 'We'll stop them where they are now.' He spoke quite casually and stood up to find his place for the night. As far as he was concerned there was no more to say.

Finally they emerged quite suddenly into open land. They stood blinking after the perpetual gloom of the forest. Sardriel shielded his eyes and stared ahead at the wind-scarred plains rising to sheer escarpments, outcrops of rocks and high, barrier ridges. The sharpest of them were already dusted with snow, and the wind smelled cold and clean, utterly different from the rich, pungent scent of the trees.

He glanced at Almerid beside him and saw amazement widen his eyes. There was no sign that human traffic had ever passed this way, let alone settled and built anything or cultivated the land.

Then the moment after, he started to order the men into companies and battalions, and began to march forward in disciplined order. Scathingly he silenced their grumbling. They were paid whatever the outcome, but they wanted booty as well. They fought for the love of battle, the testing of strength and skill. There was no satisfaction in a march like this if there were no meeting with the enemy in the end, no victory. Where was the excitement, the achievement? What was there to boast of afterwards?

But no one defied Almerid, and they continued forward, ill-temper concealed for the moment.

One of the most extraordinary sights greeted them as they breasted the rise of a long slope which must at its crest have been three or four hundred feet high. They stood gazing ahead, relief at the respite obliterated by the hundred thousand beasts that darkened the plain ahead of them.

Almerid let out his breath in a long, wordless sigh. Nothing in his life had prepared him for such a thing and Sardriel saw the wonder in his eyes. It was endless food, it was also a force of nature that could destroy them if it stampeded. There was nowhere to hide, no possibility of outrunning them. Calculation raced through Almerid's mind, reflected in his face, the concentration, the tightening of his mouth, the steady, slow breathing in spite of the climb.

Sardriel stared also. The beasts, a form of wild cattle, stretched as far as he could see. They cropped the grass and must keep moving to find more.

'We'll cut out a few,' Almerid said at last. 'We'll have to plan well. They look swift.'

Then he turned and began to give orders, strict, careful. If the herd were to turn on the mercenaries and move the wrong way half the army could be trampled to death in an hour.

The cull was achieved in a few, excellent manoeuvres, and the soldiers all ate to their fill that night, and saved for days to come, smoking the meat to carry with them. Only a dozen men were hurt, and they not badly.

Almerid grinned at Sardriel. 'Perhaps you are right to stop the barbarian here! This place has promise!'

After a further five days the soldiers spread out, one or two thousand to a group, and continued to advance across the land. They passed several highly fortified encampments and a couple of walled towns, still occupied by Irria-Kanders, but there was still no sight of the enemy.

Then on the tenth day out of the forest, just before dawn, the barbarians struck. It was as if they had been watching, and caught the mercenaries at their most vulnerable. Naturally a watch had been posted, but since they had seen no sign of barbarians, they had sunk into a sense of invincibility, and they stood at the posts, rather than send out any scouts to watch and warn.

It was still dark. Sardriel was jerked wide awake by a roar of anger and amazement, then another and another. The screaming started, and the clash of steel on leather and the whistle and thud of arrows.

He snatched his sword and scrambled to his feet. All around him men were struggling to find shields and helmets; breastplates were too cumbersome to put on when the fighting was already underway on every side and the darkness was full of cries and groans.

Every step lurched into someone else lashing out blindly, or tripped over a fallen body. There was dangerous, terrible chaos. Arrows came out of the night, invisible until they struck with searing pain, and often death. There was no enemy to see, none within reach to strike back at.

When dawn spread glaring white across the northeast sky and lit the rolling grass, there were over four hundred men dead or wounded and nothing to see of the barbarians but the churned hoof-prints of their horses.

Almerid was consumed in a black rage of hatred and self-contempt. He retreated within himself, speaking to no one but the lieutenants of the two thousand in his own division. Messengers were sent with terse words of warning to left and right of them.

Sardriel offered no comfort. Death was too bitter to be softened with speech, especially when it could contain no truth.

Almerid met his eyes just once, and that was to make clear he had understood the lesson, and that it would never happen again. Then he turned on his heel, and walked with his easy, slightly swaggering gait, and started to snarl orders to his men.

They buried their dead and treated their wounded as well as they could, but there was little hope for the survival of most of them. They were more than a thousand miles from home and this was a harsh land, with winter coming. Suddenly war was very real. Pain and possibly death lay in the future for many of those who now gathered their armour and their packs and began again to march forward. Sardriel understood what courage they needed, and how dearly they earned the treasure he had paid them.

The next skirmish was different. The mercenaries were not caught off guard, and when it was over there were barbarians dead and wounded on the ground as well as their own men. Shields were pitted by arrow points, but far less flesh was pierced. The barbarians had had to ride closer in to stab with swords and spears, which weapons they were less skilled with than the mercenaries. To add to the success, over a score of horses were taken, and they proved priceless for moving the wounded. In future every time they could take a horse they would do so.

The barbarian dead and wounded were left for their own people to bury or treat as they would, and the mercenaries moved on.

They passed more vast herds of beasts, but none quite as staggering to the mind as that first one. They also stumbled on the remains of refugee camps of Irria-Kanders fleeing westwards from cities the barbarians had raided. They must have been dead for days. Their bones were picked clean by the wild dogs that hunted in packs, and the carrion birds had taken what was left.

Sardriel was sickened by it. Almerid said nothing, but there was a tightening in his body and his hand was never far from his sword hilt. They marched in close order, and there were always scouts before, behind, and on both flanks.

More skirmishes followed through the weeks as they moved eastwards, of generally increasing success, although there were occasional sharp, ugly failures as well. The weather grew harsher. Savage winds drove across the open land from the north and east, razor-edged, bruising the unprotected skin with freezing pellets. Hail rattled on the shields and fell, coating the ground with white. The grass was withered by it and pools of water were shaded with thin, solid films of ice. The sun rose late, obscured by palls of grey cloud, arched low to the south, and set early in scarlet as if the land below the horizon were on fire.

Never once did Almerid complain, even as the wind raked the uplands, scouring the land bare, and snow piled murderously deep in the valleys, drowning, suffocating, so neither man nor beast could make their way through.

For a while the barbarians left their invaders for nature to kill the weak. But the mercenaries were forged of grim metal, and their own forests of the north had taught them to adapt and survive.

They pressed forward, and the barbarians retreated before them. By mid-winter they were deep in Irria-Kand, and the days had already begun to lengthen again when they fought their first major pitched battle. It was savage and bloody, and afterwards they laid siege to the magnificent walled city to which the barbarian leader had retreated, having months since slaughtered the few remaining Irria-Kanders and made the place his own.

For eight days the barbarians defended, but their warfare was to strike and run; they had no knowledge of the arts of mining and sapping, and now they paid the price. On the ninth day the mercenaries stormed the walls and by sundown the city was taken. They poured over the battlements and down into the streets.

For three more days the fighting raged on until at last the few barbarians left were cornered and slain. Finally Almerid and Sardriel were at the head of the score of men who burst into the last stronghold and faced the startlingly young man who stood to meet his death, no more than a dozen soldiers with him. He was obviously the leader, and yet he seemed barely twenty.

Almerid grinned. 'Ah!' he said with enormous satisfaction. 'Our warlord's son, I think. Send his head to his father. That will be a message he will not fail to understand!' He raised his sword arm as he spoke.

'No!' Sardriel grasped it and held it hard, feeling the weight of the blow that would have fallen, and the anger at being stopped.

Almerid looked at him narrowly, fury in his eyes. He was thinking of his own dead men lying unburied on the ice – hard ground five hundred miles along the bitter march eastward, and perhaps of the wounded he knew in his heart would yet die. Sardriel was thinking of the future, and the stakes of honour in the battle far wider than this one field – the final war where the weapons were of the spirit infinitely more than the flesh.

Almerid attempted to yank his arm free, but Sardriel held it with all his strength. 'Wait!' he commanded. 'This is our battle. We are deep in their territory and have a war ahead of us. There is a better use for him.'

'Trade?' Almerid said derisively. 'They have nothing we want, except their lives, and what use would it be for us to have a score of them in exchange for this one? There are thousands of them out there. I'm sure one way or the other makes no difference. Anyway, we have no common tongue. How do we tell them what we want? And like as not they'd be willing to sacrifice him anyway. They're barbarians – little more than animals.'

'Animals have their own honour,' Sardriel answered. 'And certainly their loyalties.' Almerid's arm was still pulling against his hand, the muscles straining.

Sardriel met his eyes in an unflinching stare. 'I pay you. You do as I decide. The booty is yours – I make no claim on any of that – but the prisoners are mine, unless they are a danger to your men. That is your right to decide.'

Almerid's face was still a mask of contempt. The hardships they had faced together were a bond not strong enough to hold where the conduct of war was in question.

'You'll just let him go?' Almerid said raspingly. 'He'll tell his father you're weak! I won't let you do that, treasure or not. No man says that of me or mine, not even to the barbarian!' He yielded not a fraction.

'I shall take him to the wall,' Sardriel answered. 'These men of his will tell his father what happened and where he is. He'll come, and he'll see for himself that we have the city and all that's in it.'

Almerid laughed abruptly. 'He'll find that out anyway!'

'Think ahead!' Sardriel snapped. 'We can't obliterate the entire barbarian nation! Better we drive them back, which we have done, let them taste our strength, and then make a peace with them.'

'For how long?' Almerid jeered, but there was light in his eyes again, overtaking the rage. He had glimpsed the idea.

'A generation perhaps,' Sardriel answered.

'And this city? Do we give it back to them?' Almerid enquired.

'Of course not! It belongs to the Irria-Kanders.'

Almerid grunted, then slowly relaxed his arm. 'Take him to the wall, then. But if it costs you your life, I'll take you all the way back to the sea with a barbarian arrow in you, to show your men it was none of our doing!'

'I'll write you a letter to take to them, marked by my seal,' Sardriel replied, letting go of his arm at last.

Almerid smiled sourly, showing his teeth, then turned away.

Sardriel did as he had promised, giving the letter to Almerid, then with a dozen of the best men he took the barbarian's son and his guard to the main gate of the city and let the men go, keeping the youth. They had no speech in which to communicate. Neither side had taken prisoners nor spoken a word to each other in all the marching and slaughter from the forest's edge to this day.

The guard went, understanding the bargain and perhaps expecting a ransom to be asked. Sardriel waited, looking at the youth with curiosity and finding his interest returned. He was shorter than Sardriel or the Caevans, broad-shouldered, and with bow legs, as if he had ridden horseback since infancy and it had left its shape upon him. His face was wide with high cheekbones and a broad mouth, eyes narrow as if wrinkled with looking into the teeth of the wind. After the open plains this walled city, with its constant supply of water, its sheltering walls and polished floors, its great fireplaces where peat was burned, cut from the bogs in the surrounding hills, must seem utter luxury. Already Sardriel had seen works of art in fine metal, silver, gold and copper; stones such as jasper and sardonyx carved into animals of ferocious beauty. There were skins with fur so deep they could serve as a bed to shield one's bones from the hardness of the ground. All the art and wealth of the Irria-Kander civilisation was here for the taking. It was a high prize to lose. Curiously, the barbarians had kept alive many of the younger Irria-Kander women to serve their needs or their pleasures, and they now awaited their fate at the hands of new captors.

But did the barbarian see its worth? Was there a place for loveliness, man- or God-made, in his soul?

It was four long hours before Sardriel saw the horsemen ride over the hill and come steadily towards him. There were no more than forty of them, savage men with black helmets, holding spears high in a gesture of defiance. At this distance Sardriel could only glimpse the outlines of the short, powerful bows slung over their shoulders which shot the devastating arrows.

The central figure parted from the rest and moved forward ahead of them. He stopped twenty yards away, reining in his horse.

Sardriel put his arm on the youth's shoulder to restrain him.

There was silence, but for the whining of the wind over the grass.

The barbarian would not come within spear range of the walls.

Sardriel shivered. He dared not go within arrow range of the barbarian guard.

Very slowly the barbarian leader dismounted and walked a dozen yards from the beast. It was clear he had no bow with him.

Sardriel gestured towards the waiting horsemen.

The barbarian leader turned and waved them on. They too dismounted and moved a dozen yards from their beasts, bows left over the saddles.

Sardriel took the youth by the arm, and alone they walked across the wind-whipped grass, their feet jarring against the iron-hard earth. They stopped ten feet from the barbarian leader. He had the same shape of face and body as the boy, but a skin burned dark by wind, ice and sun, and slashed with scars until its natural expression was almost obscured. Only his eyes betrayed his anxiety, and the burning relief when he saw the boy alive and unharmed. Then he looked at Sardriel, and held out his hands, palms upward. It was obviously a gesture as to what price Sardriel required for the return of his son.

Sardriel waved his hands in denial, and shook his head. He took the youth by the arm and pushed him forward, then stepped back himself.

For a moment no one moved.

Sardriel pushed the boy again, and he marched, a little unsteadily, back to his father, standing behind him as quickly as possible, not to block his line of fire, should he choose to attack.

Sardriel smiled.

Carefully, the barbarian leader held out his left hand, palm open, and with his right hand made a gesture of giving something, then he bowed low from the waist, and turned on his heel and departed.

Sardriel retreated rapidly to the wall and went in through the gate, just in case there should be a hail of arrows, but when he looked, the barbarians were gone.

Two days later the mercenaries were still exploring the city and finding more and more of its treasures of luxury for the mind and body. There were springs of water which had been built into fountains and wells to supply the occupants permanently, in any vicissitude. The surrounding hills provided fuel from the peat bogs, and there was sufficient land for growing vegetables. Some of the wild cattle had been domesticated and there was space within the walls for a considerable number of them.

But, far more interesting than that, there were thermal springs outside the city, hot, pungent-smelling water, to carry which they had built a great clay pipe under the ground leading to a vast, steaming cistern, and from this they pumped the hot water to magnificent bathhouses tiled with ceramics of extraordinary beauty. One could go from warm pools to hot, and then brisk cold ones, or be massaged with sweet-smelling oils, pots and jars of which remained.

Each of the public centres such as the palace and the court-houses were roofed with domes which lent the skyline a unique grandeur. The roads were paved, and the arena for chariot racing was like nothing they had seen before.

When Sardriel finally found Almerid on the evening of the third day after their taking of the city, he was in the central room of the palace. Its floor was tiled, and spread with thick skins, there was a fire roaring in a fireplace large enough to have roasted a pig, and others burned in twenty gold and silver holders, giving the room a glow as if seen through amber.

'I still don't know why they surrendered,' Sardriel said, anxiety pressing at his mind. It was inexplicable to him that anyone should yield a city that could, from all he had seen so far, have been held almost indefinitely against an invader who had not the skills of undermining walls, nor catapult engines to break them. And they had now examined every yard and found no weakness anywhere.

Almerid grinned, full of contempt. 'Cowards,' he said simply. 'They knew the barbarians were coming. They'd heard tales from other refugees from further east, and they just packed up and ran. Those camps we came across were probably some of them.' He gave a slight shrug, and for a moment his face reflected pity, but it was brief. He was accustomed to war and he had no time for those who did not stand their ground and live or die fighting.

'And leave a thousand of their women behind?' Sardriel said doubtfully. 'Even if they were the cowards you say, why would they do that?' A hideous thought crossed his mind that Almerid might believe they had bartered their most handsome young women for their own safety, but he dismissed it.

Almerid shook his head, smiling now. 'They aren't from this city. The barbarians have taken them in various places along the way, and kept the best. A fairly usual custom of war.' He grinned broadly, showing all his teeth. 'And these ones are skilled in the arts of the hands, with oils and the hot springs. I'd have kept them myself!'

Sardriel was surprised only for a moment. The answer made more sense. 'Then I suppose we'll have to take them with us,' he said reluctantly. 'Unless we leave them to tend our wounded? There's enough room here to care for them well, and guard our rear. It's time we moved forward. The rest of Irria-Kand lies ahead, and we must build on the advantage we have.'

Almerid lounged back in his chair, leaning against the white wolf hide that cushioned it. 'I think not,' he said simply.

Sardriel was taken aback. 'For what reason? The worst of the winter is past and there is a long way to go yet.'

Almerid crossed his legs. 'Not for us,' he replied. 'We like it here. This city has all we need – food, water, even women. It's a good place. There's room for forty thousand of us here, or more, and we can hold it against a few barbarians with nothing but bows and arrows.'

Sardriel was incredulous. 'For how long?' he said with an edge of harshness. Was Almerid demanding more money?

'Perhaps for ever,' Almerid replied casually. 'This is better than we have in Caeva. We might never return.'

'What about your own people? Your families?' Sardriel challenged, still thinking it was a bluff he could call.

Almerid's smile widened. 'We are mercenaries, we have no homes or kin. War is our business – fighting and dying – you know that. But we have had enough of it. We could live out our lives here very comfortably with no need to fight again, except the occasional skirmish with the barbarians, if they still have the stomach for it.' He waved a lazy arm around, indicating not only the room and the palace, but the city beyond.

'And your honour?' Sardriel said quietly. 'You gave your word.'

Almerid's eyebrows rose. There was no wavering in his gaze as he met Sardriel's. 'Honour is another weapon of war,' he said with a slight shrug. 'I like you, Sardriel, but you're an idealist. You live in dreams. As long as we needed to earn our way then we kept our word. But now we have no need. This is enough.' He gave a little sigh and settled deeper into the wolf fur, but his hand was on the hilt of his knife and his eyes never left Sardriel's face.

'I realise, of course, that we forfeit the last third of your treasure,' Almerid went on. 'But this is wealth enough for it, and there is no more fighting, no long march back over the plains and through the forest. Naturally, you may do as you wish. You can stay here, if you choose.' He put his head a little to one side. 'Or you may take one of the horses, two if you like, and make your way back westwards. I doubt the barbarians will bother you, if you keep going. You are no threat to them, and you have nothing worth stealing . . . except the horses, of course. Walk, if you prefer.'

Sardriel was stunned. He should have foreseen this, but such a betrayal was outside his imagination. He stared at Almerid's smiling, deeply satisfied face, and knew that argument was futile.

'You are a man without honour,' he said quietly, disgust unconcealed. Perhaps that was not wise, but the fury and the hurt that filled him was too profound to hide.

'You misunderstand life, Sardriel,' Almerid contradicted. 'I am a man who no longer needs it. I am safe, I am warm, I am well fed. I do not need that particular currency any more.' His face hardened. 'I shall expect your answer in the morning.'

Sardriel retreated to the room he had chosen, his body moving automatically, his mind numb with shock. He was consumingly angry with himself for having been taken by surprise. He should have seen such a possibility far ahead, he should have imagined or created a guard against it, although even now he could not think what.

He threw the door open and went in, closing it hard behind him and sliding home the bolt. Now suddenly the luxury of it – the warmth, the beauty, the soft ease of the bed – was no comfort at all. The betrayal beat on his senses like an assault. He was a fool, a traitor himself to the cause of God. He had wasted two-thirds of the Treasury of the Island on a single conquest, one city, when he had the men and the skill to have driven the barbarian back to the eastern rim and retaken Irria-Kand for its own people. In the ornate loveliness of this room, with its painted tiles and gilded candles, he could hear the laughter of Asmodeus.

He was still unable to sit or to rest for the turmoil in his mind when there was a rap on the door. He opened it slowly, and saw one of Almerid's lieutenants there, a man named Halmar, from the Sea Isles, with sky-blue eyes and yellow hair.

'What?' he said curtly. 'Almerid expects my answer in the morning. It's scarcely beyond midnight.'

'I would speak with you, my lord,' Halmar answered so quietly it was little more than a whisper. 'But I should prefer not to be seen. It would be safer for both of us.'

Puzzled, Sardriel opened the door wider. If the man meant to kill him there was little he could do to prevent it. If that were

Almerid's plan it was pointless, but very easily achieved. Ardesir was one against an army of above forty thousand.

When the door was closed Halmar spoke. 'I am captain of two thousand, but they are loyal to me. We have not sold our honour for hot baths or wolf skins to lie on, or sets of gold candle holders. We will go forward with you against the barbarians, for whatever that is worth. Two thousand, well led, well armed, may make their way as far as the next city, and perhaps find some Irria-Kanders there, and put heart back into them.'

Sardriel hesitated only a moment. He must either accept, and take whatever risks or gains it offered, or refuse and lose all opportunity of success, by his own decision.

'Yes,' he said aloud. 'Yes, get your men.'

'We must go tonight,' Halmar warned.

'I know. I'll meet you beyond the west gate in two hours. Will that be time enough?'

Halmar smiled. 'The south gate, in as long as it takes you to get there.'

Halmar took with them all the horses. It was his men's turn on the watch; two thousand of them rode out into the night, and by dawn they were twenty-five miles from the city and beyond pursuit on foot. They posted watch and rested for three hours, then mounted and rode again. If the barbarians observed them, they saw no sign of it.

They passed what had been an Irria-Kander camp, and saw the remnants of corpses, picked over by carrion beasts, bones white in the wind-torn grass. The land opened out till they could see thirty miles in almost every direction. A line of hills to the north was snow-mantled, shining in the low sun. At the end of the day, when sunset to the northeast stained the flying clouds scarlet, they dropped down towards the valleys and saw the first wild flowers of spring.

The breakaway army took a small town, defeating the barbarian force holding it, and swept onward, east and a little south towards less sparse settlements. They rested and regained their strength. They had lost only a score of men.

The land was wide and level, a few small stands of timber giving shelter. It was two days after that, at high noon with the wind gentler and from the south, when they saw the barbarian force in the distance, seemingly about three hundred men. Surprisingly, considering their respective numbers, they turned and began to advance. Halmar commanded his men to form into battle lines and be ready to charge, shields high against the lethal arrows. There was no sound in the silence but the wind in the grass, the thud of hoofs and the clank and jingle of harnesses and horse armour.

The battle was hard and the barbarians retreated and scattered, riding swiftly. They seemed almost to melt into the bands of trees.

The suddenly, without even a sound of warning, there were thousands of them. Sardriel turned in the saddle and saw them on every side, and he knew it was over. They fought, but there was never a chance they could have won. By sundown the barbarians' campfires mirrored the stars across the plain in number, and the bodies of the dead mounded the grass as far as the eye could see in the fading light.

Halmar was dead. Sardriel was wounded, but not badly. He gathered the score of men still upright and prepared to make the last stand. Then the barbarian leader rode towards him and in the glare of the flames from the campfires Sardriel recognised the man whose son he had returned to him, savage, brutal, a man who built nothing and planted nothing, a mortal. He lived by the laws of the wilderness of the earth, killing and being killed, like the beasts. This was only a human war.

The barbarian dismounted and walked towards Sardriel, this time coming almost up to him. He was weary, smeared with blood, and his left arm obviously pained him considerably.

He looked at Sardriel, then repeated the gesture he had made at their parting, as if Sardriel had given him something, and very carefully returned it, but held up one finger, and pointed at Sardriel himself. He indicated the others behind him and made a swift gesture of denial, then pointed to Sardriel again and jabbed at the distance. His meaning was clear. Sardriel could leave, but alone.

Sardriel bowed his head in acknowledgement, then refused. He signed that they would all go, or none.

The barbarian smiled and nodded his head several times. But it was approval, not agreement.

Sardriel stood still, his sword in his hand. The wind murmured across the grass, carrying the smell of smoke from a thousand campfires. He prayed that the end would be quick. There was nothing to wait for, nothing else to be said or done. He thought of Almerid in the city, briefly and bitterly. He was right, he was the realist.

The barbarian nodded slowly, still smiling, then waved his hands.

Was it possible? Sardriel gestured to all the men around him, and then towards the distance.

The barbarian agreed, bowing his head.

Sardriel responded, and then turned to the others. 'Go!' he commanded. 'We are free! It is a debt repaid.'

'A debt?' one of Halmar's lieutenants asked, puzzled. 'The barbarian?'

'I gave him back his son,' Sardriel answered. 'He is repaying me in kind. He will not kill me. It is against his honour.' He said the word bitterly, thinking again of Almerid. Honour was not a concept unique to civilisation after all, or even common to it, as he had believed only days ago. 'Now!' he shouted furiously. 'Go now!'

As one man, they wheeled and rode away, westward, towards they knew not where. An hour before dawn, exhausted, they slept.

Sardriel awoke to a muffled cry, and another, and another. He scrambled to rise, and found his arms pinned and felt the sharp prick of a knife at the side of his neck. The pale shafts of dawn lit a scene of horror that remained indelible in his mind. The barbarians ringed the camp and one by one they were slaughtering his men as if they had been cattle.

'You told us we could go!' he shouted furiously, even as he knew it was pointless and hopeless. They did not understand him and they did not care. The butchery went on and he struggled in vain, an agony of grief inside him, his ears filled with the sounds of death, the smell of blood choking him.

When it was over and he stood, sweat-drenched and shuddering with horror, almost supported as much as imprisoned by his captors, the barbarian leader picked his way through the dead and came over to him. His boots were scarlet and his breeches sodden red to the knees. He held up one finger and smiled, then pointed to Sardriel, and then to the distance westward where the sky was still shadowed with the last remnants of night.

Sardriel was too shattered to move.

The barbarian mimicked a tower in the air, then again and again, suggesting a city. Then he drew his finger across his throat and laughed. He pointed to himself, then to his men. He bent and picked up a handful of grass and let the blades slip from his fingers. His meaning was clear. He had as many men as the grass had leaves. He could wait, and he would. Then again he smiled and bowed, and pointed Sardriel towards the west. He was free to go. No one would harm him.

Sardriel looked across the new grass heaped with the dead and bade them a last farewell, then turned and began his stumbling, lonely journey back towards Tyrn Vawr.

Chapter Six

Kor-Assh stood at the window of the castle gallery and stared into the distance. He knew Tathea would be walking under the trees to the west of the courtyard, through the iron gate beyond the walls where the evening light would fall hazy and soft on the grass. Yet he remained where he was, gazing to the orchards and the open land rolling to the horizon. He was not ready to go yet. There was something unresolved in him which needed solitude.

The rich peace and loveliness of Tyrn Vawr touched only the surface of his senses, seductions of pleasure that did not reach his soul. He was restless to begin the battle, and understand his part in it. Time was short, and the earth, with its aching beauty, was the prize for which they fought. The touch of the wind on his face, the smell of grasses, the abundant life, unaware of its peril, reminded him with every breath that this was the final war. Beyond it there was no new chance, no other victory to dream of.

The light began to deepen and colour burned across the sky. If he did not go soon she would join the others for the evening meal, and he would not see her alone.

He went down to the courtyard and out up the slope. He found Tathea almost a mile away from the castle, standing under the trees looking up into the fork where a great branch split off. There was a tenderness in her face that caught his heart with an inexplicable ache of familiarity, as if he had seen something precious and long missed. His eye followed hers to see what she was looking at. It was a small squirrel sitting upright, staring back at her. For seconds Kor-Assh looked at them both, the little animal and the woman watching it, the last of the sunlight on her face picking out the tiredness deep inside her. There was a knowledge of pain in the fine lines around her eyes and lips, an openness to hurt that clutched at him like an iron hand.

He thought of all that Sadokhar had told him of when he had spoken of the Book. How long had she been alone, waiting? How many friends had she loved and watched die, sacrificed to the cause, or falling from it? Any loneliness he could imagine must be a sheltered pool compared with the ocean she was sailing.

Was the enormity of her mission enough to fill her heart as well as her mind? It would take all her strength, but what did it give her? What kept her all those aeons of time, all the hoping and the rejection and the fighting to hope again? Courage alone, or something more?

He looked at her face again, and saw the wounds of loneliness in it. Why could he not reach across that distance between them, or at least try to?

Then he marvelled at his own monumental arrogance. What made him suppose she would wish him to? That she was capable of suffering did not mean he had any power to heal it. Even to try might be no more than an intrusion.

The squirrel must have caught some scent of him in the air. It jerked up sharply.

Tathea turned and saw him. The nakedness vanished from her face and she smiled at him, masked and courteous again, waiting for him to approach her and speak.

What should he say? What he was thinking – the strange confusion of emotions inside him, the sense of old loyalties, not understood? The grief he felt for Sadokhar? He had liked him in a unique way, not only for his nature, his passion and commitment, but because it was Sadokhar who had sought him out and told him of the Book, and its message, sealed but remembered through the centuries, until now, the time for awakening the soul, harrowing the spirit and refining it until it was bright enough to face the Great Enemy.

Where was Sadokhar? Kor-Assh envied him his colossal calling, yearned for something as great, which would stretch the fabric of his being to the height and depth of its strength, and almost beyond. What value was anything less?

Tathea was watching him, waiting for him to speak.

'It's so fragile,' he said quietly, 'how the colour melts across the sky towards the oncoming night and the first pinprick of stars. I suppose it is the same each night, but it never seems to be.'

She looked at him, and he saw from the shadows in her eyes that what he had said skittered across the surface, and did not touch the heart. He was ashamed of himself without understanding what better he should have done. There was a terrible void inside him, driving out all other thought, and he had no idea how to heal it.

Word came of a great warrior on the Eastern Shore, not only of courage and skill, but of extraordinary wisdom. He was apparently a man of wide travel and knowledge of the ways of the sea. The traveller who told the assembled court of him did so with respect, even reverence, and he smiled when he spoke his name.

Tathea glanced across the table at Kor-Assh, and he knew what thought was in her mind. Was this man the sixth warrior they awaited, and who would read the last hieroglyph on the staff?

'Do we seek him?' he asked as soon as he could speak with her alone. Without thought he had included himself, as if it were already agreed he would go with her.

She hesitated only a moment. They were in the gallery leading to the stairs. The torches were lit, flames wavering and bending as the open windows let in the summer night, dark and fragrant with the murmuring of leaves in the courtyard beyond. 'Yes,' she answered. 'We should go.' She too spoke in the plural, and he did not know if it were intentional but it was enough.

They set out early the following day, carrying nothing but bread and water, cloaks to wrap themselves against rain, and, of course, the staff. Most of the time they rode in silence. Neither wished to speak of the warrior of the Shore, or the possibilities ahead. The sun was clear, the wind soft from the summer fields. The sky was the deep, burning blue of the middle of the year, and great cloudscapes piled light in towers and billows, high beyond imagination to the roots of heaven.

As they neared the shore on the second day, sometimes they rode single file through the narrow paths in the heather, and Kor-Assh watched the ease with which Tathea sat in the saddle.

He wanted to know more about her far distant past in Shinabar, and when they stopped to eat, he asked, watching her face as she answered him.

'We had marvellous horses,' she said, her face quickening at the memory. 'Our lives depended on them, far more than they do here.' She narrowed her eyes against the sun across the downs and the distant brilliance of the sea. 'In the desert to be caught in the open through the day is death. And you have to know the tracks from one oasis to the next.'

'Is it beautiful?' What he meant was, did she love it, but he would hear the answer to that in the words she chose to reply.

Tathea dropped her head a little, smiling. 'Oh yes.' There was passion in her voice. 'You love the sand and hate it. It creeps into everything, itching and hurting. But when you see it stretch to the horizon, blue and indigo and purple as the white wing of dawn spreads across the sky, or ribbed with silver under the moon, or you smell the heat and the bitter herbs on the wind, it's like looking into the morning of the world.'

Kor-Assh did not answer. The past was in her dreams and he knew it as clearly as if she had spoken it.

She turned towards him. 'Do you have horses in Lantrif?' Then a shadow crossed over her face the moment the words were spoken.

'A few. Mostly we travel by river,' he replied quietly, seeing it vividly in his mind – the great stretches like glass, shining, whispering, carrying the barges back and forth to the City of the Fallen Kings.

She was waiting for him to continue, watching him as if she knew he withheld much. 'You miss it . . .' she began, then read him more closely. 'You are worried . . .'

He looked away, guarding the wound inside him. 'I have left good men to govern. And they are loyal to my wife, Marilla, if not to me.' He hesitated. He could not hide for ever. He lifted his eyes to meet hers and smiled a little, self-mockingly. 'Every ruler in Lantrif has worried about the Silver Lords, who are reputed to have had powers of sorcery a thousand years ago. I think they keep the myth alive so we will always have one of them in our Council, and make very sure we do not entirely ignore his advice.'

He could see she was not certain how far to believe him, but this was not the time to tell her of the quarrels, the rivalries, the manipulation, or how he hated it. He stood up, offering his hand to her.

She declined with a smile, rising easily, and instead he held her horse for her to swing up into the saddle. Then he mounted his own and followed after her without speaking again.

The Eastern Shore had a wild, sparse beauty unlike anything Kor-Assh had known. The land was low and level, its green meadows running almost imperceptibly into the rougher grasses above the dunes, and the heavy-scented wild, yellow sea-lupins. The marble-pale strand echoed the thunder of surf that drove in from the open water, great roaring walls of blue-green, glassy ocean. In winter it would be silver grey as molten lead, laced with spume and crowned with white.

The settlements huddled into the inlets. Houses were low, built of timber, caulked and tarred like ships, bleached bone-white by wind and salt. The sea was the inhabitants' harvest, their highway and their defence. It was both servant and master.

This was like no place in Lantrif, and yet something unfolded inside Kor-Assh like an opening flower, breathing in the salt as if it were perfume, hearing the roar of waves as a familiar song, a music of living.

They were further north than Tyrn Vawr. It was just past high summer and the days were so long the sun barely dipped below the horizon and the pale fires of the Wastelands sky burned in blues and greens like the spectre of sunsets from another age.

Kor-Assh looked at Tathea as she gazed outward at the sea. It was white-crested now, whipped by the long, scythe-sharp winds that crossed the waters which stretched even to the Midnight

Lands, and the endless ice of the ancient battlegrounds of legend.

This time he did not break the spell of the moment by speaking of its beauty. She knew he shared it – it was in the way she looked at him with the light on her face and smiled, unashamed that he should see her emotion. She had spoken of the death of Aelfrith, Earl of the Eastern Shore, and Sadokhar's uncle, without hiding from him how much it had hurt. Now staring at these thundering seas reopened memories in her and wounds still raw.

'He used to tell us wonderful tales,' she said, gazing at the water and blinking. 'Some of them were funny. He had a laugh that rattled the pewter mugs on the mantelshelf. He would glare at anybody who didn't laugh with him.' She bit her lip and her eyes were bright with tears. 'He exaggerated terribly about some of his battles, but no one cared. We all knew his courage was real, he just loved a story. He wanted us to taste it and smell it as he had, to feel the ice and see the splendour and the terror of it.' She stopped and took a shivery breath.

She started her horse forward, keeping her face half away from him, and began to recount one of Aelfrith's stories, and through it Kor-Assh heard the echoes of an older time, other light on water, and passion stamped on the soul and woven into the dreams. And in spite of his will against, and all his guarding, he loved her for it.

Another mile and they passed the sprawling grey castle of Odomer. In the haze of late afternoon the lengthening sun melted the sharp patterns of the light. The jagged groynes breaking the polished surface of the water were cruel, sword-edged. The weed-darkened hummocks low as the tide's margin lifted gently on the sucking swell, the rock's storm-pitted faces disguised by a dusting of gold, shadows blurred.

Kor-Assh knew Tathea had been here with Sadokhar, and he saw in the lift of her head and the stiff angle of her back that she was thinking of him now as she stared beyond the water to the horizon where one blue faded into another. He could not imagine what it had cost her to let him go.

And yet if she were commanded this of God, what crippling of the heart and soul would there be were she to refuse? That price would be eternal.

Without warning Tathea turned in the saddle and raised her arm, signalling him forward. Then, as he reached her, she urged her horse into a gallop, and together, neck and neck, they raced across the hard pale sand by the water's edge, glorying in the speed, the sting of the salt, the horses' manes whipping in their faces.

She won by a length, and turned, for a moment victory making her laugh. It was shatteringly familiar. He had been here before, exactly like this with Tathea, before a storm which racked the skies, with a power so tremendous it broke open the roots of the earth.

He saw it in her face also, but with her it was less clouded. She remembered it with a certainty he could only grope towards, and lose again.

She turned away and spurred her horse up the slope towards the massive landward barbican. It was hewn of iron-dark stone and towered over the cullis gate and the wide, outer courtyard. The topmost battlements still looked beyond the groynes, the headland and the shoals far over the seaward approaches. But time and storms had eroded the once-titanic fortress, and the creeping tides now filled the eastern rooms, walls crumbling slowly, shell-encrusted, and the dungeons stretched far under the drowning sea, black, weed-tortuous, squid-inhabited.

This was where the warrior lived whom they had come to see. They rode up to the cullis gates side by side. The watchman challenged them, and Tathea spoke her name. He hesitated only a moment before admitting them. The cullis was winched high and their horses' hoofs clattered over the drawbridge and down into the castle yard.

They were welcomed with grave courtesy by Ceawlin himself. He was a thin man, lean and dark-skinned, white hair like spume of the sea flying up from his brow.

'Welcome to my castle, such as it is,' he said solemnly. 'We have rich food and warm beds to offer you, and the beauty of the sky and the water. But our harvest is the sea, not the land, and all our wealth is touched with salt.' He smiled as he spoke. It was in no way an apology. He had the life he had chosen, and loved.

They accepted with equal grace, and in the Great Hall Ceawlin's hospitality was indeed as good as he had intimated. The food was fresh and plentiful, but the wealth was of the mind rather than the body. Conversation was rich in the philosophy of the sea, tales of adventure and warfare, the arts of survival, and it held laughter and passion interwoven like a varied cloth. But Ceawlin's wisdom was more evident in the peace of his people than in the overt pattern of his words.

It was late in the evening and the moon was bright over the water, waves breaking luminous with foam, when finally Tathea rose to her feet and held out the staff for Ceawlin to see.

He regarded it with interest, narrowing his eyes to look more carefully at the hieroglyphs, then he looked up at her, puzzled. 'What does it say?'

Kor-Assh should have been prepared, but he was not. Disappointment was sudden and bitter. He had been certain, and now the hope was dashed and broken like fine glass against stone.

'It speaks of the future,' Tathea replied softly, her eyes downcast to hide her emotions. 'I can read only part of it myself.'

'And you thought I might read the rest,' Ceawlin responded. 'My wisdom is only that of the present, a matter of knowing the worst in men, but believing the best also. I can see deeper than some, perhaps, but no further. But I can see a prophet in you.' He spoke very softly now, a little above a whisper. He looked at Kor-Assh. 'And I think a priest in you. You will find the one you seek, but not here. But when the darkness comes, as it will, I shall hold the lights on the Eastern Shore for as long as I can. That I swear.'

Tathea bowed her head in acceptance, then looked up at him and smiled. There was nothing else to say.

Kor-Assh went to his room with his mind whirling. He had been caught up in too many emotions. Sadokhar had told him much of Tathea, and he had expected to find her extraordinary. Anyone who had sought the truth as she had could never be as other people. He would have failed himself had he not seen a mirror of all his own hungers and dreams in her. But he had not been prepared to care with the intensely personal urgency that he did. It disturbed him not only with confusion but with guilt.

He reminded himself over and over of Marilla, to whom he owed an undivided loyalty, not only in act, but in thought.

Too much was not as he had foreseen. Disappointment was sharp that Ceawlin was not the sixth warrior but, far more profound than that, raced in Kor-Assh's mind his host's words about him being a priest. What did Ceawlin see in him that he himself did not know? In what way was he a priest, that was not true of all men?

He stood at the window and stared into the darkness, hearing only the roar of the surf and the long, indrawn gurgle as the tide withdrew, and then the crash over the rocks as it came in again.

At last he turned away and kneeled down.

'Father, tell me who I am!' he prayed. 'I need to know! Help me to understand. What is it You want of me and how can I be equal to it?'

There was no answer but the salt breath of the sea, but he rose with a trust that he would not be left without a light, even if it showed only a fraction at a time. Perhaps that too was necessary, in case the whole was more than he dared face or his soul could grasp.

Tathea and Kor-Assh left in the morning and turned their horses west again and back on the path to Tyrn Vawr.

'Tell me more of Ardesir and Sardriel,' Kor-Assh asked as they rode side by side along the sand. 'And Ythiel and the other Knights of the Western Shore. Everyone knows of those who fought in the beginning, but what of the Eleven now?'

'What would you like to know?' She looked at him briefly, raising her voice a little above the surf and the cry of the gulls.

'How have they prepared for the war to come? It must require far more than military skill,' he assumed. 'Every age has its brilliant soldiers. Surely Asmodeus has powers that outweigh every weapon ever invented by man? But more than that, his goal is not the death of the body, but of the spirit. We must be armoured against terror, corruption, delusion or despair. What have they learned that will defend them? What sword can injure the creatures of hell?'

'It is not a hereditary calling,' Tathea answered. 'As each dies his successor is chosen by inspiration. They are warriors of the sword, of course, but far more than that, they are students of as much of the Book as I wrote for them from my memory. They are masters of the knowledge of good and evil, and they will not be deceived. The Island must stand, even when all the rest of the world falls. The Knights will hold our shores with courage and justice. They will guard against not only the invader who comes with armies, but those who come simply by night, with the words and the gifts of corruption.'

'And us?' Kor-Assh pressed. 'We who can read the staff – will we carry the war to the Enemy? What weapons have we?'

She spoke hesitantly, as if reaching for the answer herself. 'Ardesir has extraordinary faith.' She smiled as if at some memory. 'He has a love of good and nothing can bribe or coerce or frighten him into denying that belief, not in word, which is easier, but in act or price, regardless of what it is.'

He smiled at her generosity of judgement. 'And has he weaknesses?'

'Of course!' she said with a little movement of her shoulders. 'He is afraid because his intelligence and his imagination can see darkness that most of us cannot. But it is also his strength, because that same fear forearms him, and he wants above all to be brave.'

They rode in silence for a little distance along the wild, low, sea-bleached shore. Kor-Assh stared at the blue and gold of it. The brilliance dazzled his eyes and his ears were loud with the falling waves and the cry of birds riding the bright wind.

'And Sardriel?' he said at last.

'He has weaknesses as well. But his love of truth is absolute, and no terror or pain has ever been too much to pay, either to seek truth or to serve it. I don't think anything ever would be.'

Kor-Assh's soul ached to be part of the great battle, worthy of standing equal with such men, of having a mission as sublime, and as terrible. He wanted to be as Tathea was, and he did not know if he had the strength or the purity of spirit to do it. To succeed would be to grasp heaven; to fail, worse than he dared conceive, surely the true meaning of hell, the loss of what could have been his.

The salt wind roared around him, the surf beat in his ears, the sun blinded him, and he said nothing.

As they left the shore and went inland over the heather, Tathea deliberately rode ahead so she would not watch Kor-Assh. All her life's hunger was directed towards her love for Ishrafeli which some tiny point of light in her remembered. To lose it would be an endless night she could not endure.

Perhaps she should never have doubted the God Who had promised her that her name was graven on the palms of His hands and He would never either forget her or leave her alone. But she was weak, and human, and just now both the brilliance of the light and the horror of the darkness were too big.

So she turned to the other grief which wounded her. She thought of Sadokhar, and in her mind she prayed for him, not knowing what to ask.

As she rode she saw not the beautiful, wind-scoured shore with its ever-changing patterns of light on water, but an arid land without bird or beast, where the flat light cast no shadows and nothing lived. Then she saw Sadokhar standing on a cliff edge above a sea of formless dust, a mockery of the wild, life-giving beauty of water.

Her heart constricted watching him as he climbed down slowly, catching himself on the rock and seeming not to feel it, as if even sensation were dying in this stifling place, to which there seemed no end.

She poured out her spirit in prayer. Her words were simple, no promises, no arguments, only the plea – help him! Help him!

As they rode down into Tyrn Vawr and through the gates to the castle, Ythiel came out on foot towards them. He looked first at Tathea, then at Kor-Assh, and Tathea's heart knotted. Her mind flew first to Sadokhar, but there was nothing worse that could happen to him than already had.

'Sardriel? Ardesir?' She gasped out the words.

Ythiel shook his head, then looked up at Kor-Assh, avoiding Tathea's eyes. 'My lord, I grieve to tell you, things go hard in Lantrif.'

Kor-Assh dismounted, holding his horse's rein in his hand. 'There is a messenger? I must speak with him and learn what it is.'

Ythiel stood barring his way. 'The Lady Marilla is here, my lord.'

Kor-Assh's face changed, a subtle tightening of the muscles so small one could not have said precisely what it was, but he had retreated into himself. Part of him was already with whatever troubles disturbed his own people.

'I see,' he said simply. 'I'll go to her.'

'She is not well, my lord. The journey has exhausted her, the—' Ythiel began.

But Kor-Assh walked past him, only once glancing back at Tathea, and that too briefly for her to read his face.

Ythiel offered her his arm and she took it as she dismounted also, glad of his strength to steady her. The ground seemed hard, jarring as if she were barely ready for it. She waited a moment, unsteadily. Kor-Assh's wife was here in Tyrn Vawr. In an hour or less she would meet her and have to speak, welcome her, offer her comfort and help as she would any other guest. How could she govern her feelings enough to hide them?

Ythiel was looking at her, his face creased in anxiety.

'I'm only tired,' she said, her voice very nearly in control. Then he looked at her more closely. 'We hoped to find the sixth warrior. We didn't.' Perhaps he would believe that was the cause of her grief, the iron band that was holding her heart, tightening with every step towards the doorway already held wide for her.

It was her duty in Sadokhar's absence to welcome Marilla of Lantrif to Tyrn Vawr. No emotions of her own, no physical exhaustion were excuse. She might allow herself time to wash and change from her travel clothes, but no longer. She never had in the past given in to such weakness, and no one would expect it of her now.

She went up the stairs alone, dismissing an offer of assistance, and closed the door of her chambers. She needed every moment alone that the circumstances allowed. She realised as she took off her outer garments, then her tabard and lastly the cotton next to her skin, how she had permitted her dreams to take hold of her on the Eastern Shore. She had forgotten for these few days the reality of Lantrif, that Kor-Assh was committed to someone else, not only his bond but surely his heart. But whether it was his heart or not, honour would never allow such a promise to be broken. The day she even considered such a thing, allowed herself to dwell on it, to hope, to wish, then she forfeited that part of herself which could ever be worthy of it.

She poured water into the bowl and washed herself, then dressed in clean linen and a long tabard of blazing red. She would go down as if into battle, even if she herself were both victim and foe. She would offer Marilla all that Tyrn Vawr had to give, and she would do it as if it pleased her, or at least as if it were no different from any other guest who was hereditary lady of her people.

She found Marilla lying on a couch with servants around her

102

and Kor-Assh looking white-faced and stiff. He held a goblet in his hand and as Tathea came in he was in the act of offering it to his wife.

She was reaching for it, her ashen, pale face accentuated by an aureole of hair with the vividness of flame. She was beautiful in a fragile, blazing feminine way Tathea would never be. Her huge eyes were limpid green and her white hands seemed almost boneless, so soft were they. She wore a travelling gown of soft apple green which robbed the slight blush from her cheeks, but oddly made her look a thing of nature, an exquisitely delicate flower sprung from a frozen earth.

She turned and looked at Tathea. And smiled.

'I'm so sorry, my lady,' she apologised. 'I grieve to be an additional burden to you, when you have so high a command, and to take from you a man who could offer the Island so much.' Her eyes did not waver, but her voice trembled. 'Had I the strength to govern Lantrif alone I swear I would, but as you see, my health fails me, and my people are a troublesome race. Our contentions stretch back a long way into our history, and it requires a strong hand to prevent our quarrels from rending us apart.'

There was nothing Tathea could say except to imply her sympathy without condescension. She struggled for words, so conscious of Kor-Assh listening that his presence seemed to fill the room.

'I understand,' she said through stiff lips.

Marilla relaxed as if immeasurably relieved, and sank a little further back into the cushions behind her, gasping for breath. For several moments she was racked with coughing. 'I am so grateful,' she sighed at last. She looked up at Kor-Assh with a wan smile. 'They fear him in a way they do not me. I am stricken with a wasting illness, and I am afraid my strength fails me.'

Kor-Assh remained silent. Tathea could see in his eyes his shame at being torn in two directions, and a situation among his own people which threatened to run out of control. But he would not make excuses.

'I understand,' Tathea repeated. 'We had war in the Island for many years. It does not end easily unless you crush people, and one cannot do that to one's own.'

Marilla did not turn to her this time, and her voice was very soft and breathless, as if her power to speak was almost exhausted. 'How wise you are, my lady, and how compassionate. But I knew you would be. Your fame has spread far, although I would have come, even had you been less, for the sake of the victims of war, should we not prevent it. But I am profoundly grateful.' A tiny smile touched her lips. 'I shall not impose on your generosity for long, only until the worst of my illness passes . . . a day or two perhaps. But Kor-Assh will leave immediately, so he may return the sooner.' She let her hand fall as if she could no longer hold it up.

There was no argument to make. War in Lantrif, on their own western border, was something Tyrn Vawr could not afford, and when the main attack came, they would need Kor-Assh's armies with them.

'Of course,' Tathea said, forcing the words. 'We shall be glad for you to remain as long as it requires for you to be able to travel with safety and more comfort.'

But Marilla did not reply. She seemed to have slipped into a faint, and lay ashen-faced on the pillows, her shimmering hair spread around her like a sea of copper on the light.

Holding her head very high, rigidly and blind with tears she dare not shed, Tathea turned and walked away. She did not look at Kor-Assh, and she did no more than acknowledge the servants waiting to minister to Marilla. She hoped it looked to them as if she had withdrawn to respect their privacy, and the sick woman's need for help.

Out in the wide passage she walked quickly, and was startled to hear footsteps running behind her. At another time she would have waited. Now she did not care, and she needed the small comfort of being alone.

But the steps overtook her and she was confronted by a young woman with wild brown hair and flushed cheeks. She was a servant come recently to Tyrn Vawr, and she was well aware that she presumed in speaking so forcefully, and yet there was no hesitation in her.

'My lady, my name is Nioba. I am from the Flamen people west of the forest, and I have seen great illnesses like this before.' She stood squarely in front of Tathea. 'There is a spring in one of the groves which has healing water. My lady of Lantrif might regain her strength if she would bathe herself in its waters.'

Tathea felt her heart tighten until she could barely breathe. The last thing on earth she wanted was for this beautiful woman to regain her health, her vitality and laughter and passion of body as well as of mind.

But it was not the last thing. The truly last thing was the alternative – to have had the gift of healing in her knowledge, and to have withheld it for her own ends.

She breathed in deeply, her throat aching. 'Thank you,' she accepted. 'We shall offer it to Lord Kor-Assh.'

'Yes, my lady. It is very powerful.'

'Thank you . . . tomorrow.' The desire to escape and be alone was almost overpowering.

She would do it, she would offer healing to Kor-Assh's wife, but not yet. Tonight she needed to be by herself, to gather her strength, above all to pour out her pain and confusion in prayer and seek a peace that was beyond her to find alone.

Marilla was doubtful. She had lived so long with her frailty and her pain she found it too hard to believe it could be cured. 'The hope . . . I have had so many remedies offered . . .' she said weakly. 'I could not bear another disappointment, not only for me . . .' She glanced at Kor-Assh.

'You must try,' he said. 'I know it takes courage, but we can't turn down any chance. It may be the one that will work.'

Reluctance was so plain in her eyes, the shrinking of her body, that it was as if Tathea had heard the words of refusal.

It was the young woman from the forest who spoke, again not waiting until she was asked.

'It will work, my lady. There is health and wholeness in its waters. When you arise from it you will be truly yourself, as you were meant to be, before affliction or injury came to you.'

There was a moment's silence in the room. Everyone, Kor-Assh, Tathea, Nioba, Marilla's own servants and two of the men who had ridden with her and now awaited her orders, all were watching her, hope and encouragement in their faces.

There was no reason for her to refuse, except fear, selfish fear which would deny the very motives she said compelled her.

'Of course I will come,' she said huskily. 'I thank you for your concern and your love for me.' Again she looked at Kor-Assh.

Tathea tried to stand a little straighter, but even in this unusually warm room with the late summer sun streaming through the closed windows, she felt as cold as if it were a winter night, and she were locked in a room of stone. Old and terrible memories half stirred.

They set out next morning early, Nioba guiding them. She did not speak again, but went ahead with calm confidence out of Tyrn Vawr and through the hot, golden fields of the Heartlands towards the dark edge of the forest on the horizon.

They rode all day, each absorbed in his or her own thoughts, Kor-Assh beside Marilla, supporting her and offering her comfort and hope. Tathea rode alone, insisting Ythiel remain at the head of the company with Nioba.

It was shortly before sunset when they came to the forest clearing, a steep-sided place of shadows, damp-smelling earth, mosses crowding brilliant as velvet over the stones and in between the roots of the giant trees. The pool itself seemed like any other, springing from the forest and falling over a ledge of shining rocks to splash thirty feet into a pool barely an arm's length across, but so green it was impossible to guess the depth.

An ancient man greeted them, asking nothing, as if he already knew. He glanced at Nioba, then at the others in the company. Perhaps it would have been apparent to anyone that it was Marilla who needed his help. He went to her, his face gentle with compassion.

'Come, lady,' he offered her his hand. 'Let the waters divide the evil from you, then you will rest tonight, and in the sunrise your life will be whole and complete.'

He took her weight as she dismounted with an effort so intense every man sat forward in his saddle as if ready to help. Kor-Assh dismounted hastily, but he was still not swift enough. The old man bore Marilla across to the green water, smiling at her, murmuring words of assistance.

The others left their horses and followed, Tathea looking only at Marilla, meeting no one else's eyes.

The fading sun was gold, shifting and glittering as it fell through the leaves. There was no sound but the falling water into the pool, not even birdsong.

'It must cover you completely,' the old man warned. 'But it will be only for a moment. Hold your breath.' And very gently he lowered Marilla into the green water until there was none of her, not even her blazing hair, left above the jade-smooth, opaque surface.

Tathea could feel her heart beating. Even the wind ceased to move in the leaves above.

The old man took his hands away.

Around the place where Marilla had disappeared, the water turned dark and viscous like oil, spreading rapidly to the banks and even up the cascade until it hung suspended, too slimed and clotted to fall.

The centre of the pool boiled, and then erupted out of it a creature unlike anything human. Its head was black, and as the round, hairless skull of a great bird, crooked-beaked, sunken-eyed. Its broken many-jointed limbs hung down from narrow shoulders, as if they should have been wings, but at the ends were claws, curved for rending and tearing.

Its visage was both cruel and clever, and it held such a hatred that as it hovered above the pool, the old man shrieked and stumbled back from it.

Kor-Assh stared. It wore Marilla's gown, and copper-bright weed surrounded its leathery neck. Infinitely slowly it raised one claw and the talons shrivelled as if something were loosed from its grasp.

Kor-Assh fell to his knees, his breath strangled in his throat. He tried to crawl forward, but his strength was gone.

Nioba stepped to the edge of the pool and bent, touching her fingers to the water, and from them spread a sweet purity, cleansing the darkness to a shimmering green again, but troubled to a greater and greater whirling until it foamed and leaped in a brilliant vortex that sucked the petrified demon to itself, and drew it down into the hollows beneath, stone into the stone heart.

The water settled and once again was a limpid, perfect surface.

Kor-Assh pitched forward in a faint. The men around him were too horrified at first even to move to his aid. The old man stood unmoving, a smile like sunrise on his face, growing brighter and brighter until it was impossible to look upon him.

Nioba too shone with a radiance as if a light burned within her. Tathea crept forward past the shuddering figure of the old man, and kneeled beside Kor-Assh, taking him in her arms and holding him, rocking back and forth, too stunned to speak.

'Your love has been great enough,' Nioba said softly, her voice like the wind. 'Not once but twice. Now he is free to become himself.'

Chapter Seven

Kor-Assh awoke to feel Tathea's arms around him and see the fear and wonder in her face. Then his vision cleared and he saw beyond her to the shining form of Nioba, altered to seem a being more of light than of substance, and he heard her words as if an echo in his mind.

'Now you are free to be yourself.'

It was as if shackles had fallen from him, although he felt dizzy and stunned with relief, and elation, and fear. The question in his prayer was beginning to be answered, but it was still incomplete.

He sat up slowly, Tathea's arm still half supporting him. Then she let him go and moved back.

Nioba and the old man were hardly visible any more; they looked like shafts of sunlight brilliant through the forest leaves.

Kor-Assh turned to Tathea. He was free to love her. Everything that Marilla had been was fallen away, the bands of obligation were dissolved, shown to have been of Asmodeus' forging, there to cripple, not to strengthen. But Tathea was the Bringer of the Book. What could he do, even in the furnace of Armageddon, that could be worthy of that?

He did not even know yet what his mission would be. He could read the staff, but not understand it. What could it mean to speak the name of all things?

He stood up slowly, swaying a little, but waving away assistance. He must stand alone. Ceawlin's words 'And in you a priest' echoed in his head. What was the calling of a priest?

He mounted his horse and waited as Tathea did also, then turned and began the journey back to Tyrn Vawr, followed in silence by the bewildered Lords from Lantrif.

All the way his mind was consumed in thought. He longed above all else in existence to fight Armageddon and serve the cause of God, to pour out all his strength and his passion for life in the battle for the earth. All this made sense. Asmodeus would not have been blind to that, nor have suffered him to prepare unimpeded!

If Tathea had walked such a long and terrible path alone, if

Sardriel had suffered some way in the past too anguished to share, if Ardesir now followed Tiyo-Mah into Shinabar, and Sadokhar went through the gates of hell itself, why would he, Kor-Assh, be free to come and go as he pleased with no one to assail him in spirit?

In Marilla the enemy had been there by his side for years, unrecognised. It chilled him to the bone; it frightened him because he tasted the beginning of its power and its hate. Asmodeus knew him by name, perhaps even knew his exact calling better than he did himself.

And yet it was also a kind of release, a clean wound of truth, a setting free. He wanted to be with Tathea, and yet when he thought of her the ache inside him was intolerable. Something within him remembered an older, deeper love that held him closer than dreams, soul-deep, heart and bone of him beyond reason, beyond denial. And yet there was no way but forward. War waited on no man, no grief, no hunger.

As the first crippling horror at what Marilla had been wore off him his mind began to race again. If Asmodeus had sent her, or even created her, to bind him from his calling, was her message about the threat of civil war in Lantrif necessarily true? Perhaps not, and there was no need for him to return.

He dropped back from riding beside Tathea and spoke with the leader of the escort, questioning him closely, pressing him for details, names, numbers of men. They answered him hesitantly at first, then with increasing awareness that the trouble was actually no worse than rumour, petty quarrelling and the usual old feuds that had rumbled on for decades.

He gave them instructions and authority to act in his name, then sent them home to the City of Fallen Kings and returned his mind to the greater struggle. He tried not to imagine what Asmodeus would do because of the destruction of Marilla, or what the next threat would be, or to whom.

And there were two more parts of the prophecy to be fulfilled, one of which even Kor-Assh's dreams dared not touch, uncertain if he could bear the separation it must bring, and yet he must. Ishrafeli had not returned, nor had the Book been opened, and both must come before Armageddon.

Late in the evening after their return, Kor-Assh found Tathea in the yellow chamber above the courtyard. He had not seen her since they had ridden in, weary and dusty from travel. Deliberately he had avoided her, until he had mastered his emotions and could face her with dignity.

She looked tired. There were hollows around her eyes and an uncertainty in her when she saw him.

'We must find the sixth warrior,' he said simply. 'Perhaps it is Ulfin after all.'

'Yes . . .' She grasped the idea, her eyes searching his, trying to weigh his healing, and afraid to probe. He was startled how already he saw her tenderness, and the depth of how she could be hurt. He lowered his gaze, in case he should intrude too far, too quickly.

'We should go soon,' he said aloud. 'Asmodeus will not wait for me to gather strength.' Then he realised how unnecessary it was to say that, to her of all people. 'Tomorrow?' he asked.

She nodded.

They left the city, riding north rapidly, carrying only food, a little water, cloaks against the cold or rain, and of course the staff.

Early autumn had come suddenly. The fields were stubble where the harvest had been cut. The haze in the air carried the sharp smell of wood-smoke and the heavy sweetness of rotting leaves. The trees and hedgerows flamed with colour, scarlet berries bright as blood.

They continued northwards through the centre of the Island, past the western outskirts of Hirioth, without entering, nor did they speak of it. The trees towered high, green turning to bronze and gold, wind whispering in the leaves.

Past Hirioth the travellers started to climb up the ever-steepening incline from the softer valleys on to the high, bare moors of Celidon – endless, wind-scoured skies, vast cloud racks splashing sunlight and shadow over land rolling into impossible distances, blue into purple on the horizon. It had a terrible beauty that filled Kor-Assh with wonder.

He looked at Tathea, the fading light gold on her face, the sweet air soft around them. He thought of Sadokhar, who had loved it enough to leave it and enter a suffering he could only imagine, so that the last terrible war could be fought in the time of their choosing, not of Asmodeus'.

There were bees in the heather. A butterfly flew dizzily past, drunk with nectar. Mice and weasels scurried where he could not see them, and probably rabbits as well. Further up the slopes wild deer started and ran with their strange, awkward elegance.

A flight of wild white swans crossed the darkening blue of the sky, calling to each other, going south. He counted fourteen. He knew they mated for life, and a tug of envy pulled at him too quickly for him to bury it.

'This is what the battle is for,' he said, gazing across the land. 'This beauty, this abundance, this workmanship of God. We fight so that it will never fall into the slime of corruption and pain that would be the victory of darkness. If we cannot love this, in what

111

way could we possibly liken ourselves to its creator?'

She did not need words to frame an answer. It was in her eyes, the curve of her lips, her silence.

Past Celidon they crossed the Wastelands, desolate and stark in their own beauty. The bracken was gold, the heather, already past its flower, dark on the jagged land. Clouds, mackerel-ribbed, filtered the sun in the south, but to the north the light was clean and cold, pure as snow. Small tarns, reed-speared, reflected brilliant patches like fallen shards of sky. The mountains of Dinath-Aurer were violet, soft in the distance, colossal, like shadows over the west. Kor-Assh had never seen a land of such blinding purity, and he found emotion so high in his throat he was glad Tathea honoured the silence as he did. There was something in it too vast and too tender to break with words.

It was another three days before they crossed the border into Kharkheryll, the last bastion before the sheer drop into the ocean. It was a huge promontory jutting out into water beset by great winds in winter, lashing the seas into white fury. Century by century the cliffs had eroded, leaving caverns which echoed in the tides, sudden inlets, and rivers that ceased without warning in torrential waterfalls which roared like never-ending thunder and shot rainbows into the air.

He was tense now, and he saw it also in Tathea, although she said nothing of it. In a short time they would meet Ulfin, and have to test him with the staff. Surely he must be the sixth warrior. They knew of no one else, and there seemed no other place to seek. In fact Kor-Assh wondered why the man had not come to Tyrn Vawr himself, impelled by the spirit to offer his sword, his skill, his life in a cause which he must surely love? Only the quarrels of Lantrif and the power of the Silver Lords had held him himself from coming sooner.

And perhaps were he wiser he would have been prepared before Sadokhar had sought him. He knew that at times he had not been an easy man to serve. He had learned no patience with lies or cowardice, little tolerance with those who fell short of his own standards. He expected his lords to grasp at life with both hands and take the bruising without complaint. He gave his compassion secretly, so the receiver would feel no burden, and at least in part to hide his own gentleness from those who must hold him in awe if they were to obey him. The Silver Lords had loved Marilla, or what they thought she was! She was their hereditary liege, but they had never loved him.

Which made a mockery of their arts! They had not seen her clearly, any more than he had.

But that was something he refused to think now. It could cripple his mind and heart, and leave him of no use to Tathea, or the cause they served.

Tathea turned to him, breaking his thoughts. 'We are watched,' she said softly. 'Up on the ridge to the left, just below the skyline, and to the right in the trees. They must know who we are, or at least that we come in peace.'

Kor-Assh had been unaware of being observed. He upbraided his own inattention, but silently, leaning a little forward now and watching the horizon ahead.

He and Tathea rode steadily westwards and at last they reached the end of the track in a valley between sheer walls. They dismounted and climbed a flight of steps cut out of the hillside, leading to a castle seeming as much hewn out of the rock as built upon it.

Kor-Assh looked up at it with a sense of foreboding. It had a savagery about it as though the conceivers of such a fortress had expected to stand against the world. Once the Flamens had ruled the whole Island, except Lantrif. Then the Camassian invasion had driven them to the mountains and the forests. After the Camassians, the raiders from the Sea Isles had come, conquering much of the Eastern Shore and driving inland, ruining the ordered Imperial cities and laying them waste.

Kor-Assh saw no one, but he was certain the high, slit windows – angled outwards to give an archer a wide sweep – were manned, probably day and night.

Tathea led the way through the entrance and inside. He wondered how many times she had been here before, and when.

The cullis was left open behind them, but it could have been closed at an instant's notice, and Kor-Assh was certain the inner watchtowers were manned as well.

The visitors were welcomed and Ulfin himself came to the steps of the inner court. He was a fair, slender man with sky-blue eyes and a face that seemed to reflect laughter and tragedy in equal parts, yet curiously concealed all but the most surface of his thoughts.

'Welcome to Kharkheryll, my lady,' he said, inclining his head to Tathea. He looked beyond her to Kor-Assh. 'And you, my lord of Lantrif.' In one phrase he had told them how well guarded he was, and yet with such graciousness it could not give offence. 'Come in and eat and rest,' he went on. 'Your journey has been long. It must be a matter of great import that brings you so far.'

'It is,' Tathea agreed.

Kor-Assh turned to consider his horse, but already a soft-footed man had gone to it and was preparing to lead away both it and Tathea's. It was then he remembered what she had told him of

Flamen belief in the reverence for all beasts, for the trees and the herbs, even for the rocks of the earth. It was strange but it sat at ease in his mind, and he was startled that it should be so.

They followed Ulfin into the hall, narrower than Tyrn Vawr's, and far older. Steep iron-railed stairs led upwards around the outer wall, and high windows looked out over mountains and crags to a jagged skyline.

They were each shown rooms and offered water, little sweet cakes, and bidden to the hall by dusk.

Tathea hesitated a moment outside her door, the staff still in her hand, then smiled and went in.

In Kor-Assh's room fresh clothes had been set out, as if he were not only expected, but they had known exactly what would fit and suit him – a floor-length tunic of rich, dark fabric decorated with silver. After washing away the dust of travel he put it on. He looked at himself in the length of glass. It was highly becoming and after adjusting it to sit a little better on his shoulders he fastened the clasp. The light was already fading in the sky when, with Tathea, now dressed in purple, he made his way down again to the Great Hall where they had been invited to dine.

They were made welcome again, and offered places at the head table. There were nearly fifty people in the room, and the food served was rich and delicate, but Kor-Assh noticed there was no flesh of bird or beast, nor did anyone wear fur.

As the eating drew to a close a lone musician stepped into the centre of the floor. He carried in his hand a stringed instrument which he played not with his fingers, like a lute, but with a bow. It was an extraordinary sound, like a living soul, carrying all manner of emotions. It seemed to tell a story which ended in overwhelming tragedy, and then at last silence.

Kor-Assh listened to it intently. He could feel the music tremble on his skin and cut to his heart. He was moved by it, compelled to know more, and he turned to Tathea and saw pain and wonder in her also. He looked to Ulfin.

Ulfin smiled. 'You heard it?' It was barely a question, but his eyes were shining, almost luminous.

Lantrif had music, but nothing with the power of this. It haunted the mind, probing into the dreams and wounding places long covered over, wakening nameless emotions, memories of the soul.

'Tell me,' Kor-Assh answered.

Ulfin leaned back a little.

'It's a legend among our people,' he began, looking into the distance. 'The old gods who first found the world and loved it were here for a long time, no one knows how long.' There was a faint smile on his lips, a mixture of mockery and grief. 'They cared for it, they spoke with the beasts and the trees, the birds of the air. They knew everything by name. They watched the seasons change, the seed time and the harvest, the sleeping of the earth and the awakening.' He sighed. 'Then one morning a man came, full of curiosity and pride, and the will to change things, to place his own mark upon everything he could touch.'

Ulfin's fingers turned the goblet he was holding, catching the light in the depths of its stem, clouded blues and purples.

'He became clever,' he resumed softly. 'He multiplied and covered the face of the land. He built and he invented. He changed things from the way they used to be. And the gods watched him, and in the fire, and the stars, they saw what he would become in ages yet to be.' He twisted the glass a little more. 'His cleverness would grow greater and greater until he could unlock the secrets of life. But he forgot wisdom, he forgot humility. Above all he forgot who he was. He no longer knew his Father or his Mother. He imagined he was alone, and could do everything . . . and yet he was running ever faster towards nothing.'

Kor-Assh glanced at Tathea. He still was not certain if Ulfin were telling a story that was no more than myth, passed down for pleasure, or the core of his own faith. The light on his face touched the lines that could have been tragedy, and the sky-blue brilliance of his eyes that was laughter . . . or tears.

But she was listening with the same intensity that he was, the same urgency to know.

It was several seconds before Ulfin picked up the thread again.

'He built more and more things,' he said. 'His towns became places of iron and stone, with no leaves growing in them. He used the herbs and the trees to feed his wants, and tore up what did not serve him. He used the beasts for their labour, their flesh, their skins, their horns and their bones.' His voice dropped and became harsh with sorrow. 'He used their love and their fear for his entertainment. He looked at their beauty and devoured it for himself, as if they possessed no souls, and had no being of their own.'

His mouth quivered and pulled tight.

'He spilled out the waste of his cleverness into the rivers and poisoned them. He poured his filth into the seas in his rage to plunder the treasures of the world, until everything he touched was polluted by his greed. The earth cried out against his ignorance. In its suffering it called upon God to cleanse it of its burden.'

Ulfin stopped, still nursing the glass very gently in his hands, almost as if it too lived.

Kor-Assh waited for him to end the story, but he did not, as if he

115

needed someone to demand it of him.

It was Tathea who spoke. 'And did God hear the earth?' she asked.

Ulfin turned to look at her. 'I don't know,' he confessed. 'The old gods had gone long ago, because they knew what would happen and they could not bear it. You see, they loved the earth.' He tipped up the glass and drank the last of the wine. He looked to Kor-Assh. 'You wanted to know what the story was behind the musician's playing . . . that's it. It's a Flamen myth, an old one. But we are an old people.'

Kor-Assh did not defile the moment with speech. What was there to say?

Tathea turned to Ulfin. She had brought the staff into the hall and to the table with her. No one had questioned it, perhaps assuming she leaned on it, and it would be indelicate to enquire. It was too light and too finely engraved to be a weapon. Possibly they believed it a symbol of office, like a sceptre. Now she raised it a little, and it caught Ulfin's eye.

Kor-Assh watched her face in the light of the rush torches. The wavering of the flames made her eyes hollow and the gold in them softened her lips and cheeks until he could see the young Empress she had been in Shinabar before her quest had begun. The light moved again, harsher and a little brighter, and he saw the Isarch she had become after her conquest. Then the fires burned up, and the light of them laid bare the loneliness in her, and the years of waiting.

Was Ulfin Ishrafeli at last? And if he were, could Kor-Assh bear it? If he were not – then who? Where was he, and why did he not come forth?

Ulfin reached out and took the staff, turning it over and over in his slender fingers, touching the hieroglyphs, frowning. Seconds passed by. Kor-Assh looked at Tathea and knew what he would see. It was already too late. Ulfin would have seen the words, could he read it. They had not found the sixth warrior. He was not Ishrafeli.

The defeat was stunning, like a blow that robs the body of breath. Where else could they look? Kor-Assh realised only now how deeply he had believed it could be Ulfin. He seemed to fill every need, especially the love of the earth that surely would make him a warrior fit to battle for it against the tide of darkness coming inexorably in. He felt a moment of panic. They had lost Sadokhar, Ardesir was in Shinabar and Sardriel was on his way towards the steppes of Irria-Kand to face whatever savagery there was there, led by men or less than men.

He looked at Tathea, and saw the same bewilderment in her.

Ulfin passed the staff back, frowning, knowing that somehow a

116

chance had passed him by and been lost.

Tathea smiled, but she looked away quickly, hiding her emotions, and as soon as it was courteous to do so, she excused herself, not only to Ulfin but to Kor-Assh also. He rose to his feet as she left, but it was plain Ulfin wanted him to remain, and he had no choice but to do so. There were tales yet to be told, civilities to observe, a kindness to offer which would mask, at least on the surface, the moment of loss.

When finally Kor-Assh retired for the night he found it hard to sleep, and through his dreams the Flamen legend kept returning to him with its vision of a poisoned world where the beautiful and vulnerable creatures suffered and found no help, where innocence was laid waste and its cry went up unheard.

He turned over again and again, staring into the darkness. He got up and pulled wide the curtain, letting in the starlight, then he walked restlessly back and forth across the floor. Finally he returned to the window and stared at the night sky, pale above the black edges of the mountains. He opened the casement and smelled the sharpness of the air. High and north as Kharkheryll was, it was cold in autumn. In the distance he could hear the echo of the cataract they had passed, thundering into the gorge a mile away.

Was the tale myth from the past, and no more? Or was it also their prophecy for the future? Not essentially for the Island, perhaps, but a ruin beginning in the centre of the world and spreading outwards? If God did not answer the cry Himself, was that because He awaited a man to do so? Was this man's trust, to undo his own sins and wash clean the stain? Was that to be his burden and his gift?

Kor-Assh kneeled a long time in prayer, then he went back to bed again, wrapping the blankets around himself and trying to warm his body. He was startled how cold he had grown.

He must have drifted into sleep at last, because he awoke with a start. The room was still dark, but the light that had been in his mind was now a certainty. The Flamen legend was an ancient nightmare put into music, woven into art and preserved so that whether men chose to forget it or to remember, it could not die. Man had been given the earth as his home, but its stewardship was his test. Would he love it, nurture it, or in his blind greed destroy it, and with it himself? In all the magnificence of the blaze of stars, this one was man's, to win or lose, to make brilliant, or to darken for ever. The Flamens had known this in their music, even if their minds had grown tired and let it slip into forgetting.

As soon as it was dawn Kor-Assh dressed and went to Tathea's door, knocking softly. It had been hard to wait even this long to share his thoughts with her.

117

After a few moments she opened it, still wearing her long pale gown for sleeping, wrapped around with a robe, and her black hair loose.

'I'm sorry,' he apologised hastily. 'I have been thinking of the Flamen story all night.'

'I too,' she said, opening the door wider to allow him in.

'I think it is a prophecy, and Ulfin knows it.' He watched her face, trying to read her understanding. 'I don't know why he couldn't read the hieroglyph. Surely with knowledge and passion like that, he should be the sixth warrior? He loves the earth with a depth we can't fathom. His people have revered it more than ours.'

'I don't understand either,' she admitted. 'But I know the purity of what he says, and that if it is not prevented, the prophecy is more terrible than any ruin we can imagine.' She shivered. 'I was going to say that it is more fearful than man can make, truly a work of devils.' Her mouth pinched at the corners. 'But there is nothing higher or lower, than man. At his best he is the heir of God, at his worst the equal of Asmodeus.' Her voice dropped to a whisper and her face was very pale, her eyes almost hollow. 'There is no "them" – no creatures of another beginning, there is only "us" – angels rising or fallen.'

They remained in Kharkheryll for three more days. Tathea told Ulfin that they believed the Flamen myth, and had heard prophecies of their own which supported it. Quietly, by the light of a single torch, far into the night, she told him of Iszamber's words to her in the desert long ago, how when ruin and darkness covered the earth, the Island would still stand, because of the faith of its people, stronger than all the destruction even Asmodeus could cause.

Ulfin stared into the distance, his strange face full of courage and tragedy. 'So soon?' he said quietly. 'I had thought we had longer, but if it is not so, then we must prepare ourselves.' He turned to her. 'We will hold the north; and keep the love of the earth bright until the last sunset.' He held out his hand and she took it.

No further mention was made of the staff, and on the fourth morning Tathea and Kor-Assh set off south again across the wide sweep of the Wastelands and down through Celidon.

Kor-Assh became certain that the words on the staff for him meant that he was to love the earth and its creatures, to feel their life and their pain and to fight for their release into the wholeness that was their eternal right.

He was so lost in thought he barely noticed the passage from the high escarpments of Celidon to the gentler slopes and the first of

118

the great towns and cities which had grown up during the peace.

Midday was a glory of light across the gold of the harvested fields. Huge silken clouds shone in the west, towering into the burning blue of the sky. The land was steeped in abundance; everywhere he looked its rich, open heart lay before him.

As they rode under the canopy of Hirioth the knowledge deepened in Kor-Assh's heart that the pollution of the earth was one of Asmodeus' sharpest weapons. Man's destiny was here, not in some distant heaven or hell, and it was his care of this world entrusted to him that would determine whether he inherited other glories beyond the fire of imagination, worlds without end – or forfeited his birthright to a ruin of his own making, the darkness of the last sterility.

All the long journey Kor-Assh and Tathea had not spoken of Ulfin, nor did they now. It was enough for Kor-Assh to be with her, and yet the nature of his feeling for her also troubled him. On the brink of joy, there was always the fear that reached from something beyond him, and the nagging whisper of betrayal, an older loyalty that sealed the core of his heart.

Tathea knew the forest so intimately she found food and shelter as if without thought, though he understood that it was long years of skill. He saw her face as she bent to find a root or to choose a fungus that was edible, and he knew she was remembering her years with Sadokhar when he was a child and a young man, before the days of the Eastern Shore. He longed to be able to comfort her, but there was no ease or hope to offer, and he was afraid to intrude into a loss in which he had no place. He watched her silently, and hurt with her.

The third night in the forest he awoke abruptly to find a man standing above him. He was tall, thin-shouldered, with a high-collared cloak which fell to his feet. His head was bare and in the radiance of the moon his hair shimmered around his face almost as if it were alight.

'Be still!' he said softly. 'I mean you no ill, Lord Kor-Assh. The woman sleeps. It is you that I and my brethren would speak with. Come.' And without waiting he turned and trod on tiptoe across the leaves of the forest floor and out of the clearing and under the shadows again.

Kor-Assh sat up, but he did not go. He had no weapon except his knife, and he knew Tathea could not be injured by mortal man, perhaps not even by immortal, until her task was completed, but still he would not leave her alone.

He stood up, looking around him. She did not stir. She slept without moving at all, as if so deeply she were unaware of him, or the faint stirring of the forest. He could barely see her chest rise

119

and fall. There was no flutter of eyelids, no hint of dreaming.

The man in the cloak was there again, beckoning, impatient now. 'Come!' he said urgently. 'She will sleep until you return, and beyond. The forest will not hurt her. You know that! Be quick, there is much to speak of.'

Slowly Kor-Assh obeyed him as if drawn, whether he willed it or not. He trod softly over the grass and earth into the shadow at the further side, then beyond and into a tiny pool of moonlight where four other men stood waiting, each dressed in a cloak of sombre hue.

'I am Karguish,' the first man said quietly. 'First of the Silver Lords of Lantrif. The rest of us you do not need to know yet.'

Kor-Assh felt a shiver run through him of both fear and understanding.

'We hold the lost skills of sorcery,' Karguish went on, his voice delicate and subtle, caressing every syllable as if the words themselves held power. 'In the beginning of the world our ancestors learned the secrets of creation and destruction, and we are masters of many of them still.'

It was true, Kor-Assh knew it without argument, and yet it was also wrong. He did not know how, but there was incompleteness in it.

They were all watching him, but again it was Karguish who spoke.

'You wonder why I seek you in the night to tell you this, which all Lantrif has learned in infancy and whispered one to another in the darkness, even though they scarcely believed it, and did not understand.' He did not wait for a reply. His voice was urgent, full of emotion. 'Because the world lies in peril – not only men but beast and tree, even the stones of the ground. The last great war of all things is upon us. You know it even as we do.' He nodded slowly, his eyes invisible in the shadows. 'Tathea knows it, but there is nothing she can do. She has wisdom, but she has no power.'

Kor-Assh drew in his breath to argue, but Karguish silenced him.

'You have seen her try!' he said impatiently. 'Ardesir is gone to Shinabar and sends no word. Sardriel of the Lost Lands marches with armies somewhere at the ends of the earth – and achieves what? The barbarian harries the Empires of the west, the centre and the south, the borders crumble and no man bars the way.' He lifted a pale hand, silver rings gleaming in the light. 'But it hardly matters. The war is of the mind, not the flesh. Battles of swords are incidental.'

'We fight him with both!' Kor-Assh contradicted. 'Do you think we have not thought of that? Of course it is of the spirit, but man is a whole creature, of heart and mind, passion and intellect, body

120

and spirit. Asmodeus will fight on every level. We must be prepared on them all, and armed.'

'I know!' Karguish said impatiently. 'Your warriors are brave, and honourable – Tathea above all. But this war is not won by good intent, but by strategy, by skill, by unbending resolve, and, most importantly, by knowledge of the Great Enemy, and of the laws of creation!'

'Why do you tell me this?' Kor-Assh asked, the truth of it troubling him. And yet the core of it was missing, like a coldness. 'Do you imagine we don't know that?' he challenged. 'That we haven't talked for hours, days, discussed every method man or devil could use? He wants the whole world, the physical, life-giving beauty of it, just as we do, and he will attack us where we can see and where we cannot. But if you imagine it will be a struggle in the air between your mind and his, then I believe you have little concept of the magnitude of his power, or the width of it.' He stared at Karguish, who still stood motionless. 'The whole world must be armed with faith, or at least with hope.' He took a shuddering breath. 'And if hope is gone, then with love. Compassion is the last and best weapon against him.'

Karguish smiled, a patient, contemptuous curl of his lip.

'None of us denies your courage,' he said softly. 'Or your good intent, only your wisdom. You have not the knowledge.'

'Then why have you come to me?' Kor-Assh demanded.

'Because we are the five Silver Lords,' Karguish answered. 'And for the fullness of our power to save the earth we need the sixth.'

'Who is he?' Kor-Assh asked. His words were whispered, yet they seemed to fill the glade.

'He is not yet one of us,' Karguish said. 'We must choose him, covenant with him and teach him the arts of the mind beyond ordinary men to dream. You can be he. Then the war can begin in earnest. We need wait no longer, helpless, dancing on Asmodeus' will!' Now his voice vibrated with power. 'We can begin the real defence of life, all precious, tender and beautiful life, both man and beast. Virtue is a fine defence from day to day, but we need more than a shield, Kor-Assh, we need a sword to attack! And that blade is knowledge. Then as fast as evil strikes, we can summon the forces of creation to defend. We can dare the stars and stand face to face with the Father of Lies, and put him to flight for ever.'

He leaned forward, his long face vivid, eyes burning silver-bright. 'Have you the courage to accept your destiny, Kor-Assh? Will you be our leader, take up the weapons of power which can shake even Erebus, and drive terror and pain and death from the world and give it back again, whole, into the hands of life?'

'Life?' Kor-Assh said the word slowly, very carefully, needing to

121

be sure. His answer must stand for eternity.

'Life!' Karguish repeated. 'Joyous, wonderful, everlasting life! You can do that! There is only one question . . . will you?'

One of the other Silver Lords pushed back the cloak, showing a high brow and scarred cheek. 'Dare you?' he murmured. 'Asmodeus is terrible! He desires the death of all things, to ruin the earth, to pollute the stars beyond the furthest edge of imagination. Have you courage to think of that, and to stand with us?'

'Do you love the world enough?' a third asked, his voice lifting.

'We will stand with you, back you, but the glory will be yours,' the fourth one said.

Only one remained silent.

'Give it back from destruction into life?' Karguish repeated. He held out his hand.

Still Kor-Assh hesitated. Was this after all the great purpose of his life? Was this the tiny whisper within him that held him from giving himself to Tathea? Not a memory of love at all, but of a higher calling?

'Life!' Karguish said for the fourth time.

Then Kor-Assh knew the word that was missing. It was like a clarion call, clear as a trumpet across the sky.

'There is no life without God,' he answered, looking at Karguish. 'I am His servant, or I am nothing. You fight with the wrong weapons. I am not of you. Your enemy is my enemy, but your god is not mine. Walk the road of your knowledge, if you must. I walk the road of faith.'

Karguish stepped back. 'You walk the road of blindness!' he snarled. 'You walk the road of defeat! You could have had the love of all men for eternity! You have cast it aside like a thing of no worth.' His voice shook with rage and contempt. 'You have trampled the crown of ages as if it were paper and denied your destiny.'

For an instant Kor-Assh was swept with doubt. Could it be true?

Karguish turned back to him, his eyes wide, waiting.

Kor-Assh thought of Tathea, of all the things Karguish had not said, of mercy and patience, of trust in the love of God. 'Go in peace,' he said aloud. 'We fight our own way.'

When Tathea woke in the morning she was aware that her sleep had been different from usual. There was no sense of half-remembered dreams, no consciousness of the night. She sat up abruptly and saw Kor-Assh standing above her, his face solemn and pale in the white light of sunrise. He was looking at her, and there was something in him which had changed irrevocably. The pretence, the veil between them was stripped away.

Suddenly she was afraid, with an incomplete memory of some pain so dreadful it negated every other beauty and all but swallowed purpose: light on water, ancient stones, the gold of the sun. She dimly remembered welcoming the thought of death.

She looked at his face and her heart lurched inside her. Her body was trembling so much it took all her self-control to speak. 'What is it?' The words were a whisper.

He kneeled down beside her, but still a yard away. The rising light half shadowed his face and fell in brilliance on her. She felt as if her heart were naked to his gaze, but there was no escape. Everything that mattered was here. This was the heart of it all.

'I know that the Flamen myth will become truth if we do not prevent it, and that it matters – not for the earth, which God can make whole again and remove the memory of its pain, but for our souls, who do such things, or watch and allow them to be done. Those will be marred for ever.'

'Armageddon?' she said doubtfully. 'Is that what it is? How can there be time?'

'I don't know,' Kor-Assh answered. 'I think perhaps God will hasten time. Does that sound ridiculous? Blasphemous?'

'No . . .'

'Our chance to love the earth enough is short,' he went on, frowning. 'Whether that is our doing or not, I don't know. The Silver Lords came to me in the night . . .'

Tathea stiffened, ice touching her.

'No!' he said quickly, disappointment in his face for an instant. 'They are not of God. Did you think I should be tempted?' A tiny smile touched his lips, and his eyes were soft. 'You are right . . . I was. But not now. I know my calling is to love the earth so completely that I share its life and its pain, perhaps its death.'

Looking at him, she knew it also. It was high enough, close enough to God, large enough to encompass all he could do.

'Good,' was all she answered.

Something inside him eased also . . . She realised with a flood of joy how intensely it had mattered to him that she should understand. But was it for herself, or because of who she was – the Bringer of the Book, the one person whose knowledge was greater than his own?

She climbed to her feet and, without meeting his eyes again, walked over to the deep shadow where the dew was wet, and bent to wash her face in it. Then she found roots and berries for them to eat, and without referring to the subject again, saddled the horses and continued south.

The longer she thought of it, the more certain she was that Kor-Assh was right in the understanding of his mission. Snatches of memory came back to her of walking through the forest towards the Eastern Shore with Immerith, High Priest of the Flamens, more than five centuries ago. He had taught her so much of the love of the earth and its creatures. She had come to understand the Flamen belief that even the stones were precious, made of intelligence, the handiwork of God, not random, insensate chance. Immerith's reverence for it had left an indelible print on her soul, and she realised only now how profoundly she had accepted it.

If it were Ishrafeli's calling to love the earth, protect it from the ignorance of man, it would take all his strength, because its defilement would wound him far more than he could have any conception now.

She was still pondering this in the deepening sunlight of the late afternoon, when she sat alone in a copse on the edge of the Heartland. Kor-Assh had gone to seek food. She was aware of someone else standing in the shadow beside her. Her instinct was to be angry at the intrusion. She jerked her head up.

The figure that moved now before her was lean to the point of gauntness, yet oddly graceful. He was clothed in jerkin and hose, parti-coloured in quarters of purple and gold, and his absurd shoes had curled-up toes with bells on the ends. His face was thin, his eyes brilliant, his lips full of humour and tenderness.

She knew him immediately. From the beginning he had come to her at the darkest hour, when it seemed there was nothing left but despair, every course had been tried and found wanting. He was Menath-Dur, Lord of Hope.

'You are quite right,' he said softly. His voice was always in the heart more than in the ear. 'Ishrafeli's mission is to love the earth and all its life, to love it with his whole heart . . . and that means he must weep with it, and when the time is come, bleed with it also. He must watch with it in the long night of its grief, and climb the steps of sacrifice so that it may die, and be reborn of God, when all is renewed in its eternal glory.'

'Can't I . . .?' Then the words died on Tathea's lips. She stared at him, seeing the ache of gentleness in his eyes, and afraid of it. He knew her too well, he could read her heart, the light and the darkness in it, the fear from which she drew back even now.

There was denial in his face. He knew what she was going to ask, and even before she put words to it, he refused.

'Hope,' he said softly. 'I have always told you to hope, even when the sky is at its darkest and there is no star to follow. Now I say to you also – have faith. Trust in God, Who is wiser than you are, and can see the heavens and the earth and everything that is in them, and has ordered it all from the beginning. No matter how it seems to your human vision, who love and fear, who believe and do not

124

know, doubt not the power of God Who holds you in the palm of His hand. He has trodden the path before you and knows every cut and bruise of the way.' He turned and walked towards the trees again, the bells on his shoes tinkling faintly, and the next moment he was gone.

Kor-Assh returned with bread and apples, pleased with himself, and Tathea smiled back at him. They ate side by side in the sun, staring in silence, almost touching, feeling the warmth. She breathed in the scent of dry grass, remembered the blue sky and the tingle of heat on her skin, storing it in her heart.

That night, only a few hours from Tyrn Vawr, Tathea kneeled alone in the moonlight and poured her heart out in prayer, pleading with God that she might take Ishrafeli's place and carry his burden.

'He does not know what he has promised to do!' she cried. 'He has no idea what the pain of it will be. I know he has ruled in Lantrif and seen all kinds of corruption and deceit. He's seen people fail, probably people he loved, but he doesn't know Asmodeus! He can't even imagine the pain of the earth, the betrayal, the ruin, the innocence and beauty lost! Let me do it!'

She knew that what she dared not say, even to God her Father, was that she loved Ishrafeli so much she would protect his soul from failure, from the dark terror that might ruin what he had been in the days before life, all the passion and beauty of the love he had felt then. What if in the griefs of mortality he could not keep that fire inside him alight? The strength of his generosity of heart, the wholeness of purpose, the purity of his soul's honesty, was more precious to her than anything of her own. To have it again, to love and be loved was the star she had seen and followed all the existence she knew. If that were spoiled by the Enemy, then there was nothing left.

She waited, almost crouching on the dry earth, simply for the comfort of it. There was only silence. Eventually she crept back to her bed in the grass and lay with the tears running down her face, not daring to sob in case he woke and heard her, and yet her whole body ached to let go of the agony inside her.

Why was there no answer? Where was God?

She must have drifted into sleep. She saw the earth corrupted as Kor-Assh had said, its beauty spoiled, its beasts tortured and dying, its plants and great trees withered. Slowly it perished into a broken thing, and Asmodeus stood upon it, covering it with his filth until all goodness and beauty was violated. It became a dark core of inconceivable evil to pollute the stars, and spread forever outward with endless suffering. The hosts of hell streamed from it like liquid shadow, to devour everything in violence, chaos and annihilation. All reason, passion and loveliness was gone. In pain more than she could bear she saw it twist and spin down into an abyss and disappear from her sight.

She had no idea how long she lay there before she opened her eyes again and saw a new earth, shining with a glory that healed all wounds and blazed into the furthest reaches of the universe, and yet wrapped the innermost heart in the arms of love unimaginable. Worlds beyond worlds were spread like dew on the grass, with no end to their increase in knowledge of everlasting truth. The light of God shone in the faces of men as they trod the galaxies with life eternal, and a radiance of joy which could not be bounded. Their hearts became wide as infinity, and God called each one by name.

When she awoke, understanding filled her mind as the morning sun washed the sky. These were the choices. As the Book had said long ago, there was no middle ground – only the darkness or the light. There was no escape for her, or for Ishrafeli. She could not walk the path for him. She must stand back and allow him to fulfil his destiny, as God Himself must with all those whom He loved, whatever the cost.

The dearer they were, the greater would be their task, their suffering . . . and their reward.

For a long, shattering, sublime instant, between one beat of the heart and the next, she had a glimpse of the soul of God, and the burden of His love as He watched the children of His spirit struggle and hurt and strive to return to Him through brilliant flashes of faith and dark agonies of doubt, crying out to Him, and so often imagining themselves unheard and alone when He was closer to them than their skin.

And yet He could not relieve them of the toil, or He also took from them the prize which was beautiful beyond dreams to form.

She knew that she must offer the Book to Kor-Assh. There was a deep certainty growing inside her that he would open it again, just as it was he who had closed it before. Even so, he would grasp its fullness only step by step, learning by passion and joy and pain, as had every living soul since the first dawn of light in heaven.

She chose the first evening back in Tyrn Vawr to do so. Taking the Book out of its cupboard, but keeping it still wrapped in its blue silk Lost Lands cloak, she carried it to the quiet courtyard where she had asked Kor-Assh to meet her.

He was waiting in the soft light by the pool. He turned the moment he heard her footsteps, his face tense. He saw what she held in her arms and knew from its shape what it must be. His eyes widened.

She let the cloak slip off into a bright mound on the stones, and left the beaten gold surface shining in the last of sun.

Still he did not speak, but his face was filled with awe, and he made no move to touch it.

Tathea held it out towards him, offering it.

He stared at her, in his eyes questions he dared not even frame.

'Take it,' she whispered. 'It is time.'

He hesitated still.

She did not move, and the Book grew heavy.

At last Kor-Assh put out his hands and accepted the weight from her. The gentleness of the fading day made the pearls milk white and shot fire into the star ruby in the hasp. More as if drawn by its beauty than anything else, he put his fingers on it, and the hasp fell open.

The knots inside her unloosed. The waiting was over.

A tremor shook his body, questions teeming inside him. Already, even before lifting the cover, he knew a fragment of the sublime truth.

She nodded, afraid to speak.

He bent his head and began to read.

He did not look up, and she watched his face, the passion, the pain, the glory of all life reflected within him as the words of God settled on his heart. She saw understanding come to him, incredible, stupendous, that he himself was Ishrafeli. At last he lifted his eyes and gazed at her, and in them was such love as had shone in her forgotten dreams, from the day they had parted in Hirioth, more than five hundred years ago. The passion, the tenderness, the soul's need that had filled her, was echoed in him till it was a music between them that was more than sound or feeling, a fire that wrapped around and held them both.

He put the Book down and stepped towards her and took her in his arms. The touch of his skin was warm, the smell of him sweet and exciting and familiar, as if she had spent all her life waiting for this moment. She let herself go utterly and answered his need with all the longing of her own, his lips, his cheek, his eyes, his brow.

There was no need for questions, and yet he did ask her, as if it were conceivable she could refuse.

'Will you walk by my side now and through eternity?'

'Yes,' she said with certainty as simple as a blaze of light. 'I will.'

'Covenant with me, before God, and on the Book . . .'

She rested her hand on the Book, and he placed his over hers, slender and strong, and together they promised before God and all His angels to walk the path upwards together, all the days of time and eternity.

From Erebus there came a howl that shivered out to the furthest stars and into the empty spaces between.

Chapter Eight

Sadokhar stood shuddering, sick with horror, and then overwhelming fear. What had he done? The portal was closed. Return was impossible.

He had broken the barrier and let the creatures of hell into the beautiful, vulnerable and infinitely precious world, and now he could not even be part of the struggle against them. He was as imprisoned here as they had been.

How would Tathea manage without him? She had known at least some of these fearful beings before, but long ago. Had she still the power and heart to fight against them? Before having seen the black keys of Asmodeus he would have had no doubt . . . but now he knew her weakness as well as her strength. She was human, tired after the long years alone. One more battle might be too much.

And what of Sardriel, and Ardesir? They had been refined by the fires of life, but could anything human prepare them for what he had seen in this place?

And Kor-Assh, when he came? He was an unknown force, believed in, but not yet tested.

Should he, Sadokhar, have taken this terrible, irretrievable step? The decision had been the hardest of his life, but the way had been so easy. Was that because Asmodeus himself had willed it?

He stood staring at the broken archway with its closed door, already seeming to blend into the shattered rocks with their half-obliterated designs, as if centuries of wind and dust had eroded the meaning they had once had. But there was no wind in the leaden air, no sound, no movement of anything at all.

He turned, and everywhere he looked the same flat, glaring light showed only endless variations of rock and splintered stones. There was no sun and no shadow. A standing monolith was surrounded by flat pebbles whose height and size he could not judge because without shade they had no dimension.

There was no point in remaining here. At last he began to walk slowly out into the landscape that stretched endlessly in front of him. He did not know how long he trudged across the sand and stones – there was no way to mark the time. He passed nothing

129

alive. Each rock formation was only a variation of the last, taller or shorter, single or broken, but always the same dun-grey colour.

Still there was neither plant nor insect anywhere and the white sky never varied, nor was there the slightest wind. He was breathing, yet his lungs ached for air. He felt neither hot nor cold, and the only sound was that of his feet on the pebbles, and even they slithered and fell without echo.

Eventually he came to a jagged line of low cliffs, but there was an easy way up, and no other path to either side, so he began to climb. He half hoped there would be a different view when he reached the top and he increased his effort accordingly, leaning forward, slipping every now and then and sending little spurts of stones flying.

But when he reached the crest there was nothing ahead of him but more dun-grey dust and rocks and shale to the horizon in every direction, except for the drop behind him. Perhaps he should not have expected other, but still his heart sank as if he had hoped for some escape from the imprisonment of the mind in the endless sameness.

Was this all there was? Was hell a wide-awake oblivion, a blistering awareness of being alone in an eternal desolation?

He started forward because it seemed like action, however pointless. It gave him the delusion of having mastery over something, even if it were no more than his own acts.

There was still no sense of perspective. The light deceived. Distant things grew little closer even after what seemed hours of travel. He passed an outcrop of rock, and although he walked without turning, he seemed to pass it again. He had no idea whether it was the same one, or any of countless others that looked alike.

Once he tried marking one, intending to write something on it so he would know, but the loose rock he picked up made no imprint whatever on the surface, and he threw it away in disgust. At the next mound he tried instead to place stones in a pattern he would recognise if he passed them again. He laid them carefully in a star and continued walking.

Eventually he grew tired and sat down, leaning his back against one of the lower upright rocks. The whole pile above him looked vaguely as if it might once have been something designed by man as a form of shelter, except that there was nothing to shelter from, neither heat nor cold, wind nor rain, only the unceasing light.

He closed his eyes, and perhaps drifted into sleep, or maybe only a lessened awareness. When he opened his eyes again he saw the first other life since the Lords of Darkness who had passed through the portal into the world. A lone man was staggering towards him, his back bent by the weight of stones he was carrying. His clothes were

130

covered in dust and his hands and forearms were bloodied with gashes, his nails torn. He stared at Sadokhar with fury.

'Get up and work, you idle pig!' he snarled, his face distorted. 'What do you think makes you different, eh? Lying there at your ease, like some damn slave master.'

Sadokhar was startled. 'Work at what?' he asked, straightening up, not with any intention of obeying, but in order to be less vulnerable, in case the man should attack him, as he looked ready to do.

'Anything! Help me! I've got far too much!' The man glared back with mounting rage, his face red, his eyes bloodshot.

Sadokhar was surprised by the sense of purpose in him. What could there be that made any difference in this wasted place?

'What are you doing?' he asked.

'I'm moving those damned stones, of course,' the man shouted at him. 'Are you blind, or are you trying to provoke a quarrel? You're just as stupid and perverse as everyone else. Why did I ever imagine you might be different? No one ever is.'

'I don't see anyone else.' Sadokhar looked around.

'Well, they're in the hole, aren't they!' The man's temper finally exploded and he slashed wildly at the air. 'We don't sit around all day, as if there were for ever, you know!'

'Isn't there?' Sadokhar said bitterly.

Now the man was confused.

'Isn't there what?' he demanded. 'What are you talking about?'

'Isn't there for ever?' Sadokhar said patiently. 'Anyway, why are you moving the stones? What does it matter where they are?'

'If we don't move them far away enough they'll fall back into the hole, idiot!' The man was still shouting. 'I'd have thought that was obvious enough, even for you!'

'What hole?' Sadokhar had seen none.

'The hole we're digging, of course!' The man's voice was almost a scream now, and his face and neck were scarlet. 'You're just deliberately trying to pick a fight, aren't you? What do you want of me? Eh? Why are you doing this to me? What did I ever do to deserve it, answer me that?'

Sadokhar was beginning to get angry himself. 'I'm not doing anything to you!' he snapped. 'You are doing it to yourself. I asked you a perfectly reasonable question. I don't see any hole. I don't know why you'd bother to dig one. What for?'

'That's it!' The man hurled the last rock he was holding. It narrowly missed Sadokhar's head, striking the outcrop behind him and falling into the dust with a thud, sending up a little cloud which settled exactly where it had been before. There was no movement of air to carry it.

Sadokhar bent and picked it up, ready to use it as a weapon.

'That's right, attack me! Go on!' The man put up his arm to shield his head. 'You're twice my size, you coward! Everybody picks on me! No matter what I try to do, no one gives me any credit.' There were tears running down the dust on his face. 'Everything goes wrong! It always has . . . and it's not my fault. Even you are trying to pull my work apart and say it's no good. Destroyers, the lot of you!' With that accusation he turned and stumbled away, slipping on the loose scree, and still calling out abuse over his shoulder.

Sadokhar went after him, not from any desire to catch up with the man himself, but with the faint hope that the others he spoke of might have found some purpose in this place, and because they were the only life he knew of, other than himself. He still had seen no bird or beast, no insect, not even a patch of lichen on the stones.

Down the slope and past a vast, crumbling slab he saw in front of him a staggering sight. At least a hundred men and women were labouring in a hole, a thousand yards across and more than fifty feet deep. Bending, heaving and staggering, they moved every size and shape of rock from the floor of the hole, while others swung stone axes, chips flying in all directions, cutting out more chunks of rock. Yet others scooped up dust in bloodied hands and carried it bound in shirts and skirts up the paths that led out of the hole, emptying it out in mounds around the edge. Every one of them was cursing themselves, their neighbours, the injustice of life. Above all they cursed the God Who had made promises He had not kept, and not forgiven the sins they still hugged close.

Their faces were gaunt and they worked with a pent-up rage that spilled into everything they did, every movement, every word.

Sadokhar stood on the edge and watched them, trying to understand what they hoped to achieve. He asked, but no one answered.

Slowly he went down the steep steps dug into the side of the wall. Finally he reached the bottom and stood amid shards and splinters of rock. Many of the facets of the wall were smooth and their surfaces polished. He was startled to see shadows reflected in them, as if ghostly figures moved within the stone, taunting them, aping the gestures of those outside.

He stood watching for several minutes before he noticed that others also kept glancing at them as if it were not a trick of the light, but something of importance. He looked from the reflections to the reality, and back again, and slowly it dawned on him that they were not exactly the same. Every now and then one inside the stone was different, an effort succeeded, and something appeared like a doorway. Work redoubled, arms flew frantically, splinter and slab alike was hurled aside.

And then he looked again, and the doorway was gone. It was an illusion, an eccentricity of light and imagination. And yet the workers began again, cursing, digging, blaming.

He turned and began to climb back up the steps to the rim, a weight of despair inside him as if he were carrying lead in his heart. He would immeasurably rather have been dead, gone into nothingness, than survive in this crushing, sterile place where all life but human was gone, all labour and hope futile and nothing but anger and hate remained.

But hell did not offer the escape of death, or the peace of oblivion. Existence was the punishment . . . and a never-ending awareness of it all.

He walked on, not so much in the hope of arriving anywhere as the desire to leave the great hole and its labourers behind him. There was no sunrise or sunset, no day or night. The flat glare never changed, so he had no sense of time.

His legs grew tired and he sat down, leaning against a pile of shingle, and drifted into a half-sleep. His mind wandered and he dreamed he had fallen off his horse and was lying bruised on the hard ground. Waking was worse than anything he could have imagined. For a few moments he had been in the world again. Hell did not exist. Now the full horror of it returned with a violence that stunned his heart and crushed the light out of his spirit. It came back with the shock of the new, and yet the depth of knowledge of the familiar. He swore he would never sleep again.

But he did, measureless time later, lying in a hollow in fine, ash-like dust, as exhaustion overtook him.

He dreamed, vividly and with total, overwhelming sensation. He was drowning in mire. Dark slime covered his skin, sucking him down, the foulness of it filled his lungs, the taste clogged his mouth and throat. Bubbles of gas broke the surface with a stench that sickened him. He thrashed around in desperation to find a foothold, anything solid to cling on to, but there was nothing but the oily, viscous filth.

Then suddenly he felt a hand, slender, but pulling him with amazing strength. He jerked his head up, and through the miasma saw Tathea. She was up to her waist in the clinging ooze, but she must have been standing on something firm, because her weight was balanced so she could lean away from him and draw him forward.

His heart surged up inside him. Suddenly he could fight again, he could believe that anything and everything mattered. He opened his mouth to speak her name, but no sound came. Then she was gone and he was awake in the dust, and alone.

He staggered to his feet and started to walk. Time was meaningless.

He had no idea how long it was until at last he came to a shallow cliff and slid and stumbled down it on to a flat sea of dust. It stretched to the horizon without feature, without height or shadow. It was like an ocean in its endlessness, and yet in everything that mattered it was utterly unlike. He had loved the sea, its passion, and fury, and beauty, the teeming abundance of its life.

He could remember the first time he had seen it, when Tathea had taken him from Hirioth to the Eastern Shore, having realised she could no longer teach him all he needed to know. It had been time for him to learn from other men the arts of leadership. To do that he had to be taught first how to obey, how to follow, how to work with others and often to sacrifice his own will and ambition.

That had been so hard! He winced now at recollection of it. He also stubbed his foot against a rock and, looking down at the slow trickle of blood, realised with a sick dread how little it hurt. In this consuming sterility, even sensation was dying. What was there left when even pain was not real? Existence without life?

He sat down on the hard ground. He would like to have wept, but he had no energy, no tears.

He remembered the great storm he and Tathea had faced on the promontory. The sky had darkened and the sea risen in howling mountains of destruction. Tathea had known what it was, even though he had had no idea then. The Great Enemy had promised her that if she would turn back, taking Sadokhar with her, away from his destiny, then he would never be hurt. Long life and prosperity in the world . . . in exchange for forfeiting his promise to God.

Tathea had defied him. There had been years of peace, love and learning in the halls of Aelfrith. He could remember them now with an aching clarity – Aelfrith standing before the great fire, his mane of yellow hair grey-streaked, his battle-scarred face shining with goodwill, while he told tales of courage and the sea. He had talked of fighting on pitching decks, with the wind and water to ride, and how they had taken the long ships, a willing crew, and put to sea to chase the pirates to the world's edge.

Sadokhar had loved Aelfrith as he would have loved his father – with awe and a burning loyalty, a fierce knowledge and denial of his weaknesses. His stories fired the imagination, his courage was the ideal, his laughter filled him with wellbeing, his praise was the final accolade.

Perhaps Tornagrain had loved him as much. He was his brother's son, Sadokhar was only his sister's. Tornagrain had grown up on the Eastern Shore, and it was not unnatural he should expect to inherit the earldom, on Aelfrith's death. He was the heir in everyone's eyes, until Sadokhar came, and then what began as friendship and a bond of blood, had ended as rivalry, and in that terrible last day, betrayal.

But before that Sadokhar too had committed his own betrayal because he had fallen in love, not only with Yldyth, to whom he became betrothed, but with the life and loyalties of the Eastern Shore, with its beauties and its simple, daily decencies. He had told Tathea to leave him, not to try to force him to fulfil her dreams of uniting the Island, or fight her war against Asmodeus. She had been so angry. But she had not argued. She had used no pressure to force him. Perhaps even then she had had some foreknowledge of the weight he would bear, and part of her had been willing for him to set it aside, and grasp at happiness instead.

She had been gone for four years. By the time she came back he had regretted his denial. He understood better what it meant to serve a calling higher than one's own peace.

And two nights after Tathea's return the pirates had raided again. They had swept down out of the darkness with blood and fire. Everyone in the village had taken up whatever weapon he or she could to fight them. It had been years since there had been such a raid, and the surprise was crippling. They were caught on every side.

Only in the morning, in the smoking ruins, had it been so plain to see the path of the attack, and that it must have been aided by someone who knew the village.

Sadokhar remembered charging through the broken timbers, the charred remains of homes and storehouses, and then his amazement that the ships had not been touched. He could see the faces of the men who had come to say that Aelfrith was dead, and beautiful Yldyth too, who had wanted him to give up his calling, to deny Tathea, and for her he had done it . . . and it had lain like a stone between them.

Even now in this place of despair the grief of that night could still touch him, the sudden blaze of understanding that it was intended that Aelfrith be the victim as clearly as if it were a solitary murder. Then he had felt as hollowed out and empty as the endless dust and rubble under his feet.

After had come the rage as he realised it was Tornagrain who had betrayed them, leading the pirates in over the sea defences. Sadokhar had taken his dagger and gone after him into the fen country beyond the inland wall, miles of mists and foetid pools between shifting and unstable islands, bogs that sucked down all unwary enough to tread in them.

Hour after hour he had trailed Tornagrain until at last they had stood waist-deep in the slough, face to face.

They fought as only men can who have tested each other in

135

practice, time without number. They knew every strength and every weakness, every move before it was made. Back and forth they struggled in the slime, tripping, falling, rising again, striking until they were bloody and exhausted. In the end it was Sadokhar who had overcome, and carried the senseless body of his enemy and brother over his back. It had weighed him down, almost drowned him. Again and again his legs had buckled and they had sunk together, but always he had found a last ounce of strength, a last breath to raise them both and stagger on.

It was only when he had seen in the dark the torches of the men coming to meet them, then felt their arms heave him out of the sucking water, that he had realised Tornagrain was dead. He would never be tried for his betrayal. Sadokhar had exacted the justice the tribe had a right to. But it had been in rage and grief, not in judgement.

No one held him to account, no one blamed him. Aelfrith was buried in his own ship and the great funeral pyre lit the night as it set to sea on its last voyage. Sadokhar had spoken the final words of farewell – 'Safe harbour. Soft seas on the morning tide' – then he had stood on the shore watching, the tears wet on his face as the light of the pyre was lost on the horizon and the sea swallowed its own, until that day when the waters give up the souls of its children.

Tornagrain was buried in a traitor's grave on the land down by the edge of the fens where nothing grew but sedges and the white bog cotton, and they left him in silence to the wild birds.

Sadokhar was made Earl in Aelfrith's place, and the village was rebuilt. It was the beginning of his path to uniting the whole Island, and becoming King to all the tribes.

Now he stared at the bleak and terrible waste around him. Had his treachery also brought Tornagrain here to hell? He surely deserved that it should. Was there any blacker sin than to betray a man who had been to you father, friend and King? Sadokhar clenched his teeth. It was a sour satisfaction to think that somewhere in this desolation Tornagrain was also wandering hopeless and alone. And as anger filled him, so did despair. His own soul felt as arid as the destruction around him, as if in his torment he had created it.

He walked as long as his strength survived. There was no light or shadow, no day or night for him to judge time. Finally, legs aching and his feet bloody, he sank down and drifted into an uneasy sleep.

He became aware of a dry prickling on his skin and struggled to sit up, peering through the greyness. A wind had arisen and the dust was flying in clouds, acrid and sharp. He must find shelter or it would abrade his skin.

He staggered forward, the ground soft and shifting under his feet. He lost his step and fell, landing hard, bruising his hands. He had no idea which way to go. He could not remember any feature in the land at all. Perhaps he should simply lie down? He would be buried, choked, but what did that matter? If he could die, so much the better!

'Get up!'

It was a voice – a woman's voice!

'Get up! Come on!' it urged.

He knew her! It was Tathea!

He staggered to his feet, overbalancing in the violence of the wind and dust, but feeling for her in the gloom. His hand caught hers and clung to it.

'Come with me!' she commanded. 'Come!'

He struggled to obey, longing to be closer to her, to make out her form in the blinding dust, to see her face, but it was impossible. He could only grasp on to her hand and beat his way through the suffocating clouds.

He did not know how long he floundered forward, desperate to keep up with her, falling and crying out, gulping mouthfuls of air that choked him.

Then at last the dust cleared and he saw her, covered in fine pale powder as he was, but smiling at him.

He wanted to thank her, but what words could ever encompass the love for a human face in the wasteland of hell?

"Where have you been?" It was a child's cry, desperate and throbbing with fear.

'I've found Ishrafeli,' she answered softly. 'He has opened the Book.'

'Found him?' Now, stupidly he could weep. The tears sprang to his eyes and his voice was thick with them. 'He'll fight beside you . . .'

'So will you!' Tathea urged. 'I know it now. There is a way to escape!'

'Escape?' He breathed the word as if he had forgotten its meaning.

'Yes . . . you can, but it will be very hard.'

'How?' His voice was harsh, torn out of his dust-clogged throat. 'Tell me! I'll do anything . . . anything!' He meant it. Nothing could enter the mind of man worse than remaining here. 'Tell me!'

'Tornagrain is here also.'

'Good!' He meant that.

'Yes, it is good,' she agreed with a tenderness he could not understand. There was sorrow in it and passion, and hope. 'Because you can find him,' she went on. 'And when you have done, you can forgive him for betraying Aelfrith.'

Sadokhar did not believe it! It was impossible . . . monstrously unjust! God Himself could not forgive such a sin.

'I can't!' he protested, scalded with rage and grief. 'You can't ask it!'

'I don't, my dear,' she said so gently he heard her words more with his heart than his ears. 'But God does.'

'But it's unjust!' he cried out. 'It's . . .' He stopped. If that were the price, it was too high.

'It is not justice for him, it is mercy.' She did not move her gaze or even seem to blink. 'But for you it is what you need. Find him. Forgive him. And come home!'

'I can't!' he cried. 'It's too much! He betrayed us all! Can't you remember?'

'Yes, I remember.' There was pain in her voice, raw as the night it had happened. 'But it changes nothing. You must find him . . . and forgive.'

'No! I can't! It's not possible!'

Her hand slipped out of his and the wind stirred the dust again, prickling and hurting his skin. 'Tathea!'

But she was gone. He sank to the ground and buried his head in his hands, hurting with every inch of his body and aching to the core of his soul.

When at last he opened his eyes again he was lying exactly where he had fallen asleep. Nothing was different or disturbed. He could even see the footprints of his arrival.

He sat up very slowly, all his muscles aching. The sea of dust stretched around him level in every direction to a flat, grey horizon.

He knew that what she had said was true, bitterly as gall though it rested inside him. If he wished ever to leave, then to find and forgive Tornagrain was the only way. He climbed to his feet and began to walk.

Chapter Nine

In the clashing of air and darkness where chaos meets creation, Asmodeus strode the ramparts of Erebus and stared beyond them into the void. Hunger consumed him for the earth in its passionate, living beauty, its flesh that could know such suffering and such joy which now were for ever denied to him.

He had refused mortal life in the beginning, afraid of the pain, the risk of loss, doubting, disbelieving love, and that choice had cost him the chance of it for ever. He had sat in the Councils of Heaven, and like every other spirit, he had cast his lot. Now he had no place to rest his foot, no certainty, no sublime hope of eternal light if he stayed the course to the very end. And he hated with all the fury of his soul.

He had looked upon the earth and seen Ishrafeli open the Book, and begin to know himself. But Tathea loved him, and that was a weakness, a fatal weakness, in her armour. In the end it would be her undoing. He would find a way to use it against her. There was always a way.

In the meantime there were other matters for his attention. The Island at the Edge of the World could be left to itself for a while. Its day of darkness would come. The City in the Centre was nicely ripening in corruption, and all Shinabar was rotted to the core. Tiyo-Mah had at least done that much well. It was time to use Ulciber. Since he had chosen to disobey, and enter the world now, let him work for his satisfaction.

For Asmodeus to visit the earth too often was dangerous. Better he were seen as little as possible, until the last. Some man or woman whose spiritual eyes were open, might sense who he was. And belief in evil all too easily produces an equally powerful belief in good, and eventually in the power for good.

He did not permit any of his servants to enter Erebus, but if he summoned them none would dare disobey. He raised his voice and sent the command shivering out through the whirling darkness.

He turned and there was Ulciber, motionless in the lurid under-light of broken stars. As always his face was beautiful, skin smooth, features perfect. When he smiled it would be dazzling.

How he loved his flesh that looked so very nearly human! Only if it were cut would one see the spongy, bloodless texture, and know it for what it was.

He had wanted a body so much! But he had made the same choice as Asmodeus in the beginning, to walk away from the mortal life with its cost and its reward, its risk and its glory. Now he regretted it. He ached for a body, he lusted after it; his corrupted soul would do anything if only he could obtain one.

And he never would!

Asmodeus smiled at him, curling back his lips.

'You sent for me,' Ulciber said quietly.

Was that fear in his eyes? Good. He had every reason to fear. He had disobeyed.

'Of course!' Asmodeus snapped. 'You could not come here had I not! Since you chose to follow Tiyo-Mah through the portal, you will work for your stay in the world.' He saw the flicker of appetite in Ulciber's eyes, and he resented feeding it. But then he thought of how it would torture Ulciber to live among mortals, however weak, but who still had flesh, and will of their own, and he smiled again.

'Tell Tiyo-Mah to ally with Camassia.'

'She won't—' Ulciber began, then froze as he saw Asmodeus' eyes and lips. 'She hates Camassia,' he finished under his breath.

'Is she not infecting Shinabar with the disease of civil war?' Asmodeus raised his brows questioningly. 'Will it not bring them hatred, persecution, oppression, lies, and betrayal? In the end will a man not sell his brother for an idea, his wife for preferment, his child to save his own skin?'

'Yes,' Ulciber nodded. 'It is coming already!'

'And she agrees to all of this?'

'Much is her doing. She uses fear of the barbarian as a musician plays a fine instrument. She can wring from it a dozen tunes, each one to make the hearer do as she wishes.'

'What a shame to keep the contagion locked inside Shinabar,' Asmodeus observed. 'If you cannot persuade her to infect Camassia as well, then I shall have to find someone cleverer than you – who can!' He spat the last words with such fury Ulciber stepped back in spite of himself and all his intention to stand fast.

'If you carry a disease,' Asmodeus went on viciously, 'you give it to whoever you hate the most! Tell her that – fool! Use her! She is a mortal who has disobeyed me, but I will get every last feather-weight of worth from her before I destroy her – and she is of worth! See what she has done already.'

'Because I helped her!' Ulciber's voice was bitter. Whatever he thought of Tiyo-Mah's skills, he would never forgive her for having a body. Even if it were resurrected to hell, it still had form and

140

substance, and he had not! He had been lied to, deceived in the beginning. He had believed Asmodeus' plan for mankind, the easy path, no test, no agency, no chance of failure. Asmodeus had said the souls of men would choose it too, but they had not! More than half had chosen the beautiful and terrible path of earthly life with its sacrifice, redemption and the long journey to the light.

And Ulciber was left fleshless . . . and damned.

'Get out!' Asmodeus shouted at him. 'Go and prove your worth! Take Tiyo-Mah to the City in the Centre of the World, and spread the corruption of tyranny, violence, greed and oppression until Camassia also tears itself apart! You wanted Armageddon without waiting for me! So go and forge it then! Create it! Reap souls for me.' He held up his hand, clenched tight. 'Bring me the cruel, the cowardly, the betrayers, the deceivers, bring me the corrupt to the core!'

Ulciber smiled. 'I'll bring you those who used to be frightened and confused, ignorant of the laws of price and reward, once I have made them all you want them to be.'

'Of course you will,' Asmodeus agreed venomously.

'What about Tathea?' Ulciber asked. 'When can I have her?'

'Tathea?' Asmodeus rolled the name on his tongue. 'When she loves Ishrafeli more than she loves God . . . that is when you can have her. Now get out!'

Ulciber turned on his heel, marched to the end of the long rampart and disappeared into the clouds, shadowed with monstrous shapes of things out of the primeval night.

Ardesir rode into Tyrn Vawr shortly after dawn. It was a crisp, late autumn day and already there was frost in the air. The walls of the city gleamed pale in the clear light and the gates and arches were shadowed sharply.

He entered through the main east gate from the road to the sea, and clattered on to the smooth paved street with merchants' halls and houses on either side. Pillared façades rose in slender elegance. Ahead of him an arch spanned the street with a covered passage across. Beyond he could see the trees in half-hidden gardens, almost leafless now, and he smelled woodsmoke from kitchen fires in the still air.

He went straight to the castle on the rise in the centre of the city and into the courtyard with a sense of homecoming. The familiarity of it tugged at his emotions in a way he had not expected. He dismounted, leaving his horse for the groom, and went straight inside.

He was met with great welcome by the servants and courtiers, but when he entered the familiar upper chamber where Tathea awaited him, after the joy of seeing him well and safe, she perceived the urgency in him and cut short her greeting. She glanced not at Ythiel of the Eleven Knights but at the man beside her whose face was filled with power and vitality, whose strength was yet vulnerable, then she looked back at Ardesir.

Questions surged in Ardesir's mind. Who was this man that he dared stand beside Tathea? A quick anger seized him for the presumption. He was even resting his hand on the back of her chair, close to her shoulder, as if he might touch her. And looking at Ythiel's face in the sunlight, it seemed he did not mind. What had happened while Ardesir was away? A sudden fear seized him. Surely Shinabar was the centre from which all evil was spreading? He was the one with all the news to give!

The usual formal welcomes seemed absurd. There was not time or occasion. 'I have much to tell you that is urgent.' Ardesir was startled to find his voice hoarse. He had not realised he was so exhausted. His arms and legs ached and he was trembling very slightly. He was angry with himself. He hurried on, to cover his weakness.

'Reports of barbarian invasion and atrocity have increased so much everyone is terrified, turning to anybody they think can help them. Tiyo-Mah seemed the only strong voice willing them to fight and persuading them they could win, if only they would realise the strength of the danger and throw all their forces into the field. All dissension must be got rid of. To disagree, even to be half-hearted, is to betray one's country and to condemn one's family to being destroyed by the barbarians in ways too hideous to be named.'

His voice rose in anger and no one made the slightest move to interrupt him.

'Tiyo-Mah became Isarch in all but name,' he went on. 'She suggested a thing and they were all so frightened they obeyed. Taxes were tripled, every able-bodied man was called up into the army. The old leaders disappeared and Mabeluz, Lord of the Undead, was put in charge of everything.'

Tathea was staring at him, her face pale.

He went on to tell them about Min-Obal, the tears of the widows, and the plans they had made. He found his throat tight and he struggled to keep control of his words, hurrying before his grief betrayed him.

When Ardesir had finished it was the stranger who moved and brought him a chair and poured water for him to drink, and he accepted it with overwhelming relief, easing back and letting himself relax at last. 'Who are you?' he asked, too weary and raw with emotion to soften his tone.

'Ishrafeli,' came the answer.

Ardesir felt his body tense again. How dare anyone use that name? It was a presumption that could not be tolerated, in fact it was all but a blasphemy, especially to Tathea. Why was she not angrier? This man was mortal. The marks of his humanity were naked in his face: the fine lines from nose to mouth, and around his eyes. He had seen and felt suffering, laughter, fear, anger. He did not know God any more than the rest of them, still struggling and sometimes falling, needing each other's help to rise and begin again.

'He is Kor-Assh of the River.' Ythiel's voice cut across his thoughts. 'But he has opened the Book again, and read all that it says.'

Ardesir was stunned. The room seemed to swim around him. The Book was unsealed? Then it truly was the dawn of the end. Sadokhar had weakened the portal of time sufficiently for hell to break through, but it was not a single act of madness, creating chaos – it was part of the great plan. All that was needed now was that they should each fulfil their roles, however great or desperate, whatever the cost. If this man had opened the Book, which Ishrafeli had sealed, then in all his fragility of flesh, ordinary, as human as they all were, stumbling step by step towards the outstretched hand of God, then it was indeed he again.

Ardesir let out his pent-up breath in a long sigh, and began to tell them of Tiyo-Mah's plans to spread the same disease of oppression and civil war to Camassia, by alliance, and then the contagion of fear.

There was no debate as to what should be done. The corruption must be contained. Tathea and Ishrafeli would travel to the City and employ all their skills of argument to dissuade the Emperor Justinus from making any alliance whatever with Shinabar. He must remain apart from it, as one would from a plague-infested city. The question was only how best to persuade him.

'As Sadokhar's emissary,' Ythiel put forward. 'That would give you authority.'

'Tiyo-Mah must know that Sadokhar is no longer here,' Ardesir pointed out. 'You should go as his regent.'

There was uncertainty in Tathea now. 'The Emperor will receive us as ambassadors. The Island is rich enough he could not afford otherwise.'

'Will you tell him who you are?' Ishrafeli asked, looking at her very steadily, his eyes sombre.

The moment the words were spoken, Ardesir knew that that was what had been troubling her. Tathea was an ancient name, linked with history and legend. Her looks were plainly Shinabari. Some explanation would be necessary.

'The time for discretion is past,' Ishrafeli went on with certainty. 'And lies are not our weapons. If we pick them up then we are on Asmodeus' side, whatever we use them for.'

No one argued with him. A heavy, bright silence filled the room, but it was one in which no doubt rested, only a great sense of purpose, and the will and need to prepare.

The voyage was accomplished as swiftly as possible. Everyone was aware there was no time to waste. Tathea and Ishrafeli took with them only as many others as were necessary to give them the status required as ambassadors so they might obtain an audience with Justinus.

They were welcomed with a respect which surprised them. The Island was held in considerable esteem, perhaps because, although few had ever visited it, many had treasures of one sort or another from its wealth – fine workmanship in silver, semi-precious stones or delicate woven wools of subtle colours. All seemed to have heard of its peace, although they attributed it largely to its distance from the barbarians.

'You are very fortunate to live at the edge of the world,' the High Steward said with envy. 'Of course the Emperor will receive you, but you will understand there are many other foreign princes in the City, and courtesy demands you each take your turn.' He smiled, a shallow, professional gesture.

'It is a matter of considerable urgency,' Ishrafeli pressed. 'We bring news that must be heard soon, or be of no value.' He refrained from using the word 'warning' although it was in his mind.

'Everyone considers their own embassy to be of the utmost importance,' the High Steward said blandly. Then before Ishrafeli could say anything further, he bowed and turned away to the next supplicant, a man whose crimson silk robe swept to the floor.

Ishrafeli said nothing, but Tathea saw the dark blood of anger rise in his face. He swivelled on his heel and walked away.

As they were passing through the great outer hall with its rose marble floor and towering pillars, capitals curled and gilded, a handsome man in a purple-bordered robe approached them. His smooth face was full of confidence and he appeared to feel as if they at least half expected him.

'Guderius,' he introduced himself. He did not add that he was an Archon. His clothes proclaimed that for him, and he assumed they would know, as indeed Tathea did. 'Perhaps I may be of service to you?' he offered. His eyes swept up and down Ishrafeli's carefully chosen dark Island tunic with its silver embroidered collar, and then at Tathea's wine-red gown.

'We have lodgings, thank you,' she replied. She was more familiar with the language than Ishrafeli, who understood it, as most educated men did the world over, but had had little occasion to use it. He found the written word easier than the spoken, and the employment of colloquialisms tested his grasp.

'Of course,' Guderius agreed, smiling more widely. 'I was thinking of something you could not so easily acquire for yourselves . . . such as an earlier audience with the Emperor . . . should that be what you wish?'

He allowed the question to hang in the air, but his eyes suggested he knew very well that it was.

'And how would you accomplish that?' she asked guardedly. That he was an Archon should not make any difference.

He moved his head very slightly, indicating surprise that she should be tactless enough to have asked.

Ishrafeli caught the inflexion. 'We will wait,' he said decisively. There was no warmth in his voice and his face was still closed in anger as he took Tathea by the elbow and guided her out.

On the steps in the busy street, carts and wagons, sedan chairs and crowding pedestrians striding past them in the late sun, she turned to him anxiously. 'Are you certain? Tiyo-Mah could come any day, and we can't afford to make enemies. He is an Archon—'

'We can't afford to make friends like that!' he replied grimly. 'And don't concern yourself with our enemies. I think there will be enough of them – one more or less will weigh little in the end. It's who is with us we must be sure of.' He smiled very slightly. It was only an easing of the corners of his mouth, but his eyes held all his heart. 'Even if it is only each other.'

During the waiting time Tathea showed Ishrafeli much of the City, most especially the old parts which had been there five hundred years ago. They walked together up the cypress-lined roads, to where she had once lived. The pillars were gone, replaced by larger ones, which were more ornate, lacking the ancient simplicity.

She did not tell him about the people she had loved, and he did not ask, but she saw in his averted face as he gazed across the lemon groves and the uneven rooftops that he knew he could not share in it, and it hurt him that there was so much of her he did not know.

She ached to tell him that it did not matter, but she was not yet certain enough that he would wish her to have seen his vulnerability.

They passed one of the great churches of the Light Bearers. He wanted to go in and attend the service. She was reluctant, afraid it would hurt. She could remember too many people who had begun with faith and understanding, and been betrayed by priests who loved power more than truth, and gradually twisted the teachings

145

of the Book until they became fluid, soft to the ear and easy to obey. Music drowned out the words, loveliness of form seduced until the purer beauty of the law was distorted into other shapes, and paths that led only back into themselves.

But he insisted. 'We need to have the knowledge,' he said. His voice was not harsh, but there was no yielding in it. Now that he had opened the Book and read, he would see every bit as clearly as she did how priest-craft had corrupted it.

He looked at her unwillingness. 'Know your enemy,' he said with a very slight smile. 'We can't afford to pass by, easier as it would be.'

Tathea knew he was going to go in. She could either go with him, or wait outside. She went, as no doubt he had known she would.

Through the great ornamental doors she stared around her. The style had changed in five centuries, but it was just as overwhelmingly beautiful. The High Priest stood up and intoned words, obviously ritual and recited from memory. His singsong voice made them curiously barren of meaning, but they were repeated back to him, and gradually the rhythm and the music gained a magnificent and somnolent beauty.

Tathea gazed around the faces and saw the comfort in them, the love of the familiar. Cares slipped away as they were taught of a different and easier world. Promises were given of glory unimaginable, offered freely by a god who was inconceivable to the mind, possessing no definable qualities except total power and an infinite superiority to anything that held a physical, earthly form. Material was dross, and would eventually be burned away. No understanding was required of man, only humility, penitence and belief. Change was not expected. It was futile to imagine any of them being of worth to such a being. It was the supreme arrogance.

The congregation left, apparently comforted. They had heard what they expected to hear, and the world was, after all, as they had supposed.

There was a complacency in it which enraged Tathea. The priests were cheating the very people they had sworn to serve. It was Asmodeus' message! Man is helpless, worthless, conceived in sin and born to failure. Do nothing, and trust in the mercy of a deity who will carry you safely to a paltry reward.

The God Who had begotten your spirit in glory and Who ordained you to climb step by step all the way to the stars, was a blasphemy no one mentioned.

But surely the true blasphemy was to believe that God the Father had begotten the only offspring in the universe which could never become like their parents, but were destined from the beginning to remain immeasurably inferior? It was the negation of all love, the ultimate insult.

Tathea and Ishrafeli walked in silence for some distance, then he took her elbow and slowed her pace a little. At first she was angry, thinking he did not understand, then gradually the warmth of his grip steadied her, and she became aware that he understood very well. It was not that his outrage was less, simply that his closeness to her was greater.

That evening in the rooms they had taken she sat on the step down to the garden with its vines and lemon trees, and told him something of the Hall of Archons and all that it had once been.

A small black and white cat joined them, jumping down from the wall and ambling over the warm stones in the sun. It rolled over several times in the dust, then thoroughly satisfied, came over and rubbed itself against Ishrafeli's legs, leaving pale patches behind. Then it settled to wash itself, staring at Tathea with green eyes like jewels.

'The best of the Archons was Maximian,' she said quietly, remembering how he had been. 'He was stubborn. He never believed in the Book, but he held his own code of honour and nothing ever tempted him or frightened him away from it. In the end he gave his life so we could escape. It wasn't really to save the Book, it was more to be certain it left Camassia, because of the way it had been used to corrupt.'

'By those who used the Book to gain dominion over others?' Ishrafeli asked, narrowing his eyes against the evening sun. It picked out the lines on his face so clearly every passage of his life seemed written there.

The cat finished washing itself and lay down in the dust again and went to sleep.

'Mostly,' she agreed. 'It was the best vehicle for power then. Tomorrow we should look at the Hall of Archons, listen to them.' She slid down the step and moved closer to him.

'Yes,' he agreed. 'Of course.'

They had already purchased Camassian clothes, in case of need. Dressing discreetly in the morning they went as agreed to the Hall of Archons. They sat in the gallery reserved for visitors. Tathea was filled with a deep grief for the past and what had once been a place of passion and virtue, where ideals were argued and beliefs espoused more from loyalty than any expectation of personal gain. The longer they listened, the more it seemed a parody of that time, a façade with nothing behind it. The Archons themselves were mostly poseurs, time-servers whose eyes were more to profit than honour, and who wore their purple-bordered robes to further their own advantage.

147

There were exceptions, men fighting a lone battle against the tide. One such, named Merkator, spoke eloquently against a relaxing of the laws on financial privilege, and was overruled. His opponents jeered at him, insulted his family, and made poor jokes which were received with roars of laughter.

'Are you surprised?' Ishrafeli asked Tathea as they left.

She looked away from him. 'No. But I had hoped . . .'

'No, you hadn't,' he said quietly. 'This is the beginning of the final war, my darling. How else would they be but corrupt, here in the Centre of the World?'

She turned to him, and felt the tears prickle her eyes. The truth of his words burned inside. She put out her hand and took his, clinging to it.

The day came for their audience with Justinus. They each dressed carefully because impressions mattered. Tathea chose a hot, fierce terracotta to give light to her dark skin. She looked across at Ishrafeli in a severe, dark green Island tunic, cut with skill to sit smoothly across his shoulders and chest. He was regarding himself in the glass, readjusting the fastening, and he caught her glance.

She smiled at him and he coloured very faintly, but there was laughter in his eyes. He was perfectly aware of his vanity, and of how it amused her. For a moment it was as if they were an ordinary couple, with time for the little things.

They went by carriage to the Emperor's palace, and this time they were kept waiting only a matter of minutes before being shown into the splendid audience chamber lined with murals set between rose marble pilasters.

Justinus was a handsome man with thick hair, a clear brow, narrow nose and a mouth which only on second glance seemed loose-lipped. He was dressed in magnificent robes of silk brocade in shades of cream, embroidered and embossed in gold thread. The whole thing must have taken months of labour to make, and yet he wore it carelessly, as if it were of little worth.

He welcomed them with all the appropriate phrases, and asked them about their voyage.

'No pirates, I hope?' he said wearily. 'Travel is becoming dangerous these days, wherever you go. Barbarian tribes growing stronger in every direction. One hears terrible stories. I suppose you have them also?' He raised his eyebrows slightly.

'No,' Ishrafeli replied. 'We have had over a decade of peace, and there are no incursions on to our shores as yet.'

'You are fortunate.' Justinus indicated where they might sit, and then himself reclined on a well-upholstered sofa, swinging his feet up to make himself comfortable. He regarded them with a certain curiosity, picking idly at a dish of almonds as he waited for them to ask for whatever it was they wished, and state discreetly what they would pay him in return. He did not grant favours for nothing, unless it amused him, but to a man essentially bored, amusement was a legitimate currency. His patience was short, and the evidence of that was in his face.

'No doubt you are aware of the latest news from Shinabar, Majesty,' Ishrafeli began. The word 'Majesty' sat ill on his tongue, and it showed in faint distaste in the line of his mouth.

'Someone has invented a new musical instrument with strings to play with a bow of horsehair. I am told it squeaks like a bag full of cats fighting!' He snorted abruptly. 'So much for Shinabari – genius!'

Tathea drew in her breath sharply, and felt Ishrafeli's fingers bite into her arm. 'We have something in the Island made of a leather bag that you blow into and squeeze,' he said with a smile. 'The result sounds rather the same. I thought it was an instrument of torture.'

Justinus stared at him for a moment, then roared with laughter.

Tathea avoided Ishrafeli's eyes and kept her temper with difficulty. She understood what he was doing but she had been too long away from the need for diplomacy to find it easy.

'I must tell the Shinabari ambassador that!' Justinus said with delight. 'That will catch him on the wrong foot! Have you ever seen the Shinabari dance? It is so complicated it would be easier, and more fun, to command a fleet of ships in a storm, than learn to perform one of their court rituals.'

'I have never seen one,' Ishrafeli confessed.

'You would be no wiser if you had,' Justinus retorted. He waved his arm. 'We have everything here that anyone could want. Forget Shinabar.'

Ishrafeli disregarded the warning. 'Word is that the Isarch has acquired a new adviser.'

'Yes, yes.' Justinus flicked his fingers in dismissal. 'The old woman from the desert, widowed by the barbarian incursions, and trying to persuade him to send more men into the army. What of it? I have my own barbarian problems. I am not interested in theirs.'

'He has made her a special adviser,' Ishrafeli persisted. 'And now also an emissary, to come to your court and try to persuade you to ally with Shinabar.'

Justinus sat up a little and the almonds slid from his fingers back into the dish. 'Indeed? And how do you know this, when I don't?'

'We have friends in Shinabar,' Ishrafeli replied.

Justinus' eyes slid to Tathea. 'Indeed? And a Shinabari wife too, by the look of her!' Suspicion was sudden and sharp in his face. 'Why should I believe you? And what odds if this old woman does come here? I shall listen to her, out of curiosity, then I shall send her on her way. I have no need or desire to ally with anyone. And what would either of us gain by it? We trade already. That is enough.'

'You have nothing to gain by it,' Ishrafeli said. 'And much to lose.'

'To lose?' Justinus' voice was dangerously close to offence. 'Camassia has no need to fear one old Shinabari woman, my Lord of the Island. If you imagine so, then you are less astute and far less wise than I had assumed.' His underlip pouted a little. 'You do not seem to know much of the world at large. You should learn more before you presume to advise the Emperor of Camassia upon whom to deal with, and whom not to!'

Ishrafeli controlled his temper with an effort that perhaps Justinus did not see, but Tathea did.

'You assume that my wife is Shinabari,' he said very softly, his voice level. 'You are perfectly correct. Her name is Ta-Thea, as perhaps you recall?'

Justinus had obviously forgotten. 'Of course I recall!' he snapped. 'What of it? It's an old name, not used now. But we all know who the first Ta-Thea was! Shinabari culture might bore me, but I am not ignorant of its history, or of our own.' He shrugged. 'She brought the Book, before Ra-Nufis took it from her, and then she stole it back and escaped with it . . . God knows where. She was never seen again.'

'To the Island at the Edge of the World,' Tathea answered for herself. 'It was sealed for a space, but it is open again now. I still have it.'

Justinus stared at her, and started to laugh. Then very abruptly he stopped, his mouth sagging a little.

'What do you mean, you still have it? That was centuries ago!'

'I know how long it was,' she said very calmly. 'Yes, I still have it. That is how I know who Tiyo-Mah is, and what she can do – and will do, if you allow her to ally with Camassia. She has spread the infection of civil war in Shinabar, and she will do it here, if you give her the power.'

'Tiyo-Mah . . .' he repeated the name very slowly, sounding the syllables as if to make it familiar again from long ago. He stared at Tathea, studying her face feature by feature. 'You look like the portraits of Ta-Thea,' he said after several minutes. Then he shook his head. 'But it's ridiculous! Nobody lives five hundred years! Do you take me for a fool?' The thought angered him again. 'And why should you care if Camassia allies with Shinabar? You live on the edge of the world – what is it to you?'

'I care about Camassia,' she replied. 'I lived here once, and loved its people. I don't want to see the contagion of civil war spread.'

'Why should it?'

'Because Tiyo-Mah will see that it does. That is her purpose.'

'Why? It makes no sense.'

'Do you think Shinabar is enough for her?' she asked. 'She wants the ruin of all the world. This is only a beginning.'

'Rubbish!' Justinus said defiantly. 'Why should she?' But the first edge of fear was in his voice.

'You said you knew your Shinabari history,' she answered him. 'Do you not remember she murdered both her son and grandson in order to keep her power? And when I conquered Shinabar with a Camassian army, and faced her with it, she disappeared . . . into time. Do you think she has any love for Camassia?'

'Then . . . then she's hardly likely to come here and seek alliance now – is she?' he said as if clinging to some small moral victory.

'Not for any benefit of yours, no! So you know that if she does, it will bring you no good.'

His eyes narrowed and he stared at her fixedly. 'Ta-Thea? Can you prove who you are? How can I believe it?' He bit his lip. 'But you do look like the old painting that the Emperor Isadorus had of her. I've seen it. It's still in the old Imperial apartments.'

She looked back at him unflinchingly. She remembered it also. It was a good likeness. It caught not only her physical features, but her expression as well, the tilt of her head, the passion in her eyes and the tenderness of her mouth.

For a moment it was plain in his face that he believed her, perhaps even that he knew. Then a courtier, standing a few yards away, bent his head and coughed discreetly.

Justinus swivelled round to stare at him.

The man raised his hand, and there was a smirk of contempt on his mouth.

It was enough. Justinus was furious. He could not bear to be mocked. 'You look like her,' he said scathingly. 'No doubt you are a descendant. But don't come here with your charlatan ideas. And if you value your safety, don't try to tell anyone you have the golden Book of Ta-Thea!'

'It's not the Book of Ta-Thea!' she snapped, her eyes blazing. 'It is the Book of the law of God! I was simply the one who brought it here!'

'You?' Justinus shouted, leaning forward, his face red. 'You are forty-five, at the most! She would be five hundred and forty-five! More! The only reason I don't have you thrown out is that you claim to represent the Island at the Edge of the World, and that is a kingdom that all respect, and I would not insult their name!'

Ishrafeli stepped forward, his face grim. His body was rigid with the effort of controlling his anger. 'Whatever you believe of us, Majesty,' the word rang with no honour, 'consider the news from Shinabar, which your own ambassador will tell you is true. They are massing great armies, adding to them every day. Hardly any man escapes conscription, regardless of his age or his skills. Taxes are increasing by the week.'

Justinus was impassive. He levied high taxes himself. His eyebrows rose very slightly in a swift flicker of temper.

Ishrafeli ignored it. 'What civilian population is left is riddled with terror and betrayal,' he continued. 'They walk in fear of each other. All news is controlled by the government. They are told only what the Isarch's advisers wish them to know.'

'That is unavoidable in war,' Justinus said with exaggerated patience.

Ishrafeli was not yet finished. He held his head a little higher. 'Tiyo-Mah arrived from the desert, so she said, with a dozen or so advisers. She was no one, a widow without a name or a fortune.' His eyes flickered for a second, no more, at the grandeur of the palace hall. 'Now a few months later she tells the Isarch what to do and, regardless of how it ruins his people or wounds his country, he does it. They are at war with one another, every man suspects his neighbour. Fear and betrayal are on every street. Is that what you want for Camassia as well?'

Justinus was pale. Unwittingly he glanced again at the courtier who had smirked, and then at another, who looked back at him with an open, contemptuous smile.

'The Emperor is not afraid,' the second man said to Ishrafeli, a sneer on his lips. 'Shinabar may be too weak to stand up to this old woman from the desert, but we are made of different stuff.' He gave a little snigger. 'She can come here and try if she wants, but she'll gain nothing . . . except perhaps an education in the practical sense of Camassians. The Shinabari are a bunch of superstitious weaklings who outgrew their time centuries ago. They are dying, and their culture with them.'

'I couldn't have said it better myself,' Justinus agreed, the tension easing out of him. 'I shall grant you the courtesy of believing your warning was well meant, but quite unnecessary.' He breathed out slowly, glancing at Tathea. 'And I shall consider your fanciful claims of identity as an embellishment intended to add colour to your words. I am not familiar with Island manners.' He dismissed their entire culture with a sentence. 'Perhaps that is the way you do things there? Thank you for coming. You are welcome to stay in the City as long as you wish. Good day.'

152

There was nothing they could do but accept the rebuff and leave, walking side by side, seething with anger and helpless to say or do anything further to undo the sheer, blind stupidity of it. They had spoken only the truth, and hardly a word had been believed.

Perhaps they should not have been surprised, but even the wildest hope dies hard and leaves an emptiness behind.

Chapter Ten

'What are we going to do?' Tathea said desperately when she and Ishrafeli were alone in their lodgings an hour later. 'We've made it worse, not better. I played right into Tiyo-Mah's hands, didn't I? Why am I such a fool? This is the war to test us all. Everything there is will be won or lost for ever in this. Asmodeus is going to use all the weapons he has. There's nothing else to keep them for!' She hesitated a moment. 'I wonder where the other Lords of Sin are. Are they in other parts of the world: Caeva, Tirilis, Pera? Or Irria-Kand – leading the barbarians? Or did they corrupt the Irria-Kanders so they fled before the barbarians, instead of standing their ground and fighting?'

Ishrafeli's face was pale. The enormity of the thought hung in the room like a suffocating weight. 'I don't know,' he admitted. 'But we must learn, if we can. Perhaps there is something that holds them back, some spiritual weapon we are using even though we are unaware of it. All sin operates by our leave.'

Her gaze stayed fixed on his. It was an enormous thought, beautiful in its hope, and terrible in its acknowledgement that they held such power of failure. She found she was shivering, even in the slanting sunlight in the room.

'We are fighting in so many different ways,' she said quietly. 'But if there is a way we can hold them back, blunt any of their weapons, then we must do it. Ulciber has been the easiest to allow in. We have always been open to corruption. Perhaps delusion is the next. They are not so far apart. Anyone who has passions and dreams is in danger.'

A flash of bitter humour crossed Ishrafeli's face. 'They are the best.' He drew in a deep breath. 'I suppose the highest to climb, and the furthest to fall. We must watch for Azrub. And the others?'

'I think the earth is not ready yet for terror or despair,' she said softly. 'Please God, I hope not.'

He walked over to her and put his arms around her, holding her close to him, his cheek against her hair till she could feel the warmth of him, smell the familiarity of his skin.

It was a long time before she spoke the thoughts inside her.

'When Tiyo-Mah comes,' she began, 'we must be there and say or do something that will provoke her into showing who she really is.' The certainty grew inside her as she spoke. 'If she does, then Justinus will see, and even his courtiers won't be able to mock him into denying it.' She took a deep breath. She still stood close to him, her brow against his cheek. 'And if he sees that Tiyo-Mah is who we say,' she went on, 'then he will have to consider that I am also who I say. In fact, he may be only too eager to believe it! If one sees a force for evil, surely one doesn't rest until one finds the force for good, out of sheer terror, if nothing else?'

'Provoke Tiyo-Mah?' He pushed her a little away from him so he could look at her. 'Have we power to withstand her?'

Tathea bit her lip hard. 'God help us if we don't!' She was shivering very slightly. She was not sure she did have the power. 'But if we don't, we've given up. Then what have we left? This isn't a war we can choose not to fight . . . nobody can, but we least of all.'

'I'm beginning to understand that,' he replied, smiling at her, but his eyes were bleak.

He was a long way from understanding it yet. She knew that, but perhaps it was as well he did not. One step at a time is all anyone can bear.

She kissed him very gently, and it grew longer and deeper as he responded, because there was nothing to say except, over and over again, 'I love you.'

Five days later the City was clamouring with the news that Tiyo-Mah had arrived and was to be received immediately by the Emperor. Tathea and Ishrafeli were back in the audience chamber again to watch. It was one privilege they had yielded to bribery to buy. Were they not to be there they would have no chance to confront her.

They waited almost shoulder to shoulder with nearly a hundred other aristocrats, Archons and courtiers. There was a hush and everyone turned as the doors at the far end opened and Justinus appeared, robed in purple and gold with a coronet on his head. He walked very slowly to one of the two padded and gilded seats that stood near the centre of the room. He made an effort never once to look at the double doors at the opposite end, and Tathea realised with a start that he was nervous. Gone was the calm arrogance with which he had received her and Ishrafeli, merely ambassadors from the Island. He stood a trifle stiffly, and three times he moved his robes so they fell a little more elegantly. And still he restrained himself from glancing to see if the other doors were opening.

'Part of him believes us,' Ishrafeli whispered to Tathea.

'I wish it were a larger part!' she returned.

Any further speculation was prevented by the doors at last swinging wide to reveal nothing at all. There was a gasp from the throng, a slow letting out of breath, and then another gasp as a very old woman, shoulders bent, head almost bald, shuffled across the entrance and walked very slowly down the length of the marble floor towards Justinus. She was clad in the ancient Shinabari turquoise and copper against parchment white, heavily embroidered and encrusted with gold. An enormous star sapphire hung on a chain between her shrunken breasts. Never once did she look to either side of her. For her the crowd lining the way did not exist.

Tathea felt a tingle of both horror and pride. She had once been Isarch of Shinabar herself, and she would have entered a foreign court like this. No upstart Camassian Emperor would outshine her or seem to anyone watching to dominate the room.

She glanced sideways at Ishrafeli and saw the amazement in his face. She had tried to describe Tiyo-Mah to him, but no words could have encompassed the reality.

No one in the crowd moved at all, not a step nor a whisper. There was no pushing or jostling for position. Tathea looked at the doorway again. Tiyo-Mah would never have come alone. What size of retinue would she choose to bring, and of what nature?

It was apparent within seconds. A dozen Shinabari nobles walked in, two by two, all in ceremonial court dress dating from the time of the old Shinabar Empire, in the style of Tiyo-Mah's own days as Empress, before her husband had died and her son taken his place, and Ta-Thea taken hers, sins for which she had never forgiven any of them.

After the nobles came a single figure, tall and graceful, with blue eyes, fair hair and a face of calm and smooth-featured beauty. He was dressed in military uniform, also Shinabari, blue and white with copper breastplate and greaves and a long copper ceremonial sword at his side.

Tathea felt a chill run through her as though in a breath the heat of the hall had turned cold. Ardesir had described Ulciber, but no words from anyone else could match the reality of seeing him again. Without being aware of doing it, she was gripping Ishrafeli's arm so hard he winced at the pressure.

Tiyo-Mah was level with Justinus now, barely half a dozen yards from Tathea and Ishrafeli. She stopped, and all those behind her stopped also, preserving the distances between them, except Ulciber, who continued to come forward on silent feet, and the Shinabari nobles parted for him as if they had expected as much.

'Welcome to the City in the Centre of the World,' Justinus said stiffly. 'We receive your embassy with interest.'

157

'You are most gracious,' Tiyo-Mah replied. She did not use any courtesy title. She called no one 'Majesty'. 'We have much to say to a great nation like Camassia,' she continued. 'Together we hold the civilised world in our hands. We have privileges and duties in common.'

It was an odd way in which to address an emperor, and Justinus was not subtle enough to conceal his surprise. He stared at the old woman in front of him, in her stooped age, more than a head shorter than he. Her body was bowed, her hands clawlike, but her strength of will dominated the entire hall as if she were the monarch and he the supplicant. For a moment he did not know how to reply, which must have been obvious to those closest to him.

Tathea stepped forward, not more than a pace, but sufficient to draw every eye to her.

'The privileges and duties to which you refer belong to the Island also,' she said distinctly. 'We have fought the barbarians not only from our shores, but from within our cities too . . . without resorting to secrecy and oppression of our own people.'

Tiyo-Mah turned very slowly and stared at Tathea. Her skin was mottled dark with blood and her opaque eyes shone with a hatred as old as the first damnation. Her hand clenched on the stick she used to steady herself.

Justinus stared at Tathea in horror.

Tiyo-Mah lifted the stick as if she would strike her with it.

Tathea held her breath.

Then Tiyo-Mah smiled, drawing her lips back from shrunken gums. It was a hideous gesture. The stick sank back and rested on the marble again.

'Of course,' she agreed, her voice a whisper like the wind through dry reeds. 'Had I realised you were here in Camassia, I should have included you in my words. Even in Thoth-Moara we are aware of the nobility of the Island at the Edge of the World, and the peace that has reigned there in the last ten years. The sea is your friend. Would that we had such a defence against the barbarian, but alas we have not. We must provide our own bulwarks, with the sacrifice of our people, and their courage and loyalty to the cause.'

She turned again to Justinus. 'That is the reason we have come to speak with our cousins in Camassia, whose problem is the same as our own, that we may aid each other, and learn from each other's experience.'

Tathea had been effectively acknowledged, and dismissed. Her eyes were drawn beyond Tiyo-Mah to Ulciber, standing behind her, straight-backed, and a little taller than the nobles around him. He was looking at her. To anyone else he must have seemed full of

158

grace and charm, smiling at strangers with the confidence of one whose heart is clear.

But Tathea saw the jubilation in his eyes and the shadow of a sneer over his lips as if a darkness inside him had been momentarily visible. He tasted victory, smelled it in the air around him as he heard Tiyo-Mah's voice, and knew that Justinus would listen to her, and Tathea had no power to prevent it. It was as certain as tomorrow.

Then he looked past her and saw Ishrafeli. He was puzzled. He did not know who he was or why he was there so obviously beside her. Did he matter, or was he incidental, a courtier of sorts, an attendant? He stared steadily, and Ishrafeli stared back, eyes unflickering.

Then Ulciber stiffened and a shudder passed through his body as his soul recognised his final enemy, and he was dizzy with the knowledge. The physical world became as nothing. Spirits faced each other across an abyss, aware that one day they would do so again, without the distraction or the protection of other people, a set ceremony, and a war yet to unroll and play itself out.

Then the present closed in again with the noise and the words and the business of the moment.

Tiyo-Mah was speaking to Justinus, telling him about the atrocities in the southern desert, and how the barbarians were pressing steadily northwards. Her words were not extreme but she spoke with an intensity that gripped him whether he would or not. His face was pale and for once he seemed unaware of his courtiers and advisers around him.

'News comes to us that you also are experiencing greater activity on your borders,' Tiyo-Mah continued, her voice stronger now and the light glancing off her withered face. 'We would be most interested to hear your solutions to meeting it.'

Justinus hesitated. He had not been conspicuously successful, but he wanted to appear in control in front of this strange old woman from the ancient enemy.

'Our armies are well trained,' he replied cautiously. 'Extremely so. The barbarians are not. It makes the difference . . . in the end.'

'Precisely my thoughts,' Tiyo-Mah agreed, nodding very slightly. 'It all comes to superior discipline. That has been the Shinabari experience also.' Then she went on to relate several stories she had heard of Camassian military success in the past.

Justinus listened with evident pleasure. Even though none of them was directly attributable to him, he took the praise as if they were.

Ulciber listened and every now and then added a comment and suggestion as to how the tactics might be improved, made more stringent, civil interference excluded altogether and eventually a

159

total power obtained. All the time he drew examples of how necessary this was, and how Justinus would become the saviour of his people, a preserver of the present and also of all the wealth and heritage of the past. Every move he outlined, he also justified.

Tathea could hear it all, and understood its sweet-tasting corruption, its appeal to vanity and fear, and she could not interrupt. Justinus seemed not to hear the lies with the truth, and his pretence at consideration, reluctance, the need to be persuaded, was no more than a diplomatic game to make the decision seem his own.

Tathea and Ishrafeli left, knowing that the treaty of alliance would take its appointed time, but it was already concluded in everything but signature. Tiyo-Mah had won, and they had not raised a weapon to prevent her.

They walked home through the dusty streets in silence.

'How can we fight her?' Tathea demanded almost as soon as the door was closed and they were alone. 'I used to imagine Armageddon was vast armies drawn up against each other, covering the earth with blood and tears, and I suppose it will be, in the end.'

'That kind of war doesn't destroy the soul,' Ishrafeli replied, walking over to the cool stone jug and pouring water for both of them. 'Death is no victory for Asmodeus. He wants misery, despair, the corruption of the heart until we hate as he does, until we lash out and destroy each other, and thus ourselves.' He passed her one of the goblets. 'Would it be wrong to kill her, if we could?'

'Assassination? I don't think so. This is war, and her time when she had a right to mortal life is long past. But she's not alive in an earthly sense.'

'I thought not,' he said grimly. 'I had to ask.'

He smiled at her, and she reached forward and touched his bare arm, feeling the warmth of him, the muscle under the skin. 'We must stay here and find allies. They are here somewhere. The art will be in recognising them!'

He gave a little grunt. 'I think the greater art will be in recruiting them!' he said drily.

Tiyo-Mah and her entourage waited in the City only long enough for the formalities to be completed, then claimed that the urgencies of war required that they return to Shinabar as rapidly as possible. Messengers would come and go regularly, but Ulciber would remain, at least for a matter of weeks, to offer any advice and encouragement he could in the practical plans for getting rid of the weaknesses within Camassia which would sabotage their efforts: the disloyalties, the personal greeds and ambitions, the talk of defeat, the false information that undermined resolve.

The corruption spread with terrifying speed. It began as a call to all citizens to give their time and means to the war effort. Taxes were raised again. More men were recruited to the army, as they had been in Shinabar. Gradually all criticisms of the Emperor or of the Hall of Archons was suppressed, and complaint of any sort was branded as selfish and unpatriotic.

All news was censored. In ignorance of the truth, fear increased. Rumour spread like fire in summer grass. Any bulletin or letter of news was illegal unless it had the Ministry of Information seal on it. Anybody found passing or receiving unauthorised news documents was deemed to be an enemy of the people and liable to fine, confiscation of goods and properties and, in extreme cases, forced conscription into the army.

Violence erupted in the streets, unreasoning prejudice as fear was whipped up and unthinkingly people turned on anyone who seemed different, who spoke for moderation, or made light of the barbarian threat. It was easier to have an enemy to lash out at. It made them feel as if they had achieved something, taken some action in their own defence. Fear was released and the tension abated until next time.

Two or three moderate leaders were voted out of office, and replaced by men of more extreme views. One by one dissenting voices fell silent. One man whose courage and passion outweighed his caution had his house burned by a mob who had just heard new stories of barbarian incursions, fifty miles closer than before. Their fear turned to rage, and he was an easy victim.

Tathea and Ishrafeli stood quietly by their open window on to the cypress walk, close enough to touch each other, but without speaking. There was no need to give words to the understanding of what Tiyo-Mah had achieved. Whether the Great Enemy had had anything to do with the rise of the barbarians around the margins of the world or not, Tiyo-Mah and all her servants knew with a skill soul-deep how to find the weaknesses in every man and woman and turn them into the ugliest possibility. One of the most potent of all, and the easiest to manipulate and to spread, was fear. It overrode reason, tolerance and compassion. It ploughed judgement under and tore it apart.

Surely this was the first wave of Armageddon – not open battles with soldiers wielding swords against an army they could see, but the secret worm in the heart, eating courage, pity and faith, carrying corruption like a disease on the wind?

'How can you fight it?' Tathea asked desperately. 'There are only two of us here, and people are falling by thousands. Except it isn't really falling, it's stumbling, slithering, losing balance.' She pressed her hands up against her face, her head throbbing. 'He's so clever! So very clever!'

'Of course,' Ishrafeli agreed. 'I suppose it's comfortable to think of evil as stupid, but it's only stupid in the spiritual sense. It can never win because it destroys the very thing it fights for. There is nothing left for the victor.'

'Then we must be cleverer!' Tathea said fiercely. 'Where do we find the good?'

'In people,' he answered, putting his arm around her shoulders. 'We must find the people.'

In Erebus, Asmodeus looked over the ramparts of darkness at the churning chaos that bound him in, the nothingness of worlds that disintegrated into the void and ceased to be. Tiny like a blue jewel beyond his grasp, he saw one earth and all the life that was on it. And he smiled, his lips parted, the taste of victory on his tongue.

Tiyo-Mah had exceeded his best hopes. He would let her be, for the moment. Camassia was more ripe for the plucking than he had supposed, and her strategy had been superb. For an instant he had feared Tathea would foil her, but he should not have doubted. Tiyo-Mah knew the stakes she was playing for. She would not allow Tathea to forewarn or forearm a perfect tool like Justinus.

Flattery, ridicule, fear: they were the supreme weapons, broad enough to ruin a population, and sharp enough to wound the most subtle and complicated soul.

It was working magnificently. All through Camassia people were denying old principles of tolerance and freedom they had held for generations. The violence had begun already, and it would progress. In a few months it would be so common it would no longer occasion surprise. Retaliation perhaps? But that was good. The lust for revenge was perfect!

And there was anger, which, like fear, was the enemy of judgement.

Everywhere truth was being suppressed or denied in the name of the common good. And better still, it was being done in the name of patriotism. Convince a man that his act is for 'us' against 'them', and you can make him do anything at all. Soon there would be enough lies seeping into the heart like a black ooze that Azrub would be able to function; that was the next step. And then after him each of the other Lords of Sin could come into the world, as it was ripe for them.

When the war escalated and the soldiers panicked enough, forgot their training, forgot what cause they were fighting for and remembered only that they must kill or be killed, then Cassiodorus could enter the fray, and spread the blind, scarlet terror everywhere, until madness reigned.

But it was a long way from dark enough yet for Yaltabaoth. Men were still fighting, still believing in victory. There might be lies,

162

hatred, fear, corruption, greed, but no vast stretches of the paralysing darkness of despair, the end of all light and life, the death from which there was no return.

But Asmodeus did not want even to think of that. Keep Yaltabaoth out – for ever, if possible. Win without him.

A tiny flicker of panic inside him stilled and disappeared. This was not the way he had intended Armageddon to come about, but it would work well enough. There was no question of forgiving Tiyo-Mah or those who had followed her. No one should ever be forgiven for anything. But they had done well . . . in all respects. He was pleased. That beautiful blue orb in the sky was almost within his grasp, and getting closer every day. All he needed to do was watch Ulciber and Tiyo-Mah, and prepare for the next move.

Tathea and Ishrafeli worked to influence people, to weigh and judge who might be willing to risk their lives in the growing danger and oppression in the City. News came from Ythiel in the Island that all was well. The Islanders were preparing the defences both physical and spiritual. They were keeping trade routes open to the Sea Isles and other maritime cities, and war ships were at the ready, should they be needed. Rumours had come out of Tirilis, that most secretive country which guarded the world's treasuries, which lent and borrowed, and grew rich on other nations' trade. Loans had been withdrawn from some, and offered to others who were new and unknown, especially one named Accolon, whose face was so hideously disfigured he wore a mask out of consideration for the susceptibilities of others. The trade in money itself was gaining pace. Fortunes were being made and lost, without labour. It was no longer the lending of capital so business might flourish, it was becoming the art of gambling, so one man's greater foresight, or luck, could ruin another.

'One of the Lords of the Undead,' Ishrafeli said grimly. 'Ulciber's disciple, by the sound of him.'

'We can't go,' Tathea replied with a frown of anxiety. 'The corruption is even greater here, but we are beginning to find people who will fight.' She breathed out slowly, staring at the light on the trees. 'Why can't we find our sixth warrior? What are we failing to do? Are we looking in the wrong places? Or is he here, and we just don't recognise him?'

'I don't know,' he admitted. 'We must fast and pray more deeply. Have you prayed for that?'

'No,' she confessed, touched with shame for her omission.

'Nor I,' he said wryly. 'But in the meantime we should send someone to Tirilis. There is no word of Sardriel.' His face was light, his eyes downcast. 'I shall write to Ardesir. We have enough news from Shinabar, and there is little enough he can do there against Tiyo-Mah now.'

'Good. The caravan masters will carry letters. They can find people, even in Thoth-Moara. Send two copies, one to Tarra-Ghum also.'

'I will. But it is time we took more risks here too. We have been careful long enough. We must strike back. Tomorrow I am going to speak to Merkator.'

Tathea had known it would come, and yet it still knotted inside her now that the moment was here. Merkator was the Archon she had seen and respected before. Now he had formed a small group in the heart of the City who did what they could to help those in trouble who came to them. Because of his family and his history in the Hall of Archons, he was trusted as no newcomer could be, and he had resources of wealth and wide respect to draw on.

'Yes, I suppose it's time,' she agreed aloud. 'But I . . .' She stopped. A glance from him warned her and she smiled instead, feeling the blush warm on her cheek. 'I know!'

He said nothing, but all the arguments and their answers were in his face.

The place where Merkator had set up his quarters was a large tenement in the heart of the City, a massive stone building, now long fallen into disuse which had once formed housing for athletes who had entertained the crowds in the days of the Emperor Tiberian. The huge granite blocks were chipped, the plaster inside cracked across, but the concept still held echoes of the old magnificence. The baths underneath were fed from the City's cisterns. Fires no longer heated them, but the steam had left patches on the frescos, and the marble pillars were marked with ancient lichens from long-forgotten pools.

Now Merkator met people who were frightened, dispossessed, ill or desperate, and offered what help he could. He greeted Ishrafeli with a patient attempt to cover his own weariness.

'What has happened to you?' he asked with puzzlement. He regarded the figure in front of him, so unlike his usual petitioner.

Ishrafeli smiled, not comfortably or easily, but with wry knowledge of what he was going to ask. He had observed Merkator for weeks, and believed he understood him.

'What has happened to me? I have realised something at least of the magnitude of the war we are fighting,' he replied. 'I am looking for allies.' He saw the flash of humour in Merkator's eyes, and also the fear. He relaxed the way he stood, leaning a little against one of the pillars, and dropping his voice so low it was barely audible. 'One old woman from Shinabar has changed the way a whole city thinks, and in a while it will be the nation. She has created for us an enemy that terrifies the sense out of people, and when they become hysterical enough, offered them a way of escape. We shouldn't be surprised that they accept it.'

Merkator stared up at him. 'Oppression, censorship, corruption of the law! We have become our own enemy! What's the matter with us?' He too spoke softly, but the walls gave back the whispering sound.

'We have looked to ourselves for so long that we have no moral core except what we have created of our own,' Ishrafeli replied. 'We were given the word of God, but we took out the bits we didn't like. We wanted an easier message, and in removing the labour and the price, we also removed the reward. That left us with something meaningless, and gradually we ceased to believe in it. And that is hardly surprising, since it is an echo of our own voices, and not the truth.'

He shifted his position slightly. Above him rainwater dripped on marble.

'Our heads may believe it,' he went on. 'Because it says what we think we would like, but our hearts know it is lies. It serves well enough in times of prosperity, and even in times of some national hardship, but when the real enemy is at the door, it's shown for the sham it is, and we are left naked.'

Merkator looked at him very steadily, his brow puckered. 'You believe that, don't you!' It was a statement. 'But nobody has read the Book of God in over five hundred years – or longer.'

'Not here,' Ishrafeli agreed. 'But in the Island at the Edge of the World we have.' He saw Merkator's start of surprise and the struggle in his eyes as he wanted to believe. He bit back the words. He must not say too much yet. 'All I want so far is to help you here, and my wife is wise in the law. She will help the persecuted fight their cases and perhaps obtain some justice. It would be a beginning which would grow, others would see, and gain hope. In time more centres would arise.'

Merkator's face reflected too many defeats. There was a tiredness in him that marked the lines deep and hollowed out the flesh around his eyes. 'Have you seen Balour? He has replaced the Emperor in everything that matters. Sometimes I think even Justinus is afraid of him.'

'Yes, I've seen him,' Ishrafeli replied, recalling with a shudder the bony, misshapen body, the narrow shoulders and rodent face of the creature who had come as Tiyo-Mah's lieutenant and seemed now to govern in the Emperor's place. Even if his physical malformation, the pustulant skin, narrow eyes and twitching clawlike hands had not identified him as one of the Lords of the Undead, his almost

165

omnipotent knowledge and his endless cruelty would have done.

Merkator could not keep the fear from his eyes. 'It is a dangerous thing to do,' he warned. 'I would not have my wife do it. She will be risking her life.' There was warning in his voice but no blame, and Ishrafeli realised Merkator thought he was speaking to innocence, not knowledge greater than his own.

'I know,' Ishrafeli answered. 'Would you step back from the battle?'

Merkator hesitated only a moment. 'No . . . but—'

'Would you deny it to anyone you believed as equal?'

'No. I couldn't. But someone I loved . . .' A sudden gentleness ironed some of the weariness from his face. 'My wife . . .'

'You would protect her from being the best she can?' Ishrafeli pressed. 'For whom? Her – or yourself?'

'Myself,' Merkator admitted. 'You are a hard man!' he added ruefully.

'It is the final war – the last chance to be who you want to.'

Merkator stood up and his robes fell straight, showing the marks of the mould he had touched. 'Then you'd better bring your wife to fight our battles in the courts. God knows, there are new ones set up every week to handle the number of cases. People are being charged with one form of treason or another every day. What is her name?'

'Tathea.'

Merkator's eyes widened. 'Shinabari?' He said the word with wariness, close to dislike.

'It's a Shinabari name, but we come from the Island at the Edge of the World,' Ishrafeli replied. 'She knows Camassian law, and is prepared to defend anyone who needs and wishes it.'

Merkator breathed out. 'I'm sorry. Of course. I am glad of all help, especially if it is skilled.'

Ishrafeli soon met Merkator's wife, Belida, and understood why he would have shielded her were he able. She was intelligent, imaginative, quick to sense danger, more for him than for herself. Could she have remained apart from the struggle she would never have understood what perils they all faced. As Ishrafeli watched her slender form moving from one sick or injured person to another, strong, thin hands always cleaning, binding, stitching a wound, measuring a dose, crushing leaves or powders, he too would have protected her had it been possible. At least he would have sheltered her from the knowledge of what Merkator was doing forming a resistance to Balour, and how already his name was known.

Tathea began her task immediately. As soon as someone was arrested for any form of treason and she heard word of it, she presented herself at the courts and offered her skills to plead for them. She rose early in the morning and sat up late at night, papers spread all over the table in the candlelight, studying the laws Balour had passed and the Hall of Archons had ratified.

She pleaded, argued, ridiculed and quoted laws old and new. She reminded judges and onlookers of their history as a great Empire, a people who created just laws and lived by them, to the envy, and the mastery, of the world. She obtained release for many, mitigation of sentence for even more. But immeasurably more important than that, she created hope that the oppression could be fought against and beaten. She reminded people of who they were, of the self-respect they would forfeit if they yielded to the panic around them and joined a denial of the heritage that had formed the best in them.

Ishrafeli knew the danger to herself that she provoked, and many nights he lay awake beside her, fear fluttering and twisting inside him, not for her death, because he believed Asmodeus had no power to kill her, but for the pain she would endure, perhaps the imprisonment, the torture of her mind. But his own words to Merkator haunted him, and he knew he could not prevent her, nor should he try. Sometimes it is harder to suffer for others than for oneself.

He chose a different battlefield. To fight the courts of the law was of the utmost importance. The suffering the law caused was acute, and the eternal change to the soul of those who enforced it was greater. If the time came when the ordinary people ceased to believe in the law to the degree that they no longer paid even lip service to it, then anarchy would take its place and the City would revert to the chaos of the Pit. And surely that was what Balour was here to do?

But another product of the fear that hung over the City like smoke over a forest fire was intolerance of the weaker, the slower, those who were different from the ordinary – uglier or in some way maimed or incomplete. They were seen as hampering the war effort, a drain on the food and housing resources of the nation and contributing nothing but a lessening of the strength for the battle which every day's news bulletin brought closer.

Ishrafeli chose to work with those people. He walked the dark alleys and the crumbling tenements where they had taken refuge. He moved slowly, carefully, and it was nearly a month before he won his first sure recruit.

He was in a small square, high blind houses surrounding it, the guttering broken and the walls stained with the overflow. The well was rusted and piles of refuse stood uncollected, sagging against the stone posts which had originally supported a seat, long since rotted and fallen away.

A blind woman with brown hair shuffled towards the well, carry-ing a leather bucket. Ishrafeli went to help her as she fumbled for the handle, but she knew he was a stranger. He smelled of clean linen and soap. He carried no familiarity of the seeping damp and the refuse around the narrow streets, and it frightened her. She lashed out and lost her balance, stumbling backwards and landing awk-wardly. The bucket smashed and she screamed with fear and pain.

Suddenly other people were there, coming out of shadows, doorways, from beneath arches half crumbled. A thin man with a crooked shoulder and lame leg scrambled across the cobbles to the woman and tried to lift her, but she was too heavy for his one good arm.

Ishrafeli backed away, knowing he was frightening them.

A man with a fearful stutter tried to say something and his anxiety only made him worse. Two bare-footed children looked on with wide eyes. One of them stifled a cry which turned into a giggle, then hid her face, embarrassed.

'I'm sorry,' Ishrafeli apologised, first to the woman, then to the man with the crooked shoulder, still trying ineffectively to lift her. 'I meant you no harm.'

'Fool!' the woman spat at him.

'No call for that,' the man said to her, but his tone was chiding rather than angry. 'Can't help being clumsy. No one can. Got to take folk as you find them. Lean on me a bit – no, this side!' He looked up at Ishrafeli. 'You take her that side, if you don't mind.'

With a wave of relief, Ishrafeli leaned forward and put his hand under her elbow and she allowed him to raise her to her feet.

The man with the crooked shoulder was called Severinus. His whole left side appeared to have been misshapen from birth.

'I'll mend the bucket,' Ishrafeli offered.

The blind woman grunted. It was neither acceptance nor refusal.

Severinus nodded. 'That's fair, seeing it was you who caused it to be broken.' He regarded Ishrafeli dubiously, particularly his hands, clean and uncallused. 'Can you do it?' he asked doubtfully.

Ishrafeli took it as an offer of help. 'Thank you.'

It took him nearly three hours of cutting, plugging and gluing. He was not good at it, and his attempts occasioned much amuse-ment, but finally the job was functional, if far from aesthetically pleasing. Severinus refused to praise it, but his smile was wide, broken-toothed, and full of good humour. There was respect for kindness in it, if not for skill. The blind woman took it back, feeling all around it with her hands to make sure it was satisfactory.

'No water in it!' she challenged him at the end of her inspection, but then she too smiled, her sightless eyes turned towards the sound of his voice.

Everyone laughed, and watched while Ishrafeli picked it up and took it back to the well. They applauded when he returned with it, full to the top and gently slopping over.

Ishrafeli discovered in Severinus a compassion more whole than in many a man whose body served him far better. The blind woman, Callia, was quick-tempered and apt to be flustered when out of familiar surroundings, but she knew a wealth of stories and would entertain children by the hour, never tiring of repeating a tale, especially the parts that made people laugh or cry, or squeal with delight.

The circle grew wider, the outcast and the incomplete bonding together to help first each other, then those whose minds or bodies might appear to be immeasurably superior, but in whom fear drove out compassion, confusion clouded honesty, and old loves and loyalties eroded the courage to stand alone or work against the tide.

As Tathea succeeded in defying the arbitrary arrests, the laws were changed, tightened, and more courts were instituted. Balour called the Hall of Archons and proposed a new measure.

'The barbarians grow closer to us every week!' he said fiercely. 'They are over a hundred miles into our borders already, and another village or town falls every month, or less! At this speed, in a year they will be here in the City!' He flung one scrawny arm out. 'This is not some foreign war – it is against us – against you and me!' He was sitting on the First Archon's seat and staring over the smooth marble-topped bench in front of him. 'More than that! It is against all humanity. It is not meet or just that the army should fight it alone, or the law-keepers. This is our war!' He peered around at the rows of silent men in their white and purple robes, their faces expressionless as they waited in the safety of retreat until they should know what reaction he wanted from them. Only Merkator met his flat, yellow-brown eyes.

Balour bit his lip with small, sharp teeth. His hands scribbled on the marble top, never still, and his body fidgeted beneath his robes as one spirit fought another, gnawing his belly, cramping his heart.

'We are the ones who will suffer if there is defeat!' he went on, his voice thick in his throat. 'We are the ones who will taste victory in the end, if we win, if we destroy the enemy, drive him into the ice-bound wastes of the north where nothing lives! Into the sea at the margin of the world! As the Shinabari will drive him into the burning hell of the south!'

There was a murmur of assent all around the chamber. Heads nodded. One or two Archons shifted nervously in their seats.

Balour leaned forward. Now he was looking directly at Merkator, his lips drawn back, his sharp nose twitching. 'Therefore we must all

169

fight against the evil within our land! From this day forward all men, all women, even children, will protect the law by reporting any treason among us. Whatever is spoken against the common good of the people will be told, assessed, judged and punished. Every man's word will be listened to and weighed.' He swung his arm in a tight, cramped gesture. 'We are all responsible, all answerable – and in the end we shall all be partakers in the final victory!'

Merkator started forward, rising to his feet.

There was utter silence in the room; every other Archon was frozen in his seat.

'You will turn every citizen into an informer on his neighbours,' Merkator said, his voice trembling, half choked in his throat. His body was shaking, and he knew it was fear, but his fear of standing by silently while such a thing was said overcame all else.

Balour bowed his head and stared at him, his pointed teeth chewing his knife-thin lip. 'Do you question the right of everyone to fight this war for survival, Archon Merkator?' he whispered, his voice hissing softly.

'I question the wisdom of inviting every man to police his neighbour, friend and foe alike,' Merkator answered him. 'You invite an accusation without the need to prove its truth. Without the safeguard of law, fear will drive some, misunderstanding others, and old rivalries will tempt men to accuse where there is no evidence and perhaps no guilt.'

Balour's face twisted in a cold smile. 'You think ill of your fellow countrymen, Archon Merkator!' he charged.

Merkator also smiled. 'I think some are traitors, Lord Balour,' he replied. 'And what would be easier for a traitor than to accuse a patriot of treason . . . and so destroy him in the eyes of others, and perhaps of the law.'

The dark colour, black purple, swept up Balour's face. One or two Archons straightened a little in their seats. Perhaps a whisper of courage had stirred.

The silence was breathless.

A pustule burst on Balour's sunken cheek, and oozed down his skin. 'We will trust to the judgement of the people!' he spat. He glanced around the chamber. 'Does any man not accept that?'

Merkator swallowed, his throat and lips dry. Now the victory of an instant had passed into the void of defeat.

'I don't!' The words were irrevocable. He knew it as he spoke. He thought of Belida, then of Ishrafeli and Tathea.

Balour glanced around the room. 'Does anyone else stand with Merkator against the people?'

A score of men fidgeted in their seats. Not one looked at Merkator, each having a reason, an answer – next time perhaps, but not yet, not a useless sacrifice, not a family left alone and bereaved, perhaps a duty not yet served.

Balour slammed the mallet down on the marble, unintentionally chipping it. 'Then the law is passed – unanimously except for the Archon Merkator!'

Days went by. Merkator did not attempt to leave the City, even had he believed he could escape.

Balour watched and waited. Then on the tenth day he had Merkator arrested on the accusation of a neighbour that he had betrayed his fellow countrymen by spreading alarm and discouragement, thereby assisting the enemies of the nation. He was taken to one of the great central prisons, and the following morning came up for trial.

Tathea fought for him with all the skill she possessed, knowing before she began that it would be to no avail.

She called witness after witness, trying to establish that he had counselled courage, honesty, the healing of old feuds and loyalty to the principles of ancient Camassia.

But people were afraid for themselves, looking over their shoulders, fearing betrayal, the whisper of lies that would place them in the same dock, without help or defence.

'What did he say to you?' she demanded of one evasive woman.

'I can't remember,' the woman replied, eyes avoiding Tathea's.

'Why did you go to him?' Tathea persisted. 'You must remember that!'

'I'd heard he was giving advice,' the woman said sullenly.

'What sort of advice?'

'On troubles.'

'You had troubles you couldn't mend for yourself?'

'Doesn't everyone?'

'Probably. So you went to Merkator?'

'Yes.'

'But you don't remember what he said?'

'No. I told you.' She looked pleased with herself, relaxed at last.

'Do you still have these troubles?' Tathea smiled.

Seeing a trap, the woman shook her head. 'No!'

'Did Merkator suggest you despair, that you give in, or flee to somewhere else? It seems that what you actually did was to face your troubles and overcome them! Am I mistaken?'

The trap was sprung, not where she had expected.

'Yes – no. No, I did nothing more!'

But in spite of all the passion, the reason and the evidence she could bring, fear prevailed.

Merkator was sentenced to be stoned to death.

Tathea went to the place of execution because she could not leave him to face that last ordeal alone, even though there was nothing she could do that would help or alter anything. Ishrafeli came and stood silently beside her, and also Severinus, Callia, and a host of the sick, the crippled and the simple.

It was a desolate place outside the City boundaries. Stones lay around, many of them already dark with old blood and there was a smell of death in the air. The crowd huddled in a strange, stunned silence, no more than a dozen or so willing to take part in assisting the soldiers.

Merkator stood straight, unflinching in the fine, cold rain, his eyes wide.

Tathea stood next to Ishrafeli, and yet there was a terrible sense in which each person was alone here in this final place. She stared at an old man less than a dozen feet from her. He looked awed, as if the hideous and public execution of a man he revered took from him the last shred of understanding.

The command was shouted. The first soldier stooped and picked up a piece of rock. But before he threw it there was a movement in the crowd, and a woman pushed her way through towards the front, excusing herself as she went. She carried no stone, and she was dressed in her finest clothes. She walked with her head high, even though her feet slithered a little on the stones. It was Belida.

Tathea started forward, but Ishrafeli's hand restrained her. Her movement was instinctive, to protect, to save, but he knew it was wrong. Belida was where she chose to be.

The soldier hesitated.

Belida reached Merkator and stood beside him. He put his arm around her as she swayed, holding her closely.

There was a murmur from the crowd.

The soldier swung round, angry, then he turned back and with a cry of jubilation that sounded raucously inhuman, he hurled the stone with all his strength. It struck Merkator on the chest and he staggered back.

A woman shrieked.

Merkator regained his balance and faced them again. Tathea wanted to look away, not to see an agony she would never be able to wipe from her memory, but that would be a betrayal. Merkator was here because he had chosen to stand for his beliefs, and Belida because she loved him. Tathea must watch.

Another stone caught him on the face, crushing his cheek, then a third. He fell to his knees, trying in vain to shield Belida. More stones struck them, landing hard. Belida collapsed and lay motionless in a spreading pool of blood.

A man yelled in triumph, another in rage. Severinus wept

without shame or pretence and Callia murmured blindly, holding his arm.

A soldier stepped forward and raised a sword to finish it, and a rock caught him on the arm, drawing bright blood. The man who had thrown it turned and ran. A youth hurled stones after him.

The soldier killed Merkator in a swift act of mercy and glared at the crowd.

'You have something to say?' he challenged, his voice breaking with emotion.

No one answered.

Ishrafeli put his hand on Tathea's and together they walked out of the fallen rubble on to the steps of the street and began the long journey home.

In the days immediately following, posters appeared saying that Merkator was a martyr to the cause of truth. They were instantly torn down by Balour's police, but as fast as they were removed, others were put in their place.

Merkator's speeches were printed and became a kind of currency passed around. People remembered things he had said, and repeated them to one another. Women wound purple into their hair, the colour of Belida's dress, and were proud to do it.

Balour's men were jeered at. There were ugly scenes in the streets and they dared not arrest the large numbers that sided against them.

Public opinion was passionately divided, but Balour recruited a secret police, wearing no badge or uniform, and answerable only to him. Justinus approved it.

The country was on the brink of civil war.

Across the battlements of Erebus, Asmodeus was satisfied. Tiyo-Mah had succeeded more than he had foreseen. Perhaps he should not have doubted her judgement after all. Mankind balanced on the brink of the abyss. There were things which could have been better if left longer. The pollution of the earth came foremost to his mind. There was a vast amount yet to be accomplished in that! He had had plans to encourage man's pride and greed, and his cleverness at understanding the physical without seeing its results, to the point where the very balance of the air and the light could have been broken. The stuff of life itself could have been twisted out of shape until man dreamed himself capable of anything, and he would have created a hideousness that those alive now could not even have conceived in the darkness of their hearts. They would have deluded themselves they were masters of life and death, and denied God to His face.

173

But perhaps it didn't matter. Victory was the only real purpose. Why let it stop now just to taste it at greater length?

But he wanted Tathea. She had been a needle in his side for long enough, and that required not just death but a very special vengeance.

Not that her death was his to take. Man of Holiness held that power . . . and the thought of Him seared Asmodeus' heart and made him hate Tathea the more.

Maybe he could not kill her but he could certainly make her long for death! And he would!

The question was how to reach Tathea. She might be frightened, or discouraged, but success depended on the real weaknesses, not the trivial ones. The ones that bit soul-deep and hurt beyond any art to heal. Love. That was always the answer. Strike her where she loved!

Ishrafeli!

He was not certain how to do that yet. He would begin with the others. Isolate her. Loneliness is a sharp sword. It injured every time.

Ishrafeli was young in war. He felt other people's pain, and in his passionate arrogance he had promised Man of Holiness he would feel for the whole earth. He had not the faintest idea yet what that would mean. He had tasted merely the first drops of rain in a storm that would drown all mankind!

Yaltabaoth would defeat him! Let him once know the real darkness of despair, and nothing else would matter. He would lose . . . like all the rest.

Yes: Asmodeus would win Armageddon! Let it roll forth. After the earth, there was the rest of creation waiting!

Chapter Eleven

Ulciber looked at Tiyo-Mah in her splendid robes, sitting beside one of the numerous lily pools of the palace. These days the Isarch was barely even a figurehead. He remained in his private quarters, brooding, pacing back and forth, creating plans he never had the courage to put into action.

Tiyo-Mah stretched out her skeletal hand and took a ripe fig from the alabaster dish in front of her and put it in her mouth. Deliberately she allowed the juice to run down her chin, smiling at Ulciber.

'It is time,' he said softly, smiling back at her.

'Time for what?' she enquired, reaching for another fig.

'Time for you to pay your side of our bargain,' he answered.

'Bargain? I don't recall a bargain.' She bit into the fig.

'One day each year, your body is mine,' he said, watching her as she froze, her tongue in the midst of exploring the rich heart of the fruit.

She bit on it, sucked it and swallowed. 'And if I don't?'

Now it was he whose smile widened, showing his perfect teeth. 'Then I do not go back to Camassia and corrupt the law, make a mockery of justice and set the people at each other in violence and despair.'

'Balour can do that,' she retorted with a sharp bark of laughter.

Ulciber raised his eyebrows. 'You think Balour is a match for Tathea, when she has Ishrafeli by her side? Are you prepared to account for your failure to Asmodeus?' He watched with satisfaction as she paled. 'And if you think I cannot turn your own forces against you, then you have not dreamed the beginning of my power!' He leaned forward a little. 'Think of it, Tiyo-Mah! Why do they follow you? Love, loyalty, honour, patriotism?' His sneer dismissed them all. 'Are they incorruptible? Are they more afraid of you than of me?' He did not need to number the horrors he could create, using one man against another; she knew it only too well.

'One day!' she snarled. 'Only one! Don't exceed it. I'm an old woman, you'll burn it out, and then neither of us will possess my body.'

'I know. Now yield it!' He stepped forward, his eyes shining, lips parted.

Cautiously, reluctantly, she kept her word and as his body melted into hers, she disappeared, and only one figure was left standing, an old, old woman with wrinkled skin and nearly bald head, but lustrous eyes that stared in wonder at a sensuous world of colour and vibrancy: the sound of the water sliding over the ledge and falling into the pool below, the smell of it in the air, the heat on the skin, the dust, the texture of the lilies floating on the translucent surface. But most of all her crooked hand curled over another fig, fingers sliding over it, feeling it, savouring it, and she put it to her lips and bit.

Ulciber also kept his word, not out of honour but because it served his own cause. It fed the appetite of his spirit. Also, it was a good bargaining tool for next year, when again he would take Tiyo-Mah's body for a day. He must constantly remind her how much she needed him. It was a pleasure to watch the hatred seething behind her eyes anyway.

Balour was good. He had corrupted Camassia profoundly.

People joined factions to protect themselves. Extortion became normal practice. Citizens formed their own militias, against armed robbers or assault, but more as private armies. Certain men gained power, and others sought to take it from them.

Balour called on Ulciber, who knew of different and more efficient ways of refining the metal out of the rock, and instructed the industrial princes in them. Wealth abounded. What mattered it that the new ways polluted the land, poisoned the rivers with sulphur, leaving dead fish and beasts in its wake?

The law became more and more ridiculous as verdicts were brought in to convict those who endangered anyone's perception of his or her safety, and the guilty were excused in the name of the good of the country.

Witnesses were intimidated, men were bought and sold, sometimes with money, sometimes with promises of office, power, or that their own offences would be erased from the records.

Tathea came home late and exhausted, defeated yet again. She and Ishrafeli had heard little from Ardesir, and nothing from Sardriel. The darkness seemed to be closing in.

Ishrafeli stood behind Tathea, his arms around her, holding her close to him.

'Are you sure it's worth it?' he asked, aching for her, wishing he could give her of his own strength, the hope he gained from a hundred men like Severinus, deformed of body but burning with compassion which made them whole in spirit.

'Yes,' she said with a weary smile. 'As long as I keep trying, Balour knows he is not safe. He knows who I am, and he dare not relax. He has to watch me, just in case I win something he can't afford to lose.' She put her hands over his gently. 'And if people see me give up, who else can be expected to fight? They have to believe in something. A little hope is better than none at all.'

He stared past her to the faint gleam of the last light over the sea to the south, far beyond the rooftops of the City. It was spring again and the days were growing longer.

'And if I give up fighting, however often I lose, how can I tell anyone else to continue?' she asked. 'You can't preach what you won't do.'

'I know,' he replied, resting his cheek against her hair. 'I wish we were making more mark against Balour.'

'Balour isn't the real enemy, he's only a tool,' she said thoughtfully. 'He's being prompted by someone else, far cleverer than he is.'

'Who?' he asked. 'Asmodeus?'

'Not yet.'

'Ulciber?'

'I expect so.' She shivered a little. 'It has the sweet rot of corruption deeper than Balour knows. I can feel a subtler touch to it, far stronger.'

He held her tighter. 'We can still win. I have a thousand men and women in Severinus' chain right now, helping where they can – a word, an act, a secret gift. It's spreading. Sometimes it's no more than a hope where there was none before, but after a kindness is returned, a small change is made. When a merchant is robbed in the street, and it's a beggar who picks him up and takes him in, a blind man who brings him food, a cripple who winds his bandages, something new awakens in him. More than one has seen an instant of eternity, and that swords win only battles, wars are of the spirit.'

Tathea smiled.

'A thousand I know of,' he added. 'Ten thousand more beyond those that I couldn't name. Yesterday Callia sat all day telling stories to children whose parents have been executed. She can't see their faces and doesn't know who they are.' He held her a little tighter. 'Their parents wouldn't have given her bread in the street when they passed by, but all she knows is their confusion and their loss. Suddenly their world is upside down, and a grubby blind woman who smells of the streets is warmth to them in the cold, a voice to speak to them in the night, patience with crying, courage when they have to get up and face the day.'

Tathea turned round, clinging to him, burying her face in his shoulder. 'That's the victory that matters,' she said, too weary to weep but her tears thick in her voice. 'When the broken and the lost

177

can love the strangers who have not loved them, Asmodeus is losing.'

Ishrafeli did not answer. He knew how dangerous the warping of the law was, and that she must fight it. As long as there was at least a practice of justice, there was something for men to hope for, still a banner under which to fight, a common belief.

Ishrafeli was in the room where the old baths had been, where he had met Merkator, when Severinus came shambling in, his crooked side carried as awkwardly as always, his wasted arm held sideways. His face was ashen and tears furrowed his cheeks.

'Callia's dead!' he gasped before Ishrafeli could even rise to his feet from the table where he had been sitting with pen and paper. 'They set on her in the street! They raped her . . . and then they killed her.' He stopped, his body shaking with sobs.

Ishrafeli went to him and held him in his arms, feeling the horror shuddering through him and the anger, the fear and the grief he had no words to name.

His mind raced. Who had done it? Was it Balour, or mere chance? Or far more likely, was it Ulciber behind him, whispering, prompting? How far was the war already lost that men raped a blind woman in the street, and killed her? Ought he to fight for their souls, or were they already beyond recall?

All he could feel was Severinus' pain and his own.

'Where is she?' he said at last when Severinus stopped shaking and stood up alone, his face streaked and smeared, his eyes red.

'In the poorhouse for the dead,' Severinus answered.

'Then we shall bury her in the Field of Cypresses,' Ishrafeli said, 'tomorrow.'

'That costs money.' Severinus was sceptical. 'It's a place for the rich.'

'She'd like it,' Ishrafeli argued.

Severinus smiled, but his eyes brimmed with tears. 'She'd like it a lot,' he agreed with a violent sniff. 'She never saw a cypress, but she liked the smell of them in the sun. Do we know anyone with money?'

'Oh, I think so,' Ishrafeli answered. Already ideas were forming in his mind. 'Perhaps not tomorrow, but the day after. It will give us time to make arrangements, get the necessary money.'

Severinus' face shadowed. 'How are you going to do that? You may have to sell something. She wouldn't want that. She'd rather be buried in one of the mine shafts like those that are executed, than you give up your things for a place. So would I!'

'I'm not going to sell anything.' Suddenly Ishrafeli found his own throat aching. Callia's blind, dirty face was exquisitely sharp in his mind, and the softness in it when she recognised his step. 'Other people are going to pay for it. The Archon's wife who made a fool of herself in the square, and Callia helped her dress herself properly and leave. The prostitute she nursed when she was beaten by drunks. The merchant whose father she sat with when he died. There are dozens. It doesn't matter how much or how little, pennies will do. We'll get enough.'

Severinus was grinning now, showing all his broken teeth. 'She'd like that! I reckon she'd like that a lot!'

Ishrafeli was fearless in asking all those he knew Callia had helped in any way, telling them all he knew of what had happened to her, and where he intended to have her buried.

The Prefect of Police knocked on his door that evening, and the moment it was opened he strode in. He was a man of about fifty, burly and grey-haired. Now his face was creased with anxiety and he started to speak the moment he had acknowledged Tathea.

'You can't do this, sir!' he stated bluntly.

'Do what?' Ishrafeli asked with slightly exaggerated care.

The Prefect's face reddened a little. His shoulders were very stiff. His hands were clenching and unclenching by his sides, although they moved no closer to his sword. 'You can't go around telling everyone that that woman was raped and murdered!'

Ishrafeli's eyes widened but his voice was very steady. 'Wasn't she?'

The Prefect breathed out noisily. 'Probably, from what I hear . . .'

Ishrafeli stared at him. 'Are you saying that you are not enquiring into it? Are rape and murder no longer crimes here?'

The Prefect changed his balance, rocking a little on the balls of his feet. 'Of course they are, sir! But we have no real evidence, and you're stirring up a lot of feeling. You're making it very difficult for us!'

'Difficult to do what?' Ishrafeli asked, very polite again.

Tathea looked from one to the other of them, but she did not interrupt.

'To keep the peace!' the Prefect replied, easing back onto the flat of his feet again, satisfied with the answer.

'The peace!' Ishrafeli repeated the word. 'A blind woman has been set on in the street by four men, raped by them all and then beaten to death. Is that the "peace" you feel the need to keep, Prefect?'

The Prefect's face burned scarlet. 'We work by the law, sir! We don't go out and stir up people to anger so they execute their own vengeance. If we do that, we'll have everyone out there deciding who's innocent and who's guilty of everything. It'll be chaos.'

'I asked for contributions to buy her a place to be buried,' Ishrafeli pointed out quietly.

'You told them how she died!' the Prefect shouted, suddenly losing control of his temper. 'You're doing that on purpose!'

'To achieve what?' Ishrafeli raised his eyebrows.

'To—' the Prefect began, then stopped abruptly.

'What?' Ishrafeli pressed. He knew what the man had been going to say.

'To rouse up feeling,' the Prefect retreated. 'You're making it very difficult for us to keep the law. We'll find whoever did this, and we'll have them tried the proper way.' He took a deep breath and let it out slowly. 'You leave us to do our job! Just say she's dead. Don't go whipping up feeling. It's a warning, that's all. I'm sure you don't want panic in the streets, or people taking the law into their own hands.'

'I want the law in your hands.' Ishrafeli looked down at the Prefect's clenched fists. 'Don't let go of it!'

The Prefect started to say something, then changed his mind.

'No, sir,' he said grimly instead. 'You bury this woman tomorrow, and do it quietly. No more than a score of people. That's official!'

'A score?' Ishrafeli said with sarcastic innocence. 'Perhaps you'd better send soldiers to keep away the rest. A lot of people may wish to pay their last dues to her. Who will you let in? The first twenty to come? What if an Archon should be late, or a Captain of the Guard?'

The Prefect's chest was rising and falling rapidly, his face red all the way down his neck.

'She was a blind beggar, for God's sake!' he exploded.

'If no one comes, then you'll have no trouble,' Ishrafeli pointed out with a tight smile.

'I'll send men!' The Prefect jabbed his finger towards Ishrafeli's chest, but he did not touch him. 'And if I hear you saying a single word about revenge, I'll have you arrested!' It was a pointless threat and he knew it, but it gave him a pretence of power and he swivelled on his heel and marched out before it could be stripped from him.

Scores of people did come to the Field of Cypresses in the wind and the intermittent sun, but Ishrafeli barely cared about that. Callia had loved, that she had been loved in return was a greater blessing to the living than to her now.

What mattered was that the Prefect could no longer ignore the crime. Two days later the news was announced that four soldiers had been arrested and were to be tried for the rape and murder of the blind woman.

None of the lawyers wanted to prosecute the case. The men accused were on brief leave from the army after having served on the battlefront against the barbarian. This was the first time they

180

had been home to the City since leaving nearly a year ago.

Tathea had no hesitation in taking it for herself. Ishrafeli was tireless in seeking evidence, witnesses, means of assuring or protecting those who were afraid, bullying those who placed their own comfort before the duty of testifying. He came home exhausted and sat almost motionless in his chair in case he should distract her study of how best to argue the case.

Sometimes he brought Severinus with him, knowing the cripple needed to feel as if he were part of the fighting. There was nothing Severinus could do, but he seemed more at ease if he was with them, watching Tathea, willing her to find a way to win.

The trial was held in the great hall of justice. Crowds of people poured up the shallow steps from the forum, filling the courtroom and packing the corridors outside.

Balour himself presided, sitting in the high, carved judge's seat, his rodent face peering over the bench into the room, shifting, watching, his sharp-nailed hands never still.

He brought the proceedings to order the moment the doors were closed and, glaring at Tathea, spat out the command to begin.

The four soldiers stood at ease in the box reserved for the accused, their bodies relaxed, their faces calm, one even half smiling, as if he had no fear of being found guilty.

Tathea controlled her temper with an effort. Already the trial was threatening to run out of control, and she had not yet even spoken. In her mind their arrogance, their certainty that the law was corrupted beyond even the respect of lip service, was a supreme victory for Asmodeus.

She looked at the man who was to represent them in their defence. She could see only the back of his head as he sat bent over his papers. He was slender, with thick, fair hair.

He straightened up and turned very slowly to look at her, and suddenly she was cold. She gazed into the wide, blue-grey eyes of Ulciber. He smiled, and the strength drained out of her so it was all she could do not to collapse in her seat. She willed herself to face him, to remember the powers that supported her as well as those against. She must concentrate, think, fight.

She turned back to the front. 'My Lord Balour,' she began, her voice steady, a stranger might have even thought without emotion, 'a blind woman of the streets, without money or status, but who worked to help the sick and the lost, was attacked by a group of men, raped, and then beaten to death. I intend to show this court that the men who did this thing are the four who stand here accused. I have witnesses and evidence to that end.'

Balour's lipless mouth spread in a smile, cold as a polar wind. He nodded very slowly, a silent indication to proceed.

All day into the early evening Tathea called person after person who testified to Callia's whereabouts – not that they were in doubt, but she knew the importance of correctly identifying the victim, and it gave her the chance to show in emotional terms the kindness and simplicity of the old woman's life. By the time Tathea had finished, the common people in the gallery listening were caught in the rage of the crime and hardly one of them even moved position on the benches, let alone thought of leaving.

By the end of the second day, without a single interruption or challenge from Ulciber, the lawyer for the soldiers' defence, she had proved, both by witness and by physical evidence, that the four soldiers accused were indeed the ones responsible. And yet Ulciber showed no concern. His face was as smooth as if he were at his own dinner table, well fed and sipping wine with friends. Even Balour had not done more than nod comfortably, his hands moving with only their usual perpetual twitch.

Tathea was worried. The enemy never slept; certainly he never retreated.

That evening Ishrafeli said nothing to her of it, but she felt his tension as if it had been words, touch, a passion within her own skin. She could give him no reassurance. Her fear was even deeper than his.

On the third day Ulciber rose to his feet at last and began the defence, smoothly, easily, with a smiling face. His first witness had nothing to do with the event at all, nothing even to do with Callia. Indeed he began by conceding with graciousness that she had been a good woman and had performed all the kindnesses Tathea had attributed to her, and no doubt many more as well.

Then he asked his witness, a burly man with a quiet voice and scarred, weather-burned skin, to introduce himself and tell the Lord Balour and the court something of his life. Ulciber interrupted him only once to ask, quite casually, if he were acquainted with the accused men, to which he received a denial.

As the man spoke Tathea began to perceive the path of the defence and nausea ran through her. The man was a soldier of long and honourable service. He had been one of the leaders of new recruits on the long march north to the barbarian frontier. He described the desolation he had seen, the long lines of exhausted refugees fleeing from the battlefront, frightened, bewildered, carrying what few possessions they could on their backs, leading even tiny children by the hand, stumbling, crying, lost.

Then he described the burned villages and the trampled and torn-up crops, the bodies of the dead left unburied because there was no one left even to perform that decency.

Lastly he told in simple and unflinching words of the horror of battle itself, how the hordes of savage horsemen swept out of the dawn, hair flying, voices screaming high and animal-like on the wind, the rain of arrows that pierced the flesh through to the bone, long before a lance could be raised, let alone a sword. He described the pain, the maiming. He told them what it was like to fight beside a friend, and the next moment see him dismembered in front of you, his entrails spilling out and his life gushing scarlet on to the earth, and be too helpless and sick to do anything but stare.

Not a man or woman in the room moved. Tears ran silently down their faces and they clung to each other in paralysed grief.

'Thank you,' Ulciber said gravely when at last the soldier finished. 'I think you have told us a small portion of what it is like to be a soldier in battle. It is a life we who live safely here are spared from even imagining, worse than the most terrible nightmares of any of. us.'

'It changes you,' the soldier said succinctly. It was three words, but it was the sum of everything Ulciber wanted the court to understand.

'And our men,' Ulciber asked softly, his voice a purr, 'how do they bear such things? What do you do to help them survive?'

'They have to do more than survive,' the soldier replied grimly. 'They have to fight back, slaughter the barbarian in turn. Kill them wherever they find them.'

'The men, the warriors?' Ulciber sounded as if he were merely clarifying.

The soldier gave a grunt, his face now a little paler, his shoulders hunched. 'All of them, women and children as well, if you find a camp. It's natural. They've seen what the bloody savages did to ours!'

'I see.' Ulciber nodded. For several moments there was a stunned silence in the room. Even Balour's twitching hands were still until a spasm overtook him, then his nails on the bench were like the sound of rats' feet on a floor. Never once did he take his eyes from Ulciber.

'And when young men have seen and done such things,' Ulciber resumed at last, 'how do you teach them to be the people they were before, to have pity and decency, to govern their emotions and treat others with respect?'

'You don't,' the soldier said harshly, anger and helplessness in his face. 'You can't. No man sees those things and comes back the same as he went. You thank God if he comes back at all.'

Ulciber turned to Tathea and bowed, smiling at her and indicating that she might question his witness if she chose.

She stood up slowly. She could not tell this Camassian crowd that years ago she had marched across the Shinabari desert and fought side by side with their soldiers, smelled the blood till it sickened her, felt the horror and the exhaustion, the pain of wounds. She could even have pushed back the sleeves of her robe and shown them the scars on her arms, thread-fine now, almost invisible. But none would believe her. This was a battle of passion, not logic. She was a woman, rape was a crime against women, war was men's battle to protect the entire nation. She had lost almost before she had begun.

Still the truth must be spoken, whether a dozen people heard it, or one, or none at all.

'So in the horror of war against the barbarian you taught young men, like these accused, to slaughter the women and children of the enemy, as they had seen their own women and children slaughtered?' she asked levelly.

'Yes . . .' The answer was honest, but she saw the shadow of reluctance in it.

'Because the enemy are barbarians?'

'Yes.'

'And are our men equal to the barbarian?'

'Better.' That was said with confidence.

'And how are they different, other than by being more efficient at butchering women and children?' she said quietly.

There was a low rumbling around the room, fear, anger, dismay. Emotions were raw and too confused for thought, and it frightened them. She could feel it, like the heaviness in the air before a great storm.

The soldier struggled for an answer that made sense to him. She saw it in his face, as did everyone else in the room.

Balour leaned forward, opened his mouth, and then closed it again, waiting. Ulciber did not move but sat with his beautiful fingers steepled in front of him.

'It's war!' the soldier said bluntly. 'It changes people. We learn to do terrible things. If you're saying we're no better than the men we fought against, maybe you're right. That's the price.'

She felt a rush of pity for him so intense for a moment she floundered for words. He was like a thousand other men she had marched and fought beside, shared food with, talked with over the campfire, and owed her life to in the heat of the battle.

'I know,' she said softly, her voice thick with memory and pain. 'And it's too high, but we know of no other, except to be conquered and lose all that we have built and fought for over the centuries. The tragedy is that when we become the barbarians ourselves, then we have lost just as surely. Whatever soldiers have seen or done, whatever they have endured to protect us, it is still a crime to rape a woman and murder her here in Camassia. That is what makes us

184

different from the barbarian. We know better. We may do it in war, and that is grievous enough, but we do not do it in peace.'

There was a rustle of ease around the room. She had offered them an escape from the turmoil of conflicting passions and fears. They were not barbarians after all. There was safety of mind, of conscience.

Balour's face darkened, the purplish hue creeping up his cheeks, the thin hair on his scalp bristling.

'We are not at peace, woman!' he said sharply. 'Haven't you been listening? These young men leave their homes and their futures and go to the northern frontiers to fight to protect the rest of us.' He leaned further forward over the marble. 'They are taught to commit acts of war in our name, to drive back the barbarian any way they can, and we are equally responsible with them for what becomes of them!' He looked at Ulciber. 'Is that not your argument?'

Ulciber was as calm as a summer dawn. 'Yes, my lord, it is,' he agreed. 'These men were ordered by us to raid the enemy villages, to put them all to the sword. They began by being as terrified and repulsed by it as any of us, but brutality becomes a way of survival, and in time it is no longer alien.' He turned to Tathea. 'The first time it is an order, they have to be commanded to do it and there is no choice but to obey, or to die themselves. The next time it is not quite so hard, and by the fifth and sixth it has become habit.'

Tathea looked at Balour, who was smiling, the tiny points of his teeth showing between his lips. Then she looked at Ulciber again. 'Orders?' she said.

'Orders,' he repeated with sublime confidence. 'In the army if you do not obey, you forfeit your life. They had no choice.' He looked up at Balour and smiled.

Balour smiled back and inclined his head minutely, or it might have been only a spasm.

'There is always choice,' Tathea replied steadily. 'Sometimes it is terrible, and the price is death. That is the measure of your spirit, when the cost is all you have. Anyone can choose right when it comes cheap, but do not say there is no choice. We are better than that – all of us. We cannot choose to be beautiful or clever, to be talented, even to be loved, but we can choose to do the best, the bravest, and the most beautiful things we know. Callia chose it.' She gestured towards the accused in the box. 'These men did not.'

Balour sat up very straight, his chin high. He looked directly at Tathea.

'Then I shall decide for you,' he responded, his voice thin and flat, 'as is my duty to the nation. The men are not guilty. Set them free.'

Tathea had expected it, but in spite of Ulciber, she had allowed herself to hope. Now she felt as if she had been hurled from a galloping horse. The ground had risen and bruised her, knocking the breath from her body. She had failed Ishrafeli and Severinus. She had failed Callia.

She heard the roar of mixed elation and fury around her, as the court erupted in emotion.

Balour banged his gavel on the marble but for once no one took any notice of him. Men and women were pouring out into the street shouting, cursing, jostling and knocking one another.

The soldiers were escorted out and disappeared. Ulciber was nowhere to be seen.

Tathea left her place in the court. She knew where Ishrafeli would be, and the fury and distress he would be feeling. Even though he had seen injustices all around and had heard Tathea speak of her lost battles before, he had hoped. Perhaps it was foolish, and against all the chances, but he cared so passionately he had allowed himself to believe. Now he would be angry and crushed, trying to help Severinus and not knowing how to.

She found them outside in the small yard at the northern entrance. They stood silent, blank-eyed and stunned. The apology died on her lips. Words would help nothing yet. Together they walked under the archway out into the streets. It was a mild evening, the unblemished sky pale violet overhead, still touched with colour toward the west. It bathed the shabby walls with a temporary healing.

They passed little groups of people standing around, but here and there some were running, as if carrying urgent news. It was not until they were about a mile from their home that Tathea realised what was happening. A crowd was gathering with distinct purpose – ordinary working men, builders, traders, artisans, middle-aged family men. There was a deep, implacable anger in them. Many carried knives or cudgels of some sort, and their faces were dark with anger.

Now she realised what the building was they were intent upon – a brothel! Ishrafeli pulled her to a halt.

'They're going after the soldiers!' he said with horror. 'They must be in there!'

She knew it. Perhaps it had all been inevitable from the moment they had been arrested.

Severinus was scarcely listening. He was oblivious of the world around him. Everything he knew was inside himself, a huge, consuming emptiness too vast to allow room for anything else.

'They're going to execute them!' Ishrafeli's voice was rising, close to losing control.

There were thirty or forty men in the crowd now and there was a low growl from them like a pack of animals scenting a kill. The impetus driving them forward was unstoppable.

The first of them reached the door, hesitated only a moment, then put their shoulders to it, heaved, stepped back and charged. It splintered off its hinges and fell under their weight. They poured into the narrow passage, pressing behind each other, pushing.

There was surprisingly little noise, no shouting. The rage was too deep, and yet there was a hysteria below the surface like a pent-up scream, such a thin skin guarding it, it would take only a scratch for it to well out and fill the night with agony of confusion and pain.

'They're going to kill them!' Ishrafeli shouted. 'We've got to stop it!'

'You can't!' Tathea caught at his arm, clutching fabric and feeling the muscle iron-hard underneath. 'Ishrafeli! You can't stop it! It has to run . . .'

But he had pulled away. 'We've got to!' his voice choked. 'They'll kill them!'

'I know.' She plunged after him, trying to catch his arm. 'Don't interfere, you'll only make it worse! Do you hear me?'

'I've got to!' he said, half over his shoulder. 'Think what it will do to the law if they murder them! Think what will happen to these men. They're ordinary people, decent most of the time.'

Severinus was still somewhere ahead of them, swallowed by the crowd closing in. It was nearly dark and there were torches everywhere, more and more flaring as new people joined, tense, pushing and jostling.

Ishrafeli broke away from Tathea and she could not hold him.

There was an eruption of noise. Half a dozen men emerged from the doorway, dragging the soldiers with them, whose faces were contorted with terror, eyes and mouths wide open, gagging with fear. One of them either refused to stand, or could not. His arms and legs thrashed around, but he was lifted and carried as if he had been a child, his weight nothing, his violence irrelevant. Somewhere behind them there were women screaming.

The torchlight shone red on the blades of three broadswords. The crowd came to attention and sudden order, for all the underlying frenzy, as if this were to be a ritual.

Ishrafeli had reached the front. Tathea saw his dark head a little above those around him. Then Severinus was there, crooked-shouldered, using his good arm.

'For God's sake stop!' Severinus shouted. 'Stop, before you become just what they are!'

The whole scene froze except for the flicker of torch flames in the breeze.

187

One of the men turned his sword handle toward Severinus, offering it. 'Do you want to?' he asked. 'I guess you have the right.'

'No!' Severinus' voice was quivering. 'I don't want it done at all.' Perhaps it was the red torchlight moving on his features, but it seemed as if he were enduring a struggle within himself so intense the muscles of his face were contorted with its savagery. 'I don't want us to kill them at all. The law found them not guilty.'

One woman yelled out a torrent of blasphemy. Another howled, like an animal in pain.

Ishrafeli stepped forward beside Severinus.

'Damn the law!' the man with the sword shouted furiously. 'Everyone knows it's a farce! They're guilty as the damned. You of all men know that! Or does friendship mean nothing to you – decency? Does nothing matter any more?'

Severinus swayed on his feet. Ishrafeli caught him, supporting him in his arms. But it was Severinus who spoke. 'Everything matters – the law, the army, you, me . . .' He swallowed. 'Callia. But this isn't the way!'

The man's face was stricken with disbelief, his voice choked. 'The law has betrayed us. We are taking it back from men who are not worthy to act in its name. What they do is a mockery of everything that makes life decent. If we do nothing, then we're part of it!'

'No, we aren't!' Severinus argued, shaking his head wildly. 'We know what they are. Maybe we should try them again, or . . .' His face crumbled with exhaustion and misery. 'But I know that if we drag them out of their houses and kill them in the street, because we don't agree with the verdict, then we destroy the law just as much as they do!'

His voice was drowned in a roar of anger. The crowd did not understand; it was naked in their faces and in the hard angles of their bodies and their clenched fists.

'It's time we made the law decent again!' a voice shouted from one in a group of men in tradesmen's rough clothes.

'If we don't, it's no good to any of us!' another added.

The man with the sword faced Severinus. 'If we let them get away with this, it'll happen again. Next time it could be my friend, or my family, or his!' He pointed randomly into the crowd. 'Or his! Or anyone's. It's too late to save the blind woman, but what about the rest of us, eh? If you don't care about that, at least don't try to stop us!'

'You can't . . .' Severinus began, but he was overwhelmed, pushed and shoved roughly. He lost his balance and stumbled. Ishrafeli went down with him.

Tathea charged forward, shouting and punching her way

through until she was next to him to support some of his weight, hopeless and pointless as she knew it was. Others were pushing towards him also, angrily, threatening him in their fury and their frustration at being balked in their need for action, justice, the illusion that they had some kind of control.

Ishrafeli scrambled to his feet, refusing to lean on Tathea.

'How dare you?' he shouted furiously. 'Hasn't this man suffered enough, that you attack him now? He's only trying to save you from yourselves!'

One man waved a knife in the air, his face dark with anger. 'Then get him out of my way! We've suffered too! This is our city, and it's time we took it back again, and made the law something that protects us all! We're a laughing stock, and we won't take it any more!'

Ishrafeli rounded on him. 'And what will you be if you murder these men in the street?' he shouted. 'Dozens of you, breaking into a brothel and hauling them out to kill, because you don't agree with the verdict of the court? Is that your idea of justice?'

'My idea of justice is that rapists and murderers get executed,' another man shouted across them both. 'If you'd let them free then you're no better than they are!'

There was more shouting, rising closer to hysteria. A woman started to sob in fear, and another joined her. Someone began to scream.

A stone was hurled and only just missed Ishrafeli, but it fell long, and clipped another man on the elbow, causing him to bellow with pain.

The shouting grew louder, out of control. People were shoving more roughly. A punch was thrown, then another. Retaliation was immediate. Within moments there was a tangle of fists and curses, men fighting with all their pent-up helplessness and frustration – the outrage at injustice, the fear for themselves and those they loved, exploding in the need for action.

The four soldiers were lost in the mêlée.

Severinus was staring in horror at what had happened around him, too bemused to protect himself.

On every side people were fighting, some of them with knives. It was as if a madness had taken hold of them. The driving need to lash out had swept away all reason.

Tathea lost sight of Ishrafeli and panic seized her. She struck out, desperate to reach him, terrified that he could be trampled by the mob.

She found him, battered and indescribably angry, but Severinus was gone. They fought and stumbled their way through the darkness and the flaming torchlight, the noise of blind rage. Finally they reached the comparative safety of an alley leading to a flight of steps up the hill. They huddled close, protected by each other's bodies.

'You can't help,' she said at last, her mouth half muffled by the top of her cloak where it tied around her neck.

'I lost Severinus.' His voice was shaking with grief. 'They killed him. They didn't give him a chance.'

Tathea moved even closer, putting her arms around him. 'I know.' She nearly added that Severinus had fulfilled the giant in himself, but Ishrafeli was too caught up in ordinary, human grief, and guilt for his own part in what had happened, to hear that now.

They stood motionless for a little while longer, then turned and walked the rest of the way home without speaking again.

She fell asleep still holding Ishrafeli close in her arms, but when she woke he was sitting on the bed in the hard morning light. He was dressed as if he had already been out. His face was pale, the lines in it cut deep. She saw in his eyes that there was something yet worse that he needed to tell her.

All thought of her own feelings vanished. She sat up and put out her hand to his shoulder.

He shook his head fractionally, but something inside him eased at her touch and he put his hand over hers. 'They found the bodies of the soldiers an hour ago. They were hacked to pieces.'

She leaned forward very slowly and buried her face in the side of his neck.

She felt his arms slowly close around her. But it could not undo what had happened to Callia, to Severinus, to the people and the City.

The public reaction over the next days was not as everyone had expected. There was no jubilation, no sense of victory or restitution. Ordinary people were shocked by what they had done, and horribly, bitterly ashamed. Balour and the courts had made a mockery of the law, and then they themselves had made it worse.

If the people did not uphold the law, then it was of no value for anyone. The boundaries that created a civilised society were destroyed. If those who believe in the law do not abide by it, or they feel it wrong, then how can they expect it to protect them from those who do not believe in it at all?

The most startling thing was the number who were no longer willing to obey Balour. Their fear of him became less than their fear of the anarchy they had seen within themselves. They had been conquered by a moment of darkness within, something close to chaos of the soul, and they drew back from the brink.

Weapons were laid down. The first, stumbling steps were taken towards peace.

Asmodeus watched, and planned, and bided his time. The seeds of division he had sown between Tathea and Ishrafeli were beginning to grow. He would reap the harvest yet!

Chapter Twelve

Sadokhar continued his journey through the wastes of hell because as long as he was moving at least at times he had the illusion that something could change. He might find Tornagrain, though everything within him rejected the idea that he could even look at him except with loathing.

The more he saw of the inhabitants of the endless dust and rubble, the less did he imagine any of them leaving. He watched them digging, cursing, quarrelling with one another in useless fights. Not once did he hear a word that perhaps they had brought this upon themselves, and change within might produce something better, if not escape, then at least a mode of life more bearable, even constructive. Each was consumed with self-pity, justification for all they did, which at the same moment was also self-disgust. Never did he see a minute's compassion for another, a hand reached out in kindness, or a word of encouragement offered. They were crowded together, sometimes banging into each other clumsily, and yet each was desperately and utterly alone.

Watching their futility, Sadokhar lost his temper.

'Fool!' he shouted at one man who was picking rocks off a pile and throwing them on to another. 'Why don't you build something useful? What's the point in that? It's just stupid!'

The man swung around to glare at him, the sweat glistening on his bald head. 'Build?' he yelled back, his face red with exertion and rage. 'Build what? A house? Do you want to stay here? You're the fool! Idiot! Cretin! Why should I stay here? It's hell! Hell!' And he laughed maniacally and started to fling more rocks around, careless of where they landed.

One hit Sadokhar on the leg, drawing blood. Sadokhar stooped and picked the rock up, weighing it in his hand, then hurled it back, striking the man on the shoulder so hard he lost his balance and fell over, letting out a stream of abuse so violent and filthy Sadokhar was startled. In that moment he realised how hell had taken hold of him also and he had become part of it. The desolation he saw on every side was the reflection of what was within.

193

It had touched him so quickly he had gone from pity to rage in moments.

But then the greater the light in a spirit, the more rapid the descent into darkness can be. He knew that and he had allowed himself to forget it.

He walked over and held out his hand to the man to help him up. 'I'm sorry,' he said. He meant it, not so much in compassion for the man as regret for himself. He had behaved badly, and that was an injury to his own soul.

The man stared at him in stupefaction. No one apologises in hell. For some reason it frightened him. He did not take Sadokhar's outstretched hand but went a step back instead.

Sadokhar shrugged and walked away.

Some time later – there was no manner to tell how long – he reached another cliff. It was perhaps forty or fifty feet high and jagged-edged, as if once eroded by wind. It stretched as far as he could see to left and right but a hundred yards away there was what seemed to be an opening. In the shadowless light it was hard to be certain.

Still, there was nothing else to do. He had no idea how far hell extended, if there was an end of it to reach. Perhaps it was all a region of the soul, and had no physical existence? That was a thought too hideous to contemplate. He would drive himself mad. The only thing was to keep on moving, past exhaustion or misery or any kind of disappointment. He must imagine there was purpose. Tathea had promised him there was . . . He must believe . . . There was nothing else.

He trudged on. His leg was sore where the stone had hit it, but not as much as he would have expected. As he had noticed before, physical pain was dulling, as if it were part of a real world that was gradually fading away.

But the break in the cliff seemed to be genuine. He stopped and stared up. There was a steep gorge leading up, easily climbable, and apart from a few outcrops and scree beds it seemed clear all the way to the top. He set out with renewed energy.

Sadokhar was a little more than halfway, stumbling on the loose stones, when he was vividly and terrifyingly aware of a living presence in front of him, blocking the way. There was no shadow, but still a suffocating sense of the light being sucked away.

His fingers lost their grip and he slid backwards, pebbles falling behind him and rattling down the way he had come. His breath rasping in his throat, he lifted his head and looked up.

Towering above him was a creature more hideous than anything he had imagined. It was almost human, and yet it was not. It stood on two massive legs. At first it seemed as if the muscles rippled, then before his horrified eyes the flesh broke open and a new limb emerged, skinless and bleeding, only to be consumed again leaving nothing behind except a putrescent scar.

He tore his eyes away and looked up at the body, which was naked, entrails pulsing, swelling and retracting, forming obscene new shapes, and then losing them again. The skin was scaly, bubbling, purple-dark. A sickly stench came from it, filling the air.

Repulsed and helpless to avoid it, Sadokhar looked at the face, although in his heart he knew what he would see: the fractured, misshapen torment of legion souls locked together in eternal hatred, fighting for mastery of one body and never holding it.

The creatures roared with laughter. More rocks broke loose, crashing down into the gorge and rattling away.

'Where are you going, little man?' it demanded.

Sadokhar straightened up. If this was hell, what had he to lose? The creature, Lord of the Undead he might be, could hardly kill him! Then a hideous thought occurred: he might consume him, and Sadokhar could end up imprisoned in that filthy skin also, never to exist alone again!

He recoiled in terror, his limbs shaking, panic exploding inside him, skin crawling as if covered with maggots. The scream choked in his throat as his legs buckled and he slipped helplessly on the stones and fell backwards.

'Frightened?' the creature said with relish, stepping towards him. 'You should be!' Even as he spoke another mouth erupted out of his cheek, gaping open. 'I am Ozmander and this gorge is mine!' it shouted, and then retracted and shrivelled up. The eyes skewed round and a third and then a fourth eye appeared, bulging out of bleeding sockets. Another mouth protruded from the neck and stretched wide, screaming. 'If you want to pass,' the first mouth yelled above the others, 'you will have to pay me!'

'Pay you?' Sadokhar gasped incredulously, scrambling to his feet, careless of the bruising and cutting of his hands. 'With what?'

Ozmander curled his lips off broken teeth. 'I'm bored! Entertain me!'

It was absurd. If it had not been so obscene it would have been laughable. But Sadokhar had no heart to laugh.

'Climb up that rock face!' Ozmander commanded, pointing to a steep, jutting side with no crevice for even a finger to hold.

Sadokhar looked at it and knew he could not.

'Go on!' Ozmander jeered. 'You want to pass me – do as I say!'

'No one could climb up that,' Sadokhar protested.

'Then no one can pass me!' Ozmander rejoined with a leer.

'Then I'll have to find another way.' Sadokhar started to back down again and when he dared, turned to leave.

'Wait!' Ozmander shouted after him, his voice crumbling the rock and sending pebbles dancing.

Sadokhar stopped. 'What?'

'If you can't climb up the rock, then crawl over the scree there, and get up that side,' Ozmander shouted after him. 'You can do that!'

Sadokhar looked at it. It would be tedious and slippery, but as Ozmander had said, quite possible. He climbed back a little way.

'And if I do?' he asked.

'Then I might let you pass!' Ozmander grinned, showing all his jagged teeth. 'Or I might not.'

Sadokhar stood still. 'Not good enough,' he said. 'What's beyond there?' He pointed. 'That could be entertaining for you.'

Ozmander's face contorted and his body writhed under its skin. Ulcers cracked open and oozed blood.

Sadokhar was sickened. He knew the souls within must have looked on the light, and deliberately chosen evil, cruelty and lies, feeding on the pain of others, and yet still he felt a pity for their damnation, self-chosen as it was. But he knew better than to trust them.

Ozmander strode forward, his arm outstretched.

Sadokhar jerked back so quickly he fell and rolled several yards down the scree, bruising himself and landing hard against a stony outcrop. He was startled by the sharp pain of it, crying out involuntarily.

'It hurt you!' Ozmander said gleefully. 'It hurt you! I saw it! You can't deny it!'

Sadokhar staggered to his feet, feeling warm blood on his back. 'Yes,' he agreed, straightening up only slowly. 'I can feel. Can you?'

Ozmander's face twisted, his mouth slack, and in that instant Sadokhar knew he had scored a victory. He smiled widely. 'I thought not!' he jeered. 'Crawl up your own scree slope! I'm going to find another way around. I don't care where I go anyway.'

'There's no other way!' Ozmander yelled, starting down after him. 'You'll not get around! You'll be stuck here for ever!'

'I'm stuck here for ever anyway!' Sadokhar called back as he slipped and slithered down the gorge. He could hear Ozmander bellowing after him, but it seemed he was in some way tied to the place, because he did not follow.

Sadokhar walked for what seemed like miles along the base of the cliffs, and nowhere was there more than a crevice here or there, every one ending in sheer walls.

Finally he slumped down in exhaustion, his body aching, his feet blistered raw. He had to face the possibility that the vile Ozmander was right, and there was no way up except through the gorge.

Or perhaps there was no way up at all? What lay beyond, anyway? Everything or nothing? Tornagrain could be anywhere, far ahead of him on the cliffs, or on the plain behind, scrabbling around futilely in the dust like those he had seen, angry, self-pitying, blaming everyone else for their fate. There was no end to the cliff. He could go on like this for days – had there been days or nights in hell – or he might find a path up in the next hour.

But there was one for certain if he retraced his steps back to where Ozmander waited. And who was to say that if he found another way there would not be some other creature of hell waiting there for him?

He had promised Tathea. There was a kind of cleanness to returning, a resolution that had a balm within it, even in facing Ozmander.

He set out walking, this time with purpose and intent. He would do whatever was required to pass him, even submission to his ridiculous demands, if he had to, because it was the way forward, and he was not going to give in, not to Ozmander, not to anyone.

Ozmander was exactly where he had left him, standing in the middle of the gorge, blocking the way. He gave a bellow of jubilation as he saw Sadokhar struggling up, sliding on the shale.

'I knew you'd be back! I told you there's no other way! Now you'll do as I tell you . . . and more!'

Sadokhar gritted his teeth and kept on climbing. He must fix the purpose in his mind, think of Tathea and the fighting of Armageddon, what victory would mean, and the way back into the world again to be part of it, with those he loved.

He reached Ozmander and stopped in front of him, looking straight ahead.

'I can't climb the rock face,' he said bluntly. 'So that order is a waste of time. I'll crawl up the scree, if it's what you want.'

Ozmander grinned. 'I've changed my mind.' Now his voice was soft, like a score of whispers. 'See that pile of stones there?' He pointed to a scattered heap. 'Move them over to the other side, one at a time. Pile them up carefully.'

Sadokhar swallowed back his anger and bent to obey. There were over two hundred stones. It took a long time, but he persevered.

'Good,' Ozmander said when he was finished at last.

'Now let me pass,' Sadokhar asked.

Ozmander squinted at him with a bloodshot eye. 'I don't like them there. Put them back where they were. One at a time! Carefully.'

Sadokhar lost his temper and charged forward. Ozmander stopped him with one arm, flinging him back with such force he lay on the ground winded for several moments before he could climb to his feet again, bruised, just as angry, but wiser.

'Why do you want to stop me passing?' he asked.

'It amuses me,' Ozmander answered with a sneer. 'Once you've gone, I'll be bored again.'

'If I refuse to obey you, you'll be just as bored,' Sadokhar pointed out. 'Why don't you come with me?'

'Because there's nowhere to go, fool! If you want to waste your energy, that's your stupidity – not mine.'

'Have you ever been past here?'

'No. There's nothing to see, just more rocks, more dust. Why should I bother?'

'There might be something else . . . if you looked!'

Ozmander thrust his hideous face forward. 'There's nothing,' he hissed.

Sadokhar backed away, gagging in the stench. He went a hundred yards or so and stopped to think. Obviously Ozmander was not open to reason; for him this was simply another way to be obstructive, and just as entertaining. Physically Sadokhar could not overpower him, he was immensely strong. There did not seem to be any way to deceive him, and there was certainly no way to bypass him. Perhaps there was some part of his emotions to reach. Plainly he could be angered, or amused. Could he hope?

Sadokhar stood up again and climbed slowly back to where Ozmander was waiting.

'Ready to move the stones?' Ozmander asked with a leer.

'I would, if I believed it would get me past you,' Sadokhar answered. 'But I don't. You don't know what lies beyond the cliff, so you don't care.'

'You don't either!' Ozmander pointed out. 'I told you, there's nothing there . . . or anywhere else.'

'Yes, there is!' Sadokhar put all the passion and certainty into his voice that he had felt as he had clung to Tathea in the sandstorm. 'There is a way out, and I'll find it. You can come with me if you want . . . or stay here. But I'm going.'

'You're lying!' Ozmander accused. 'There's nothing out there.'

'Yes, there is. An angel told me.' How else could he explain Tathea?

'Angel!' Ozmander's eyes opened wide but his face was a mask of derision. 'There are no angels in hell.'

'Because you haven't seen any?' Sadokhar managed to get just as much ridicule and derision into his voice, and he saw the first flicker of doubt in Ozmander. He ploughed on, to make the most of it. 'I have. She told me of a way out . . . ahead.' He straightened up, holding his head high. 'I mean to find it. If you like it here, then stay. I'm going.'

Ozmander's eyes blazed with hope, and then doubt. Anger suffused his face and his veins bulged. His lips curled in a dozen different expressions as he fought within himself. His body began to twitch, and then within his skin the muscles heaved and the organs began to displace one another.

Sadokhar watched with a sick fascination as it became more apparent that the different personalities imprisoned within his body were attacking each other with ever increasing violence as rage mounted inside them and exploded uncontrollably, tearing each other apart, some to stay, some to go.

Ozmander's right arm swelled and the muscles writhed, tearing it out of the socket at the shoulder. His face distended, eyes swivelling wildly, skin purple. His lips curled back off his teeth and a foam of dark blood appeared, dribbling down his chin. His cheek ballooned out and burst open as another head broke through, the half-formed mouth already cursing. He lunged forward as if to grasp at Sadokhar, fingers outstretched like talons.

Sadokhar backed away quickly, stumbling in his haste.

Ozmander let out a howl and began to claw at his stomach, tearing away the skin till the blood spurted in dark gouts. His whole body jerked and heaved, and his head was now on almost backwards.

Sadokhar was moved to pity as well as horror, but he was helpless to intervene. Ozmander started to speak in a dozen different voices, shouting, snarling, lisping as the blood oozed between his lips, arguing that there was hope, there was no hope, cursing as one tyrant wrenched at another within him, each determined to force its will upon the others.

Ozmander fell to his knees. His other arm reached across and tore the dislocated one at the elbow, ripping it off and letting it fall to the stones, blood pumping.

Sadokhar tried to speak, but no sound came from his lips.

Ozmander gouged with his nails and tore his bowels open, spilling them on to his thighs. His right leg swelled and the skin split, showing the bone white, the muscles writhing. With his remaining arm he gripped his other leg and heaved at it, pulling it out at the hip and the flesh broke away. He threw it at Sadokhar, who leaped aside to let it strike the ground with a sickening squelch.

All the while Ozmander was still swearing and fighting with himself: 'There is hope! We must go!' 'There is none! It's pointless. Stay here!' 'Do as I say!' 'It's all lies!'

Sadokhar could do nothing until at last Ozmander lay twitching on the stones in a dozen bloodied places, organs and entrails ripped out, limbs broken, torn off his trunk, head twisted on his neck, face blotched, eyes and mouth red, still moving. He should have been dead, but there is no escape from hell, no oblivion.

His stomach clenched with pity and revulsion, Sadokhar side-stepped as widely around the filthy pieces of flesh as he could, scraping himself back against the rock face. All the time he watched in case some dismembered hand could still reach out and grasp him.

Then when he was finally past he turned and scrambled on up the path, careless of bruising himself or tearing his skin as long as he got away from that fearful thing on the ground.

At the top of the gorge where the steep sides fell away, he stared around him, hardly realising he was holding his breath in the agonising hope of seeing something different from the endless dust and the flat horizon.

There was nothing . . . nothing at all but more dust and shale and spaces of barren stone, shadowless. It almost broke his spirit.

'There is a way!' he shouted. 'There is a way.' And the silence swallowed his cry.

Nothing moved.

Sadokhar set out to walk because there was no point in remaining where he was. He tried to picture Tathea's face in his mind, clinging on to the vision of it, and the words of her promise. There was no reason or sense to anything. He must believe in miracles, because that was all that could rescue him. Somewhere he had read that there was no height of heaven nor depth of hell where God could not reach. Then He could reach even here! He must!

He raised his face to the flat sky. 'Father – help me!' he cried aloud. 'Help me!'

The sound did not even echo.

He trudged on in the dust, his feet aching, his back sore. He did not know how long he went on before he realised an extraordinary, incredible thing: it was growing dark! In fact he could hardly see ahead of him. He stopped and turned slowly to stare. It was dark all around! Then dimly over to the left he saw something flicker – a light, a flame, as if someone had lit a campfire.

He started towards it rapidly, increasing his pace until the ever-deepening night forced him to move more carefully. By the time he was within yards of the fire he could see it plainly, and also that there were at least a hundred people sitting around it in a huge circle, but each so close to his neighbour that there was no room at all for anyone to make their way in.

None of them turned as Sadokhar approached. They were all apparently oblivious to everything except the blazing fire and its light and warmth. Sadokhar realised suddenly how much the warmth mattered. It was bitterly cold. Outside the circle the wind seemed to bite into the flesh and the darkness was now absolute. He was shaking with cold, his whole body shuddering.

Two men moved apart just enough for him to squeeze in and sit down and the warmth reached him, enveloping him, easing the ache out of his bones. It was marvellous. All his muscles relaxed and he found himself smiling.

He did not know how long he sat there basking in the heat before he became aware of someone moving on the outside, first one place then in another, trying to get in, and always denied. Each time he came between two people they would move almost indefinably closer together, excluding him. Then he would back away a little, his shoulders slumped, and try somewhere else, always to be met with the same refusal. He looked beaten, shaking with the cold.

Sadokhar could not bear it. He stood up, leaving his own place, and shuddering, stumbling in the dark, he went to find the outsider.

He had gone more than halfway around the circle, ignored by everyone else, when finally he found the shadowy figure. Sadokhar was between him and the fire, and when he turned in amazement, his face was clearly visible.

It was a long moment before he believed it. It was Tornagrain. He was haggard-eyed, there were streaks of grey in his hair, but he was still unmistakable. Not only that, but he knew Sadokhar in the same instant, and his features suffused with joy. He stepped forward, his voice hoarse with emotion, and long disuse.

'Sadokhar!' He held out his hands.

Instinctively Sadokhar clasped them. So much of friendship came back in a wave – danger and laughter shared, victories and mistakes, all the wild learning of youth.

Then he remembered Aelfrith, his death, Yldyth's body in the burned house, the pain and the ruin and the loss. Rage boiled up inside him and he let go of Tornagrain and hit him as hard as he could, feeling his fist connect with bone with an impact that jarred right through him.

Tornagrain staggered back and fell.

Sadokhar strode forward. 'Get up!' he shouted furiously.

Tornagrain scrambled to his feet, hesitated a moment as if to speak, then, seeing another blow coming, struck back.

Again and again they hit each other until suddenly Tornagrain stopped and held his hands wide, moving backwards and away. He shook his head. His face and neck were smeared with blood but he did not seem seriously hurt.

Sadokhar was out of breath, and bruised. Without any warning the whole thing had become ridiculous. Tornagrain was the only soul in hell that he knew, and the passion and hate of the Eastern

Shore was years ago. Tornagrain might not have changed since then, but Sadokhar had. The war for the earth was what mattered, not old sins already paid for over and over again. The betrayal was Tornagrain's grief, not Sadokhar's. He should have let it go then, not treasured it up all this time, to the crippling of his own heart.

He held out his hand, palm up.

Tornagrain hesitated only a moment, then came forward and took it, holding it tightly, his eyes steady and straight.

Sadokhar found himself smiling.

Then he saw a look of horror on Tornagrain's face, and the instant after felt a stinging blow on the back so violent it knocked the breath out of him and left him gasping. He swung around and saw that a dozen of those who had been sitting around the fire had risen and were bent on attacking himself and Tornagrain. It seemed that as long as they were fighting each other, they had been content, but now in the sight of some sort of peace, they were enraged.

In moments they were both fighting the strangers, arms and legs flailing, rolling on the ground, beaten, bruised and all but suffocated. As another numbing blow landed on his chest Sadokhar rolled over and tried to get up, and it came to his mind how idiotically pointless this was. There was nothing to be won or lost.

But it went on. He managed to land a severe blow on the face of the man nearest to him, a visage made hideous by fury and hatred. The man fell backwards, allowing Sadokhar to get to his feet just in time to kick another man in the act of strangling Tornagrain.

The next instant he was knocked over himself and the air driven out of his lungs by the force of his landing. Then Tornagrain was attacking the man who had struck him, and being kicked and punched by two more.

Sadokhar could see they were vastly outnumbered and not all the courage or the anger imaginable would be enough to help. Almost without realising what he was doing, he prayed, not only for himself, but for Tornagrain also.

Then he heaved himself up and lashed out again as hard as he could. He was aware of Tornagrain being badly beaten, struggling to hold off an attack on Sadokhar. His face was covered with blood and he was limping badly.

'Go!' he shouted, gasping for breath. 'Get out! I'll hold them . . .' He was cut off by another tremendous blow to his head, and fell back with three men on top of him, pummelling and kicking his body. Sadokhar hesitated. The anger slipped from him and all his will was to save Tornagrain, as if the betrayal, the raid, and the deaths had never happened. He moved forward.

202

'Get out!' Tornagrain yelled with the little strength he had left. 'It's all I can give. For God's sake, take it . . . and go! Please!'

A man with streaming hair and savage, contorted features lunged towards Sadokhar. Sadokhar raised his foot and kicked him as hard as he could, throwing all his weight into it. The man let out a scream and fell back, clutching his stomach.

But there were others behind him.

Sadokhar ached to help Tornagrain, but he knew he could not. Perhaps the best he could do was to accept his gift. Maybe that was what he needed more than physical help.

He raised his arm in a salute, as they had when they fought at sea together on the longships of the Eastern Shore. He stood long enough to know that Tornagrain had seen it, then he turned and ran, his feet flying easily over the dust, barely leaving prints on its powder surface. There was no dawn, only a slow return of colourless light.

It took him nothing like as long to reach the plain with the great rock piles and outcrops than it had to go from it, and then at last to find the one which held the portal. He was overwhelmed with relief, almost joy, to recognise it. It was unmistakable: there were hand-cut slabs, paving stones made by men, not random nature. The arch of the portal was carved with lily flowers as beautiful as daybreak after a lifetime's darkness.

He stumbled in his eagerness to reach it, and be through. Hell was behind him. Tathea was right: he could forgive Tornagrain; he could even grieve with real pain that he had left him behind. All his hatred was gone, and nothing remained except the memory of friendship, and a grief that it had been broken . . . no anger, no pleasure at his pain, just regret that justice demanded such a price. He would have remitted it now, had he the power.

The door was open!

He walked through, his feet silent on the dusty flagstones. The arch above him was lost in shadow, but there was light ahead. He increased his pace. Where would he emerge? Sylum again? Would Orocyno still be there? How long had he been gone? He had very little idea. It would be wonderful to see Tathea, and the others.

The light was growing stronger, but no sun! What time of the day was it? Shouldn't it be summer now?

He started to run. There was still dust under his feet, and bits of loose rubble here and there. The arches were broken, crumbling. But there were no ivies, no moss, no green at all.

He burst out into the open.

It was the same flat, shadowless light as before, and the grey dust of hell spread out in front of him all the way to the white horizon. There was no air, no wind, barely any sensation under his feet, no sound except a roaring, crackling in his ears as if a sea of despair were closing over his soul and drowning him, yet leaving him witheringly, hopelessly alive.

He fell forward on to the dust, crumpled up, desolate and utterly, heart-achingly alone.

Chapter Thirteen

Sadokhar had no idea how long he sat staring into the despair of hell. He was too wretched to move. What was the point?

Hope died hard. There was nothing any sense or reason offered, and yet the pain of having believed still filled him, as if he could not let it go. He did not want to leave the place he had so passionately thought was the portal. He could not accept that it had gone.

He became aware only slowly of how tired he was. His body ached, his feet and legs were bruised, and caked in blood and dust. There was nothing to do, nowhere to go, no purpose in anything any more.

He drifted into a sleep which was hazy, full of vague discomfort and the desire to weep, without the energy to do it.

He opened his eyes at last to an image of mounds of debris, the sour smoke rising from them darkening the air. As far as he could see in every direction it was the same – hills and waves of every kind of detritus, and the smell of it knotted his stomach.

He did not move. There was no way to escape it, and no purpose in trying.

Then he saw her, walking towards him like a shadow over the sea of filth. She was slender, head high, as beautiful as the hope of redemption.

'Tathea!' He started to his feet, plunging through the waste towards her. He reached her and clasped hold of her fiercely, passionately, as if she were life itself.

She put her arms around him, but he could barely feel them. Then, with a wave of horror that broke sweat on his skin, he realised that his own arms closing around her body could crush her by accident, so fragile was she, so insubstantial.

Why? When she had come before she had been so strong it was her power which had pulled him out of the mire and held him up during the sandstorm!

Was this how it was going to be now – he would be less and less able to feel her, to touch her or hear her? What if one day he would not even know she was there any more? Then hell would be truly endless. That would be the last damnation.

Why? Was it because he had failed somehow? Or was hell doing this to him? Or worse! Was it she who was weakening, her faith slipping away as Asmodeus and his creatures won the earth? If Tathea lost her belief it would be like God ceasing to exist!

Sadokhar clung to her, gently, saying her name over and over again in his mind, as he buried his face in her hair, but no sound came to his lips.

He heard her voice in his heart rather than his ears.

'You have forgiven Tornagrain, but it is not enough,' she said softly.

'I did! I forgave him!' his heart cried. 'I did it!'

'I know, my darling, I know!' she whispered. 'But to forgive, and walk away is only half. You must teach him why he was wrong. You must wait with him until he understands and becomes no longer the man who would commit that act, or even think of it. You must guide him to honour, and love, and greatness of spirit. You have learned forgiveness; that was for yourself. Now you must teach redemption – which is for him.'

'I . . .' he began. The idea was monstrous. It was too much!

'You must!' She held him more fiercely, but he could hardly feel her any more. It was only the tightening of her arms, of her shoulders and the way she leaned even closer to him that made him sure. 'Tornagrain must come back. His work is not yet done.'

'I can't!' It was a cry of despair, torn out of his heart and his flesh, out of his soul. 'I can't!'

'It is the only way,' Tathea repeated. 'You come out together, or not at all. It is the truth . . . for both of you.' She loosed her hold on him and looked up, meeting his eyes. 'Please?' she whispered, her voice growing faint. 'I can't ask again. You have all you need to come back to me, to the world. I love you, Sadokhar, and I need you . . .' Even as she was speaking she was moving away from him. She tried to hold on to him, but her hand slipped out of his.

He could not bear it. He called her name, but his lungs had no air. He could not move his feet from the filth in which he stood. All around them the smoking debris was piled high, the air was dark with the fumes of it.

She was helpless. Her face twisted with anguish as she was drawn back into the smoke and in moments she was gone and he was alone again.

He sat down suddenly, his legs too weak to hold his weight. He bent his head and covered his face with his hands. He did not know how to begin! What she asked was too much.

When at last he looked up it was light and he was back in the rubble beside the portal and the dry, dust-white land stretched all around him. If this was the only way, then he must try. He staggered to his feet and set out.

He did not count the time it took him to go past the rock outcrops, the huge excavations where the people were still digging and swearing in everlasting rage, or over the flat plains towards the cliff. He dreaded going up the gorge and seeing what was left of Ozmander. His imagination raced on to whether he was whole again and barring the way, or if he had in some way managed to sink into unconsciousness.

But even before Sadokhar reached the narrow pass he could see the broken limbs, the scattered entrails and the blood exactly as he had left them. In the world they would have been consumed by flies and maggots by now, but there was no life here, not even the minuscule beasts of the air that cause dead flesh to rot.

He stopped, thinking he could smell it in the air, but it was only the illusion of what he expected, not reality. He stared at the head, a dozen yards from the disembowelled torso, and the limbs misshapen and twisted, and felt more pity than revulsion.

Then with a sick horror churning his stomach he saw the fingers move, scrabbling in the dust.

He took to his heels and ran, scrambling wildly up the scree slope, falling and clambering up again, fighting to keep his balance, oblivious of bruises and gashes.

He reached the top breathless and collapsed on the level ground, gasping with relief. His feet and shins were covered with blood, even his hands were torn, but he was aware of no pain. He was losing sensation even more rapidly.

But there was no time to waste. After only a few moments he rose again and started to go the way he had before, even though as far as he could see there were no features to distinguish any direction from another.

Eventually it began to grow dark and he started to turn from side to side, seeking the fire.

Then it was there, just a spark, so tiny he was not sure if it were illusion born out of the passion of his mind.

He began to run, floundering in the dust, falling and sending up choking clouds which half blinded him.

But the fire was real. It grew stronger as he came closer to it, and he started to shout. 'Tornagrain! Tornagrain!' How dare he not be here, after all Sadokhar's labour and pain to find him?

At first he could see no figures. Nothing moved. Disappointment and anger engulfed him, taking his breath away.

Then he heard a sound, very slight, then out of the darkness there was a flurry and a shout.

'Sadokhar!' It rang with joy, like a trumpet call.

He spun around, and there was Tornagrain, his face radiant in the firelight. 'You came back for me!'

Sadokhar was filled with shame because it was not true. He had come back for himself, but he wished now with all his heart that it had been for Tornagrain. He gulped, and forced a smile to his face. If it was not the reason he had come, then he would at least make it why he stayed.

Looking at Tornagrain's battered face, which was scarred and bruised still from the fight, Sadokhar was overwhelmed with how much he truly wanted to tell him everything that mattered and make him understand it, make him see the beauty of what was precious and true. Now, he could not bear the thought of leaving him behind in this place of agony. He knew what it was, he had tasted the bitter dregs himself. They would find the portal together and it would have to let them pass!

Tornagrain reached him and clasped him by the arms. He struggled for words, and found nothing which was enough to express his emotions.

'Yes, I did come back for you,' Sadokhar said, trying to keep his voice firm and strong. He could feel Tornagrain shaking. He had been here for years! Could he ever imagine leaving this place? What blind, stubborn courage had sustained him?

'For what?' Tornagrain whispered, daring now to meet Sadokhar's eyes. 'What could we do? I'm tired of fighting. There's nothing to win . . . or lose.'

'Yes, there is. There's everything,' Sadokhar argued. 'There's a way out.'

Tornagrain's eyes filled with tears of pity. 'No, there isn't. Don't you understand that? We chose our path in life, and now we have what we earned.' He frowned. 'Why are you here? You seemed to have so much! No one is punished blindly. How did you die? At sea in some great battle? Is the world still . . . as beautiful?'

Sadokhar was overcome with loss so intense it dizzied him. 'Yes,' he gulped. 'On the Island, at least. Walk with me and I'll tell you.'

'Walk?' Tornagrain was confused. 'Why? There's nowhere to go.'

'Yes, there is. Don't argue! Just do it!'

Tornagrain laughed sharply. 'You haven't changed. Just as bossy as ever.'

'I united the Island,' Sadokhar told him, taking him by the arm and pulling him along in the dust. 'I was King of it all. I got into the habit of being bossy, and I did it very well.'

'And modest as always too!' Tornagrain's voice was thick with mockery, then sudden and urgent pain. 'So what happened? How did you come to end here?'

'I didn't die,' Sadokhar replied, then as he saw Tornagrain's look of disbelief he snapped back: 'Do you want to know or not?'

'I want to know!' Tornagrain returned. 'Why are we walking so quickly? Where do you think we're going? It's getting light!' He looked around them in surprise, shading his eyes against the white glare. 'God, what a wasteland!'

Sadokhar began by telling him about the night he was born and his mother died, and how Tathea had taken him to Hirioth and cared for him and taught him all she could, until it had been time for him to learn the arts of war and leadership which she could not show him alone.

Tornagrain did not interrupt; much of it was familiar to him because he had been there. Looking back now, knowing what had followed, he saw that the account was also threaded through with the pain of all that he had betrayed and lost for ever. It was a silent and terrible ghost between them.

They walked rapidly through the dust, side by side. Tornagrain had not the faintest idea where they were going, nor why, but he offered no more argument.

'Tathea taught me it was my destiny to unite the Island,' Sadokhar went on after a while, 'long enough for there to be peace in which we could find and teach the warriors who would fight the final war against the Great Enemy.'

'Final war? You mean there'll be peace after that?' Tornagrain was incredulous.

'No. There'll be the end of the world in its present state,' Sadokhar answered, not looking at him. 'The Great Enemy is not the barbarian, it is far older than any man. It is Asmodeus, the son of God who denied the light and fell to the darkness that has no end.'

Tornagrain stared at him, slowing to a stop in amazement. 'The end of the world?' he repeated through dry lips.

'Yes. If we win it is ours for eternity. If we lose, then it is Asmodeus' to turn into a different kind of damnation that would spread to the stars.'

'How . . . how do you fight?' Tornagrain asked. 'What can you do?' There was pain in his eyes, and knowledge of the long despair of hell.

Sadokhar told him how Sardriel and Ardesir were prepared, and that Kor-Assh was coming, and of the Knights of the Western Shore. Then he told him how they had realised that time was Asmodeus' ally, and thus their enemy. He described the great golden Book, and how Tathea had seen Asmodeus' keys of the world on it, and for a moment lost her faith and became old and weak.

Tornagrain listened white-faced, not speaking. Neither of them had begun to walk again.

209

'What did you do?' he said hoarsely.

'I remembered the doorway Orocyno had gone through into the past,' Sadokhar answered, looking sideways at him. 'And I thought perhaps I could provoke the angels of hell to start Armageddon now, while we are ready.'

'Oh God!' Tornagrain gasped as the enormity of it hit him.

Sadokhar smiled bitterly. 'And that is how I came into hell . . . alive! And how Tiyo-Mah and the Lords of Sin and the Undead went into the world.'

Tornagrain stared at him, his eyes dark with horror and understanding.

Sadokhar started to walk again, impatient with delay. 'Come on! We've miles to go yet!'

'If you can go back through it into the world again, why haven't you?' Tornagrain asked, catching up with him.

'Because I've damned well got to take you with me!' Sadokhar snapped. Anger welled up inside him again at Tornagrain because he did not understand that it was his sin that held them both here. Then honesty compelled him to look at the truth. He lowered his voice a little. 'Besides, if we are going to win the war, I'll need you. Tathea came to me in a vision and told me of the darkness that Tiyo-Mah is spreading through Shinabar and Camassia.'

Tornagrain matched him stride for stride. 'What kind of darkness?' he asked.

Sadokhar told him all that Tathea had said of the corruption and evil in Thoth-Moara and the City in the Centre of the World, how lies were passed from man to man until no one knew the truth, and fear twisted everything.

He saw the sorrow in Tornagrain's eyes, in the lines of his mouth and the tight skin across his cheeks. Even through the dried blood and the darkening bruises, the grief in him was naked. Perhaps only now he was realising how much he loved the earth, now when it was gone from him, and in danger of destruction so nothing would be left of it but its pain. Perhaps too he felt the weight of his own betrayals.

He walked for a long time in silence, absorbing the enormity of what he had heard, trying to understand it and find some way of bearing it.

'Who is Tathea?' he said at last. 'Who is she really? How does she know these things?'

If Sadokhar had told him in life, he would have mocked the idea, but here Tornagrain knew the existence of the spirit outside mortality only too achingly well. It was a simple thing to speak to him of Tathea in Shinabar over five hundred years ago, of her journey of the spirit where she had found the Book, and how she had brought it back to the world, and all but a few had rejected it.

'She kept it?' Tornagrain said in wonder. 'For five hundred years?'

'Yes.'

'And you were born to open it again?'

'No.' That was difficult to say. 'I used to think so, but it was Ishrafeli himself, once he knew who he was, once he understood and was prepared to commit to serve God all his life, with everything he has or will ever have.'

'And Armageddon?'

'They are fighting it now.'

'Will they win?'

'I don't know.' It was the first time Sadokhar had admitted that to himself. They were at the mouth of the gorge going down on to the lower plain. Somewhere about a thousand yards away the twitching pieces of Ozmander lay in the dust, still alive, still sentient . . . feeling God knew what. Would the whole beautiful world end like that?

'We have to go down here,' Sadokhar said as calmly as he could. 'You will see something repulsive and pitiful. He tore himself apart . . . I didn't do it.'

Tornagrain did not understand. 'Tore himself apart? Who?'

'Ozmander, one of the Lords of the Undead,' Sadokhar replied, starting down the slope, slipping a little on the loose stones. Surprisingly, he could feel pain again. A sharp chip cut his foot and he gasped as the jagged hurt of it shot through him. 'He was legion . . . a score of damned spirits all locked together in one body, hating each other, always fighting for dominance.'

'Why did he tear himself apart?' Tornagrain scrambled to keep up with him. 'Did you make it happen?'

'Yes. It was the only way to get past him.'

'Why did you have to?'

'To find you, of course!' Sadokhar kept his face forward so Tornagrain could not see it.

'You were so sure I'd be here?' There was an edge of emotion to his voice but Sadokhar could not tell if it was resentment or pain, or both.

'Where else would you be?' Sadokhar said with sudden bitterness, then as quickly regretted it. 'Tathea told me I couldn't get out without finding you,' he added.

'I see.'

'No you don't.' Sadokhar knew they were near Ozmander now, but he did not look at Tornagrain. He scrambled over a patch of loose scree, keeping his balance with difficulty. 'It began for myself.'

211

'And now?' Tornagrain asked. 'And if you lie to me I'll push you the rest of the way down this damn gully!' That was pain too, trying to disguise itself.

Then Sadokhar heard a gasp as Tornagrain saw Ozmander's head lying in the dust, hideous, deformed, but still moving, still alive. One arm lay less than a yard away now, and the eyes were looking at it, willing the fingers to drag it closer, worming in the dust, crawling half-inch by half-inch.

'Come on!' Sadokhar shouted, beginning to run, and jumping from one pile of scree to another.

'For God's sake! What is it?' Tornagrain cried out, flailing his arms to keep his balance and leap out of its way.

'What we become, if we cling on to what is monstrous inside ourselves,' Sadokhar answered. 'He's us, after a thousand years of sin.'

A shower of rubble spattered around him as Tornagrain slid, landing half on top of him.

They picked themselves up and kept on, neither turning even once to see what might be behind them.

Tornagrain's question still hung between them, demanding an answer.

'No, I wouldn't leave without you, even if I could,' Sadokhar said honestly. 'God in heaven, how could you leave anyone here if you knew a way to get them out?'

They reached the bottom of the gully where it opened on to the plain, and together they started to walk across the broken, lifeless rock.

There was no way to count time, except as a matter of weariness when legs could endure no more. Then they lay and rested, sometimes drifting into a kind of sleep. It was in one of these half-dreams that Sadokhar acknowledged to himself that he must begin the struggle towards teaching, and to do that he must first understand for himself. He sat up slowly. If he waited until he had the right words he would never begin.

'You know why I am in hell. Why are you?'

Tornagrain stared at him, then looked away. 'You of all people should know that!'

'It doesn't matter whether I know,' Sadokhar answered. 'It's whether you do that matters.'

'Why? I thought you came to get me out ... for whatever reason!' He still kept his face averted, eyes on the horizon, his mouth tight as he fought to control loneliness, the passionate overwhelming need to be loved, in spite of everything.

'I did,' Sadokhar said hoarsely, wrenched inside with a hundred memories of friendship before the betrayal. Now only truth, clean and hard, would serve. 'And the reason doesn't matter, except to me. This is about you.'

Tornagrain swung around to face him. 'I thought it was about you getting out so you could fight Armageddon!'

Sadokhar smiled bitterly. 'I can't get out without you – and you can't get out without understanding why you are here.'

There was silence. Nothing moved as far as the eye could see across the endless, grey-white plain.

'I'm here because I betrayed you,' Tornagrain said at last, his voice very quiet, but there was no hesitation in the words.

'And Aelfrith,' Sadokhar added. 'And everyone else who died, or lost anyone.'

Tornagrain did not answer for a long time. It was as if a wound inside him was bleeding.

Sadokhar waited. There was nowhere to go until this was done.

'I know,' Tornagrain said at last. 'I thought you had forgiven me.' He looked at him. 'Was I wrong?'

Sadokhar faced him without blinking. 'No. But forgiveness is not enough.' The words were harsh, but now that it was begun it must be completed or it meant nothing; all the pain was wasted.

'For God's sake, what more is there?' Confusion filled Tornagrain's eyes and face as if hope had given him new power to feel despair all over again.

Sadokhar looked at him steadily. 'Understanding . . . and change. You have to become different, so that even if exactly the same things were to happen to you, you would never do that again, but far more than that, you wouldn't want to!'

Tornagrain stared back at him, eyes narrowed against the glare. Everything in him was pleading for help.

'Did you want to be Earl of the Eastern Shore so much?' Sadokhar said at last.

Tornagrain turned away, looking at the horizon. 'I did at the time,' he admitted quietly.

'And now?' Sadokhar pressed.

'Now I'd give anything to undo it . . . but that isn't enough, is it!' It was not a question. He knew the answer.

'No,' Sadokhar agreed. 'To be sorry is good, it's necessary, but it isn't everything. You must see envy for the ugliness it is. You must let go of all selfishness and come to know without question that everyone else is as precious, as real and as important as you are, as capable of joy and pain.' He sighed. 'Or if they aren't, that's God's judgement to make, not ours.'

Tornagrain said nothing for a long time, but his thoughts were clear in his eyes and lips, and the way he moved his hands in the dust.

'Tell me what has happened in the world since I left it,' he said at last, standing up and stretching, wincing as his muscles cramped.

Sadokhar rose as well and started walking, conscious of his blistered feet and the abrasions on his legs, and glad of the pain. He began to recount all the history he could think of.

'Tell me of these warriors,' Tornagrain pressed. 'Sardriel and Ardesir. Who are they and what are they like? And Kor-Assh – you said he would come also. How will they fight? Tell me about this Tiyo-Mah, and the Lords of Sin.'

Sadokhar told him all he could, digging deeply into himself and uncovering a sense of desolation at his own loneliness for those he had loved more than he knew. It lay naked in his words, and he kept his face ahead as they trudged over the dust and climbed laboriously up slithering scree and rubble, and slid down the far side again.

'What can I do to help?' Tornagrain said when Sadokhar fell silent at last.

Sadokhar looked at him. 'To get out?'

Tornagrain's stare was level. 'No, to help you fight Armageddon. If you can come here to choose the time of it, I can stay, if that's what it takes to do my part.'

Sadokhar stopped abruptly, amazed.

'You would?' he said in disbelief. 'You'd stay here, even if the portal would let you through?' The enormity of such a sacrifice appalled him, and yet the beauty of it scorched away refusal.

'If I have to.' Tornagrain's voice trembled. 'I want to do something to fight for the world, even if I never see it again. I want it to survive, to have resurrection and glory. I'll give anything I have for that.'

Sadokhar looked in his face and believed him. 'You must come back into the world with me,' he answered. 'There's nothing to do here.'

Tornagrain's voice was high-pitched with hope. 'Into the world . . . with you?'

'Yes,' Sadokhar replied, then he looked away, his eyes suddenly swimming with tears. 'Now come on!'

Tornagrain obeyed and they plodded through the clinging dust, leaving a seemingly endless trail of footprints behind them.

'I wouldn't mind if it were sand!' Tornagrain said abruptly. 'I could fool myself that somewhere at the end of all this there was going to be a great, clean ocean with roaring waves, white spume and a wind that sings in the ears. The only noises here are the ones we make. Have you noticed that?'

'There's nothing else alive,' Sadokhar replied. 'Man is the only living thing that can deserve hell.'

Tornagrain shrugged. 'I wonder if we all got together, we could make something decent of it?' He smiled suddenly. 'That'd be a poke in the eye for damnation – wouldn't it? Nothing would grow, but what if we built something beautiful out of the stone? Or even told each other stories? What do you think?'

Sadokhar thought that if they had the will to do that they would not be in hell, but he did not say so. Instead, he entered into the game. 'Stories,' he replied. 'Definitely. You can't wake up and find your work undone. The moment you speak it begins to come alive. Do you remember Aelfrith's stories of his great voyages to the northern seas and the battles?'

'I remember the monsters!' Tornagrain answered with a grin. 'They got bigger and had more legs with every telling!' If the name of Aelfrith caused him any pain it was not in his face, as if his resolve had melted the hurt from it and he could remember the joy. 'I never cared whether they were literal,' he went on. 'The truth of adventure was what mattered.' He plunged into retelling one as they walked, putting in all Aelfrith's heart and imagination, and adding a little of his own.

When he came to the end, Sadokhar began one of his favourites, a wild, roaring battle on the ice of some legendary fjord with glittering peaks against a wan sky and an enemy half man, half beast.

'They ate them!' he finished.

'Cooked?' Tornagrain said in amazement.

'The first time I heard it – yes,' Sadokhar agreed. 'Later they were raw!' And he started to laugh as if they were again in Aelfrith's hall by the fire with the wind and the stars outside, and the sea crashing on the Eastern Shore in the endless music of the earth.

Tornagrain started to laugh as well, and they stopped walking and stood still, a little bent over to catch their breath.

Sadokhar wiped tears and dust off his face and slapped Tornagrain on the shoulder. 'A definite poke in the eye!' he said with profound feeling. 'Come on!'

They continued walking steadily. At one point they were obliged to pass between two vast quarries like craters in the rock where once people had laboured to dig their way out just as futilely as those Sadokhar had passed before. They were so huge the ends were invisible and there was no alternative but to pass on a relatively narrow neck of land between them. It was perhaps fifty yards across, and marked with jagged outcrops and towers.

They were level with one of these when a dozen people, men, women and youths, stepped out from behind and barred their way.

'We mean you no harm,' Sadokhar said civilly. 'Please allow us to pass.'

215

A broad-shouldered woman with a bulging stomach stared at him aggressively, hands on her hips, fingers close to a knife in her belt.

Sadokhar held his hands wide to show that he had no weapon, and Tornagrain beside him did the same. 'We mean you no harm,' he said again. 'Let us pass. We intend to go, let it be without injury to any of us.'

'You threatening us?' the woman asked with surprise and anger, her face twisted, mouth ugly.

Another woman, older, stepped up beside her, and a man came on her heels. A youth rocked back and forth as if to launch himself in an attack.

'This is ridiculous!' Sadokhar said sharply. 'We simply wish to pass. What difference can it make to you if we do or not? We have nothing for you to take, and we want nothing of yours. Stand aside and let us go.'

'Or what?' the youth demanded. 'You'd beat us, stab us? What?'

'Force our way through,' Sadokhar replied, not certain if they had the strength to do that, but meaning to try. Nothing, even of hell, was going to stop him reaching the portal and taking Tornagrain through it. There was no price too high to pay if it would allow them to join the battle of Armageddon.

The woman threw her head back and bellowed with laughter. Then without any warning she pulled the knife out of her belt and launched herself at Sadokhar, arms flailing. The blade was dull in the flat light, but he could see its razor edge very clearly,

He stepped aside and aimed a hard blow at her shoulder, intending to numb her enough so she would drop the knife, but she was too quick. She twisted and fell to one knee, just at the same moment as the youth kicked at Tornagrain and caught him on the shin. The next instant there were half a dozen of them thrashing around in the dust, punching and kicking, gouging, cursing.

Sadokhar did not know how it happened, but one minute he was grappling with the woman, holding her wrist with the knife in her hand, the next her whole body heaved, her wrist turned and she was driving the knife into her own belly.

He was furious with her. He could never have denied the act, but he had not meant to do that! He watched in horror as the flesh tore open, gushing blood. She screamed, a terrible, rending cry, and her unborn child emerged from the ripped womb, struggled to breathe, made one desperate sound, and then died.

Sadokhar was paralysed with horror. What had he done? He had killed not only her, who must have chosen to be here, but her child who could be guilty of nothing!

216

The others stood staring at him, their faces hideous with accusation.

He would have given anything, paid all he possessed to have undone that moment. He looked at the dead child where it lay in the dust and blood of its own birth, its mother half curled around it, her belly gaping open.

'God forgive me!' he whispered, shame consuming him. He was barely aware of the touch of Tornagrain's arm around him.

'Come,' Tornagrain said gently. 'There is nothing for us to do here. We must continue our journey.'

'Look!' Sadokhar said, furious with Tornagrain for not understanding, but overwhelmingly with himself for in one act condemning them both. 'In God's name, can't you see what I've done?'

'Yes, I see it,' Tornagrain replied levelly.

Sadokhar swung round on him in rage. 'Are you going to tell me they are creatures of hell, so it doesn't matter?' he accused, his voice choking almost incoherently.

'No.' Tornagrain faced him, his eyes unflinching. 'Of course it matters, whoever they are. Their sin doesn't alter your act, or the fury that gripped you. Only what you feel now can do that. God judges what you are, but also what you mean to be. If what you said about forgiveness is true for me, and it is, then it has to be true for all men, including you.'

'I didn't mean to do that!' Sadokhar said, still staring at the bodies, his voice shaking. 'I was angry . . . but I didn't know she was with child! I could never have . . . I didn't know she would die! I only wanted to be able to pass!'

'I know.' Tornagrain pulled him to his feet and urged him forward beyond the rest of the group. 'We must go onward. We have things to do, a battle to fight.'

Sadokhar resisted.

'Are you going to let one mistake, however terrible, stop you from going on?' Tornagrain said grimly. 'Where is your courage? Where is your trust?'

Sadokhar was still stunned. 'What?'

Tornagrain stared at him fixedly, daring him to look away, to evade the demand of his eyes. 'I betrayed you, for my own jealousy and ambition. Worse than that, I betrayed the ones you loved . . . and you learned to forgive me. Are you greater than God?'

'Of course not!' Sadokhar said roughly. 'But—'

'But nothing!' Tornagrain cut across him. 'Are you sorry? Sorry to your heart and gut and to your soul?'

'Yes!'

'Then God can forgive you. Now stop standing here and find your courage to go on and fight the war you told me about. There's no time to waste in indulging ourselves. Come on!'

'I must bring the child,' Sadokhar said hoarsely,

'Then I'll help you.' Tornagrain was the first to turn back. It took Sadokhar longer. He could not bear the thought of looking on it again, but he knew he must. He could not leave this place of horror until he had done so.

He lifted his head and stared. The ground was simply dust, no blood, no child, only a small group of angry, sullen men and women, faces filled with inexpressible hatred so deep it twisted their features until they were barely recognisable as having once been human.

Then he understood. They were here because they were what they had chosen to be, seeing the light and the darkness, tasting them and knowing the meaning and the difference. There is neither birth nor death in hell. No child can enter damnation.

He felt Tornagrain's hand on his arm again, a strong grip, firm, not to be denied. 'Come.' His voice was warm, there was friendship in it – but stronger even than that, there was knowledge of himself, and of the presence of God, even here in this place. 'We must find the portal and try it again,' he insisted. 'You and I are forgiven, because we have understood, and chosen the light. But we have work to do, and battles still ahead of us which we must help win. We can't be forgiven for not trying – not when we know, and the weapons are in our hands.'

Wordlessly, but with a sudden lift of the heart, a coursing of blood through his veins, Sadokhar went with him, walking even more rapidly, running a step or two, certain of what was ahead and eager to be there.

The portal looked as it had when he had watched Tiyo-Mah go through it into the world. He hesitated, his mouth dry, his lungs tight.

'Courage!' Tornagrain said, a faint, twisted smile on his mouth, his hands clenched, and only because Sadokhar knew him did he see the fear in him, the terrible, consuming knowledge that he faced Heaven's judgement, and Hell's, and the decision was everything.

'Come!' Sadokhar stepped forward and side by side they went under the shadow of the archway. This time there was a door, heavy, iron-black. Not only had Yaltabaoth taken the key, but the keyhole itself was gone. Sadokhar raised his hand and touched it, then leaned his weight and it swung open. Breathless, shaking, they walked through and across the stone flags, past curved pillars that had guarded the great days of Camassian architecture, and saw ahead of them another door, standing ajar, and beyond it, light.

Sadokhar prayed in his soul that it would be the beautiful, beloved world, and he heard Tornagrain's indrawn gasp beside him.

He pushed it wide and took the last step, afraid to look. He felt the breeze on his skin, cool . . . sweet.

He opened his eyes and saw the ruins of Sylum in the amber and violet of sunset. There was a vine curling over the broken stones, its tendrils biting deep, gold trumpet flowers slender as horns. He stared at the damp soil at the roots and saw a worm slide into the mould, sleek and living in the beautiful earth.

His face was wet with tears as he turned to Tornagrain and saw him come out of the gate and then stop, blinking in the air. He saw Sadokhar and moved forward again. First his hand, then his foot seemed to shimmer as if he had reached some barrier, and as he pressed forward through it his whole body glowed. It was like breaking the surface of a pool, liquid and shimmering.

And then it was gone, and he stood in amazement at himself, at his own flesh, whole and complete. He stretched his hands, breathed in deeply, filling his lungs, and gazed around him. He could taste, touch, hear the far, bright song of birds. The scars on his cheeks were the wounds of the soul – healed at last.

It was the most natural thing, the only thing, to put their arms around each other and hold so tight they were almost bruised.

When they stood back Sadokhar saw Orocyno a dozen yards away, staring at them, his head skull-like, his body so thin he seemed barely to have substance at all. And even as they watched him, the last of the sun shimmered on his robes, the wind fluttered them and they rippled as if silk, and then water, and then no more than a mist with the light on it. And when they looked again he was gone.

There was nothing else, just life, and beauty, passion, and the greatest of all battles to be joined.

Chapter Fourteen

In Camassia the fighting died down. There seemed, at least for the moment, to be a desire for peace. Tentatively at first, trade resumed, people planted and began to repair and to rebuild. But it was uneasy, always teetering on the brink of violence again.

Ulciber was not seen, but Tathea knew better than to imagine he had gone. This was the centre of the world, the heart of the greatest population. He had succeeded brilliantly even if only for a while. He would retreat, but only to regroup before another attack, cleverer and more skilfully planned.

Was the slow, twisting corruption of Tirilis his doing also, aiding the natural subtlety of the Tirilisi? There was only occasional word from Ardesir, and he dared commit little to paper.

And yet Tathea felt an inner peace, almost a radiance, when she thought of Sadokhar. Something inside her had eased. A long battle was over, and she would not have another meeting with him in vision, struggling, sharing his agony. It was as if he were no longer there, and yet he was not dead.

She stood now in the amber light of evening watching Ishrafeli working with a farmer, trying to convince him that the labour was worth it, that he would reap what he sowed, that he should keep faith with the future. She looked at him with an ache of love so deep she was racked with it, because she saw the belief in him that they were tasting the beginning of victory, and it filled her with a loneliness that was almost beyond bearing.

She had tried to warn him. So many times the words were in her mind, but never found her tongue because of the division it would make even deeper between them. Standing by the wall of an old town in the calm of the last light, seeing the arch of heaven unbroken by cloud, the radiance ascending for ever, she knew this was the eye of the hurricane, not the end. Armageddon was not over in this way, and not so easily.

Ishrafeli would not have said it was easy! The dead were countless, not only here but in Shinabar as well. No one knew how many souls had chosen irrevocably the downward path.

But as she watched him now, talking to an old man about his

221

vineyard, she saw the straightness of his back in spite of the long hours he had worked in the heat and dust, and it cut her to the heart that he was going to be so hurt when this did not last.

Asmodeus would strike again. The question was not 'if', only 'where?' and 'how?' Her imagination was crowded with ideas, but she knew the past well enough to be certain he would surprise them. It would come when they were unprepared and vulnerable, wherever they were weak. The waiting was part of the trial.

Ishrafeli concluded his conversation with the old man and walked up the incline towards her. She saw when he was still yards away the guardedness in his face. It was nothing to do with what had been discussed, it was because he feared the darkness in her.

He stopped but did not put out his hand to touch her as he would have done automatically only a short while ago. Now he told her what the man had said, and something of the solution he had offered.

'Good.' Tathea tried to invest her voice with enthusiasm, but he knew her far too well to be deceived.

'What is it?' he demanded, suddenly the raw edge of his hurt naked. She had excluded him, and he did not hide from it any more. 'If you disagree with me, say so!'

'No, of course I don't—' she began.

'Then what? Don't look away from me! Anyone would think you didn't want peace. People are rebuilding, sowing crops again, working with each other.' He gestured towards the vineyard and ploughed earth beyond, furrows shadowed deep in the fading light. 'The civil war is over. Isn't that what you want? Or do you see some glorious victory which we've missed? What is it, Tathea? At least be honest with me.'

What should she tell him? That Asmodeus was far stronger, far cleverer than anything he had yet shown? The war was real, the earth itself was the prize . . . and they could lose!

Did Ishrafeli know that?

She looked at his face in the last of the sun, at the lines etched deep, and the loneliness in him. She ached to hold him in her arms and simply be close, to forget words, true or false, just to be with him in the intimacy of touch.

When the new attack came, he would be so hurt. And there would be nothing she could do to protect him from the grief, the disappointment, the jarring shock to the faith he had now that the worst was over.

She looked at him, and saw the isolation in his face. She had already waited too long to answer. He knew she was concealing knowledge, and that in itself was half a lie.

'Of course I want peace,' she said almost with conviction. 'Peace is the real victory. I don't have to look anywhere else for it. It's here in the rebuilding and replanting.' She stopped. She could see in his eyes that he knew it was not the truth. In that instant he had understood that the war was not over, and that she knew it, and had lied because she wanted to comfort him.

He looked away, but he did not move. He stayed beside her, and she was aware of his emotions as if she held him in her arms. She could do nothing to help either of them.

With disbelief Asmodeus saw Sadokhar and Tornagrain break back through the portal. At first he was too amazed for any other emotion to find room in him. Then as he saw the two men stand together in the light and wonder and vitality of the world, their bodies whole, he was consumed with a rage so violent the dark sweat soaked his skin and his soul burned with a hatred like the corrosion of all matter. The thunder of stars breaking apart in the throes of death was split by the high, thin scream of his fury.

It was Tathea's doing! The power of her love had taken her spirit to Sadokhar even there! Damn her! Damn her to torment inconceivable! He would make her suffer until she begged for oblivion! Until she would deny God to His face, rather than survive another hour of the pain Asmodeus would inflict on her!

She had robbed him of the soul of Tornagrain which should have been his! Had he not already won it fairly in terrible sin, unforgivable? And she had not only taught Sadokhar to forgive him but – infinitely more than that – to change him – to redeem him! She had likened herself to God! Only He could do a thing like that!

But the war was not over yet! God may have won the battle on that other world, in among the olive trees, but this was still Armageddon here, in this world, and it was going well. But he must hasten the ruin of Tathea. The wound like a knife blade in his body would twist and turn inside him every moment until he did.

How? The answer was plain. Her greatest strength was also her profoundest weakness. She loved many people, but most of all, the man Ishrafeli, who had been Asmodeus' enemy since the Great Council in Heaven, and would be until he was finally destroyed, and the earth a smoking ruin to darken the stars.

And Tathea must see every moment of it! She must watch them all die, one by one, Ishrafeli last of all, and then know that it was she who had lost the earth to eternal night, every living and beautiful thing in it gone.

That would be enough! That would satisfy him.

He must turn his attention to Tathea again – now!

He stared across the abyss of darkness at the tiny blue jewel of world. He had gone there once already when Tathea had left the forest. It was too soon to go again. Someone, some man or woman with a vestige of spiritual vision might recognise him, and begin to understand his plan.

Ignorance was still the greatest of his weapons. People did not believe in him: he was no more than a figment of nightmare, an excuse for man's own weakness, something to laugh at, to frighten the superstitious.

Ishrafeli had tasted power, and he liked it! Why not? He was a man, which meant he was just like Asmodeus in all that mattered. They were brothers, as all men were, from before the foundation of the world, cut from the same cloth, born of the same eternal Father. He had but to look in His own heart to understand them all! There might be a coating, an outer shell of compassion or belief in an eternal good, but crack it even a little, and underneath there was the same love of power, the hunger to control, to feel that elemental thrill of dominion and know yourself invulnerable.

Ishrafeli was obeyed, needed, admired. And so far Tathea was happy enough to see him taste and roll it over his tongue. But the time would come when she would like it less. Let him begin to become arrogant with it and in time he would corrupt her also. But if not . . . better still. If her old wisdom, the facts she had learned over all the years, were strong enough for her to see his error and be disillusioned in him, it would destroy her. She would not bear it.

If Ishrafeli fell, be it ever so slowly, then there was no heaven for Tathea to hope for. She was still human, and the need for love was beginning to undo her. Because he was there, warm in the heart and the flesh, with his passion and his need, his laughter, his courage, his pity, his urgency of life, in the end when she had to choose, she would love him more than she loved God.

The dark mists swirled around Asmodeus, gaining and losing shape, forever missing true form, as he himself would never have a body of flesh.

The plan was working. Tathea had lied to Ishrafeli, denied the truth she knew rather than lose some part of the closeness to him by telling him what she believed he was not ready to understand. And in doing it she had opened a gulf between them that would be the beginning of death for her.

But there were other things to be done before the final victory. Sardriel and Ardesir must be destroyed. Apart from their closeness to Tathea, they were dangerous in themselves, and deserving of punishment. They had defied him, Ardesir with his arrogance, his persistence in spite of fear, his belief, always his belief. And Sardriel, complacent, reason-loving Sardriel, who imagined the truth would preserve him, who thought he had already endured the ultimate loss and it had somehow made him invulnerable.

Well, he would learn differently! He had still to taste the pain of real failure, far deeper than some savagery on the steppes of Irria-Kand. He would learn the bitter knowledge that he had betrayed not only those he loved but himself, his own inner purity of soul. Then let him speak of pain, and he would know what it meant!

He could deal with Sadokhar later. Tornagrain hardly mattered. What was he but a soul already damned, only escaped hell by some mischance which would have to be put right? After the final victory all the world would be hell!

Asmodeus clenched his fist and punched it into the air. Far below him the darkness spiralled downwards with a new violence, dissolving half-shapes and erupting into others, only to lose them again.

The plan was already forming in his mind, details becoming clearer every second. Tathea's heart would break, her soul would surrender at last, a ruined thing he could hold in his grasp for ever.

For Sardriel he would use Azrub. Asmodeus' lip curled at the thought of the golden dwarf with his disgusting appetites, the lewd gleam in his yellow, goat-eyes. But he had skills that were necessary, and much as Asmodeus hated satisfying anything in him, there was no other way.

He raised his voice across the yawning spaces and summoned him.

Azrub stood shimmering just in front of the parapet beyond which lay chaos. The cold light played on the diamond panes of his sleeves and his white hands fluttered. He looked eager, and only very slightly afraid. Not enough . . . damn him! But then he was damned! He would never have a body either, which was why the filth in his soul fed on the lusts and dreams of others – and would do so for eternity.

'I have work for you,' Asmodeus said abruptly.

Azrub inclined his big head. 'Of course.' He oozed satisfaction. He licked his lips and there was a sheen of sweat on his skin.

Asmodeus decided to torment him a while. 'In the Lost Lands,' he said, watching Azrub's face.

'The Lost Lands?' Azrub was surprised. 'What for?'

'To delude them, fool!' Asmodeus snapped. 'What do you think I want you to do, frighten them out of their wits? You wouldn't know how!'

Azrub's heavy eyelids half closed. 'Delude them into what?'

'Do you need me to tell you?' Asmodeus said with mock disgust. 'I thought you could read the secret longings of everyone? Isn't that how you create for them the illusion of what they want?'

'And what do you want?' Azrub asked.

Asmodeus suspected sarcasm; worse than that, insolence. But he would bide his time for revenge.

'Sardriel is Lord of the Lost Lands,' he said with exaggerated patience, as if Azrub were a fool. 'I want the Lost Lands in your grasp, deluded, weakened for invasion by Siriom of Kyeelan-Iss. His greedy soul lusts after their wealth. It always has. Make them ripe for his plucking.'

'You want Siriom's soul?' Azrub asked.

'I already have it, imbecile!' Asmodeus shouted at him. 'I want Sardriel! If his own lands are invaded he will go to them! Then you can have him. When he is separated from Tathea and Ishrafeli, you can enter his heart and read the loneliness there, and then weave a delusion that he will choose above all reality. Then I will have him! Sardriel, the lord of the pure truth . . . pledged to a delusion!'

'I see.' Azrub shifted his immense weight from one foot to the other in his excitement. 'I see!' Sardriel was sweet prey indeed – perhaps the ultimate conquest.

'No, you don't!' Asmodeus glared at him, his face dark with loathing and contempt. 'You see nothing! If Sardriel chooses delusion over reality, then I can take the Island at the Edge of the World! And I can make Tathea watch it! When that falls, then the whole earth will be devastated, a ruin like the dust of hell. She will believe God Himself has abandoned it – and that will finally bring her to her knees before me.'

'I'll do it!' Azrub said softly, licking his lips again. 'I'll do it!'

'Of course you'll do it!' Asmodeus swore. 'Not because you want to, or because you understand. You'll do it because I tell you to!'

But Azrub was smiling as he bowed, and hurried away without asking leave. He knew Asmodeus' heart as Asmodeus knew his, and he understood the craving that devours from the inside.

When he had disappeared, Asmodeus stood on the shadowed battlements of Erebus and stared at the emptiness above him, then at the whirling and dissolving darkness around, the roaring of dissolution and the changing shapes of chaos. He thought of the bright, endless worlds beyond, glory upon glory, where even the tiniest beasts that fly and swim and know nothing but the few inches around them yet had bodies, substance, and were perfect in their own measure. And he gave way to a rage that howled and thrashed and bit the air till the ramparts shook and the void yawned beneath and the broken fragments of matter shivered into tinier pieces and fled into the night.

And it changed not a single fact. When at last he picked himself up, everything was exactly as before, except he hated himself even more profoundly, and hated Tathea with a bitterness unto death.

But he knew of another ancient, undying hate, and he knew how he would use it. He sent for Cassiodorus, Lord of Terror.

He did not come bright with glittering arms like Azrub, but walked the full length of the battlements, slowly, as if he were on parade, his cloak swinging behind him, the dead light on his thick, curly hair and his broad, arrogant face with its brutal mouth. He stopped in front of Asmodeus, just short of insolence. There was no servility in him, no submission, but even he could not forget who was master.

'You have work for me?' he said quietly.

'Of course,' Asmodeus said acidly. 'Did you think I wanted your advice?'

'It is yours, if you do.' Cassiodorus lifted his brows very slightly; again it was almost insolence, but not quite.

'I don't!' Asmodeus snapped. 'I require your obedience. You chose to follow Tiyo-Mah through the portal and begin Armageddon . . .'

Cassiodorus flinched, just a tiny movement of a muscle in his cheek, but Asmodeus saw it and it satisfied him.

'. . . so you will earn your place in our victory,' he finished.

'How? What do you want me to do?' Now there was definitely obedience.

Asmodeus smiled. 'Shortly the barbarians will attack Camassia again, far more powerfully. There will be fear across the country like fire over dry grass. They will look to a greater leader for their armies.'

Cassiodorus sighed with the pleasure of anticipation. It was in the brightness of his eyes, the slight flexing of his shoulders. 'You want me to lead the barbarians?' he asked.

'The Camassians, fool!' Asmodeus grated between his teeth. 'I want them taught to become more barbaric than their enemies. I want them to believe that any act whatever, no matter how bestial, is justified in the fight for survival. I want them to descend below the savages until they have become subhuman, with no way back to sanity or the ordinary decencies of life – not ever!'

Cassiodorus breathed out very slowly. There was admiration in his face, and something almost like respect. 'Good,' he said in a whisper. 'Very good. But it is not my usual way.'

'Then change!' Asmodeus retorted, half turning away, as if their business were concluded.

It scalded Cassiodorus' pride. If Asmodeus needed him, let him pay for it! 'Why?' he asked.

Asmodeus whirled around, eyes blazing. 'Because I tell you to!'

Cassiodorus had every intention of obeying. He relished the prospect of so much slaughter, battlefields of it, blood and terror everywhere. But he would exact a price, all the same. 'Then give me something in return,' he said insolently.

227

Asmodeus took a step towards him, his face beautiful in form and hideous of expression. 'You have the pleasure of satisfying your appetite,' he hissed. 'That is what you live for. Do you imagine I don't know you? I can see every violent and obscene thought within you, every titillating joy as someone else cowers in terror. I know you as I know my own heart!'

Cassiodorus felt violated by those clever, intrusive eyes, as if his being had been stripped naked for all to see. Rage boiled up inside him and spewed forth.

'Of course you do!' he yelled, choking on his own tongue. 'Because you are the same! Only you can't go to the earth yet, in case you are recognised. There are thousands of good souls there still. It's too soon for you. But I can!'

An equal fury exploded in Asmodeus. This rebellion was intolerable. He hurled the power of his rage in black violence, but it bounced off Cassiodorus as if his shining hunger for fear were an armour, and he threw back his head and laughed, a long, shattering sound high in his throat, like the bray of an animal, as primal as blood lust.

Asmodeus roared back at him, drowning him in sound like the breaking of rocks as continents collided.

Cassiodorus was touched for an instant by fear himself, but he knew his usefulness. Asmodeus might destroy him one day, but not yet! 'I want Tathea!' he screamed back. 'She beat me in Parfyrion – in front of the court. Let me have her now!'

'She's mine!' Asmodeus said, his voice cold and dark.

'I don't want to kill her, just let me cause her pain!' Cassiodorus pleaded.

'If you kill her, I'll banish you to live among the dead, who know no fear!' Asmodeus swore. 'You'll starve . . . slowly!'

'I won't kill her! Just make her wish I had!' Cassiodorus swore, his face pale, his fists clenched. 'Give me that, and I'll make the Camassian army murder every living thing. They'll tear the barbarians limb from limb, rape their women and eat their children.' He was shaking with excitement, his bold eyes shining, his lips parted.

Asmodeus looked at him and his gorge rose in disgust.

'Then don't stand here talking about it! Get out!' he ordered. 'Get out!'

He watched as Cassiodorus hesitated only a moment, then turned and obeyed. He walked jauntily, going the full length of the battlement before he disappeared, swallowed in the clouds of dust.

Asmodeus hated him because his rage reminded him of his own: savage, uncontrolled, consuming. He wanted him gone.

★　★　★

Ishrafeli was wretched, but there was nothing he could do to bridge the gulf between himself and Tathea. The ache inside him seemed to touch every part of his being. It took all the mental strength he possessed to control his thoughts and direct them towards any sort of useful act. She had lied to him. He knew exactly why; he understood perfectly. She wanted to protect him from pain she feared he could not bear. She was afraid he might not endure it, that he might fail. But she had not only thought it of him, she had denied the best in herself, that white fire of integrity within her soul, and the burden that lay between them.

It was evening, and he was sitting in the garden room with her, talking a little stiltedly over the events of the day – small things, details achieved or to be attended to. A breeze rustled the leaves of the lemon trees and whispered in the grass. Sunlight slanted across the floor and made bright globes of the ripe apricots in the bowl on the table.

There was a knock on the door and Ishrafeli stood to answer it. He pulled it ajar, then wide, shock and delight sweeping over him. Sadokhar stood in the entrance. It had been over two years since Ishrafeli had seen him in Lantrif, but he looked far older than he had then. There were pale streaks in his hair, but it was in his face that his age showed most: the lines cut deep from nose to mouth, the sensitivity of his lips, the slow pain and wisdom in his eyes.

Wordless with emotion Ishrafeli threw his arms around him and they clasped each other. Then Sadokhar broke free and as he came into the room Tathea stared at him in such wonder and joy she could barely speak his name.

'Sadokhar,' she whispered. Slowly at first, she took a step towards him, then another, then clung to him with all her strength, and he to her, as if even here in the City, freed from hell and enfolded in life again, he needed to hold her with all his strength.

Perhaps he was remembering. From his face, the tenderness in it that shone like the last, aching light of the sun across the sky, the thoughts in him needed no words.

Then Ishrafeli realised with a start that another had followed Sadokhar in. He was utterly different. He was not quite so tall, and leaner of build. He stood with a certain grace, but it was his face that arrested the attention. It was lean-boned, his eyes were wide and dark grey, his nose broad at the bridge and strong, his mouth scarred beneath the lower lip. There was strength in his face, for good or ill, and immense passion, hunger for all manner of things. And yet there were other wounds also, as if he had endured suffering beyond description. His dark hair was blasted with white.

He hesitated, uncertain how he would be received, his eyes on Tathea, barely noticing Ishrafeli.

This must be Tornagrain, who had betrayed Sadokhar in his youth on the Eastern Shore. Tathea had spoken of it to Ishrafeli in whispered words in the closeness of the night, and told him that Sadokhar could leave hell only with Tornagrain beside him.

No wonder Tornagrain hesitated now. What uncertainty, what guilt must hold him? Ishrafeli stared at him in wonder, and then an incredible awe grew inside him. He was looking at the face of a man who had been redeemed from hell and returned to the earth to walk again in a mortal body, a man who had drunk the fullness of the grace of God.

He heard Tathea speak. Sadokhar stood aside and Tornagrain walked forward.

Tathea looked steadily at Tornagrain, then she held out her hands to him. Ishrafeli saw the tears wet on his cheeks, and that he could think of no words to say.

He wanted to look at Tathea himself, honestly, with all the old intimacy. In looking at Tornagrain's face he had understood both the darkness and the light in a new way, and he ached to share it with her, as he would have anything that mattered, good or ill. But they had both built the gulf now, her lie, his failure to understand the path of Armageddon and the power of Asmodeus.

He smiled, and looked not quite at her. He welcomed Sadokhar and Tornagrain and offered them food, then listened to all they had to say, hearing the urgency in their voices, the passion and hunger to join the battle that filled their words and every line of their physical presence. They sat in the room with its warm, earth-toned walls, the small table with terracotta dishes filled with slices of cheese and rough bread, fingers caressing the textures as if they would never tire.

'Did you come out through Sylum?' Tathea asked eagerly.

Ishrafeli was not jealous of her love for Sadokhar – he understood it too well for what it was – but the ache of his own loneliness became greater. He loved her with an intensity, a wholeness that threatened to drive from his mind even the passionate good he sought, and had dedicated himself to fight for. The room seemed oddly distant, and Sadokhar's answer to come from far away.

'Yes,' he nodded slightly. 'And Orocyno was still there, but I think he passed into nothingness as we used the portal. It had weakened him until finally he faded away altogether.' He leaned forward towards her. 'There are things of the Island I think you need to know. We went to Tyrn Vawr, of course, but secretly, to speak with Ythiel and the other Knights of the Western Shore, and saw much that concerns us. Perhaps because it has happened slowly we noticed the changes more than they.'

'What changes?' she said quickly.

Sadokhar turned to Ishrafeli, startling him. 'The Silver Lords are stronger in Lantrif since you left. I heard them spoken of with a respect I had never observed before.'

Ishrafeli felt a chill, as if someone had opened a door into a winter night, and yet nothing had changed except that the wind was rising a little and the light fading. But he remembered the night in the forest when Karguish and the four other Silver Lords had asked him to become the sixth and complete their power. He knew now that they had found the last man and the circle was made whole. They had dredged in the secret places and reformed the ancient secrets of the earth and air, and again were using them to bind rather than to free, to get and not to give.

He rose and lit the candles, aware that Sadokhar was looking at him with anxiety, and perhaps the beginning of understanding.

'And in the south Siriom is building armies in Kyeelan-Iss,' Sadokhar went on. 'More than he can need for any threat against him or his people. Mile by mile he is spreading his boundaries and, more worrying than that, he is bribing mariners to bring Lost Landers to Kyeelan-Iss, those who could sail the Maelstrom and take others back through it to Orimiasse.' He had no need to explain his fear. Siriom had long hated Sardriel and all to do with his kingdom and his people. He did not know the reason why, but it lay in some rivalry bitter and deep.

Ishrafeli asked him more, and the four of them talked long into the night. Sadokhar was full of questions about the war in the City and how peace had come, and what had happened to Ulciber and the Lords of the Undead.

'We don't know,' Ishrafeli confessed. 'No one has seen Ulciber in months, but that doesn't mean he is not here, waiting. No one has seen Balour either.'

'But he is not gone,' Tathea said quickly, glancing at Ishrafeli, and away again, her face suddenly tight and a little pale. 'He too will be waiting for another chance. The Lords of the Undead can't be destroyed.'

'Yes, I think they can!' Sadokhar looked from one to the other of them. 'I fought one of them in . . . in hell.' He said the word with hesitation, and there was a pallor to his skin as he did so, almost a greyness.

Ishrafeli saw Tathea wince and her body recoil as if she had been stricken with a pain deep inside herself. He reached out his hand towards her, then at the last moment withdrew it again, remembering the distance between them, and the pain was as deep within him.

'I defeated him,' Sadokhar continued, staring into a distance only he could see. 'The Lords of the Undead are legion souls inside one body, trapped together. They can be made to fight one

231

another, and tear themselves apart.' His eyes were hollow, almost blind to the soft room around him in the candlelight. 'Ozmander dismembered himself in front of me.'

'They can die?' Tathea said with disbelief.

'No . . .' He did not meet her eyes. 'No . . . he was still alive.'

She reached across and touched his hand, asking nothing more.

Sadokhar looked up. 'We can fight them! We must. Not only for ourselves, but perhaps for them also. Free the best in them from the worst . . . a chance for each to choose for himself again, perhaps better this time.'

Tathea nodded.

Tornagrain had not spoken yet but his eyes had followed every word and his agreement was not only in his face but in the angles of his body, the stillness of him and attention to every word. Now he was looking at Tathea, and his gaze fell beyond her to the staff, only dimly discernible propped against the wall in the corner.

It was Sadokhar who realised what he was seeing, and rose to his feet. In trembling hands he carried it back and offered it to Tornagrain. 'Can you read what it says?' he asked, his voice suddenly caught in his throat.

There was total silence in the room. Even the wind outside had dropped. The candle flames burned straight as lances.

Tornagrain took the staff and turned it slowly. 'Only one line,' he said, looking at Sadokhar, then at Tathea. ' "When the man of hope forges a sword from the dust of hell".' He stopped abruptly, seeing the light in her face, a joy and amazement as if she had seen a vision invisible to him.

She reached out and put her hands over his on the staff, and her touch was warm and surprisingly strong. 'Welcome!' she said fervently. 'Welcome at last!'

Sadokhar was beaming. 'I should have known!' he said, clapping Tornagrain on the shoulder so hard in his enthusiasm he almost bruised him. Ishrafeli held out both his hands to Tornagrain and clasped his wrists warmly, then slid his hands until they were on the staff beside Tathea's.

In a quiet voice Ishrafeli read the staff: ' "When the man of courage enters and leaves where I am not: when the man of faith embraces terror to himself: when the man of truth hungers for a lie, and casts it to the deep: when the man of wisdom has spoken the name of all things: when the man of hope forges a sword from the dust of hell: when the woman of love has kneeled in the ashes and taken up My burden, then shall I come and receive My own.'

The candle burned up, filling the room with radiance, and a brightness of certainty descended upon them.

★ ★ ★

Within days of Sadokhar's return, Sardriel also arrived in the City. He was leaner than when he had left the Island, his face burned by sun and wind, a weariness in his eyes. There was no air of victory in him, rather a silent and deep understanding of loss, as if he had had many months of solitude in which to learn every corner of its nature, and how to bear it.

But when he saw Sadokhar he came as close to losing his immaculate composure as anyone had ever seen. The emotion radiated in his face and his rare smile was beautiful to see. He wanted to know everything that Sadokhar had experienced, and only afterwards did he tell them of his march through the forests and over the plains, and Almerid's betrayal, then his own long journey back.

No one questioned him or spoke about the judgements of the losses. The knowledge of them in his face was more profound than anything they could have said. It would have been insulting even to try to share the feelings locked within him.

Ardesir came only a few days later, bringing news of Tirilis and of Shinabar. He arrived in the evening, having walked up from the dockside carrying only a small, leather satchel, his sandals slapping on the warm stones of the floor. He found them sitting together on the steps by the lemon trees.

'Ardesir!' Tathea rose immediately, her face alight with pleasure at seeing him. The others stood also eager to welcome him, to offer food, a chair to sit in, and above all to tell him of Tornagrain, the sixth warrior, even before they asked for news.

'The bankers of Tirilis have lent money for trade all over the north,' he replied at last, when they allowed him to speak. 'For their own ends, of course. But I heard nothing of any of the Lords of Sin or of the Undead. However, I think Ulciber may have been there before I was. The marks of his skill are bedded deep.'

No one interrupted, but he saw their agreement in their faces.

'Tiyo-Mah has gone from Shinabar!' he added jubilantly, his face alight with victory. 'No one knows where she is, but not in any of the great cities. The civil war was terrible, and the peace is still uneasy . . . but it is growing!' A radiant hope lit his thin face. 'Perhaps we are winning after all!'

Tathea looked at him with a deep and spreading pain. In spite of the weariness around his eyes and the hollow of his cheeks, there was a youth inside him, a kind of innocence. In fact as she looked at those she loved here in this quiet, familiar room with its ancient colour so reminiscent of long ago, she felt a terrible separation from all of them. This was not victory, and she alone knew it. Armageddon does not end in peace in the mortal world.

How could she tell them?

She was here, warm, comfortable, physically safe, and with those she loved most in all the aeons of her life . . . and she had never felt more isolated.

What if this were hell: immortal loneliness, each alive, but with a glass wall between them, seeing but never touching, hearing the words but never the heart?

Or what if the war were over after all? Not won – but lost? And it continued for ever, growing a little less bright every day, until one calm evening like this, the realisation came that they were damned, there was no resurrection. It was all just a slow fading that never ended!

They were talking together, of the Island, of Lantrif again. Without making a conscious decision she stood up, murmuring some excuse, and left the room. She needed solitude; the enormity of the night was hardly large enough to hold the tumult inside her. She went to the door and down the steps, through the lemon trees, glad of the shelter of the cypresses beyond. Here no one could see her even if they were to go to the window and look.

She stared upward at the pinpricks of the stars. Those were the worlds beyond worlds, filled with the creations of God – unreachable, except by the will, the hunger, and the pure courage of the spirit.

She could not do it alone. The weight of the darkness was crushing. Without the deep, passionate, gentle touch of another soul there was no strength to continue, no will to draw on, nor prize to win.

The journey had been too long and she had no glimpse of the end, only hope.

There were six of them now, and yet deeply and unendingly as she loved them, in her understanding she was as alone as a mother with small children who could not know the enormity of the power of the evil they faced.

Then as she stood in the silence except for the wind in the trees, an old promise came back to her mind, as clear as a voice speaking. 'Your name is before My eyes, and I shall not forget you, nor shall I leave you alone!'

Her heart overflowed and the cry was torn from her soul: 'Father – help me!'

The stars wheeled in silent glory. The wind stilled in the branches. A certainty filled her, and slowly she walked up through the lemon trees across the patch of moonlight towards the steps and back into the house. She went straight to the bedroom and waited for Ishrafeli.

She had no idea how long it was, but eventually he came, closing the door softly behind him. Then, seeing her, he stopped.

She stood up and walked over to him, but did not touch him. She must be honest; there must be no pressure of physical intimacy. She looked into his face.

'This has to stop,' she began. Her voice was level, but caught a little emotion. 'I love you more than anything else, except God Himself, and I will not let this distance lie between us.'

He did not move. She could see the pulse beating in his throat. The silence seemed almost to roar in the room before he answered. She felt her heart pounding.

'How are you going to cross the distance?' he asked.

It was as if he had struck her. She could scarcely believe it. But she did not look away. This was the moment of testing.

'I am not.' She almost choked on the words. It was win – or lose – everything on earth that mattered to her . . . and what was even heaven without him? 'You are,' she said. 'This is not the end of Armageddon, it is only the middle, the eye of the storm, the false peace before the greater part, which is still to come. The world is neither won nor lost yet. We must wait, keep our courage and prepare ourselves. I wish it were not so.' She gulped, the pain inside devouring her. 'At least part of me does, the small, childish, human part. The better part knows that whatever God's plan is, it is as it should be – as it must be. I have loved you since the journey before life, but I cannot deny the truth for you. We must face it . . . because it is.'

Something inside Ishrafeli lit with a joy that burned like the light of stars. 'Why did you wait so long to say that?' he asked, his voice scarcely more than a whisper. 'Did you think I was afraid? I am . . . but not so afraid that I can't face it.'

The tears filled her eyes and spilled over. 'I'm sorry!' She had judged him wrongly, weighed him short. Perhaps it sprang from love, her desperate hunger to protect him, but it was still a wrong she had done him.

He smiled, wry, half-humorous, but his eyes too swam with tears.

'Then I suppose I shall forgive you.' He leaned forward and kissed her long and deep, and then again, and again, as if he would never let her go.

The chasm beneath Erebus roared and spewed out the ruin and rubble of worlds high into the air to blot out the last vestige of light.

Asmodeus stood on the parapet as it shattered and regained its form, and cursed in the bitterness of his soul. He would destroy both Tathea and Ishrafeli one day. He was not finished – far from it! This was merely the end of the first wave, a time to cosset them into blindness, a laying aside of weapons so that when it began again it would be even harder to bear.

He was glad he had given Cassiodorus leave to hurt her. He did not know how he intended to do it, but as long as it left her alive so she could taste to the last dregs of the wasting of the earth and feel every moment of pain, he did not care.

Then an idea came to him in the thick darkness of the air. He would use Cassiodorus, Lord of Terror, to destroy Ardesir. He was the perfect tool. Ardesir was clever, resourceful, he never gave up or gave in, but he knew fear. He understood it deep into his bones. And he loved Tathea; it was a friendship that meant more to him than any other. He saw in her a light that shone in no one else.

Yes. It would work very well. There were a score of ways of doing it . . . it would be simple. All it needed was to give the order. He could compel Cassiodorus to obey. That in itself would be satisfying.

And after Cassiodorus' spreading of blood and terror, the bestiality of total war over the earth, there would be enough despair that Yaltabaoth could come at last. He was the last and the strongest of the Lords of Sin, but he was also the one who could touch Asmodeus himself.

A twinge stabbed him somewhere deep inside. He could not afford ever to doubt his own final victory. This world was his! It was his right, which God had threatened to take from him. That was what this eternal war was about. Despair was his one vulnerability. If he granted the possibility of defeat it could be the beginning of it becoming a reality.

Yaltabaoth did not believe he would win, because despair was the core of his nature. And for that Asmodeus hated him even more than he hated God.

Again the chasm churned and erupted torrents of gas, stones and consuming darkness, shrouding the sky and blackening the stars.

Chapter Fifteen

It was the middle of the day and Tathea was stooping at the fountain to wash her face in the cool water when the first messenger came. He was a stocky man riding a grey horse, with sweat on its flanks as he pulled it to a halt. The words came gasping from his mouth.

'There are riders in from the north, and from the forests right up to the snow line in the west,' he said breathlessly, swinging his leg over the saddle and dismounting. 'And as far as Irria-Kand to the east! The barbarians have attacked! Tens of thousands of them, maybe hundreds of thousands!' He swung his arm wide, his body shaking. 'Whole towns have been swept away as if they'd never existed. There's nothing there now but ruins. You can smell the stench of burning from miles away. God knows how many there are of them. They're everywhere.'

Tathea looked at Ishrafeli sitting on the stones in the dappled shade, a plum in his hand. He rose to his feet and walked over to the rider. His face was pale and full of pain, but there was no doubt in his eyes.

'Thank you for bringing us the news,' he said to the man. 'Rest yourself and your animal, then go home, do what you need to. Make your peace with God.' He offered the plum, but the man scarcely saw it. Instead he simply remounted, awkwardly as if his limbs were stiff, and rode away.

'Is this what it will be?' Ishrafeli asked when they were alone again, his voice rough-edged with horror.

It was a question. He was watching her, looking for some kind of answer.

'It's not . . . not the real attack,' she fumbled towards the truth, trying to see it for herself as well as to console him. 'Killing us all does not serve Asmodeus' purpose.'

'Doesn't it?' he frowned. 'One by one, with pain and terror?' His face tightened. 'Reduce us until we deny God?'

She said nothing. The quiet peace of the courtyard with its carved stone seats, the bright water spilling over into the green bowl – it was like a dream from which they would awaken so

237

desperately soon, the last shreds before reality tore it away.

'Isn't that kind of fear his weapon?' he asked. 'What will we do when we have to face these barbarians – uncounted thousands of them? Isn't that when we will betray ourselves?'

Tathea searched his face. Had he meant to include themselves in the destruction that he could see ahead? She saw in his eyes the knowledge of the weakness, the pain, the courage and the dissolution to come, and it sickened her with fear. She searched frantically for anything at all, any way to avoid it, escape the loss, the exhaustion, the overpowering darkness ahead. And she knew there was none. The light lay beyond it, and there was no other path.

'I don't know.' She kept her gaze on his. 'But it isn't what Asmodeus does that destroys us, it never is; it is what we do because of it. I suppose that's the best and the worst of it. In the end, we will always know that we could have won.'

He touched her gently, the tips of his fingers on her cheek. 'We will . . . not all of us, but some of us . . . enough to count.'

Days after that, news came in from Irria-Kand as well. The barbarians were pouring across the plains, pressing south as well as west, and had taken every city right from the edges of the Caevan forest to the borders of Camassia itself. The survivors of their ferocity huddled in their thousands in makeshift camps across the vast, wind-torn plains, and the first snows would kill heaven knew how many of them. The barbarians roamed in armies on horseback, ten thousand strong, looting and burning what little was left.

And word came across the sea from Shinabar that the desert cities had been attacked and pillaged, every man, woman and child put to the sword. It was total war on every side. People wandered in the streets of the City in the Centre of the World as if struggling to waken from a nightmare. They spoke to each other saying the same things over and over again: it could not be true! There must be something else, some other explanation. This was too much to bear.

But the days of disbelief were short. Suddenly Balour reappeared in the palace, calm and filled with a certainty that curbed the rising panic. He woke the people out of their daze of denial and gave them a sense of purpose. He directed their anger into something that looked like hope.

Every able-bodied man, no matter how old or how young, or what his profession, was drafted into the army. The entire populace must devote themselves to the war. The very survival of the world was at stake. No price whatever was too high to pay, because if they lost, then all the art, the science, and the culture of humanity would be swept away. Mankind would be plunged into an age of moral and intellectual oblivion. Millennia of beauty and accumulated learning would be swept away as if they had never existed.

Every day more people answered his call, at first hundreds, then thousands. By the end of a week there was barely a single voice which did not respond.

In Shinabar Tiyo-Mah reappeared from the desert oases with the same rallying cry to unite all the people to save themselves from the blood and terror which threatened to obliterate them and all their works as if they had never existed. She had with her Mabeluz, who had stood beside her in her earlier power, and other Lords of the Undead, Accolon and Indeg.

'Our people have been massacred!' she was reported to have said. 'They are part of us, as we are of them! We will be revenged!'

And she was answered overwhelmingly. Support poured in from every side, men, money, labour, above all unquestioning obedience.

A young Shinabari brought the latest news to Tathea, Ishrafeli and the others as they sat late in the quiet room beside the lemon trees, planning what next to do. It was to Ardesir he spoke, simply because he knew him.

'The Isarch is nowhere to be seen,' he said breathlessly. 'Tiyo-Mah has three new generals, and they are like no one you have ever seen.' His face became even paler and the fear was printed on it so deeply it was as if another presence had entered the room. How could they be worse than the Lords of the Undead?

'Describe them!' Sadokhar ordered.

The messenger looked to Ardesir.

Ardesir nodded, but stiffly, presentiment telling him what was to come.

The messenger gulped air. 'One is big, with tight curly hair and a face that is handsome in its own way, I suppose, and yet there is something in him which frightens me more than all the ugliness in the world.' He shivered although the room was warm. 'I feel foolish standing here telling you, but there is a brutality within his eyes and his smile, which makes me wish I had never seen him. I dream he is looking at me, and I waken trying to scream, but my throat is closed.' He stared at them helplessly, willing them to understand and not despise him.

Tathea knew exactly how he felt. Her dreams too had been haunted by him.

'Cassiodorus,' she said gently. 'You are right to feel as you do. Don't blame yourself. You would be foolish not to. Who else? A dwarf with yellow eyes like a goat, and white hands which are never still?'

The messenger's face was sheened in sweat. 'No . . . no one like that.' He was trembling a little. His face was pinched and white.

'Another soldier, almost beautiful, fair-skinned and tall. He moves with grace and there is nothing brutal about him. He speaks softly, and no one has ever known him raise his hand against anyone. I don't know why he is a general at all – he is far more like a courtier. He frightens me only because Tiyo-Mah listens to him all the time, and those I thought to be good men become evil in his presence.'

'Ulciber,' she answered him. 'You are right. He cannot act for himself, but he corrupts others. Who else? You said three. If it is not the golden dwarf, then who is it?' She asked because although she believed it must be Yaltabaoth, she had not thought there was yet enough despair in the world for him to do his work. Perhaps it was a measure of the scale of destruction in the desert that he had now appeared.

The messenger shook his head. 'I haven't seen him, I've only heard. He is leading the armies south already. They say he is lean and dark with black hair that is ragged like something torn or unravelled, and that he wears black and his face is like the end of all hope.' He shook his head, embarrassed for his words but unable to take them back.

'You speak accurately,' Tathea assured him. She had not seen Yaltabaoth since that terrible battle on the Western Shore, but she had never lost from her mind the sight of him, or the sound of his war cry on the wind. She looked at Sadokhar, who had seen him enter the portal. The others knew nothing of his nature except what was printed on his countenance, but they also made no mockery of the messenger's words, and she saw the flicker of gratitude in the young man's eyes.

After he had gone, they turned to her. It was Sadokhar who spoke. 'Where is Azrub? Is it possible he is there, but no one saw him?'

'Can it be that he has no part in war?' Ishrafeli asked, frowning. 'But what is Ulciber doing there? He is the Lord of Corruption – what is there left to corrupt in Tiyo-Mah?'

'He won't corrupt her,' Tathea replied. 'He will advise her how to corrupt others. She is brilliant, but he is better than any mortal could imagine.'

Sardriel frowned, his face tense. 'But where is Azrub?' he persisted. 'If he is not in Shinabar, then he is somewhere else. Would Asmodeus concentrate all his forces in one place?'

Ishrafeli's eyes were dark, his mouth tight. 'No. Shinabar alone would never be enough for him. He hungers for the whole world. Irria-Kand has already fallen to the barbarians. Perhaps in their place on the eastern rim, they were bound to be the first. Shinabar may be next, or it may be Camassia. But one of the Lords of Sin will be sent here, surely? Ceava is mostly forest, and individual

240

settlements. He may bother with them, or he may simply allow them to be separated off, and wither away. We knew Tirilis has long been his.'

He looked directly at Tathea. 'I know Iszamber prophesied long ago that the Island at the Edge of the World would stand after all the other nations had fallen, because of the light of faith, but Asmodeus will have heard the prophecy too . . .'

She nodded. 'I know. He won't let us be. Of course he won't. It is possible that is where Azrub is . . .' It hurt even to say the words aloud that he should set his strange, impossibly heavy feet on the soil of the land she had loved so dearly. The Island, in its wild, sea-swept beauty, would be the ultimate prize, because it had nurtured the truth.

For a long moment silence held the room, then Ishrafeli spoke.

'They will not remain together for long. At least one of them will come here. Perhaps Ulciber again? This is the beginning of the end. Asmodeus is grasping the whole earth. We must do what we can to defend it all.' He hesitated before he said the words, even though by now they all knew what they must be. 'We also cannot remain together.'

'Someone must go to Shinabar,' Sadokhar said softly. 'Tornagrain and I will. We are used to war, and to the creatures of hell. We are best suited to face the Lords of the Undead.'

Ishrafeli glanced from one to the other of them. 'Agreed,' he said with a slight inclination of his head. He looked to Sardriel.

'I will search for Azrub,' Sardriel answered. 'I will begin westward. There is nothing left to the east for them to destroy.' His voice was level and precise as always, but there was a tightness in his body, and his hands were shaking. In that moment Tathea realised how profoundly he felt the loss of Irria-Kand, and his own failure, though there was nothing he could have done, and all of them here knew that.

Again Ishrafeli nodded. 'Good.' His voice was rough with emotion. 'Send messages if you can, although we none of us know where we shall be.' He turned to Ardesir. 'Tomorrow we shall consider what we can do here. One of the Lords of Sin will come. This is too great a task for Balour. Asmodeus will never leave the City to such a creature. He is only preparing the way.' He looked at each of them in turn. 'We shall not sit together like this again . . . until it is before the face of God.' He smiled at them, passion in his eyes. 'Let us eat together, and then pray. Remember what it is we fight for, and that whatever the forces against us, God is for us and will never leave us alone. We are His children, and are greater than the darkness.'

Tathea rose to prepare the food. No one came to help her, and she returned with bread, cheese, fruit and wine. They ate in silence. Everything that needed to be said had already been spoken between them, and it seemed right that now they were left with their thoughts.

Afterwards, when the last of the wine had been drained, they stood in a circle and repeated the covenants they had first made in Tyrn Vawr, in the beginning, then with solemn prayer bade each other farewell and took their leave, Sardriel westward, Tornagrain and Sadokhar south, Ardesir into the City.

For Tathea to part again with Sadokhar, even seeing Tornagrain go, was hard. In these few days she had known a different man, and come to love Tornagrain with the bond born at least in part from the knowledge that he was the next warrior chosen by God to fight beside them. But it was that same knowledge which now made it necessary they separate. The war was greater than any of them, and they could be together in spirit only if they gave to it the best and the dearest they possessed. To withhold anything would be to betray the light, and in the end lose each other in the way which could never be undone.

She went to bed and clung to Ishrafeli silently, feeling his arms around her, the strength of his own need, and pain, knowing that he understood it just as she did. All the knowledge of eternity did nothing to ease this wound now, only to make it as inevitable as the movement of the stars. It was part of the laws by which all things exist, and which bound even God, otherwise there could be neither light nor darkness, heaven or hell.

The call for more men went out through the whole of Camassia. New soldiers were recruited by the score, the hundred, even the thousand. A hysteria gripped the land. Tathea, Ishrafeli and Ardesir scoured the streets for word of Ulciber, and heard none.

Everywhere in the City and around it the movements of men, armaments, food and horses, increased. Roads were blocked by wagons. The sound of marching feet echoed in the streets and there was hardly a woman anywhere who was not hiding tears as fathers, husbands, brothers and sons put on whatever armour they could find, and went to answer the call.

Ardesir moved among the manufacturers and financiers, arranging agreements, all the time listening for Azrub, and learning nothing.

Ishrafeli was in one of the nearby towns, seeking news and trying to secure the water supplies from accidental damage, remembering that whatever the war on the frontiers, those left behind still needed to survive. More than that, supply lines must be kept whole and there must be places where the injured could be cared for. Someone had to till the land, reap the harvest and store the grain, or the army could not be provided for either.

Five hundred years ago Tathea had been in the streets to watch the Emperor Isadorus ride by in triumph with armies from half the world paying tribute. He knew war; he had been a victorious general at the height of the Empire's power. Never before or since had it had quite that glory. Now she stood in the crowds again as a new army marched past and she felt the reverberation of thousands of feet in unison.

The thin, miserable figure of Balour, Lord of the Undead, was taking the salute as the army marched past him. They were disciplined because they were Camassian, and it was part of their blood and their heritage, but untrained, not like the legionaries of old. These were men taken from their homes, their farms, their workshops, and thrown without preparation into camps and given only the briefest of instruction before they were sent out to meet the severest need, wherever the barbarian invasion had done the most damage. The military was not their career; it was the last attempt to save their nation from being submerged beneath a tide of destruction. They were an army of last resort.

Tathea looked at their faces and tried to imagine each one as someone's husband or son. Yesterday, or the day before, they had been individual, sleeping in their own beds, with family around them, driven by the necessities of life, but answerable only to those. Today they were anonymous, one among thousands, even moving their feet in unison, and to order, never mind the rest of their comings and goings, their will to act, their speech, the multitude of choices one makes every day. They would taste fear, loneliness, anger, physical exhaustion and pain; at its worst, terror, mutilation and death. What would it make of them?

After the conscripted troops came the élite, the professional army, led by the general who would be in command of the entire battlefield from east to west. The crowd stared. They were entirely women and children and a few elderly men now past fighting even a rearguard action. Had the best not come last they might not have waited, but this was what would put heart and hope into them, the courage to keep up the struggle.

Tathea turned as they all did, and saw the magnificent red roan horse prancing, too full of fire to walk sedately, as might a lesser beast. On his back rode the commanding general, the sun gleaming on the metal studs of his armour and on the sword at his side. His helmet was crested in scarlet, like those of the old legionaries, and his red cloak billowed around him.

But it was his face which transfixed her with a sickening lurch of memory older than life. Cassiodorus! Suddenly she was back in a prison cell and that same face was staring insolently at her, the brutal mouth, the bold, searing eyes that looked inside her, stripping her soul bare. She had outwitted him then, and he had sworn never to forget her.

Now, out of all the women milling at the pavement's edge, his eyes found her and held. His smile widened, triumphant. She saw his tongue come out and very slowly lick his lips, while never for an instant moving his gaze from hers.

She felt cold and sick, as if he had somehow violated her. All the years since then ceased to have reality; they were back in Parfyrion, eternity before and around them, locked in an enmity that would never cease until one of them no longer existed.

She turned away. If Cassiodorus were leading the Imperial armies it could only be to the destruction of their souls, because that was all Asmodeus wanted. In spite of his arrogance, Cassiodorus was his servant. Then her work was not in the City any longer, it was wherever the battle was being fought – and that question was now answered. She must go after the army, watch and wait, learn Asmodeus' tactics and guard her own weapons. Now was the time to tell herself over and over again that God asked of no one more than they could give. No matter how impossible a thing may seem, God knows the end from the beginning, and His ways are certain.

At the house Tathea found Ardesir and told him what she had seen, and how she had no choice now but to follow Cassiodorus.

'You can't go alone!' he said in alarm.

'Ishrafeli is not back,' she answered quietly. 'I can't wait. The army moves out tonight.' In a way she was almost glad there could be no goodbyes. She was even glad Ishrafeli could not come with her. He would be her hostage to fortune. She was not sure she was strong enough to see him threatened, hurt, and still be true to her purpose. Better that she was not put to such a test. Perhaps that was the mercy of God, Who knew her strength and her weaknesses perfectly, that He did not give her that last burden to bear.

'I'll come with you,' Ardesir said without hesitation. 'You will need me.'

She could not deny it, and it was too late for pretence. She accepted and they made their preparations, packing only a few extra, heavier clothes for when they were further north – breeches and jerkins, and stronger leather boots.

Tathea left Ishrafeli a letter to explain what she had done. The necessity of it he would understand. It would be harder for him than for her. She had made the decision. It was he who would return, expecting to find her, and discover he had been robbed of the parting, even though he must surely have known one day it

244

would come, but he might not have foreseen it so soon.

She left the letter where he could not miss it, propped up on the bed by the pillow. She walked around the room slowly, looking at things for what she knew could be the last time, things Ishrafeli would see when he returned: the way the light fell on the round surface of the bowl, a worn patch on the tiles of the floor just inside the doorway, the smooth wood of the table. She touched the door above the handle almost as if she could feel his fingers there when he would come in, and find her already gone.

It was time to leave. She would not look at the bed again, where she had lain in his arms so often. But it made no difference: it was as if she could reach out now and touch him; his presence was as real to her senses as to her mind and heart. She expected to hear him speak, to feel his hand on hers, the warmth of him.

But this is what war was, the real war – parting, giving up what is so dear it is woven into your life and tearing it out leaves agony behind. The world was to be won or lost. How could the price be less than everything?

Ishrafeli knew that, he had always known, it was only a case of remembering again. She could not be less than that now.

'Please, Father, look after him!' she said aloud, then added in a whisper, 'And if it be possible – bring him back to me!' Then she turned and went out, closing the door and walking away.

Ardesir was waiting for her. It was time to go forward. 'Don't think, or you'll never have the strength,' she said in her mind. 'There's no choice . . . just do it!'

Chapter Sixteen

As with any army, there were camp followers, and it was easy for Tathea and Ardesir to join them and mingle invisibly with the other medical assistants, and with the wagon masters, and armourers who moved in the wake of the legions.

Three days out from the City and moving rapidly north, Cassiodorus gathered the men for a great rallying speech. They filled a wide, natural amphitheatre in the shallow hills, and he stood on a slightly rocky ledge ten or a dozen feet up, surveying the thousands of men before him. He was a magnificent figure, light glistening on his armour and catching his hair like an aureole. Behind him, to the west, the sky flard gold and violet above the scarlet orb of the sun. The breeze carried the scent of summer grass.

Every face was turned towards him as he began to speak.

'This is a war no one can escape!' His voice echoed around the huge space but every word was clear. 'We march against the forces of violence and madness which would destroy everything millennia of civilisation have created. We stand together, every man loyal to those beside him, obedient to the one call that is to all of us.' He raised his arm high, fist clenched and there was a shudder of anticipation throughout the massed assembly. 'We fight for the survival of the world!' He punched the air. 'Survival!'

'Survival!' the army reverberated back to him from a hundred thousand throats.

'You don't know yet what you face!' he went on. 'You are civilised men, decent, with homes and families, farms and shops. You plough, you sow and you reap.' Suddenly his visage darkened. 'You are going to face barbarians who are more bestial than any animal you have imagined!' He slashed his arm across the air. 'Men who create nothing, build nothing, sow nothing. They take what they want, and destroy what they don't. They have no morality, only appetite!'

The hush of fear settled over the crowd. No one fidgeted any more.

Tathea stared at Cassiodorus' face, and beside her Ardesir shivered and moved closer to her.

'Be proud of your courage!' Cassiodorus cried loudly. 'You are the forces who will save the world! Later generations will look back on this time and wish they could have been part of the greatest war that was ever fought! They will envy you, at the same moment as they know that they might not have been equal to such a test. It is a great thing you do, not only for your country, but for all mankind!' He smiled, this time hesitating long enough for a reaction.

He received it. Somewhere one man cheered, then a score, then everyone. A wave of sound rose into the air, gathering volume until it was like the roar of the sea.

Cassiodorus held up both his arms, but it was minutes before the sound subsided.

'Brave men! It is my honour to lead you.' His face darkened. 'But you do not yet know what it is you face, because you have met nothing like the barbarian, even in your dreams. You imagine something like yourselves, only perhaps different to look at – wild-haired, dressed in skins and speaking an alien tongue. But you still imagine a human being, with a life and hopes and dreams.' Without warning his voice rose to a roar. 'He is not!' Then dropped till every man strained to hear him, and the vast space was filled with a rustling stillness.

'Dreams are a human thing.' His voice vibrated with passion. 'Ideals are what make you a man, and not an animal.' Again he slashed his arm in the air. 'The barbarian is not a man! He looks like one, he apes your appearance, but judge him by what he does! See the devastation! See the ruin and the pain, see the tortured corpses of your own people littering the villages and fields where he has passed.'

Ardesir's hand tightened on Tathea's arm. He did not know he was doing it, but his fingers bit into her flesh. She did not care. She felt the same bitter understanding rising inside her.

'Since the beginning the barbarian has waited!' Cassiodorus thundered on. 'Now is his hour. Unless we stand against him, stand against wave after wave, use every weapon we have, to the last man, then he will sweep over us and conquer the world.' His face shone; the evening light on it made it seem like a mask of gold. 'Make no mistake . . . it is the world we fight for! This is the great and final war – good against evil – light against darkness – the forces of civilisation against the tide of their barbarism! If we lose, then there is nothing left. It is the end of humanity! We must win whatever the price. We must exterminate them!' Again he raised his arms high. 'Survival!'

The cry went up over and over again around the massed men – 'Survival! 'Survival!' – like the breaking of a great sea against cliffs.

Staring over the forest of arms Tathea saw Cassiodorus' shining face, the taste of victory already on his thick, curved lips.

'It's so nearly the truth,' Ardesir said bitterly.

'The best lies are,' Tathea replied. 'Asmodeus' plan begins as only a slight twisting of God's, but by the time you have followed it to the end, it is hideously different, the negation of everything that has value.'

They turned together and walked in silence back towards their own part of the camp, the enormity of what lay before them dwarfing words.

It was two days before Tathea had the opportunity to take even the smallest measure against what Cassiodorus had said. She and Ardesir had discussed it, and made what plans were possible. They separated, to be more effective. She was helping the women who cooked for the soldiers, lugging heavy cauldrons of stewed meat and vegetables, ladling it on to dishes and passing it around. By the end of the evening her back and arms were exhausted, and she was glad to sit down on the grass out of the cold wind and eat bread and a little stew herself.

'You have a man here, husband perhaps?' a voice said out of the shadows.

She looked up and saw a centurion just beyond the firelight, the flames' reflection dancing on the studs in his armour and catching the red of his cloak.

'No. But it's the cause of all of us,' she answered. 'Where else would I be?' She ate the last of the stew and put the bowl down.

He came closer to the fire and she saw his face. It was blunt, wind-burned, an old sword scar down one cheek. He looked closer to fifty than forty.

'Have you fought the barbarian before?' she asked.

'Not like this,' he replied, squatting down and warming himself. 'Just a few bands of them, here and there.' He frowned, the firelight showing the pale skin of his scar, puckered a little, and the curve of his mouth.

'Were they so terrible?' she asked, seeking an opening to begin what she needed to say to as many as she could.

He shrugged. 'Seemed ordinary enough then. But things have changed.' He smiled at her, showing a chipped tooth. 'Don't be afraid. We'll win. We have the discipline, and that counts for everything in the army. We won't break, or run, no matter what they do. Just stick towards the back, and you'll be fine.'

'I'm not afraid of being killed,' she said quietly.

'Then what?' He looked at her with compassion. 'Tortured? We'll never allow that to happen. Don't let yourself think about it.'

249

How could she tell him the real fear that lay behind everything? 'If the barbarians have no hopes or dreams, no morality that tells them certain things are wrong,' she began tentatively, 'and we behave the same way as they do, in order to beat them, then they are dead, and we have taken their place.'

He did not understand. 'We've no choice,' he reasoned, gently, remembering she was a woman. Perhaps he had a wife, or daughter of his own. 'You heard what Cassiodorus said, didn't you? This is the final war . . . for survival! Don't you believe that?'

She tried again. 'If we use the barbarians' weapons and morality to defeat them, in what way will we be different from them?' She leaned forward and put another piece of wood on the fire.

He was puzzled.

'We will have become the new barbarians, without dreams or ideals either,' she said, watching him.

He shivered in spite of the fire roaring up again and catching the new wood. 'You don't change that quickly . . .' he said, but there was no conviction in his voice.

'Yes, you do,' she answered. 'One act of brutality and you are not what you were even moments before. It's not long before you can't go back. If you slaughter a barbarian village, women and children, when they were no threat to you, how will you look at your own family when you return home? How will you tell your children that they must not retaliate with violence if they are cheated or robbed of something, or someone angers them?'

'Who are you?' he asked, his voice sharp with a new confusion. 'Why do you say these things?'

'Are they not true?' she countered, staring at him across the firelight.

'We're fighting for our survival!' he tried again to explain.

'Are we?' She broke the last of the bread and offered him half. 'If we behave no differently from the barbarians, then the only thing whose survival is certain is barbarism itself. Maybe they had dreams, and a code of honour once . . . maybe they still do, it's just different from ours.'

The centurion took the bread, his eyes steady, his fingers touching hers in an ancient gesture of unity, as if the sharing of food were a bond between them. She smiled at him, and ate, knowing they did not understand each other.

Through the next weeks as they pressed northwards and the weather grew colder, both she and Ardesir had more such conversations with other soldiers. Many did not get as far. It was uncomfortable for them to think of the enemy as just like themselves. It made the act of killing too personal, something for which one took a different kind of responsibility.

Others were disturbed, able to acknowledge that one's humanity was defined by one's own acts, not by the threat or the failings of another.

'We are making a difference,' Ardesir said one night as they sat in the dark beside the fire, huddled in blankets, surrounded by the myriad sounds and movements of the camp. Within a thousand yards in all directions, a city of men slept or lay awake, lost in their own thoughts and loneliness. There had been no battle yet, only the fear of it, and the certainty.

Tathea did not answer. She was not sure enough, but she smiled at him. They both needed to hope, and perhaps there was cause.

The morning was sharp and brilliant. The dawn shadows fled across the snow and the bare trees were black fretwork crusted in glistening ice, the pines a hidden, scented gloom under a canopy. The whole earth seemed jewelled overnight and the fire of the rising sun blushed amber and peach on the distant peaks.

The order to break camp was late. Tathea and Ardesir walked a short way into the forest for fallen wood to build a fire and cook grain into flat cakes to carry with them. The next place might not afford the same forest to glean from.

They heard a thump and slither as they climbed up rising ground, and stopped short.

'Snow melting?' Ardesir asked in a whisper.

'No.' Tathea shook her head. 'It's far too cold for anything to thaw.'

'What? Soldiers?'

She said nothing, but moved forward, treading silently and keeping within shelter of the trunks of pines. The slope opened up ahead of her and she saw what she first thought were two soldiers rolling in the deep snow. Them, as one reared upright and shook, she realised with a bubble of laughter that they were bear cubs. She held up her hand and Ardesir stopped beside her, pleasure lighting his face and his body easing from the tension. He let his sword arm fall.

The first cub took another hefty swipe at the second, and the two of them slithered and tumbled down the slope, squealing with what might have been fury, or equally well sheer delight at the joy of being alive.

For minutes Tathea and Ardesir stood side by side watching the cubs play, then a movement at the further edge of trees caught Ardesir's eye and he froze.

Tathea saw it with horror: three soldiers armed with bows and arrows.

The cubs heard no noise, no scent even in the still air. They went

251

on playing, oblivious of steel-tipped death yards away. One of them cuffed the other, turned tail to run, and stumbled over his own feet and somersaulted, shaking his head.

The soldiers shouted with laughter and applauded them.

'Thank God!' Ardesir breathed fervently, and Tathea added the same, frightened that it meant so much. A minute's innocence shared was a light in darkness within. She waved at the soldiers and called out a greeting.

They waved back, and they all watched the bears scamper off into the forest, then they turned, each to look for their own wood for fires. Even dry oat cakes and melted snow would have flavour today.

The first sight of the barbarians came in a sudden swooping attack by eight hundred mounted men riding hard, harrying the outer columns. They fought with bows and metal-tipped arrows, which they fired standing in their stirrups. Within the space of ten minutes nearly two hundred Camassian soldiers fell.

There was chaos as men stumbled over the injured and dying, attempting to save themselves, or to help others. It was not possible to tell if any of the barbarians were even wounded, much less killed.

It was the first time many of the men had seen the reality of battle, and the pain and confusion in the growing darkness was terrible beyond anything they had dreamed. There were no brave words heard now, no pride or boasting, only the agonised horror at the fragility of life and the obscenity of what can be done to living flesh.

It was a wretched night, cold and moonless, with an edge of ice to the wind. Tathea spent all of it moving from one group of injured men to another, trying to do for them what little she could. Many of them would die long before they reached any Camassian outpost with warmth, food or help. She could see in their faces that they knew it as well as she did, and lies were of no comfort.

Those who were unhurt were bitter with anger and guilt that they had made no retaliation, and swore they would never be caught again. In future scouts and outriders would be better prepared.

And so they were – but even with warning, many were killed by barbarian arrows. It was the third attack before any real success was tasted, and that was obtained by laying a trap and closing it with well-shielded men in the heaviest armour. By the end of that encounter thirty-two Camassians were dead or wounded, but over twenty barbarians were lying on the ground, and another thirty-four captured. All of them were put to the sword and their bodies left for carrion.

'They killed them all!' Ardesir said desperately, as again he stood by the fire, shivering, holding a blanket around his shoulders. 'Ordinary soldiers did it, men we've marched with, eaten beside!'

Tathea was more used to the exigencies of war. The smell of blood, the feel of blisters on her feet, aching muscles, the constant sounds of pain and the knowledge of helplessness brought it back as if it had been five weeks ago, not five centuries.

'We need the bandages and ointment for our own men,' she said, staring into the yellow flames. 'They wouldn't have lived anyway, not out here. It's brutal, but perhaps less cruel in the end than leaving men to bleed to death, or freeze.'

Ardesir started to argue, then fell silent.

The encounters with the barbarians continued as the army moved north and east. Sometimes they were merely skirmishes, a few score involved, half a dozen wounded or dead, and the men longed for a big, pitched battle that would crush the invasion and mark a turning of the tide. But they never saw more than two or three hundred barbarians at a time.

The weather was raw this far north. Grey skies were torn ragged by wind from the east, knife-edged and heavy with rain. The land was rough, low-lying marshy stretches divided by belts of pine trees and tangled scrub. There were few hills and they offered little vantage point because of the vegetation. The next valley could hide anything.

The army had been away from the City for almost three gruelling months of marching, sudden attacks and retreats, sleeping hard and cold, eating poorly, when they came upon their first experience of what the barbarian was truly like. It had been a restless night and Tathea slept only fitfully, rolled up in her blanket on one of the few dry spots of ground she could find. She was dimly aware of men coming and going, stepping softly, but it seemed as if they did so with more purpose than the usual anxiety and wakefulness of a camp so near the enemy. It occurred to her that perhaps Cassiodorus had chosen a scouting party from among those recruited from this type of terrain, who would be familiar with its dangers, but it was only an idea, half a dream.

When she finally rose, stiff and shivering, it was broad daylight, and the wind out of the east rustling the pines carried the cold scent of snow from the higher ground.

She looked over towards the centre of the camp and saw Cassiodorus standing at the flap of his tent. His physical presence was an illusion. Like all those who had followed Asmodeus from the beginning, he would never have a body of flesh. He could neither truly live nor die. The tent was not for his comfort, but to mark his leadership, his superiority. Wherever it was set up marked the heart of authority.

He stood broad-shouldered, the pale light catching the sheen of his armour. Even at this distance the confidence in him was like the warmth of a fire. She could see how the soldiers kept glancing at him. He was their one source of knowledge and hope in this nightmare land.

He could not, at this distance, have picked her out from any of the other drab, ordinary women who followed the army, but he was not limited by flesh; his spirit always knew where she was. The arrogance of his pose was a deliberate message to her.

She had only just turned back to her task of packing when she heard the night scouts ride in, not wearily as usual, but with a speed that scattered idlers in their path and made Cassiodorus stride towards them, speaking even before they dismounted to tell their news.

Everyone in the camp was startled. Word spread like flame, and with the same searing pain. They had come on a village half a dozen miles away. Animals prowled the streets and carrion birds settled unafraid on the corpses. The ground was soaked with blood and there was not a man, woman or child alive in the place. Some had been trampled or beaten to death, some slashed with swords, but others were dismembered, brutally, unnecessarily, as if it had given someone pleasure to do it. Women especially were left naked and some even disembowelled. Now the dogs and foxes tore apart what was left of them, dragging limbs and flesh, fighting over the pieces, snarling and wrenching, gulping down what had so recently been warm, beating life.

The men stood around in little groups, horrified into a kind of stupor. Suddenly the atrocity of it was unbearably real. Then as the wave of sickness passed, rage took its place.

Cassiodorus judged his moment to exactness. He spoke with grief and a passion of indignation.

'This is what we fight against!' he cried out hoarsely. 'They are not men who do this to harmless villagers, women and children like your own families . . . and make no mistake, they are just like your own! They were going peacefully about their lives – working, building, farming the land – and they were slashed to pieces where they cowered, begging for mercy, from creatures who are less than animals. The beasts of the forest kill to eat, as you or I might! These barbarians kill because they take joy in it! They have forfeited their right to be thought of as men!'

He needed to go on no longer. His voice was drowned in a roar of agreement, rough with terror and outrage, shrill in the damp air. Faces were white, bodies shook and hands were clenched tight on sword hilts.

The order was given to march north on the trail of the barbarian, as deep as necessary into his own lands. Revenge must be swift and total.

It was two nights and three days before the army caught up with them in their own encampment. It was just after sunset in the long twilight of the north when they fell on nearly two thousand of them, including women and children. The slaughter was hideous. Nothing was spared. The men were killed where they stood, the children at their parents' feet. The old women were butchered with the rest, the young kept alive to serve the soldiers' pleasure.

A few held back, horrified, but Tathea was helpless to affect the tide of destruction. She knew Ardesir would fare no better, and dared not think of the danger he would draw upon himself by trying, but words were their only weapon.

She stood alone beside the fire after dark, shuddering with cold, wrapping her woollen cloak tightly around her, hearing the wind moaning in the pines. She could not bring herself to offer help to the few wounded, or even to grieve for the dead. Let the legions bury their own.

She heard footsteps, and swung around, hoping to see Ardesir. Then her flesh froze as she looked into the triumphant, sneering face of Cassiodorus. There was a brightness to his skin as if the victory created a kind of glow inside him. He stood with his arms folded across his broad chest, the dark stains of blood splattering his tunic and armour, but no helmet over his close-curled head, and the firelight burnished the gold in his hair.

'Taste my victory, Tathea,' he said very softly. 'I told you I would win. How many souls do you think have chosen their path to hell today? A thousand, two thousand, five?'

Suddenly she knew what the scouting party had done three nights ago, as he meant her to. It was there in his eyes, the curl of his lip.

'It wasn't the barbarians who tore the villagers apart, was it?' Her voice was shaking, her words clumsy on her tongue. 'It was our own men! You sent them . . . so this would happen!'

His smile broadened, showing his white teeth; his eyes shone. 'Of course,' he agreed. 'Killing barbarians in battle is pointless. You surely didn't imagine that is why I came, did you?'

There was no need to answer him. Their understanding was as old as good and evil.

He threw back his head and roared with laughter, a shrill, hollow sound which settled on the heart like the touch of death.

She turned away, but it made no difference: she could feel him in the night, as if in the darkness he would always be there.

Chapter Seventeen

The army pressed on along the borders, marching in close order but with outriding scouts. The weather grew colder and the east wind drove across the open spaces. Cassiodorus allowed them little rest and less shelter. Tathea knew why. She watched him as he looked at the men huddled in little groups around the campfires at night, shivering in blankets, faces pinched. He felt neither cold nor exhaustion. He had no flesh for pain, or for pleasure. She was not sure if he saw the beauty of the earth or the sky, as she did, or if they were merely a presence to him, without glory. Was it just another world to defile, to pollute with violence and filth until he saw in it a mirror of his own soul, a desolation in which he was at ease, because nothing in it reflected the Glory of God?

Was that what Asmodeus wanted all worlds for, not their life and their beauty, not even to have and to hold, but simply to defy Heaven, to inflict the ultimate wound upon the heart of God Whose soul's name is love?

Yet if Cassiodorus pressed these men too hard, they would die of illness or exposure before he had fully corrupted their souls. Tathea stared across the tussock grass, combed by the wind, and wondered if he realised that.

The answer came to her in a way she had not expected, with the weight of a physical blow, stunning her after a hard day with several skirmishes and little ground covered. Over twenty men had been killed and another thirty-five wounded. She was slumped by the campfire alone, exhausted, feet sore and muscles aching, when a man came and crouched beside her. For an instant she assumed it was Ardesir, then she looked at him and saw the centurion she had spoken with at the beginning of the campaign.

'What is it?' she asked, thinking he wanted medicine of some sort.

In the firelight his face was haggard, his eyes rimmed in shadows. He spoke so quietly she could barely hear him. 'We made a mistake today . . .'

That was hardly worthy of comment. She would have dismissed him, but for the agony in his face, the fixed, terrible staring of his eyes.

257

'What?' she asked softly. 'What mistake?'

'We found a settlement and attacked it.' He winced even as he recounted it now. 'We killed everyone – even the children . . . and the women. Thank God, at least we didn't . . .'

They both knew what it was he had not said.

'Isn't that what Cassiodorus ordered?' she said bitterly, turning away from him. She had said and done all she could to prevent that. 'I told you that you'd become the same as the barbarians . . . now you are.'

'You don't understand!' He was half sobbing the words and he reached out and grasped her arm as if to stop her leaving, although she had not stood up. 'I don't want to be! Most of us don't! Somebody attacks you, you fight back. It's going on all around you . . . and . . .'

She remembered his face that first time and how much she had wanted him to see the truth, and the bitterness of failure twisted inside her. 'So you massacred a village of barbarians,' she said. 'Perhaps you didn't really want to, but that hardly counts now, does it? This is the last war, there are no tomorrows in which to do better. You've got to choose which road you are on today. If you behave like a barbarian, then that's what you are. I know perfectly well it may cost you your life to stand against it! It will cost you your soul not to!'

'You don't understand!' There were tears of despair in his face. 'They weren't barbarians! They were our own people! It was a Camassian village! We got lost in the wind and the snow . . . we attacked our own! I looked down at them, and I saw faces just like mine, like my father's – and, God help me, like my mother's!'

She stared at him, at last reading the horror truly. Was it shame in his eyes, or only terror?

Beyond the fitful circle of the light there were shapes moving, men restless, unable to sleep, too cold or too frightened.

'Why are you telling me?' she said, almost under her breath. 'I can't absolve you from that.'

'I know! Hell itself can't!' the man replied. 'But you can do something about it.' His eyes were pleading, his features crumpled as if something were broken inside him. 'You can tell me what to do now. I know it's the end. I don't suppose any of us are going home.' His voice caught, but he mastered it. 'I don't want to die with that sin on me. I used to think I was a decent man . . . a bit quick-tempered, maybe, a bit lazy now and then, but not bad . . .'

'Can you find twenty other men like you?' she asked. 'Whom you know, from your own town, perhaps?'

'Yes. Why?' Hope flared in his eyes.

'Can you find this village again?'

258

He nodded.

'Bring them to that gully beyond the outcrop, before dawn,' she replied.

'Do you want spades?'

'No. I just want good men, who have families of their own.'

'Oh . . . God!' Now there was a glimmer of understanding in him. But he did not argue. He rose to his feet awkwardly and stood very straight for a moment, as if he were on parade, then he disappeared into the shadows.

There were twenty-five of them when Tathea, the centurion and Ardesir set out without torches to retrace their steps to the village. They moved in near silence. It was imperative no one saw or heard them go. It was a bitter night, the ground ice-hard, grass crackling under their feet.

An hour later the first pale light of dawn painted it in streaks of white and grey, mist-edged, sparkling where the clear light struck the frost. It had a translucent, ethereal beauty no tender south could have offered. An hour later the rising sun shone pure as snow on the white wings of migrating birds, and in the sharp silence the creak of their wings was a kind of music.

They found the village. Scavenging animals had already scented the slaughter and as the soldiers stepped out of the shelter of the pines a wild dog lifted its head from a corpse and snarled warningly, then saw the number of them, and loped off. Further away carrion birds rose in the air, and descended again to tear with beak and claw.

The men moved forwards slowly, as if dazed. In the cold daylight it was easy to see that it was a Camassian settlement. No barbarians tilled the ground like this. They were nomadic, and these houses, rough as they were, had been built with the intention to remain. Blinded by snow, in fading light, perhaps it would have been easier to mistake, but now the truth was hideously plain. There were bodies everywhere, fallen where they had been caught by surprise. Men lay with spades and scythes in their hands, or tools of woodwork, chisels and mallets. A group of children had been cut down as they played. A dozen skittles were scattered over level ground, a wooden ball several feet away.

The soldiers walked among them, stiff and grey-faced.

They found nearly thirty women separately, a hundred yards away, also all dead. It was now that one of the soldiers could control his passion no longer.

'Cassiodorus is right!' he said in a thick, choking voice, breaking the silence of that terrible place. 'They aren't fit to call human! They must be wiped out before they spread any further south. If we

259

don't stop them, they'll destroy the whole world.'

Another man muttered a prayer, and made a holy sign of his faith. 'You're right!' he agreed, his voice trembling. 'This is an abomination.'

'They must be exterminated – like a disease!' another added. 'Cassiodorus spoke truly, we shouldn't have doubted him.'

Tathea glanced at Ardesir, and saw the resolution in his face, unwavering, filled with misery.

'Would you say that the men who did this have forfeited their place in humanity?' she said very clearly.

There was a unanimous growl of assent.

She looked at the centurion, and he met her gaze squarely.

'That they have soiled the good earth, and no longer deserve a place on it?' she pursued.

'Yes,' came back the answer clearly.

'Perhaps they were frightened, confused, badly led . . .' She was shouted down before she could finish.

'They're worse than animals!' one man said angrily, his rage and pain directed at her, because she argued. 'Animals kill to eat. These . . . creatures kill for the love of it! For God's sake look at the corpses, if you don't believe me! Look at them, woman!'

'I have looked,' she answered him. 'And I see people killed by broadswords, not arrows. There's not a single arrow here! I see no hoof-prints in the ground. I see the women separate, as if they had been going to be kept alive . . . until something changed their captors' minds. Tell me what you see!'

They stood staring at her in ashen silence. In the distance came the snarling and barking as wild dogs fought over the flesh. Far above them, dark against the blue of the sky, a skein of wild geese went over. The cold wind moaned as it passed through a tree.

'What are you saying?' It was little more than a whisper, yet the idea behind the words came like an avalanche.

'You know what I'm saying,' she replied.

'We wouldn't . . . do . . . this!' The man covered his face with his hands. 'God! That would mean we are no better than they are . . . not even any different!'

'We're not,' the centurion said softly. 'God forgive us all.'

Slowly some of the men looked at each other. Others could not bear to, but stood motionless, absorbing the horror, not of the scene around them, but of that within. They had looked into their own souls, and seen the barbarians they despised looking back at them.

The centurion was the first to move. He walked forward into the middle of the group in the freezing sunlight, looking from one man to another. 'There are spades and mattocks here. We've a lot of

260

graves to dig. Two of you take sticks and beat the dogs off. Get on with it! It'll be hard work; the ground's like iron.'

They stared at him.

'Come on!' he shouted suddenly. 'We killed them . . . we can bury them decently.'

One man shifted wretchedly. 'We thought they were barbarians!' he said, almost swallowing his words.

'No.' The centurion looked at him with pity but he yielded nothing. 'A man is a barbarian by his actions, not his birth. And a man is a coward who cannot face what he has done. Find a spade!'

Ashen-skinned, the man moved to obey.

The centurion glanced at Tathea, saw the softening in her eyes, and walked on.

They returned to the camp in silence, travelling the last thousand yards separately, as if they had merely been out foraging. But each man carried in his heart a burden that weighed him down. He had seen what he could not forget.

Two days later the soldiers were forty miles to the north and east and their scouts had reported a large barbarian encampment, possible a thousand or more men, with their women and children.

Cassiodorus stood in front of the men, swaying a little on the balls of his feet. His eyes gleamed. He gazed at the thousands of soldiers marshalled in front of him.

Tathea stood far at the back of the vast throng, with the other women and servants, but even so she knew he was as aware of her as if they were alone again in the room in Parfyrion.

Cassiodorus raised his arms. 'Go to your places,' he cried. 'Eat well! Rest! At midnight we march. We shall fall on them at dawn and not one of them will be left alive. Not a man to murder any more of our people, not a woman to breed more fighters and killers, not a child to grow up for revenge! Go now, and prepare yourselves for victory!'

'Victory!' came back the shout as fists punched into the air. 'Victory!'

At midnight, in the flare of a thousand torches, they began to move out, rigid, obedient, heads high. Twenty-five men were left, led by the centurion with the broken tooth. They stood stiff-backed, eyes forward, motionless. Seeing them, the last legion hesitated and looked to Cassiodorus.

He smiled, but it was a cruel pleasure that lit inside him, like the anticipation of a hunger to be filled.

'Did you not hear the order?' he said quietly, but his voice carried in the sharp, still air.

'I heard it,' the centurion answered. 'Those are not from the tribe

261

that attacked us. They are not yet our enemies, and I will not fall on them and slaughter them for no reason. We say this war is to save us from being destroyed. If we do the same thing, then we have destroyed ourselves.'

Cassiodorus raised his eyebrows. Almost unconsciously he ran his tongue over his lips. 'Do you refuse?'

The centurion was white-faced, and Tathea could see in the torchlight the knuckles on his clenched hands shining where the skin was stretched tight across them.

'Yes we do,' he answered. 'We will not obey an unjust command. We fight against the barbarism that slaughters women and children and destroys those who are no threat to us.'

Cassiodorus' face remained unchanged. 'I give you a last chance to obey a command in the field of battle,' he said distinctly.

There was a flurry of wind, ice-edged, the clouds crossed the moon and then passed, the torches flickered and then became brighter and harder.

'We will not,' the centurion repeated.

The men behind him stood rigid, as they would if they were awaiting an enemy attack they knew they could not survive. They had looked death in the face before and found strength from each other, and from within themselves.

Seconds passed as Cassiodorus realised they would not be panicked. Rage filled him for an instant, then it was succeeded by triumph. 'I charge you with mutiny and cowardice on the field of battle!' he shouted, then turned to one of the centurions he trusted most. 'How say you, Catullan, are they guilty?'

'Guilty!' Catullan replied without hesitation.

Cassiodorus looked beyond him to the other legionaries, rank upon rank of them stretching away into the darkness until only their helmets were distinguishable in the flare of torches. 'How say you?' he repeated.

Tathea looked at their faces. They were cold, weary, caught by surprise. No one had expected mutiny.

There was a moment's silence, then they spoke. 'Guilty,' they answered. They did not know how to give any other verdict. They also did not realise yet what hideous judgement was laid upon their comrades in that single word.

Cassiodorus' huge body relaxed and a smile made his face repulsive. He looked across at Tathea as if this whole bitter campaign were a duel between them, and all the blood and pain, the tens of thousands of men involved, were incidental, the tools used in its accomplishment, not living people.

'You are all witness to what has happened,' he said, his voice ringing in the still air. 'Mutiny in the field has only one punishment.' He looked at Catullan. 'We march on the enemy camp immediately. You will carry out the executions, and then catch up with us at the river.' Without waiting for an answer, he turned, his head high, a slight swagger in his step.

No one else moved.

Tathea had known what must come, and yet it was still both a victory, and a price which, now it was real, was almost beyond paying. For an instant she allowed herself to hope that the centurion charged with the execution would refuse to obey. That would be the ultimate prize. She stared at his face, the realisation in it, fear making it slack. Her heart tightened as she understood he would never find it within himself to defy Cassiodorus, even at this terrible price. He would think about it, weigh one sacrifice against the other, and then yield.

He turned to his men. If he looked at their faces or wondered what they wanted, it was nowhere visible in his demeanour. He made the decision for them and gave the command.

They closed ranks around the twenty-five and, with swords drawn, marched them in a tight phalanx through the trees and over the ridge until they were out of sight.

The women and camp followers turned to one another in bewilderment.

Ardesir came striding across the icy grass towards Tathea, his face creased, his eyes dark and angry.

'Didn't you know he'd do that?' he demanded when he was close to her. 'They're going to murder those men.'

'I know,' she said, wishing she could avoid the blame in his eyes. She was tired and cold, and bitterly aware of what was happening beyond the ridge. She felt as if she could hear the blows falling, even though there was barely a sound except the wind in the branches, and the shuffle of feet as the remaining people began to move off at last.

She looked past Ardesir. 'Hurry!' she said to one of the women. 'Mix in with the others. Don't be caught alone!'

The woman had no idea what she meant.

'Get out!' Tathea heard the panic in her own voice. 'Now! Quickly! You know what they did! Don't you realise that when they come back they'll see that? Maybe we'll never get home, but if we do, do you think they'll let you live to tell people?'

'But it was an order,' the woman argued. 'What else could they do?'

The old man next to her understood. He gave Tathea a glance of gratitude, then dragged the woman away, muttering a curse at her stupidity.

'We'd better go too,' Ardesir said bitterly. 'Why should they spare

263

us? They don't know that nobody in the City would believe us.' He strode after the others, head down, face into the wind.

She caught up with him, walking with difficulty over the rough tussocks of the grass, the iron-hard ground jarring her body. She was tired deep within herself and his anger hurt. She tried not even to think of Ishrafeli, to wish he were here where she could meet his eyes and know he understood. She had no idea where he was, even if he were still alive.

'What did you want me to do?' she demanded, matching her stride with Ardesir's. 'Let them go on in ignorance, making no decisions?'

He kept his face averted and his voice was quiet and strained when he answered. 'Did you ever imagine they'd stand up to Cassiodorus? You know what he is. Didn't you know what would happen before you spoke?'

'I thought I did,' she admitted. 'Does that make any difference?'

He stopped, swinging around to face her, his eyes wide and dark, his shoulders hunched against the cold. 'You knew they'd fail, and you still put them to the test?'

She wished she could answer him differently. The dark landscape, with its leaden sky obliterating the moon, and the glimmer of snow-patched grass in the red torch flare, the wind keening through the branches of the trees, was a perfect mirror of the loneliness she felt inside herself. But it was too late in time to retreat now, or for gentle answers that were less than the truth.

'I didn't know, and I could have been wrong . . .' She ignored the scepticism in him. 'Now is the time for them to choose. There isn't always a tomorrow for you to do better.'

He looked stricken, as if the one thing he had trusted had let him down with no reason and no warning.

She had to show him, even though it would mean miles more tramping over the frozen grass, through the trees and down the scree slopes, slipping on the loose earth and stones, then more forced marching to catch up with the others again. 'Come,' she said, holding out her hand.

She led the way back, walking carefully to keep within the shelter of the trees, unseen all the slippery way back to where the executions had been carried out. She did not want to see it, and she knew he did not either, but there was no escape now.

When they reached the place it was grey dawn and the men who had done it had gone. The dead men lay on the scarlet snow, hacked to pieces by broadswords. They were twenty-five against a hundred, and they had stood still for their slaughterers.

Ardesir drew his breath in with a great sob, and in spite of himself, let it out in a cry of pain.

'Look at them again,' Tathea said quietly. 'Look at their faces.'

It was minutes before he could do it. The wind whined through the trees and dark, carrion birds circled overhead. Then he walked forward, his footsteps crackling on the ice and bent over the nearest one where he lay, his body contorted in his final physical agony.

Ardesir forced himself to look at the face, and slowly something changed in him, a searing peace broke open, a light that burned, as he recognised the victory in each of them, complete and untouchable.

He looked up at Tathea, the tears on his face wet only for a moment before they froze. 'But what about the men who killed them?' he asked. 'Are they lost for ever?'

'I don't know,' she said honestly. 'Probably. They can't go home after this . . . not as long as anybody knows what they did, and why . . . the truth about the massacre of the village.'

'You mean they'll murder everyone who knows?' His face was ashen grey.

'I don't know. But that's what Cassiodorus intends.'

'What can we do?' It was a will to fight, and a cry for help.

She shook her head. 'I'm not certain. I wish I were. I wish I knew how far we were from the end . . . what's happened to the others . . .'

Ardesir put out his hand quickly and took hers. He was shuddering with cold, and yet there was warmth in the gesture that neither the snow, nor the east wind could destroy.

'Just go on,' he said firmly. 'These have won, and the others aren't lost yet. But even if they were, there comes a time to let go.' He rose to his feet. 'Come on. We've a long way to catch up.'

Cassiodorus led the army to destroy the barbarian camp exactly as he had said he would, and then on again to victory after victory until the barbarians were decimated, their women and children driven into the forests. Even their horses were scattered to the hills, which were now sheeted with snow in the deepening winter.

The Camassian borders were safe from invasion again and the people could begin to rebuild. The army began to return to the City in the Centre of the World. Less than half the men who had set out were fit for the long march home. Another thousand at least would follow later, when they were able, but many were maimed, blind or disfigured. Above all they had memories of slaughter that had crippled their souls. They had seen and done things that they could not bring back or undo, and all the wine, the violence, the excuses, the celebrations did not expunge from them the nightmares that each lapse of vigilance allowed back. Cassiodorus had won, and the victory shone in his face, in the wide, bold smile on his mouth.

It was over a month before they entered the City, and immediately a triumphal march was planned so that all Camassians could celebrate the release from the grasp of fear. Everywhere there was excitement, jubilation, wild words of praise for the returning heroes. Nothing was too good, too rare or too expensive to give them. They were the saviours of the nation, more, of all mankind. Camassia had turned the tide for civilisation.

Tathea and Ardesir came in quietly. Their triumph was far smaller, a few score of souls who had fought and died terrible deaths for the light they had grasped, a few hundred more who had seen some kind of honour better than simple slaughter, and perhaps returned wiser or braver than they had left. But there was no boasting to be done, no flags to wave, no flowers to throw, even had it been summer, and blooms for the picking.

They separated themselves from the other camp followers with a brief goodbye, and walked side by side throughout the busy streets, speaking to no one. This was a day to release all the pent-up waiting and fear. Tomorrow was time enough to look more closely, and perhaps think of grief.

In spite of her weariness and her blistered feet, Tathea found herself walking more and more rapidly along the familiar streets. They were easy to tread after the long, uneven country roads of the march home. They had heard no news of the rest of the world all the long campaign. There had been no word of the Island, the Lost Lands, not even of Shinabar. And she knew nothing of Ishrafeli. It was the thought of him, which she had tried to keep from her mind all the bitter, weary days of the fighting, which now willed her feet up the flights of steps towards the house, even though her muscles were shot with pain and her chest ached to catch her breath. She did not even think of Ardesir a yard behind her, nor stop to wonder what he hoped for.

She threw the door open and was dizzy with joy when she saw Ishrafeli standing in the room beyond. The winter sun was clean and hard on the lines in his face, his cheek, his mouth as he smiled slowly, allowing himself at last to believe the moment was come.

She threw herself into his arms and clung to him, feeling his grip around her so strong it hurt, and yet nothing could be close enough. The ache of familiarity was in the smell, the taste, the touch of his skin, the sound of his voice even before he spoke. And yet the memory and the dream of him had been so powerful she had to pull away and look into his face to assure herself of the reality, wait for him to speak, to say something unforeseen and beyond the control of her longing.

He looked at her very carefully. 'It isn't your battle to win or lose,' he said at last. He kissed her gently again and again. 'And we

266

haven't time for the self-indulgence of guilt,' he added with a wry smile. 'I think the end is coming swiftly.'

She stared at him. 'Is it?' She was frightened now. She wanted more time to share with him, to think, to plan, to find a way to bear the future.

'I believe so,' he answered. 'I'm afraid too, but what lies ahead is far, far better than anything that could be behind.' He took both her hands in his, then suddenly closed his eyes as the knowledge of what was to come overwhelmed him, and it was she who held him close in her arms and could not let him go.

Cassiodorus led his triumphal march into the City at the head of the entire army and the people went wild with relief after the terror of the months of waiting. The streets were jammed with young and old cheering, waving banners, calling out. Ribbons flew from every window, children were carried aloft, girls threw kisses, scarce winter flowers and sweetmeats at the feet of the soldiers.

Cassiodorus rode a red horse and his armour was beaten and scarred, stained with blood, but still the bronze studs gleamed in the fitful sunlight and his golden hair curled like an aureole around his head.

The cheers were deafening.

Behind him came the pick of the legions, red-crested helmets tossing, cloaks ragged, stained, but swinging as they strode, broad-swords at their sides.

After them came the recruits drawn in because of the national peril. They had left home as ordinary men. Now they had tasted a whole new world of terror and exhaustion and had learned things they could never put away. They looked neither to right nor left, avoiding the eyes of their fellow citizens, and in front of them they carried long poles, each topped with the decapitated head of a barbarian, some women, some even children. Above a score of them looked up triumphantly at the thing he bore as a trophy.

Tathea turned to Ishrafeli beside her and remembered another time when they had seen the beginning of a war, in a world apart from this. The only likeness between then and now was that Cassiodorus had been there also, and she had looked at his face and seen the triumph in it because he knew that destruction was certain, and the undying evil in him had fed on it. He had sworn he would remember her for ever. Here, today, he was keeping that promise.

They were in front of the forum where once the Emperors had taken the salute. Now Cassiodorus reined in his red horse and dismounted so he could climb the steps.

The crowd ceased its roaring, faces turned towards him, waiting.

267

At this moment he could have asked anything of them at all, and they would have given it to him.

Tathea glanced at Ardesir, perhaps a dozen yards away. His face was pinched with revulsion and the lines from nose to mouth were deeply carved, his lips drawn tight as if he tasted defeat and the hurt of it were draining his strength. She longed to comfort him, but the distance was too great for her to cross without drawing the attention of the crowd waiting for Cassiodorus. And even if she were beside him, there was nothing that she had not already said.

Cassiodorus raised his arms, the muscles of his shoulders bulging under the tunic and the armour.

The crowd was silent.

'My fellow citizens of Camassia!' His voice rang clearly, every word distinct. 'Salute your victories! Your men have marched into the unknown, beyond the threatened borders of our nation, and pursued the barbarian who would have engulfed us . . . and beaten him in his own land!'

A wave of sound rose almost like a wall, cheering, shouting, whistling, and he let it roar around him as a tide of water, buoying him up. It had all but spent itself before he signalled for them to let him continue.

'We have driven the barbarian back into the wilderness where he belongs!' he cried. 'And in such a way he will not lightly come upon us again. But – and I say this to you as your friend – he is not beaten for ever! We have shown even the proud Shinabar that civilisation can win! At least Camassia can . . .'

He was overtaken by another burst of cheering, and his smile showed he welcomed it. He waited until they were quiet again before continuing.

'. . . but we must remain on our guard. There are other barbarians. Irria-Kand has fallen and already become a wilderness, as we would have. But we have beaten them, and we can do it again, if – ' he held up his hands, palms upward – 'if we keep our strength, our courage and belief in our cause. We must remain loyal, above all else.' He stopped long enough for another great cry of agreement to roar up from the crowd.

He glanced over towards Tathea.

'We must purge ourselves of the traitors amongst us who would yield to pandering to the enemy, to telling the lies that subvert, weaken and in the end betray.'

The crowd was puzzled. There was hesitation, then the slow, ugly rumble of anger.

'You can hardly believe me?' Cassiodorus raised his voice till it seemed to reverberate from the great walls of the furthest buildings around the forum and wash back over them, penetrating to the

268

heart. 'And yet it is true! Ask your own husbands, fathers, brothers! Ask them if there was not a woman among the camp followers who went from man to man, seeking to convince them the barbarian was human, a man like themselves! Ask them! It is the final war, my friends, good against evil, for the survival of mankind. And it is as old as sin itself.'

The crowd remained silent, frightened, huddled together.

'Look to your history!' he shouted, his face darkening. 'She was among you even in the days of the great Isadorus! She tried to weaken him, to unman him of his courage and his decision. It was she – Tathea – who led the great Alexius into Shinabar, and finally to the Island at the Edge of the World where he was murdered in her cause. And she is here again!' He flung out his arm, pointing at her.

Every head in the crowd turned.

Ishrafeli tightened his arm around Tathea, his body shielding hers.

But it was Ardesir who stepped forward, walking up the steps as if he had been invited. The confidence in his manner was so great that no one reached out to prevent him, or even to question who he was. He stopped half a dozen steps up, just short of Cassiodorus, and turned to face the crowd.

'Cassiodorus is right: this is the final war between good and evil!' His voice also carried, but it was the passion in it, the fierce, driving certainty that held them. 'What is lost now will remain lost for ever.'

There was a growl of anxiety, fear mounting in the crowd.

Tathea stared up at his face. Surely he must know he had not long before Cassiodorus would stop him? A few moments at most.

'But good and evil do not struggle for cities or land,' he went on. 'Not even for the life or death of man. This is the real war we are in, the eternal one that is for victories far greater than the things of this world.' His face grew suddenly tender. 'The beautiful, ephemeral things we touch and hold so dear.' He leaned forward over the rail of the steps. 'This is for our souls! We are not fighting for a few miles of territory, or a few years of peace or wealth. The end of this is heaven . . . or hell! Glory goes on to eternity, to more and more perfect light and knowledge and a joy that has no measure. Damnation is the loss of every precious and beautiful thought, belief, every hope of love or life, every understanding of the ways of God.'

Not a man or woman moved and all their faces were upturned towards him.

'The Great Enemy is the master of lies,' he went on. 'He would have you fight for the things you see, and use his weapons to do it, and so lose the real prize.'

269

The rumble from the crowd grew louder. People stared from Ardesir to Cassiodorus, and back again.

Cassiodorus made a move as if to attack, but some fire in Ardesir made him hesitate.

Ardesir leaned further forward, his thin face alight. 'It is not the miserable barbarian at the borders of the world who threatens you, the ignorant, shattered men and women whose heads are skewered on your spears. It is the barbarian in your own hearts that led you to pick up the weapons of atrocity.' He gestured towards the shrunken, bloody trophies still held aloft. 'They know no better! They were savages who lived in the night. We stand in the full daylight, and yet we stooped to the same bestiality they did! That is the Great Enemy's victory over us! Of course Tathea sought to save us from that! And she did save some. There were those who defied the order to massacre settlements that offered us no threat . . . and Cassiodorus had them hacked to death for their mutiny.'

The crowd was stunned, turning to one another in horror.

'They were your own men,' Ardesir went on. 'Ordinary citizens. I saw their bodies where they lay.' His voice broke but he was unashamed of his emotion. 'And I saw the men who did it to them. You will find no one else who knows, because they killed them all lest they told you. But look in their eyes, and you will see the Enemy's victory over them.'

Cassiodorus would permit it no longer. He swivelled on his stand and took a step down towards Ardesir. His face was twisted with rage, and the hatred burned in him with such heat his skin glowed with it, his eyes blazed and the sun on his golden hair seemed to set it alight.

Ardesir turned to face him. The courage he had sought all his life had come with the knowledge of true darkness. Cassiodorus came down another step, and still Ardesir did not move nor did his glance waver. Cassiodorus was less than a foot from him.

Ardesir smiled, as if he knew something Cassiodorus never would.

Cassiodorus put out his hand, fist clenched, his thick lips drawn back to show his teeth. He was so close Ardesir must have felt the heat of his body and smelled the odour of his skin, the sweat, the stale blood on the leather of his armour.

Cassiodorus' fist touched Ardesir's shoulder and the sneer on his lips grew wider.

Tathea gripped Ishrafeli so tightly her nails dug into his skin and drew blood, but neither of them was aware of it.

Cassiodorus lifted his fist and swung it wide, then smashed it across Ardesir's head . . . and the unbelievable happened: it went straight through as if his arm were an illusion, not flesh at all.

Slowly horror filled his face. There was a gasp from the crowd. He drew back and lifted his other arm, but the awful knowledge was there inside him even before he tried to strike the blow.

Ardesir understood. He reached his hand forward and laid it on Cassiodorus' mighty forearm and saw the muscles ripple, waver and begin to dissolve.

The crowd was frozen, struck dumb.

Cassiodorus opened his mouth as if to scream, but the sound did not come.

Tathea struggled to breathe, and beside her Ishrafeli was rigid.

Ardesir spread both his arms wide.

Not a soul in the crowd stirred.

Ardesir closed his eyes and then clasped Cassiodorus, chest to chest, belly to belly, knee to knee, and Cassiodorus tried for a hideous moment to struggle, to loose himself from the grip, but his body was already melting like wax in a furnace. His armour was hollow, buckling, folding in on itself. The gauntlets and greaves fell off, the breastplate slid down.

Very slowly Ardesir swayed, then he sank to his knees and collapsed forward to lie sprawled on the empty armour, his face stripped of all strength and filled instead with a peace beyond the power of earth or hell to touch.

Ishrafeli took a step forward, then stopped. There was nothing for him to do now.

With a force she could not have imagined, Tathea was aware of Cassiodorus ceasing to exist. At the moment of dissolution his spirit vented all its years of hatred upon her. She no longer saw the forum in the City and the gathered crowds, but the souls he had destroyed with fear, wandering white-faced, in memories of the terror which had robbed them of eternity. Some she knew – people who had loved and laughed in the earthly realities of life, but whose courage had failed the test. Some had scarcely realised, until it was too late, that fear was their undoing.

She felt an ever-increasing cold bite into her, hard and sharp as steel, and in spite of all her efforts to see, the darkness closed around her so thickly she could touch it. It crawled over her skin and clung to her as if it would never leave.

Someone was shaking her. She tried to pull away, crying out. The grip tightened, but she could see no one.

Cassiodorus was all around her, his hatred beating in her mind, hard-edged, violent, blinding with pain.

She felt a stinging slap on her cheek. She was being shaken so roughly she bit her tongue and the stab of it made her gasp. There was blood in her mouth. A voice called her name.

'Tathea! Tathea! Listen to me! Make him go away . . . you can!

271

Command him, in the name of God!'

She tried. 'In the name of God, I command you to leave me!' But there was no sound except in her head. There was dizziness all around, a whirling, then a breaking of the darkness and she saw Ishrafeli's face, and the fear in his eyes.

'It's all right,' she said hoarsely. 'He's gone. I don't think he exists any more. I didn't think that could happen to him.'

Ishrafeli said nothing.

She remembered Ardesir and the prophecy on the staff, 'when the man of faith embraces terror to himself'; she had seen its literal fulfilment! Tathea leaned forward slowly and put her hand on Ishrafeli's shoulder and clung to him. It was victory. The first Lord of Sin was gone . . . and so was the first warrior of God. It was glory, and grief, and the beginning of the end. Now, more than ever before, they would need courage.

Asmodeus was stunned. He had not believed any of the Lords of Sin could be destroyed, let alone by such a man as Ardesir. How could it have happened? He, of all of them, was a coward! What had suddenly given him the courage to face Cassiodorus, of all the enemies his soul had known? He might have believed it of Ishrafeli, or even of Sardriel, perhaps of Sadokhar – he was brash and hasty enough!

Could it be the ridiculous answer that only a man who knew the full measure of fear, and overcame it, forged for himself the weapon to destroy Cassiodorus? That would be like God: that was His sense of mortality! If it had not been so bitter, so vile, it would have been laughable.

It was Tathea's fault! It was to defend her that Ardesir had stepped forward, and for that she would pay, again and again, to the last moment of her existence. But how? His superb plan to make her love Ishrafeli more than she loved God had not succeeded! He did not understand it – it should have worked sublimely. He would think again, harder!

So what was most precious to her? What was the one thing she could not exist without? He knew the answer. Not Ishrafeli – but God! The centre, the purpose of it all.

He must make her believe that her entire perception of earth and heaven was false: shatter her faith. Without that she stood alone, and would be as easy to destroy as a child lost in the night – and that is what she would be!

If she relied upon God – then take God away! Simple!

He laughed aloud, the sound of it cannoning off the walls of Erebus and shooting away into the gloom.

But first he would get rid of Sardriel. For that he would use

Azrub, the Lord of Delusion. He could create the dream that filled Sardriel's heart. Asmodeus knew him so well! He still yearned for the woman Elessar, dead these many years. He carried her in his heart, twined through the fibres of it so he could not let go without tearing himself beyond healing.

Asmodeus stared into the roaring chaos without form or sense, a blind, wheeling oblivion, and summoned the golden dwarf to him.

'Azrub!' he roared. 'Azrub!'

Why did he not come instantly? Why was he so slow to answer the summons of Asmodeus, the second son of God? 'Azrub!'

Azrub appeared next to the wall, rubbing his white hands together.

He hated Asmodeus because Asmodeus knew him. He saw inside his being and read his lust to feed on the desires of men, watching their hunger and their need. Seeing them fulfilled by mirage, and then shattering it and leaving them alone and broken, stilled the ravening appetite inside him and took away some of the rage at what he could never possess for himself. Only Asmodeus could give him the chance to satisfy his craving, before it came back, redoubled, to gnaw at his vitals.

'What keeps you that you dare to hesitate in obeying my command?' Asmodeus shouted at him, and clouds of dust rose high into the air and were torn away by the winds of destruction.

Azrub knotted his hands even more tightly together. 'What is it you want?' he asked, standing on the sombre battlements of Erebus, and smiling.

Slowly, relishing every detail, watching him with eyes that bored through every guard and pretence, Asmodeus told him precisely what he should do to destroy Sardriel, now that he had gained power in the Lost Lands, and the ground was prepared.

'Yes . . .' Azrub's lips curved up, showing the stumps of his teeth. The satisfaction of lust gleamed in him, like sweat on the skin.

Asmodeus was revolted almost beyond his power to control. His soul was sick with it.

'Without what pleasure I allow you, you will starve,' he said in little more than a whisper. 'You think you cannot die . . . don't you?'

'We none of us can die,' Azrub replied, but there was something in Asmodeus that troubled him, sent a cold trickle of fear inside him.

'No, because we have not life, as mortals have!' Asmodeus said with a voice more bitter than wormwood. 'But we can be destroyed! If you doubt it, go seek Cassiodorus. He does not exist any more.'

Azrub's yellow eyes widened almost imperceptibly. The Lord of Delusion knew lies from truth.

'I know what destroyed him,' Asmodeus went on now quite calmly. 'I will loose it upon you if you disobey me again – after I have watched you starve for a season or two, or three.'

Now Azrub was truly frightened.

Asmodeus knew that Azrub would obey him only as it suited his own purpose. Very slowly Asmodeus smiled and the darkness above Erebus emptied and spread out a cloud of dust and filth that obscured the wheels of stars a million miles away.

'I will give you the best prize of all,' he said gently, watching Azrub's white hands and his glittering eyes. 'I will give you Tathea!'

In spite of himself, Azrub drew in his breath and his tongue shot out to lick his lips. It was beyond his power to hide his appetite, and he hated himself for his weakness. It was as if Asmodeus had stripped him naked to watch what above all he would have kept private. His soul burned like acid. But a prize like Tathea . . .?

'What do you want me to do?' he responded. 'Tell me!'

'Win Sardriel,' Asmodeus answered. 'And when you have corrupted him to choose the dream of his heart over reality, then we can take the Island at the Edge of the World, because he will corrode its soul.'

'That is not Tathea,' Azrub argued, shifting his vast weight from one foot to the other in his raging hunger and the fear that it might not be met after all.

Asmodeus loathed having to explain himself to this foul creature, but it was the only way to be certain of him.

'When I have the Island,' he said, glaring at the dwarf, 'then I will make her see the whole earth a ruined waste that even God no longer loves, and is powerless to heal. Then she will taste the ashes of despair, and her soul will die. Now go and obey me! Or I shall allow her to destroy you instead. Get out!'

Azrub turned and slunk away, but he was smiling, and his white hands rubbed each other faster and faster as he disappeared into the night.

Chapter Eighteen

Sardriel left the City in the Centre of the World and sailed first to Tirilis in his search for Azrub, the golden dwarf who was Lord of Delusion. The land of shifting money, of debts and promises, seemed the place most fertile for his twisted arts.

A dozen times Sardriel heard word of him, but each time he reached the town or the city, he was mistaken or too late. He met blind denial, laughter, meaningless apologies. Months went by fruitlessly.

Finally, on the western shore overlooking the sea towards the Island and beyond the Maelstrom and the reefs, his own Lost Lands, he heard a whisper that Azrub might be in Kyeelan-Iss. The thought weighed heavily in his heart: knowing the hatred Siriom bore him, and the hunger for revenge that had consumed him ever since Sardriel had first entered his hall, fear already touched him for the Lost Lands. The sea had guarded them against all human foes, but not even the Maelstrom was proof against Asmodeus, and surely his dark hand would not hold back now?

He sought out a Lost Lands ship in the harbour and took passage on its return voyage. He stood on the deck as they cast off and put to sea, staring at the blue water ahead.

'Siriom of Kyeelan-Iss has landed in Orimiasse,' the master of the ship said beside him when they were alone.

Sardriel was not surprised. Some part of him had already known. He turned to the master and saw the hollow lines of his face.

'We don't know how he crossed the Maelstrom,' the master went on. 'He brought only two ships, but nobody in the Lost Lands has the will to fight him.'

Sardriel was surprised only by the fact that Siriom came with no army. It seemed to make so little sense. He forced his mind to think. This was a time for reason, not emotion. 'But he is still there?'

'Yes.' The master nodded.

'How did you escape?' Sardriel asked him.

The master shook his head as if he barely understood the answer himself. 'I was at sea when they landed. By the time I put ashore it

275

was all over. There are hardly any occupying soldiers, just a score or so, and Siriom living in the Prince's House on the hill. I only stayed an hour or two. No one tried to stop me leaving. It was as if they didn't care.' His eyes were pleading, still hollow with shock. 'You must lead us, make us fight again – be the people we used to be! Better we die defending ourselves than live as passive slaves to Siriom!'

Sardriel did not argue. These were his own people, his battle-ground in a way Irria-Kand or Camassia never could be. Perhaps he had always known the fight must end in the Lost Lands. He loved them with heart and blood and bone as he could love no other place. 'Yes,' he said, facing forward again. 'Of course.'

A week later, at last he heard the roar of the Maelstrom in the distance, different from any other sound on earth. It was the primal fury of the sea raging in a vortex that had never ceased since the ocean had been formed out of chaos.

He could see it already in his mind's eye as he stood facing west towards it. It was the call of home, deeper than the conscious mind. The mountains of shimmering water towered into the air, drowning the sky, white-crowned with spume. The green depths were hollowed out like tunnels into the belly of creation.

Yet they would survive. After the noise, the battering, the drenching, bruising, all-consuming water, they would at last be spewed out at the far side, beaten and exhausted, but alive. The men would haul up the sails again and set course for the harbour of Orimiasse with its quiet houses set on the steep hill, and its sunset-coloured ships at ease. He knew it, savoured it in his heart as if it had already happened.

The reality of the Maelstrom left his body bruised, exhausted and cold, but this was slight compared with the deeper coldness that filled him when at last they approached Orimiasse.

The helmsman skirted wide around the headland, avoiding the harbour, as if they were merely a deep-water fishing vessel coming into its own mooring. They put ashore in a further bay. Sardriel had agreed with the master that he should put out to sea again immediately, and return every ten days.

As Sardriel's foot touched the pale sand, he was already dismissing emotion and trying to judge his wisest way to act. He must learn all he could: the nature of the occupation by Kyeelan-Iss, and why there was no resistance, if indeed that were true. He had friends here in this quiet bay. He would seek them first, and learn whatever they could tell him.

The way was familiar, the path winding in and out of the wild sea lupins, which were heavy with perfume, the bleached driftwood like white bones in the twilight. The mounds of sea pinks were almost colourless now as the glowing sun burned and died on the horizon, the echoes silver across the arch of heaven.

Sardriel reached the door and knocked. There was no sound but the surge and wash of the sea as it glimmered on the shore.

It seemed a long time until the door opened and a man he had known since youth stood facing him, blinking as if uncertain what he saw.

Sardriel stepped into the light. 'Farramon . . .'

'Oh! Sardriel.' Farramon's expression cleared, and he pulled the door wider. 'Come in.'

Sardriel accepted, and was startled to see the once-handsome interior of the house dull, filmed with dust. The carpet in the centre of the floor which he remembered as sea green was blotched with stains. Could the occupation of the enemy have left such marks in less than two months?

He looked more closely at Farramon, but he could see no sign of tension or grief in him. He seemed relaxed, almost indifferent.

'I suppose you've come back to join us now,' Farramon remarked. There was no discernible emotion in his voice.

'Yes.' Sardriel stood uncomfortably, trying to ignore the neglected room. Had some fearful loss robbed Farramon of all feeling? 'We must stand together and fight . . .'

'Fight?' Farramon shook his head. His confusion was so vivid that Sardriel stopped. Why was the thought of resistance extraordinary to him? Did he imagine victory impossible? Perhaps it was, in the physical sense, but the time was past for that. This struggle was of the spirit, though he should not have assumed Farramon knew that. His thoughts turned to his cousin, whom he had left as lieutenant in the place when he had gone to Tyrn Vawr to join Sadokhar. 'Where is Okanthar? Is he still in Orimiasse?'

'Okanthar,' Farramon repeated the name slowly. 'No. He's dead. I think he was in the boat that went down. We lost a few people then. It was a shame.' His face showed only slight emotion.

It caught Sardriel with a bitter grief. Okanthar had been a strong and honest man, with the same love of truth as Sardriel himself, which was why it had been easy to entrust the government of the Lost Lands to him. He would have stood against Siriom whatever the odds. His loss was more than that of an ally gone; Sardriel was aware of a new and more complete loneliness than even a moment before.

'We must gather our forces and fight—' he began.

'Fight whom?'

'Siriom, of course!'

'Why should we fight Siriom?' Farramon asked, his eyes puzzled.

'Because he has invaded our land!' Sardriel replied, and saw the moment he had spoken the words that they were useless.

Farramon shook his head. 'No he hasn't! He is only visiting us! It is an honour he comes with such a court. And we have plenty for everyone. The Lost Lands have never been so rich.' He shrugged and extended his arms. 'Look around you! We have abundance of everything.'

Sardriel saw only poverty and neglect. He looked at Farramon and met the eyes of a stranger. Yet there was no cunning in him; his expression was transparent. He believed what he said, preposterous as it was.

'Was he invited?' Sardriel asked, keeping the anger from his voice with difficulty.

'Invited?' Farramon frowned. 'I suppose so. I can't remember. Anyway, what does it matter? He has come with great gifts for us, and naturally we offer him our hospitality. What else would you have us do?'

Sardriel swallowed. Doubt and unreason seemed to be in the room like a creeping chill. 'What gifts did he bring?' he asked.

'All sorts of things!' Farramon replied. 'Bales of silk, wool, hides from the north, jasper and malachite, good wine, grain, honey. Can't you see?' He pointed to the bare walls of the room, then to a stack of wood by the door.

Sardriel could not force himself to answer.

He stayed overnight, sleeping in the room Farramon's wife offered him with pride. He found it cold, stale and uncomfortable. In the morning he left and walked slowly, miserable and confused, up into the town of Orimiasse. The steep streets with their winding steps were long familiar. This was his home, where he had been a child and a young man. This bright harbour, with Siriom's ship lying at anchor, was where he had set sail to learn the mystery, the power and the harvest of the sea. He had climbed the hill behind him times beyond number, and stood on the great cliffs at the edge of all known land. The remembrances of his father's father lay in the shell garden in the hollow that looked on eternity.

He stood in the sun and stared around him, unnoticed by passers-by. There were a score of subtle differences. The dark nets were spread across the narrow streets, but dry, as if they had not been used. The soft colours of the houses were faded, not with the sharp light, or the salt wind, but with lack of care. There was none of the sense of urgency he remembered so keenly. People were idle as if there were nothing worth the effort of doing. He looked in vain for anger or grief. There was not even the sullen helplessness of a conquered people.

If anyone recognised him they gave no sign. Yet, with his high cheekbones, his level stare and passionate mouth, they surely knew him? Were they silent for fear of betraying him?

A few yards away a woman sat on a low wall eating a loaf of stale bread, crumbling it in her fingers and putting it into her mouth. She smiled as if it were delicious to her, her eyes far away, full of dreams.

The longer Sardriel looked, the more people he saw going about purposeless tasks, apparently absorbed in them. He enquired what they were doing, feeling foolish, half expecting to be told the obvious. The answers chilled him more than ice on the wind could have done, because they made no sense. He saw a man banging nails into chunks of wood as if he believed he had built something fine. With a sense of dazed unreality he walked past three old men sitting on upturned boxes, staring across the harbour at the idle ships at anchor.

'I wonder what they have for us this time,' one of them said dreamily.

'Fruit, I expect,' the second answered. 'Or honey.'

'More like hides.' The third pursed his lips thoughtfully. 'That very soft leather that feels almost like heavy silk.'

Questions poured through Sardriel's mind, relentless logic, and he looked at the old men's faces and saw bland pleasure, contentment. The fire and the passion were gone, the capacity for hunger or pain, indignation or the driving need to believe.

He left them and walked away, back along the shore. Were they paralysed with fear? Were there hostages held somewhere? Why was no one fighting? Why could he not even sense anger in the air, or desperation, even hate? No one cared! It was as if he were the only person who could see what had happened. He was in his own land, among his own people, and he had never been so alone.

Where could he turn for an ally? Farramon was blind, like a man overtaken by madness. The master who had brought him would not be back for days. Sardriel stared around him at the bright water whispering against the piers and curling over on to the sand by the shore, crunching on the shingle. He looked up the narrow streets where more nets were hung to dry like black lace against the pale walls of the houses. Was there anyone else in Orimiasse who was awake to the ruin, or was this his own private descent into nightmare?

One decision became more and more inevitable as he thought about it. He must find Siriom and face him. It was fourteen years since they had parted in Kyeelan-Iss. They had known each other only a month, yet in that time they had marked each other's lives for ever. Each had dealt the other a wound that would not heal. Without seeking it, Sardriel had won the only thing Siriom wanted and could not buy with any art or price on earth, the love of his wife, Elessar. She had been coerced into marriage, profoundly against her will, to save her people from invasion by the strongest forces of Kyeelan-Iss. For their sakes she was obedient to Siriom in his hall and at his table, but she would not submit to his bed.

When Sardriel, new to Sadokhar's court, had gone as emissary to try to win alliance between the two kings, in spite of all their will against it, he and Elessar had fallen in love. Siriom had seen it in their eyes, their faces, even the echoing movement of their bodies, and jealousy stormed through him until it consumed the last shred of honour left. He used lies and deceit to manipulate them to one place at the same time, and appear to be adulterers. He was King, Sardriel was his guest. To have abused hospitality in such a way was treason and a crime unto death.

He told Sardriel that if he rode away in peace and never returned then Elessar would live. Of course he accepted.

He told Elessar that if she came willingly to his bed, as often as he should wish, and filled his every desire, then Sardriel would live. In agony of revulsion she too accepted. But the misery of it broke her health, and two years later she died in childbirth, and her baby with her. It was only then that Sardriel learned the price she had paid for his life, and the grief had changed him for ever.

Now he must think of the present and see what manner of creature Siriom had become, how good or evil had altered him.

It was evening when he finally walked up the steep street, between the walls of the houses, softly coloured with the reflection of sunset. Above him the remnants of the once delicate nets were strung across from window to window. No one had worked on the snags and tears, or taken out the broken pieces of weed. A few doors were open, but only from one did he see the flicker of firelight, and from none of them was there music. He could hear it in his mind, not the lutes and low, throaty pipes of the Lost Lands, but the rippling harp of Kyeelan-Iss that Elessar had played.

He let its beauty soothe and hurt him, wakening old dreams that lay crushed in his heart, and allow himself to feel, and the pain of it washed through him until he reached the Prince's House.

There were guards on duty, but they made no demur about letting him in. The iron fretwork gates closed behind him and he went on up the steps and through the archway inside. He imagined Siriom would be in the Great Hall with its long windows that looked towards the twilight over the sea. He was not mistaken.

The doors were open but there was no sound from within. He assumed Siriom was alone, but even before he saw the figure of the King of Kyeelan-Iss in the carved chair, deliberately reclining, he was aware of another person. His eyes were drawn to him in spite

280

of the power and the enmity of Siriom, and all that lay between them.

The other presence was the dwarf, broad-shouldered, squat and immensely heavy. His weight seemed to bear down as if his flat, archless feet must leave an imprint even on the stone flags of the floor. He was dressed in a curious tunic of diamond-shaped panes of different shades of gold, and it seemed never to be quite still because he was endlessly moving his stubby, white hands. His eyes were not human, but liquid yellow and goatlike.

He smiled as he saw Sardriel, and his tongue wet his lips.

It cost Sardriel an effort to tear his gaze away and look at Siriom instead. He felt an oppression in the room like damp on his skin and the air clogged his lungs. Speaking was so difficult that for a moment he did not, and it was Siriom who broke the silence.

'Is that you, Sardriel of the Lost Lands?' He leaned forward a little, peering, although there was plenty of light. His lips puckered in a grimace of satisfaction. 'I knew you'd come. Wherever you were in the world, you'd hear of this sooner or later.' His voice was low in his throat, without timbre, thin for so heavy a man. He had grown pot-bellied with time. His face was pasty-white and his black hair sparse so his scalp showed through. But it was his eyes that held Sardriel's attention. They were opaque, clouded over. His head moved, questioning, searching for the smallest sound of movement or breath so he could place Sardriel in the room.

'I'm here, Siriom!' Sardriel responded grimly. 'In front of you! And yes, I came when I heard. It's a poor kingdom you hold. What wealth is it to you when the people are idle and neither toil nor serve? What kind of fool breaks the thing he has stolen?'

Siriom faced the sound of Sardriel's voice, placing him exactly. His hands grasped the arms of his chair, his body tense. 'The kind who remembers old injuries, and repays them tenfold!' he hissed. 'I don't want your wretched islands to take their prosperity! I want them ruined. I want you to watch your people blunder around in the darkness and fall to their knees, idle and deluded, grasping dust for treasure. And I have it! Look around you and see that I do! Taste it! Smell it in the air! Know it in your soul, Sardriel!'

The acrid odour of hatred was so sharp in the room it burned the eyes. The years of jealousy had piled deep; the knowledge that Ellesar had despised him, and now was beyond his reach to win, or to hurt, had corroded all that was left of him. Sardriel knew who had given him his wish. He turned to the dwarf. This was Azrub, Lord of Delusion, who had come through the portal of hell with Tiyo-Mah.

Looking now at his face, with its lustre of pleasure, Sardriel was repulsed in a way he had never felt before, as if something filthy

281

had touched his body and crawled inside him. He must break it. He must never allow this abomination to know his heart.

He turned away, looking again at Siriom. He wanted to tell him that this was only the middle of the war, not the end, but he had no words to convey to this wreck of a man that truth was a clean and beautiful thing which no amount of lies could tarnish, no matter who believed them. Above all, Siriom's victory was a mirage which he saw because he wanted to, a reflection of no more substance than those created by Azrub.

But Siriom had forgotten what truth was and he no longer understood the words.

Sardriel knew he would be wasting his thought, and he turned away again, leaving without further speech. He must plan how to begin the struggle to tear the illusion from his people and bring them back into the pain and the joy of life. They must begin to fight their bondage before it wound so deep around them, into their flesh, that they no longer had any strength left.

It took him many days to find anyone with whom he might begin. Everywhere he went it was the same. Men and women drifted in idleness, staring at the untended fields, smiling vacuously as if they saw beauty and meaning where there were only boats riding at anchor, torn nets, weeds growing in the rich earth choking the crops, animals wandering from one pasture to another untended.

No one knew what any individual saw with the eyes of their dreams, except Azrub, because it was he who had woven the delusion which bound them.

Sardriel watched and listened. He struck up conversation with one person after another, always probing, seeking for some spark he could reach to ignite a fire of reality. He was on the beach with the tide racing in, surf white at the blue edge of it, salt sharp on the wind, when he saw a young man with a piece of driftwood in one hand and a knife in the other. He kept staring at the half-finished work as if uncertain what more to do with it. It had a kind of beauty, like the flight of a bird, and yet the wings were incomplete.

'The wood has a character in it,' Sardriel said, looking at it more closely. 'If you go against it, it will break and become meaningless. What is your name?'

'Helik,' the young man answered, struggling for comprehension as he stared at the wood again. 'You see a pattern, a form?' he asked.

'Yes . . . don't you?' Sardriel watched him closely. What had Azrub caused him to see in the bone-white branch in his hands? Was it the wood any more, or some precious artefact from the fabric of his dreams?

'I thought to be a great artist, once,' Helik said quietly. 'In stone . . . in marble, or some such. Perhaps rock crystal, or quartz. It is strange now that I can do it.' He held up the wood for Sardriel to admire. 'I cannot remember how I learned. Isn't that odd?'

'Memory is hard to explain.' Sardriel stood beside him on the sand. 'I heard a story once, from a traveller on the other side of the world.' As they walked up the slope to the dunes he began to repeat to him the tales that a poet he met on the long journey alone across the steppes had told him of the ancestors of the Irria-Kanders. They had thought themselves gods, and forgotten the fragility of the balance between life and death. Nearer the sea they sat down, sheltered from the wind where the scent of lupins was heavy in the sun.

Sardriel told stories of deceit, and how men had wasted their substance in pursuit of that which had no value.

The light faded and the air grew cold. Sardriel was aware of it but Helik was still imprisoned in the world created by Azrub's art. The rising tide washing high just beyond the dunes, loud in their ears in the gathering darkness, did not reach through the golden walls of deceit.

Sardriel picked up the piece of driftwood which had fallen where Helik's hands had let it slip.

'What is it?' he asked.

'This?' Helik noticed it again and frowned. 'Rose quartz. I was going to carve a bird in it, but it is very hard. I'm afraid I'll shatter it.'

'Where did you find it?'

'Here, in the sand.'

'Rose quartz . . . in the sand?' Sardriel said doubtfully.

Helik turned it over and over in his fingers, touching the wood's grained surface where the water had eroded it. He frowned.

'Does it feel like quartz?' Sardriel asked.

Helik held it out. 'What do you think it is?'

Sardriel took it gently, hesitating for some time. The air had the strange, luminous quality of twilight over the water, the fiery, reflected glow from beyond the horizon. 'I think it looks like rose quartz,' he replied very quietly. 'But it feels like driftwood. And it is important to know the truth, because the grain of wood is nothing like the crystals of quartz. If one were to try to make form in it, supposing it to be wood, and it were crystal, it would shatter.'

Helik concentrated fiercely, drawing his brows together, running his fingers over the surface again and again, feeling the grain, the denseness of the knots, the bare smoothness of the branch where the water had polished it.

Sardriel waited. Would the stories he had told jolt some fragment

283

of Lost Lands discipline and belief too deep for even Azrub to mask for ever?

He was afraid Helik was slipping away from him. Would he break the concentration if he spoke?

'Is it warm?' he said impulsively. 'Like a living thing, or cold, like mineral of the earth?'

Helik looked up at him. 'What are you trying to make me see?' The words were charged with emotion. His fingers were clenched on the wood, knuckles white. 'Who are you? What is it you want here?'

If Sardriel were to speak now, and say the wrong thing, he would have to begin again with someone else, and he felt time pressing hard upon him as Azrub's hold tightened.

'I am a Lost Lander returning from abroad,' he replied. 'And what I want is to know more clearly than I do what it is that I see or touch. If I don't, I may be injured, and so may those I care for.'

'Injured?' Helik repeated the word, still turning the wood over and over in his hands. 'I haven't felt pain in days ... weeks, actually.'

'That is the purpose of the story of the Irria-Kanders,' Sardriel explained. 'They realised what mistakes they had made only when it was too late, and they had already changed too far to go back.'

'Really?' Helik frowned, trying to read in Sardriel's eyes the spirit beyond the words. He smoothed his fingers over the driftwood wing. 'What is it you see?'

'Wood,' Sardriel replied. 'Bone-pale, wind- and sand-polished wood, cast up by the sea. It is as beautiful as rose quartz, but that is not what it is.'

Helik lifted his eyes very slowly to Sardriel's face. 'You are right ... it is wood. I can see that now.' He stared around him. The last echo of daylight high in the sky showed the empty, marble-pale sand, one boat pulled above the tide, its net spread across the bow end and left trailing 'Where is everyone?' he asked, puzzled.

'Gone home,' Sardriel answered.

'Home? Then why haven't they taken the net?' Helik asked with disgust. 'It's torn. No fisherman would leave it like that!'

'He can't see the holes in it,' Sardriel replied.

Helik looked not at the net, but at Sardriel. 'They're gaping.'

'I know.'

Helik did not question it. Something within him already knew. He turned and looked towards the hill as if he could see the town beyond, and Sardriel understood the slow clarifying of the vision inside his mind but he could only guess how much it hurt.

The following morning the light was bright and hard, and the wind came in cold off the sea. It was choppy, white-capped, but not a day on which a mariner would fail to put out. Yet Helik was the only one to be down by the wharf ready to sail. Sardriel stood a little apart from him as his friends stared with incomprehension.

'What are you doing?' the oldest asked, a man with grey streaks in his hair.

'Going fishing,' Helik replied. 'If you mended your nets instead of leaving them spread out like that, you could come too. It'll be good fishing today to the north.'

'We don't need any more fish,' the man replied patiently. 'It's foolish and wasteful to catch what you can't use.'

'We have no fish,' Helik replied. 'There's only grain, and not much of that.'

'The silo's full of grain!' one of the other men said in amazement. 'And there's enough fish in the ice house to feed us for a week!'

'The silo's nearly empty,' Helik said tartly. 'And there's nothing but ice in the ice house. Look at it again.'

There was now a group around him, half a dozen or more, and their faces reflected dismay turning into anger.

'This is not like you, Helik,' one said calmly. 'Why are you being so contentious?'

'Why can't you be grateful for the plenty we have now?' another asked, shaking his head. 'The only thing we haven't got in the Lost Lands is a warm shore to grow fruit!' He laughed. 'That's about the only dream left that hasn't come true!'

'Dreams!' Helik said sharply. 'That's all they are. Can't you see that? I don't know how it could all rot so far in a few days – or weeks – but it has. Look around you!' His voice was rising higher with anger and an edge of fear. He swung his arm wide, gesturing towards the harbour where no sails were lifted, no ships loaded or unloaded. Men and women sat around talking to each other, laughing. They did not even seem to feel the chill of the wind off the water.

The oldest man frowned. 'Pull yourself together, Helik! You are speaking irresponsibly. It's not like you to criticise your fellows. You had best go out on your own, if you are still bent on putting to sea. Taste the wind and the water a little. Think hard on your ways, and come back to us with a better heart. Be grateful for the plenty we have. Siriom has brought us many gifts. He is welcome to stay as long as he will. We have plenty – are we to begrudge him a few days' hospitality?'

'He's been here more than a few days!' Helik argued. 'It's been . . .' But as he strove to remember how long, the truth eluded him.

The others were looking at him with anger.

Sardriel waited. Should he intervene or would that only make it worse? What could he offer Helik that would take the place of friends – and make standing alone bearable? Nothing . . . and he knew it.

Slowly Helik turned from one of the men to another, then looked beyond to the harbour. The fight for decision was naked in his face.

'Siriom brought us nothing,' he said at last, 'except confusion, a disease of idleness as if we can't even see what's in front of us! When did you last do any work – put to sea, fish, mend nets, plant or weed or gather crops?' He turned to Sardriel for support.

Sardriel came forward. He could not deny that small comfort.

'Siriom has been here for weeks,' he said quietly. 'During that time you have changed your lives. You no longer do anything but sit around and talk and dream. Why?'

They looked perplexed. 'We do all that is needed. You can't mend a net that isn't broken, or pull weeds where there are none.'

Sardriel did not answer. He walked away and went with Helik down to the shore. Together they manned the ship and spent the daylight hours on the sea, returning at twilight with all the fish they could carry.

For five days it lasted, and Helik tasted the dregs of loneliness. His friends showed little anger towards him, and behaved as if he were as invisible to them as the slow neglect of nets, the fields, the littered streets, or the unkempt clothes of their own appearance.

Sardriel went alone to the shell garden on the cliffs to consider what next to do. When he returned he found Helik with the oldest man who had once been his friend. They were standing together in the late sun. He saw them when he was still a hundred yards away, where the path levelled off from the steepness of the hill and the sea grass was worn by the passage of feet.

The man passed Helik a cup of water and Helik took it with a smile, putting it to his lips and savouring it as if it were wine. Then he passed it back and put his arm around the man's shoulder.

They both became aware of Sardriel, even though he had not moved. They turned and looked at him. There was no victory in the older man's face, simply a blindness. The same blank-eyed stare was in Helik, but the tension had gone out of his body, the anxiety, the pain of being separate.

'Have some wine?' he called, holding out the cup.

Anger washed over Sardriel like a breaking wave, and then was gone again, leaving only failure behind. He had asked too much, and asked it of the wrong man at the wrong time. Perhaps it was his fault as much as Helik's.

He stood on the shore in the sunset wind, seeing the dark blue of the sea and the bright dazzle of light on the water, the single boat pulled up the sand, the net still across it, unmended. He knew why Helik could not bear the loneliness, because it twisted inside him also, a void impossible to heal. Only he had seen a greater truth, and to let go of it would have been a loss that could never be recovered.

He would have to begin again, with someone else and be wiser. Time was too short to fail again.

Chapter Nineteen

This time Sardriel chose a family with many members so no one would have to stand alone. The strengths of one would sustain the weaknesses of another. He befriended them one by one, using logic with the father, charm with the mother, tales of history and remembrance of old hardships, bitter winters long past for the grandmother.

To the daughter, Katina, who was thirteen years old, he told the tales he had heard in Irria-Kand, and shared his feelings of sitting around the campfires on the vast, wind-torn steppes.

She sat with dark eyes intent on his face as the sun faded in the west and the breeze painted rippling brush strokes across the shining surface of the sea,

'What did you eat?' she asked him. 'If there were no rivers, there can't have been any fish.'

Eminently logical. 'No,' he agreed. 'But there were huge herds of wild beasts, sometimes so vast they darkened the plains, and when they moved the ground trembled.'

'That sounds terrifying!' she exclaimed, her face eager.

He smiled. 'Yes it was, and wonderful. I hated killing them, but it was necessary for our survival. There were roots of plants and occasional grasses, but not sufficient to feed an army.'

She regarded him with fascination. 'Did you march every day?'

'Almost. Sometimes there were terrible storms.'

She frowned. 'If there was no sea, what did it matter?'

He tried to describe for her the thunder that had roared around the horizon on every side and the lightning that had rent the sky with fire, creating walls of flame that raged across miles of land in a matter of hours, leaving it a smoking ruin.

She sat white-faced, her eyes never leaving his.

'Were you terrified?' she whispered.

'Yes,' he said frankly. It did not occur to him to lie.

She leaned over and slid her cool hand over his. 'You're safe now. That never happens here.'

How could he tell her of the fires of the soul which were infinitely worse? 'Good,' he said softly. 'I think with the sea we have enough.'

'We haven't had a storm for ages,' she replied.

'We will have,' he said gravely. 'There will be terrible storms to come, and it is right that there should be.'

'Why?' She was guarded, uncertain. 'My father says this is good. We have plenty of fish and calm weather, and everything we need.'

'We need storms as well,' he said carefully, holding her gaze.

'Why?' It was not contentious. She wanted to know, and she would believe his answer. He must be very careful in what he said and it must be the exact truth.

'Because we are children of God,' he said. 'There is nothing we cannot do, if it is right, but we have to learn strength and courage, we have to learn wisdom and test our faith. Anybody can sail on calm waters, it's the storms that test us.'

She shifted a little in the sand, holding her arms around her knees and staring at him. 'Men and women both?'

'Of course.'

'You're not just talking about wind and lightning, are you.' This was a statement.

'No. I'm talking about good and evil as well.'

'Do I have to choose?'

'We all do. If you haven't chosen, and the Great Enemy doesn't know your name, then perhaps God doesn't know it either.'

Katina scuffed her fingers in the sand. The scent of the lupins was hanging in the evening wind on the last light. 'I can't think of anything more terrible than for God not to know my name. I think that's about the worst thing that could happen to anybody.'

'Yes,' he agreed. 'I think it is.'

She looked up. 'That's what you're trying to make us do, isn't it – my family, all of us – make us look at what's real, and choose?'

'Yes.'

She leaned forward quickly and kissed Sardriel on the cheek, her hair brushing his skin.

He sat motionless, almost as if he dared not acknowledge the gesture in case she denied it.

The last light splashed fire across the sea and the sky above faded to indigo. A white gull landed close to them and stood still, staring in curiosity.

'Don't move!' Katina whispered. 'Don't frighten him!'

Sardriel obeyed; he would not have moved anyway.

The bird put its head on one side and regarded them with interest. It took one step, then two and stopped. Sardriel was surprised how large it was. Riding the air the gulls seemed only flashes of movement, a gleam of wing in the light.

'Isn't it beautiful?' Katina said under her breath.

It was, but the curved, yellow beak was hard and sharp, a

considerable weapon, and there was power in the huge span of folded wings. Nature had built it for the wind and the sea. It nested on land, but the ocean and the sky were its realm. Now its curiosity wanted to see what these strange creatures were who sat without moving and seemed to want nothing. It took half a dozen more steps towards them.

Katina was smiling, her eyes wide with wonder.

The bird cocked its head to the side again and made a soft, gurgling sound in its throat.

'Hello,' Katina said very quietly.

There was no sound but the rushing of the waves and the barest murmur of wind in the grasses behind them.

Seconds passed into minutes. The sun slipped beneath the horizon and the spilled gold faded from the water. The bird chunnered softly and bobbed its head, then turned and walked flat-footed a few steps, spread its wings and soared up into the last of the reflected radiance across the arch of the sky, growing smaller and smaller until it was only a gleam, a star in the dusk.

Katina moved a little closer until she could lean against Sardriel's shoulder and, as if unfeeling of the galling chill, they sat together until the first stars glittered above before rising and going side by side back inland.

But it was not so easy to deal with her family's reactions to truth. Fear frayed their tempers and they began to quarrel. Old loyalties broke apart, leaving misery, and blame. They responded to pain with anger, lashing out because the reality was too bitter to acknowledge.

Sardriel retreated, dazed with guilt for their pain, and because he had forced them all, against their will, to see a truth they could not cope with. Had he been wrong to have done that? Would either wisdom or compassion have stayed his hand?

He walked alone out on the stone pier. The bright, choppy water was on either side of him, the wind of its surface cold to his skin, the gulls crying overhead. He had been certain when he began that if he could only make a crack in Azrub's power of delusion he would begin to break it all. The first few people to see the truth would tell others and the web they were caught in would unravel and set them free.

He had failed with Helik, because he was alone, and he needed acceptance more than he loved any truth. And it seemed he had failed with Katina's family also, because for all their ties of blood and marriage, in their confusion they turned upon one another.

He had forced on them a test they were not strong enough to meet. They had looked at the ugliness of Sardriel's reality, and it

291

had found the weaknesses within them, and they had let it go again, choosing unity and the façade of peace.

What right had he to do that? If they chose an illusion in which they could achieve at least some virtue, some kindness, had he done them a greater injury by stripping it away?

It was the last thing he had intended. Could it be that his own passion for truth was actually a kind of pride? Did he imagine himself invulnerable to dreams, to the longing for love, for days when there were no battles to be fought, and it was all right to laugh, to look at beauty without the ache of fear that it would be destroyed?

Siriom was still an invader. Azrub was still an emissary of the last destruction, but was this the way to fight? Or was he perhaps doing exactly what they would have wanted in forcing people to meet his own standards of truth, and letting them be broken when they could not?

He narrowed his eyes against the sun off the water, which was so glittering sharp it hurt, and felt it go through him like a darkness that took hold and drove out the light. Everything he knew or could imagine, hung in the balance, the whole marvellous, passionate, beautiful world with its power to become a heart to beat in the silent wheel of the stars – for good or evil. They must not lose!

He must not fail here in the Lost Lands which were his own battlefield. They were small, intimate, bright as a jewel in the sea, but that was irrelevant. In the end it all came to a struggle between one mind and another, elements that barely took up any space at all. This was between himself and Azrub. He must take up the weapons of war again and return to the fight with words of truth.

Katina worked as well, with the dedicated fierceness of innocence, trying to convince others to let go of the sweet ease and waken to the coming storm. She used Sardriel's words about choice. Again and again she told them who they were, but they were not willing to hear the meaning it carried.

Some resisted with smiling indifference, clinging to the visions that danced in their senses as one grasps a dream in the night and refuses to see the daylight. Others reacted with anger and defended their comfort with retaliation.

It was one of these who had shoved her impatiently when she would not be silent. He had seen only the illusion of green grass and bright sunlight, not the reality of the crumbling cliffs, nor her body overbalancing and sliding helplessly beyond the ledge and over to fall broken and bleeding on the stone below.

Only one among them even realised what had happened. Reality burst in upon him with desperate horror and he ran, heart pounding, muscles on fire, to find Sardriel. The others heard only the cry of sea birds, and continued in their smiling dream.

She was still alive when Sardriel reached her, but he knew she had not long. She had little pain because the life was already slipping away from her as he cradled her head in his arms.

'Sardriel, is that you?' She was struggling to see through the gathering darkness in her eyes.

'Yes,' he said gently, the ache in his throat choking his voice. 'Yes, I'm here.'

'Am I dying?' she asked.

He had never told a lie. How could he begin now with Katina? She alone had picked up the weapons of war he had offered them all, and gone forward without hesitation to do battle.

'I am . . . aren't I?' she whispered. 'I can hardly see you . . .'

'I'm here . . .' He held her more closely. Moving her broken bones could do no harm now, and she was beyond pain.

'I don't want to die yet!' She took a shaky breath and coughed. 'I haven't done all the things I needed to! How will God know if I am any good? I haven't sailed the storms yet.' She took another breath, shallower this time. 'Can't you help me? You can do so much . . .'

What truth was there now to tell her? His limitations, his fears, his so real humanity? What comfort would that be to her? She was a child, she should have been at the beginning, not the end!

'No,' he said softly. 'I'm just another warrior in the struggle, just as you are. But I shall have to fight without you from now on, for however long I have. Your part is done, and you did it well.'

'Did I?' She could not see him, her eyes were already blind. 'Will God know who I am?'

'Oh yes . . .' He could barely control his voice, and the tears were wet on his face.

She smiled, but there were no more words. The last silence enfolded her.

He picked her up and carried her home, stumbling and blind.

They buried her in a quiet place on the shore with the wind carrying the smell of salt and the call of birds, the ceaseless breaking of water over the rocks. The family was united at last, not so much in the recognition or understanding of reality or the breaking of Azrub's web, but in anger against what had happened to the Lost Lands that no one shared their grief except Sardriel and the one man who had run to fetch him. The rest were unaware that anything was lost. They wandered on in their dreamlike state, smiling, growing thinner as they ate food they only imagined was there, and let the boats rot, the weeds grow, and dust and the rubbish gather in the streets.

It was Sardriel who climbed up the steep hill to the Place of Remembrance on the crown of the cliff that overlooked the last ocean, and then dropped the few steps to the ledge where the shell garden nestled above the boom of the surf.

The priest of the shrine must be dead. Perhaps he was one whose mind Azrub could not reach? Maybe his only hunger had been for truth.

Sardriel gathered the shells from where they were stored and chose a perfect bivalve of the palest pink, almost translucent. Then in the custom of the Lost Lands he carved Katina's name on one half and his own on the other. He divided the shell gently. 'I covenant to serve your people with the truth, to love them and to mourn with them for their dreams,' he said quietly. 'I promise to fight for the world, the best and the worst in it, and to ride the storms, so God will know my name as well.'

Then he cast Katina's half into the void of the ocean and the sky, and placed his own in the garden. He chose the place carefully, close to a bone-white piece of driftwood, and saw there another shell with the name 'Tamar' on it. Tathea had laid it here over five hundred years ago for her mother, and another for her son, before she had set out to find the sage who had directed her to her journey of the soul.

Sardriel stared into the blue of infinity. There was no line where the sea met the sky. Grief for Katina consumed him, for that which she could have been had life given her the time. He bent his head and wept with all the passion in him for the loss of a child dearer to him than he had known or wished, and then for other loves older and deeper, and for the loneliness in his soul.

Then at last he lifted his face. The sun was dazzling, but he did not turn away from it. White sea birds rose in the air, riding the currents, soaring upwards until they were almost invisible against the burning blue.

Why had God allowed Katina, or anyone, to be torn from this life before they had had a chance to learn its lessons, or to measure themselves against its glory and its pain, and make all their choices? There must be justice in it . . . but where?

Beneath him the waves roared in and crashed against the cliff base, sending sheets of foam high into the glittering air, hanging for an instant, then falling, diving back into the white spume of the cauldron below.

Had he wronged Katina in giving her such a bitter choice to make? What of the others who had failed? Should he have shielded them, defended them from the reality? No! No – he had no right to judge who would and who would not succeed – or even what measure of the battle any man could or would fight.

Then gradually as he cried out to the infinity, demanding to know, peace came to him, and a knowledge as clear as if it were in words. It would be just if men were judged not only according to their acts, but according to their wishes also, for good or ill, all the things they would have done, were they to have had the time and the power. Surely that was the measure of who they truly were? They would have done good, but not had the means, only the love and the courage and the generosity of heart. Or they would have done evil, but were afraid of the consequences, or denied the power. That was just as much the truth of their eternal nature.

The warmth of the light became part of Sardriel's being, filling the spaces where doubt had rested before, becoming a certainty of such sweetness he wanted only to rest in it, to remain in this clean and shining place until he belonged to it for ever.

As he stared into the blue haze where the sea must somewhere meet the sky, he became aware of Katina as if she were with him. He could see her in the distance, just beyond his strength to call, but she knew he was here on an island of time. Eternity was not behind him and yet to come, as he had believed, but an ocean encircling him. Time was man's perception of a profundity too deep to grasp except in dream. He was simply separate for a necessary space, so that glory and darkness could both come to pass. Without choice there was no meaning to it all, and no purpose.

Until his time came to rejoin that greater reality he must return to the battle here and take it up again with greater energy, more courage, more trust in God Whose presence he had glimpsed in a moment of splendour that shattered unreason for ever. And above all he must have more confidence in the power of love, whatever the cost, the grief, or the time.

Truth was the only thing that could save the Lost Landers – or anyone else over the face of all the worlds that could ever be.

He turned and walked back towards the path, and the long way down through the wild grass to Orimiasse.

Sardriel worked with a new vigour. He was tireless, using all the skill, the logic and the passion he possessed, to teach the beauty of truth and the deeper treasure of identity, and the glory of courage to face the fact and let go of the illusion. More joined him, especially the man who had brought him the news of Katina's fall. Gradually they began to labour again, to mend the nets, to make certain ships were seaworthy. Women pulled up the weeds, tilled the ground, tidied the wind-blown rubbish and mended torn clothes, swept steps and streets.

★ ★ ★

Siriom went out less and less often. Most of the time he sat in the high-backed chair in the house on the hill and thought of his new empire, and how much it must hurt Sardriel. Then he smiled. Occasionally he walked in the streets, dressed in silk and embroidered robes so full they disguised his round belly. But the pleasure in that was waning. He could see only dimly; sight was more a matter of light and shadow than clear outlines. And since last time he'd gone out, everyone thought they wore silks and velvets; his magnificence caused them no wonder or envy. He had learned that there was no joy in a reality he could not share.

Azrub saw defeat moving towards him. At first he refused to believe it. His will was stronger than any mere human's. He knew the power of hunger, of longing for the impossible. Had he not lived with it since before time began? He saw it in everyone, even Asmodeus himself, and he felt it in the core of his own bowels, that ache that could never be torn out. He had the gift to read the body and the mind of men from the darkest fantasies of nightmare to the sweetest longings of the soul. He could create the illusion of them all! What else would anyone want beyond their dreams made real?

And yet Sardriel was breaking the illusion!

But Azrub had one more exquisite card to play. It would be easy, and very, very strong, unbreakable by the simple wills of the Lost Landers. There was one thing they all still wanted: a warm, sunbathed, sheltered shore where they could grow the fruit this salt-laden, wind-cleansed island could not provide.

And flowers! He could make the land lush with blossoms of gorgeous colours, a paradise for the eye, sweet-scented and warm to the flesh. The blue water would dazzle. He knew just the shore to create it, on the further side of the island where the surf thundered in with a thousand miles of unbroken ocean behind it.

He stood at the window of Siriom's great house and stared down at the streets of Orimiasse, and the harbour beyond. There were ships idle there, but there were some busy as well – too many! Men and women were working, no longer seeing all the dream, only parts, fragments here and there. Before he could go for Sardriel himself, he must deal with them.

He closed his yellow eyes and concentrated, summoning his vast power to create the illusion. The next man to pass the outer shore would see not the waves crashing on bare sand and rock, wind-scoured surf and the steep cliffs above, but a sheltered bay with calm seas, trees laden with fruit ripe for the picking, and gold, scarlet and wine-coloured blooms like the fire of sunset and the blood of the earth.

He stood there working on it, reaching into all the dreams he had seen, adding to them, polishing the images in his mind. Over and over again his tongue came out and licked his lips and his smile grew wider and ever more satisfied as he deepened the probe. He tested their appetite and how it could betray, as a man savours a vintage wine.

But the best was yet to come, when he faced Sardriel – and that had to happen, sooner or later. He almost dreaded doing it, because then it would no longer lie ahead where he could see it, play it out in his mind, rehearse it a score of different ways. The anticipation was delicate and delicious far beyond this simple exercise. These other Lost Landers were good enough people, but foot soldiers, expendable. Sardriel was one of Tathea's great warriors . . . and even better than that, he was a man who had made a god of truth. But he was vulnerable! Ah – he was so vulnerable! Azrub knew it and a groan of pleasure escaped him as he thought of the final ecstasy of holding that prize in his mind as long as Sardriel's life lasted.

Siriom was nothing, a fool whose dreams were cheap. Azrub bothered with him only as a necessary instrument, deluding him some times, not others, as it suited his purpose. Now he could be forgotten altogether. Let happen to him what may.

He succeeded. Less than two days later a fisherman far out from the shore thought he saw something quite new, and sailed closer in to look more clearly. The roaring current carried his boat towards the reefs, and he was too wise a mariner not to turn early and back away. But he made sail for Orimiasse immediately, and he had barely dropped anchor before he passed on the incredible news.

An expedition was mounted to climb the hills and scale the cliffs at the far side and investigate, then bring back word. By the end of a week, half the men on the island had been there, and a force was busy cutting a path down the cliff so every woman and child could go there too, and bask in the luxury of it, each in his or her turn, and thank a beneficent providence for such an unforeseen blessing.

Not everyone embraced it. A few reached the top of the hill and looked down at the last, wild shore of the world, and saw it as it was. But they were a minority, and no one wanted to listen to them. Sardriel knew the strength of Azrub's power over the mind, no matter how passionate the will not to be deceived. The longings of the heart could always weave a vision for the eyes, and who would choose a bitter reality for ever?

The time was coming when he would have to face Azrub and put to the test his own strength of faith, his love of truth above all, and see if he was equal to wounding the Lord of Delusion sufficiently to limit his usefulness to the Great Enemy. If he could break

Siriom's delusion, force him to see the reality and his own loss, the emptiness of his victory, then half Azrub's hold on the people would be broken too.

Then perhaps Azrub would enter the battle himself, and turn and face Sardriel.

He was not sure he would win, only that he would fight to the last instant of his strength. He would enter the battle with a perfect belief in the cause of God, but no unshakeable trust that he himself could not be overcome. That was a price he half expected to pay. Many men would die in Armageddon, in the end perhaps all. He must judge his time well and his going must be at the dearest possible cost to all who served the Father of Lies. All his thoughts were on the last confrontation, as he walked up the street towards the Prince's House, and Siriom and the beginning of his plan.

Sardriel went straight up to the door and opened it. There was no guard. Siriom knew that the web of delusion was sufficient.

Sardriel found him sitting in the carved chair, as he so often did, relishing it, trying to taste the power it should have invested in him, and now no longer seemed to. He looked up sharply as Sardriel came in, recognising his step. His eyes flickered for a moment in fear. He never forgot what he had done to him, and because he was eaten by hatred himself, he believed that Sardriel must be also.

Then another emotion took hold of him, deeper even than fear, a sort of abandonment to the inevitability of his own death, and the fierce inner joy that in accomplishing it, Sardriel would finally be equal with him . . . grovelling in the same slough of bitterness, self-loathing and at last despair. Elessar would not have loved him if she had seen him then!

'What do you want?' he said, sitting a trifle further back in the big chair and looking up towards Sardriel's dark, weary face, a shadow in the mist of his vision. He remembered when it was young and smooth, eyes innocent as he had ridden into Kyeelan-Iss. He saw again the wonder in him as he had gazed at Elessar, and her understanding of the blazing love of truth in him had sat like gall in Siriom's soul.

'To show you the further shore where the fruit grows, and the flowers,' Sardriel replied.

'Why?' Siriom asked. 'I have servants to bring them to me.'

The tone of Sardriel's voice changed. There was wonder in it, and something terrifyingly like pity. 'Have you really no idea who Azrub is?'

Siriom felt a brush of fear. It was ridiculous. What did it matter? Azrub had given him the thing he wanted most in life, revenge upon Sardriel, and asked little enough in return. 'I don't care!' he said loudly, and knew it was a lie the instant the words were spoken.

But Sardriel's voice was insistent. 'I'll take you to the further shore, and I'll show you.'

'And if I don't come?' Siriom demanded.

'You cannot afford not to come,' Sardriel answered. 'You need all the knowledge you can possibly have. All rulers do, but most especially those who play a dangerous game, and for high stakes.'

Siriom did not trust him. After all that had happened Sardriel had to hate him! Any man would. But he was obsessed with truth; it was part of his pride. To lie would destroy his self-belief, and he would not do that, even to exercise vengeance for Elessar. Siriom agreed, and hauled himself to his feet reluctantly.

'I'm not climbing that hill,' he warned. 'I'm taking a horse!'

Sardriel made no demur. Instead he held out a pale blossom – delicate, five-petalled like a star, and smelling cool and sweet.

'What is it?' Siriom asked irritably, aware more of the scent of it than the shape.

'A windflower, from the hollows of the shore,' Sardriel replied. 'You've smelled them before, even if you haven't noticed it.'

'I've noticed it!' Siriom snapped, taking it from Sardriel and peering at it closely. The perfume was exquisite. He could just make out the soft, rich petals, easily bruised.

'I'm bringing it with us,' Sardriel replied, taking the flower back. 'To the tropical shore.'

Siriom was dismissive. He knew every step of this house, and he walked ahead of Sardriel, so no one should mistake who was in command. He ordered the servant to find his horse and saddle it.

They went in silence, Sardriel walking a little ahead so the horse would pick its way where Siriom could not guide it. Siriom hated the sensation of being carried faster than his eyes could discern the changing shapes. It was unpleasant, even a little frightening. He was not in control.

They neared the top and the wind in his face told him they were facing the last great ocean at the end of the world. Then he realised it was something far deeper than that which caused the fear grasping at the pit of his stomach.

The wind was sharper now. He could hear a roaring in his ears and the cry of birds, and smell the salt.

'You'll have to dismount and walk now,' Sardriel said, offering his hand to help him. 'But the path is smooth all the way down. There are steps, and a rail on the cliff side. Even old women accomplish it safely.'

Siriom said nothing, but he obeyed. He stayed close to the cliff wall and gripped his hand on to the rail like a vice, shuffling his way down a foot at a time. He could feel the warmth as he got lower. This was a tropical paradise, as Azrub had promised. The sea was not a roar at all, only a murmur. The music was not the harsh cry of gulls but the liquid song of birds of wild and strange colours, their feathers like jewels. Even his eyes could make out the flash of scarlets and blues amid the trees.

He stepped on to the level at last and turned his face towards the sun, basking in its heat. No wonder great juicy, fire-skinned fruit grew here, with flesh that dissolved in the mouth and sweetness to run over the lips. He smiled even as he thought of it.

Sardriel was beside him. Why had he brought them both here? Was this real, or another of Azrub's delusions? He did not know the difference any more – perhaps he never had! Azrub was playing with him! To him it was a game, something for his own appetite!

Sardriel was holding something in his hand, a pale, withered thing.

'What's that?' Siriom demanded, a terrible fear gripping him as reality and delusion melted into one another.

'The windflower,' Sardriel replied, passing it to him.

'What's the matter with it?' Siriom said, gulping. 'It's dead! What have you done to it? It was . . . beautiful! Why did you destroy it? Are you threatening me?' That was it. That must be what he meant.

'No.' Sardriel sounded more sad than angry. Or was it pity? No. Never! It must be hate, it had to be.

Siriom wanted to speak, but no words came to him.

'It died,' Sardriel replied very clearly, each word falling like a stone into still water. 'They are very delicate. They shrivel up in the cold.'

'But it's hot!' There was a note of wildness in Siriom's cry. He heard it himself and tried to suppress it. 'It's tropical!' he insisted as doubt crowded in on him with greater terror.

'It feels hot to you.' Sardriel's voice cut into him like a knife into flesh. 'Azrub is the Lord of Delusion. He can read your soul and weave a fabric out of your dreams strong enough for you to believe it. But he cannot deceive the windflower. It still dies. If you walk out on that shore, you will see calm, bright water. You will feel the sun on your face. But if you walk into the sea, the surf is real, cold and strong. It will smother you and drag you under. If you believe Azrub, and not me, then do it and prove me wrong.'

Siriom blinked at him, at the withered flower in his hand. What was the truth, who lied? Was there anything real? Was even Sardriel himself real, or was he part of Azrub's delusion as well, and there wasn't even any revenge?

He turned towards the shore, the limpid water under the dazzling sun. It was beautiful, like jewels poured from an endless treasure.

He looked again. The bird flying up against the sky was a gull, blazing white, an ordinary seagull! He looked down slowly and the wind was cold on his face. It was surf that pounded in his ears, boiling, thundering surf. He did not need to turn behind him to know the trees were gone, the fruit, the gaudy tropical flowers.

'You have mortgaged your soul to an illusion.' Sardriel's voice beat in his head. 'In the end, however far into eternity that lies, truth will be the strongest. The power of dreams cannot outlast it.' The words were like death in the air. 'All Azrub's promises will fail and then you will be alone with whatever is left.'

The thought was unendurable. There was nothing left – nothing at all, no victory, no revenge, no love or power, not even any dreams.

Siriom turned and started to run, panic mounting inside him as his feet floundered in the sand and stumbled. He must find Azrub and somehow, anyhow, make a better bargain. He did not even bother to look at Sardriel behind him. He must get away from this place and begin again. New arrangements must be possible, something he could do so that Azrub would take care of him, make the illusion last.

The sand was fine and soft, clinging to his feet, dragging as if it would hold him down. He struck out and overbalanced, falling hard, knocking the breath out of his lungs. He got up awkwardly and began again.

He thought of death, and waking up into eternity! There was eternity . . . If there was a devil, and there was, then he could not cease to exist. Perhaps there was a God! What if God were the stronger, the God Sardriel believed in, Who endured no lies, no delusion, no excuses?

The thought was so hideous the beating of his own heart all but choked him. He fell again, arms flailing wildly, sand in his face, in his mouth, breath almost suffocated in his chest. He crawled the last few yards and found the bottom of the path up the cliff again. His horse would be waiting at the top. He would make it carry him back to the town as swiftly as it could. He would go into the Prince's House and lock the doors. Azrub would come whatever he did, and at least that would keep Sardriel out.

The steps were harder to climb than he expected. His legs ached; the muscles stabbed him with pain. His feet were tender, blistered. He must keep moving, but it was difficult. The top seemed impossibly high above him. He was barely halfway. The wind was cold, and it buffeted him in all directions, upsetting his balance.

How much further was it? He stepped back a little to look. The wind was fierce. Sardriel was right – damn him – it was cold, clean and salt-edged. The roar of surf on the rocks below was deafening. It seemed close, even though it was over a hundred feet below, perhaps two hundred now. He craned his neck upward to look.

Could he make it? It seemed so high, so far above.

He felt his foot slip as the earth crumbled beneath him. He flung his arms out to regain his balance, and made it worse. His other foot lost its purchase on the step and he pitched sideways, grasping the air.

Sardriel saw Siriom's arms swing wide, carrying him further backwards. Then his legs buckled and he fell hard on the edge, thrashed desperately for long, terrible seconds before he arced over and fell twisting and kicking till he landed on the foam-drenched rocks below, motionless. The next wave thundered in, crashing and rising in towers of foam to hang pendant, like diamonds, then sank back into the ocean, and the rocks were bare.

Sardriel stood with the wind and sun in his face and the pounding of the surf filling his ears. The weight of pity inside him did not ease. He did not know if even the mercy of God could fill the emptiness in Siriom's soul. Perhaps somewhere in eternity . . .?

Then he looked along the water's edge and saw the glittering figure of the dwarf walking slowly towards him. He stopped seven or eight yards away from Sardriel. The light shimmered on the diamond-shaped panes of his tunic as the wind moved it.

In spite of the noise of the sea, when Azrub spoke his voice was soft and sibilant, and it fell with perfect clarity, every word as if spoken with no other sound in the world. He smiled; it was an expression of infinite obscenity. 'You want to see what I can do for you . . . as if you did not already know it in your heart.'

'You can do nothing for me,' Sardriel replied. 'But for the world, you could serve truth, instead of lies.'

Azrub's face did not change by even a flicker. 'The truth is that man will always follow the illusion, if it is sweeter,' he answered. 'Reality needs courage, and man is a coward. It needs tolerance, compassion and infinite power to forgive, and to hope. But man is narrow of vision, quick to judge and even quicker to condemn.' His voice filled the air. 'He forgives nothing, and hopes only for the answer to his own needs. You are a realist, a worshipper at the altar of truth. You know I am right. You have seen it too often to deny. You know it and you know I know it too.'

'Man is all those things,' Sardriel conceded. 'Every possibility is there for him, and he has the power to decide. Maybe even you had that . . . once.'

Azrub's smile widened. 'So decide, Sardriel! Look at what I can give you, for the rest of your life. All you have to do is take it! Go back to the Island at the Edge of the World, to the beautiful city of Tyrn Vawr, and live out your days. Or take reality,' he went on. 'Be alone in the wasting of the world as all creatures wither and die and darkness covers the earth, and the end of all things, until

Asmodeus rules. Then you will have nothing! You . . . and all your kind.'

The sun fell glittering on his tunic, so bright Sardriel blinked and turned away his eyes. Then he looked again and Azrub was gone. He was alone on the pale sand with the wind and the surf, gentler now, still a glory of blue and white, as pure as the morning of creation, sweet to the taste, the salt like a perfume.

There was a figure walking along the shoreline towards him, slender, moving with infinite grace as if every sense took joy in the living ocean and air and sand. Her dress was somewhere between blue and green, and her hair blew back off her face in the wind. It was Elessar, exactly as he remembered her, with all the laughter, the pain, and the dreams. His heart lurched within him. This was what his life had hungered for since the day they had met; it was the purpose of all his long struggle since then. Friendship had been sweet, but his heart had been alone, disciplined, closed when he dared not look or listen to its pain.

She was just the same: her eyes, her mouth, the curve of her neck just as his soul remembered. He fought to dismiss it, knowing it was Azrub's delusion, and yet the bliss of it enwrapped him and his heart burned within him, his body shook and he could not breathe.

She was still coming towards him. When she reached him he would feel her touch, smell the warmth and the sweetness of her skin, as he had in imagination, God knew how many times.

Had he the strength to resist it?

Perhaps not. Perhaps his resolve would melt like wax before the fire.

He could hear Azrub's voice in his ears. 'All life long! All life long!'

The words were there on his lips, but without sound.

Elessar was still coming towards him, smiling, eyes soft with the same longing that consumed him in a pain almost beyond bearing. He reached out his arms. She was nearly there.

She touched him. Her flesh was warm, the pulse was beating in her throat.

She was not real! But, dear heaven, every sense in his body was burning with the knowledge of her. She was Azrub's creation, torn from the dreams of his soul.

He took a step backwards and saw the shadow of hurt across her face.

'No . . .' he said.

'Take her!' the voice of Azrub urged. 'She is the reason you have kept the laws that restricted you, robbed you of your freedom and your pleasure. She is your reward! Look at her! Touch her.'

'No!' Sardriel shouted, stepping backwards again. The stricken look on Elessar's face was like a physical blow, even though he knew it was Azrub who created it. 'No!' he said again, turning away from the dream and staring out at the wild blue of the sea. The tears in his eyes almost blinded him. He heard rather than saw the thundering foam as the waves broke. 'You're wrong. I love Elessar; to be with her is the blessing I want above all others. But I strove to keep the law because I loved it. It is good in itself, whatever the gain or the loss.'

Azrub screamed at him, but his words were torn away by the wind. Elessar was wavering, as if Azrub could not hold the power to make her real. Azrub was still shouting.

Sardriel looked back at him, the sea washing white and cold around his ankles. 'No!' he answered. It was the hardest thing he had ever done. As he watched Elessar she faded, growing thin until only her eyes and the echo of her hair were left. It was like life itself slipping from his grasp.

He hesitated. Could he let it go for ever, dream or not?

Azrub's voice was in his ears, in his mind. 'Keep her . . . keep her!'

Sardriel put his hands up to his face. 'It's not real! It's not Elessar!' He moved back again, and the sea swirled around his legs, drawing him to it in a close, deep embrace. It was not cold any more, only infinitely pure, vast as the tides that sweep the earth, and he welcomed it, sinking into its arms like a pilgrim come home at last to a measureless peace.

The sea breathed a great sigh, filled with all the wild, sweet scent of infinite space, of winds that move for ever, salt-clean, light on water and the fires of heaven. It reared itself up and reached out its shining grasp after the golden dwarf. He was dragged screaming, buffeted, bruised and choking into its devouring mouth. It sucked him down into its belly where there was darkness and no air, deeper and deeper into the silence of its smothering heart. It imprisoned him under the weight of it until his flesh was torn away and his bones were crushed into a tiny space that a child might hold in its hand, but so heavy that even the rocks gave way beneath it, and it was swallowed into the earth.

Asmodeus paced the ramparts of Erebus and cursed Azrub with a raging disbelief that he could have failed! He had had everything, every skill and chance to win! Sardriel had been in his hands! His weakness was glaring, a wound wide open – and still Azrub had not won! It was almost impossible to grasp, and yet as he stared down at Sardriel in the arms of the ocean, his body held in a shining peace, he knew the victory of his soul, as sweet as heaven, a radiance that never fails.

He was consumed with a white-hot rage. Now he would go down there himself! He would accomplish what first Cassiodorus, and now Azrub had failed to do. He would loose such horror as the world had never seen.

Chapter Twenty

The southern barbarians of the desert swept north into Shinabar. They were fought at every step by the forces of Tiyo-Mah, led in the field by Mabeluz, most violent of the Lords of the Undead. The carnage was fearful as one city after another fell.

Tiyo-Mah retreated to the secret oases. In the wake of defeat thousands were slaughtered, and Indeg, Lord of the Undead, feasted on disease and spread the filth of pollution over the land and the water, killing birds and beasts.

The Shinabari armies were driven eastwards into Pera, plundering and destroying as they went.

From the steppes of Irria-Kand, cheated of the conquest of Camassia, the northern barbarians swept east and south into the upper borders of Pera, where Balour, most cunning of the Lords of the Undead, arrived and offered his services to create a defence out of the land itself.

Threatened with tidal waves of ruin on all sides, the Perans accepted, and vast, poisonous earthworks were created in a matter of days. Balour showed them how to mine for substances which erupted and turned the lakes to acid, others which tainted the rivers, until hundreds of miles were choked with dead fish and even the plants withered and rotted. Terrible weapons were created out of minerals and salts dug up – explosions which killed a hundred men at a time.

And using such things was the fourth Lord of the Undead, the ingenious Accolon, who had taught even the subtle Tirilisi how better to corrupt the banking systems of the world to get greatest power. The ruin was not only the people but the plants and beasts and the earth itself.

It was Asmodeus' challenge to Ishrafeli, and if he did not respond, then the Lords of the Undead would go on to befoul ever wider and wider circles until they tainted the whole earth. They were creatures of filth in body and spirit, but they had once been human and he could not simply destroy them, or he forfeited the best in himself also.

This was the moment when at last Ishrafeli began to perceive

307

what it meant that we should call each thing on the earth by name. He could ignore none of it: the great and the infinitesimal, the brave and the cowardly, the glorious and the foul must all be understood and their victory sought, their pain accepted. The words were becoming reality.

He must go to Pera where the tides of war met in the last great convulsion.

He disembarked at the main sea port and travelled inland, pushing his way through the tide of refugees seeking any escape from the horrors of war behind them, a devastation not seen anywhere before. The land was poisoned, corpses of the dead choked the river and disease filled the air. Plants and trees withered. Blight infested the fields.

He pressed south from the sea, passing more people every day, many of them almost at the point of collapse. He saw a woman of about thirty, half holding up an old man who limped so badly his right leg barely touched the ground. Every few steps she spoke to him, and he answered with effort.

A child cried wordlessly, hopelessly, and no one had the strength to comfort it.

A young man with hollow eyes led a group of a dozen or so. When he drew level with Ishrafeli he spoke. 'Are you waiting for someone?' He could think of no other reason why anyone would be moving away from the town and the sea where lay escape.

Ishrafeli shook his head. 'No. I am going inland.'

'Don't!' the young man said quickly. 'You'll starve.' He put his hand on Ishrafeli's arm and his grip was tight. 'The land is dying.' His voice cracked. 'Poisoned. The rivers stink and nothing grows. Whoever you loved is either dead or they will come this way towards the sea. There is nowhere else.'

Ishrafeli pulled away because there was an air of madness about the man, and the smell of fear clung to him. But his fingers gripped the more. 'It's true,' the man urged.

Ishrafeli had not doubted it, but if he had, looking in the man's face would have destroyed the last hope. 'I believe you,' he said softly. 'I must still go.'

'You can do nothing.' It was not a protest but despair. He was simply trying to warn because there was an honesty in him and a pity that would spare another needless pain. 'No one can heal this,' he went on flatly. 'The land itself is dead . . . the water, even the air, for all I know. The smell of death is everywhere. Nothing grows, not even grass. The few creatures that still live now will not last long.'

'What happened?' Ishrafeli asked.

'Mining to build weapons,' the man said grimly. 'But the minerals

308

poisoned the rivers. They sent up fumes that clouded the air. Trees died, and winds blew away the good earth. There's only death left.'

There was nothing to say. Ishrafeli started to walk because there was no point in remaining motionless. He could not go back and he could not help. Whatever there was to do lay ahead of him.

He moved steadily in the dry heat. The road was good, laid by the best engineers in the world, level and straight, paved with tiny bricks even better than the old Camassian ones from the high days of the Empire. The passing feet of refugees fleeing the carnage of war were following in the footsteps of centuries of traders and pilgrims of the past, and made no more impression on the stone than they had.

He met a woman with a troop of children, huddled together at the side of the road, faces gaunt with hunger and exhaustion. Several of them whimpered with misery.

Ishrafeli stopped and went back a step. The woman stared up at him, longing for any word of hope. He had no idea what her beliefs were. All he saw was the same hunger and thirst that he felt, the same pity and the same fear of pain, failure, and loneliness that was common to all humanity.

'I know it hurts,' he said gently. 'But it isn't pointless.'

Her eyes begged him for understanding, but the children were looking to her, and she would not admit to fear in front of them.

'The physical pain is only for a space,' he went on. 'Then all will be restored to a wholeness greater than before. This trial is to the bitter dregs of all there is, but we are nearly at the end.'

'Are we? Are you sure?' She searched his face intently.

'Yes,' he said with certainty. 'Just a little longer. Don't give up now. The prize is worth even this . . . infinitely worth it, I promise.'

There was authority in his voice, in his bearing, as if he knew some deeper meaning, and she did not question it.

She smiled at him, tears of relief in her eyes. 'Thank you.' She started to get up. He held out his hand to help her, and as he pulled he felt the lightness of her body. There was no weight to it under the fabric of her dress. She must have been hungry for weeks, if not months. He had a sudden certainty that she had given most of what she had to the children. Some of them may have been hers, but it was impossible they all were. He passed her the bread he had left, and she took it with thanks. She looked at him for a moment longer, then called the children to her and began to walk towards the city and the sea, her head up, a child by each hand, the rest following close behind.

Ishrafeli increased his own pace, his thoughts growing deeper and more inward. He had known since returning from Kharkheryll the nature of his part in the great plan, but again and again he had been surprised as the depth of it had opened up before him. Always it had become subtler and more dreadful, calling for greater endurance, more profound passion of commitment and sharing of suffering. He began now to wonder exactly what God required of him in this tortured land and if he would be equal to bearing it.

He walked, passing more people who were struggling now, sometimes even one at a time, lonely, broken, often injured. He did what he could to help, but it was desperately little. He could not afford to share the food he had or he would not accomplish his goal. There was nothing to offer except patience, two hands to rewind a bandage, and a calmness inside which for a few steadied the fear and gave an instant's feeling that they were not alone.

Night came. His legs ached and his feet were blistered walking in the dust and heat. He went off the road to the side. There was no grass, but he found a place where he could create a hollow in the dry ground and try to sleep.

In the cold ashes of a fire he saw the small bones of a domestic animal, probably a pet dog, killed to be eaten. For a moment he was overcome with grief, not for the animal whose suffering he hoped was short, but for those whose hunger had reduced them to such an act. Killing a dog seemed such a betrayal of trust, of the silent companionship given unconditionally, and asking so little in return. It was a sign of the disintegration of the decencies which held life together. Hunger was stripping away the layers of civilisation and leaving bare the soul beneath.

People were crowding each other along the road, many of them with wagons piled with household goods, bedding, clothes, pots and pans. Some even attempted to take with them treasures where others were content with just their lives. Now and again there was a cart carrying sick or injured, or the very old. Children made their way the best they could.

He saw the blind rage of despair and self-pity as well as honour, and those who stole from the weakest and most vulnerable, those who would murder their own to survive.

To the south where Mount Sorah rose above the plain, the horizon was stained with smoke, and the wind carried the smell of burning and of death.

Ishrafeli was in the wake of the Shinabari army now. It seemed that in fury they had scorched the earth itself, poisoning and polluting until nothing could live, friend or foe. Now there was no spoil even for the victors. The plants were withered or uprooted. He saw dead animals by the sides of the road, even dead birds. There was an unnatural silence over the earth except for the occasional buzzing of flies.

A faint wind arose, not enough to stir the dust around his feet.

Then he heard a great cry that came from the heart of the earth and filled his mind and body until he was one with it. 'Oh Lord, how long? How long must I endure?'

He was robbed of breath by grief for the innocence betrayed, the perfect loveliness of it wounded beyond healing. He bent to his knees, tears choking his voice.

'Father, let it end! Whatever it costs, help us – let it be over. Tell me what I must do, and let it be soon, please let it be soon!'

And as he kneeled he saw the agony of the world as he had never imagined. Every land was laid waste by the greed of man, plundered of its treasure to feed the wants of a moment. Its creatures were tortured and killed, baited to entertain the cruel, used to exhaustion then slaughtered for their flesh. In their broken bodies he saw the suffering of millions beyond counting.

The charred carcasses of men and beasts, stark in the heat of the sun, and a myriad flies carried the message of death. Few were left living, and those that were, wandered stunned and bewildered, prey to scavengers who stole from the weak to feed themselves. Orphaned children cried in terror beside the corpses of their parents. The wounded and maimed struggled to escape, and were left behind as the tides of war overtook them.

In the wake of ruin, starvation stalked the land and men murdered one another to eat the corpses. The stench of plague hung thick in the air. Somewhere around here would be Indeg, but Ishrafeli heard no word of him, even though he asked.

He was drenched with the agony of it. Sweat poured off his body.

He lifted his face to the sky and shouted till his lungs were bursting. 'Let it end! It is too much – let it end!'

And the voice of God replied in his soul. 'Go to each of the Lords of the Undead and persuade them to come to the ravine below Mount Sorah. There I will break their bodies and free their souls from each other so they may choose again.'

'I can't!' Ishrafeli cried, everything in him recoiling from the horror of it.

'Yes, you can,' the voice of God replied. 'With My help you can do anything I ask of you . . . and you know that.'

Ishrafeli crouched low on the ground. 'I can't! To look into the hearts of the Undead would be to see hell through the eyes of those who have chosen it for ever!'

'I know, but I have looked on them . . . and loved them. So can you.'

Ulciber heard Ishrafeli's cry, and willed himself to appear and stand on the earth in the ashes of Pera on his tireless and beautiful feet that had no sensation of the ground, and envied the corpses that lay rotting in the sun. He envied even the flies that clustered on them. They did not rise in buzzing clouds as he passed, as they would have for a man of flesh and blood.

He knew how hot it was, but the sun did not burn him, nor did he smell the acrid fumes of the smoke and the reek of death.

'You don't have to suffer it all,' he said quietly. 'I have power over the Lords of the Undead. I am greater than they, and I can make them go to Mount Sorah without your having to face them.'

Ishrafeli rose to his feet and stared at him, recognition coming slowly to his eyes. 'Ulciber . . .'

Ulciber smiled, a warm, radiant gesture with a flash of white teeth. He saw the exhaustion in Ishrafeli, the loneliness and the vulnerability, the capacity for pain.

'You don't have to do it,' he said again. 'There is an easier way which is just as good. You don't need to suffer any more.'

A flash of hope shone in Ishrafeli's eyes. Ulciber understood it perfectly. He too was tortured by that brightest of all the stars of heaven, the guiding fire in the darkness. He dared to hope for a mortal body, even though he had chosen Asmodeus' path and denied the steeper path of God. It was not too late; this was a final chance. What did it matter if it foiled the plan of Asmodeus? That was irrelevant now. What if it cost this man in front of him the glory he had sought all his life, and which was now almost in his hand? If he broke this bright spirit, darkened its light for ever and sent it crashing from heaven to hell, like Asmodeus before him – or only to some grey, middle mist of eternal chances lost – that did not matter either . . . if Ulciber won a body of flesh to keep, capable of immortality!

'It isn't fair,' Ulciber said softly. 'You are being asked to pay more than anyone else. You don't need to. It will all be just the same in the end.'

'No it won't!' Ishrafeli said fiercely. 'God does not ask anyone to suffer needlessly.'

Ulciber laughed. It was a soft sound like the slithering of scales over stone. 'You have no idea what it will be like for you, no conception at all. You can imagine only one man's pain at a time, one man's guilt, a shuddering nightmare, horror at his own deeds. You will see a score at once, and it will break you!' He said that with pleasure. He would like to see that inner beauty broken and stained, spoiled for ever . . . but only after he had given Ulciber his power, his body!

'They might not be released if they didn't go of their own will,' Ishrafeli said.

Ulciber felt triumph soar inside him! Ishrafeli was wavering. He was considering it, turning it over in his mind.

312

Ishrafeli stared at the beautiful, ageless face in front of him. Was there an easier way to get the Lords of the Undead to Mount Sorah? Could he not use one evil force to destroy another? Would it not be an exquisite irony for Ulciber to serve God's purpose?

And the voice of God whispered, 'They are not two evils. The Undead are still My children. They must choose, not be coerced, and you know that just as I do.'

Ishrafeli closed his eyes, shutting out Ulciber's face. 'No. It cannot be done your way. God's way is the only one. Now leave me.'

'Yes, it can—' Ulciber started again.

'Leave me!' Ishrafeli said with absolute certainty; it was rock hard in the set of his shoulders, blazing in his eyes.

Then Ulciber knew that he had lost. He let out a howl of fury that cracked the burned beams of a house a mile away and sent them crashing down, charred wood and ash flying in the air. He had been so close, so very close . . . and it had still eluded him. He wanted to lash out, to break Ishrafeli now, to beat his living flesh until it was bloody. And the scalding fact that God could resurrect him, never again to be injured or hurt, was like a knife paralysing his hands, and tearing his mind apart.

'You will wish you had accepted me,' he hissed between clenched teeth. 'I will make you pay for this so dearly you will beg me to offer you the choice again – beg me on your knees! And I will refuse you!'

Ishrafeli gave a wry, sad little smile. 'If I've already been through the torment you describe, I can't think it will matter so very much.'

Ulciber clenched his fists till the nails gouged into the spongy flesh of his palms, cutting and drawing no blood. 'Oh, it will!' he promised. 'I swear by the pains of hell, it will!'

Ishrafeli turned very slowly on the road west, leaving Ulciber alone in the dust, a shimmering figure to appear and disappear at will, but never to feel the ground under his feet or the air on his face or in his lungs.

Ishrafeli kept on walking on the hard, arid roads until they petered out and he was on grassy tracks churned up by the passing of massed feet. The few trees were dead, shorn of leaves, and the rolling land was unbroken by outcrops or streams, only a few dry gullies bleached pale with some chemical showed where once there had been water.

Gradually he became aware that there was noise ahead as if a distant flock of geese were milling on the ground. Then as he looked up he realised that of course it was men. He had come to within a mile of one of the main camps of the central army. Here he should find Mabeluz, the first of the Lords of the Undead, and begin his task.

He stopped in the road for a moment, gathering his strength. He thought of Tathea. She was always in his mind and heart, and the loneliness of being without her was his heaviest burden. Yet he would not have wished her to share this, even though he knew she would have taken it all for him were it possible. Better he think of the task ahead, and face it, no matter though it should carry him to the last boundaries of hell. There was no other way forward. He remembered what Sadokhar had said about Ozmander and the power of hope, and he knew what he was going to say to the Lords of the Undead.

The outer edges of the camp were only yards away now in the broken dunes and tussocks, and any moment he would encounter sentries. They must already be aware of him. He thought of the creature who had led the armies to do this. Whoever it was was not a madman, a creature with no notion of what he did. This was conscious and deliberate hatred of an order outside humanity.

How would he find the strength to meet this, and not turn away? What if he could not bear it? What would his loss cost? He had not even thought of that before, because neither he nor Tathea had allowed themselves to think of anything but victory. Would his defeat alone be enough to make this beloved earth a dark star for Asmodeus? Did all of them have to win? Or did God have some other plan which He could use were any of them to prove not strong enough, not brave enough, were any one of them to find his own survival more precious to him than the task he had chosen?

The battle was terrible and final, and Asmodeus must also believe he would win!

Ishrafeli stood in the dust with the noise of the camp ahead and saw a sentry turn and stare at him. The man's face was burned by sun and wind and scarred by battle. His expression was one of arrogance, as if he were so sure of his own superiority he had no need even to put his hand to his sword. But his look demanded answer.

'I have a message for General Mabeluz,' Ishrafeli accounted for himself, trusting Mabeluz was here. If not, he would look foolish and have to make excuses. He raised his arms. 'I have no weapon.'

The sentry regarded him with little interest. 'From whom?' he asked sceptically.

'Regarding the other lands,' Ishrafeli replied.

The sentry raised his voice and called a soldier over. 'Take him to the general,' he said wearily. 'Watch him. He's probably telling the truth but you never know. Some of these people are desperate, and they don't care any more. They'll try anything. Kill him if he's lying.'

Obediently Ishrafeli followed the soldier up a slight incline, passing surprisingly few men. They were ragged and dirty, many of them wounded. They stood and sat around meagre campfires cooking what little food they could scavenge from a ruined country. Their enemies and most of their friends were dead, and there was nothing left to win or lose. The flower of them lay darkening a thousand miles of battlefields between here and Thoth-Moara.

Ishrafeli passed among them in safety only because he was with an armed soldier. They reached the heart of the camp. Mabeluz was in a magnificent dark red tent, large enough to accommodate a bed and a table with several chairs. The Undead had no physical sensation of hunger or weariness like mortal men. These were merely the trappings of leadership to impress the army. The sentry and visitor passed through the open flap and Ishrafeli stopped as his escort explained who he was.

Mabeluz was certain enough of his power he felt no fear. He turned slowly in his woven leather chair to look at the newcomer with curiosity. His head was huge, almost bald, and his skin was coarse and dark as if suffused with blood, purplish-grey and covered with old scabs where ancient pustules had broken. His features were cruel, his eyes so small only the pupils showed, like an animal's, but there was sharp, human intelligence in them, probing already for weakness, the point of vulnerability, the wound or the need he could use.

'Well?' he said with a grating voice as if his throat were constricted. 'What is your message?' Then as he stared at Ishrafeli the dark blood drained from his skin. His hands clenched and his breath caught in his throat. 'You!' he said hoarsely. He half rose in his chair, then fell back again, sweating. The smell of his terror and hatred filled the air.

Ishrafeli looked into his face and saw beyond the revulsion of the surface to the souls within. For a moment time ceased to exist. He saw overwhelming, drowning misery, an anger that lashed in every direction, wounding, hurting wherever it could. He saw the self-hatred which needs to tear down and devour anything strong or clean, the hunger to destroy anything it does not own, to ridicule and shatter dreams and break belief. The accumulated pain washed over him, filling his flesh and his bones until he was so weakened he swayed and almost fell. It was blinding, endless. Every instinct in him was to pull away, to wrench himself from it.

And yet he felt a pity also, an agony of lost light, of chance after chance denied, of selfishness and cruelty that at last crept into every corner and drove out even the imagination of love.

He saw the legion of souls who had spent life crushing the hopes of others now imprisoned in the same body, filled by hatred, locked together in eternal violence.

315

But he knew what to say.

There was a sneer on Mabeluz' thick lips. He had already decided to have some amusement by humiliating Ishrafeli in front of the soldier who had conducted him here. He drew in his breath to begin.

Ishrafeli spoke first. 'I came to offer you freedom from each other,' he said quietly, but his voice was as steady as the earth itself.

Mabeluz froze. 'What?' Then before Ishrafeli could speak he glared at the soldier. 'Get out!' he screamed. 'Get out!' Then when the man was gone, he looked again at Ishrafeli.

'Freedom from each other,' Ishrafeli repeated softly, meeting Mabeluz' small, dark eyes until he could not look away. 'Is that not what you want . . . all of you?'

A maze of expressions crossed Mabeluz' face: disbelief; hope; fear because Ishrafeli knew who he was; and even greater fear that he might offer such a thing, and give birth to such a fire of hope that would burst the soul, only to quench it again.

Ishrafeli waited. The grief inside him was twisting harder with every second that passed. He saw the individual souls within Mabeluz, each tiny step towards the darkness they had taken: a mockery of someone weak whose dreams were precious, the manipulation of someone whose need was too great to bear alone, the cruelties, the scalding shame, the degrading of those without the guile or the courage to read him and withstand. Each choice was small, but made knowingly. There had been no pity given, no burden shared, no mercy and no forgiveness.

'I can give it to you!' Ishrafeli repeated with an urgency that surprised him. He wanted to free these souls from each other. Maybe some of them might change, take even a single spark of light. Even one would matter.

'You can't!' Mabeluz said with a sneer, but he could not keep the hope out of his eyes. 'It's not possible.' His voice was rough. He was used to domination. No one had challenged him in centuries. His pain was his own secret. Now here was this man who had conquered the darkness and was creating in him a terror greater than anything he had ever known, because suddenly he offered him light as well. He hated with a white-hot fury, the deeper burned into his being because he was helpless against it. He did hope! Damn the man to everlasting agony – he did hope!

'There is a price—' Ishrafeli began.

Mabeluz threw back his huge head and bellowed with laughter, a harsh, ugly, grating sound. The men standing duty outside cowered away from it.

'Of course there is!' he spat. 'What do you want?'

Ishrafeli remained perfectly still. 'If you are freed from each

316

other, I will have at least part of what I want. But the price is not paid to me; it is the natural cost of casting away the bond that holds you.'

Mabeluz was watching him as a beast watches its prey, head motionless, eyes unblinking. Ishrafeli could feel his need like a miasma in the air, rank and sour. It knotted his stomach.

'What do we have to do?' Mabeluz asked, his breath rasping in his throat, his neck bulging.

Ishrafeli hesitated. He was walking the blade's edge. If he slipped now he lost everything. He must make Mabeluz go to the ravine below Mount Sorah, but no matter the temptation, he must not stoop to lying.

But how close was a misunderstanding to a lie? If he willingly allowed Mabeluz to be misled, was that not at heart the same thing?

'Tell us!' Mabeluz demanded, the veins in his face and neck protruding, pulsing with dark blood.

'You must go to the ravine below Mount Sorah,' Ishrafeli answered. 'And wait there until all the Lords of the Undead come to you.' That was the exact truth.

Anger, confusion, the desire to believe and the rage against mockery followed each other across Mabeluz' hideous face. 'Do you take us for fools?' he shouted suddenly, clenching his huge shoulders and half rising in his seat. 'What can going to Mount Sorah do for me, or for anyone? You think I can't see through you? You don't care about me. You want glory for yourself, so you can say to your God that you destroyed me!'

Ishrafeli stared at Mabeluz, steeling himself to go deep into the souls inside him, to smell and taste the individual misery of loss, the need to torment in order not to drown in a sea of self-loathing. He searched for any light, any mercy or honour that still lingered, and found nothing. Every act was soiled by selfishness as if a tide of filth had risen over them all.

Mabeluz stared back. The only movement in the slime of his mind was hatred, and the knowledge of pain.

Ishrafeli prayed for strength, clinging to the thought of God, to the word of life, the light and the breath of Him in the soul. He had said it was possible and Ishrafeli could do it – therefore he could.

'You know what this war is for,' he said steadily. 'It has nothing to do with death, or the ruin of the land. They are only means. The end is the last confrontation between the forces of God and of Asmodeus. Neither of them will undo what you have chosen.' It was brutal, and he felt as if he had kicked a broken animal as he said it. The words burned his tongue. 'You have tortured the earth, and done it knowingly, but if you go to the ravine, the earth will break the shell that holds you together. Like every other creature of God, you are immortal, but your souls will be separate again. Perhaps some of you will choose the light at last.'

'We can't be released,' Mabeluz said after a moment or two. 'The undead can't die!' But there was hope in his voice in spite of his denial. He hungered, starved to be contradicted. The plea for it filled his eyes.

He told Mabeluz what he wanted to hear, and it was the truth. 'The earth can break your body, the fire of its heart is strong enough.'

Mabeluz was afraid. 'Then what? What happens to our souls?' he whispered.

Ishrafeli knew that the answer must be the truth, whole and clean. One slightest stain of deceit on it and it would all slip away.

'Judgement is not mine,' he replied. 'You will go to the kingdom whose laws you will keep. But alone, you are free to make your own choice; together you are bound by the lowest of you.'

Mabeluz was going through some kind of turmoil inside himself as the spirits attacked each other with a violence which distorted his features; his body writhed and the sweat broke out on his skin.

Ishrafeli stood by helplessly. He could neither ease Mabeluz' pain nor make it shorter. The tent grew dark as if the light outside had faded, and the stench almost overpowered Ishrafeli. He had to exercise all the self-control he possessed to stop himself from retching. To watch the creature in front of him drowning in darkness was worse than anything he had begun to imagine. And he knew that if he looked away, tore himself apart from knowing it, then Mabeluz would not believe him, and he would have lost.

Suddenly the silence was split by a scream. 'Help me!' Mabeluz foamed at the mouth and all the skin on his face and head twitched. His eyes rolled and the blood oozed and dribbled between his lips.

'I can't help you,' Ishrafeli said desperately. 'Not even God can make you what you don't want to be! I can only tell you the truth. Go to the ravine, and free yourselves from each other, then choose again. Put away the hate and the lies and the cowardice.'

Rage flashed in Mabeluz' little eyes, and a brilliant flare of cunning.

Ishrafeli stepped back as if he had been struck, sickened by it. For a moment there had been hope, and the darkness was the more intense because of it. Despair washed over him. He felt his own strength drain away until he was dizzy. This was pointless. He should leave Mabeluz to his damnation. He had tried! Surely that was enough?

'Going?' Mabeluz asked with a bitter ring of triumph, as if being

318

abandoned were some kind of victory for him.

Ishrafeli jerked his head up. 'No, I'm not going!' he said savagely. 'I'll stay until you have the courage to face the truth! It's your only escape. That – or stay locked together for ever. This is your chance, it won't wait. Time is short – but you know that! You all know it, perhaps better than I do.'

'And if I go to Mount Sorah the earth will free us?' Mabeluz implored. 'You swear? Why would it, after what I've done to it?'

A score of thoughts rushed through Ishrafeli's mind, memories of glory and destruction, wonder at the mercy of God. 'Yes,' he agreed gently. 'It will.'

The silence was thick.

At last Mabeluz rose stiffly to his feet, knocking over the small, wooden table behind him. 'I'll go. You said all of us?'

'Yes.' Ishrafeli felt hope surge up inside him, and tried to repress it, not daring to let it overtake him, knowing the darkness was so close.

'What about Balour, Accolon and Indeg?' Mabeluz asked. 'How will you bring them?'

'The same way I brought you . . . with the truth.'

Mabeluz turned and blundered out of the door, reeling as if his legs were weak and his mind befuddled.

Ishrafeli left the army camp escorted by soldiers, and walked steadily westwards in the wake of where the battle had been fiercest. There was no doubt in him that Mabeluz would go to the ravine below Mount Sorah. He could leave him behind and go forward to search for the others with a peace within him, a certainty of the spirit. The sun still scorched his face, his clothes stuck to him, the sand abraded his skin raw, but he knew God would provide the strength to do all he had to.

Weary to the heart he began the journey back through the trail of destruction and famine left behind the armies across Pera into Shinabar, searching for Indeg. The sparse trees became even fewer. Farms and small villages had been looted and the dead lay where they had fallen. Some were stripped by wild dogs, others Ishrafeli saw with churning stomach had been cleaned of flesh by the skill of a human-held knife.

In the oases he saw famine where men and women stood skeletal thin with bloated bellies and hollow eyes. He could do nothing to help them.

At each place he asked after Indeg, and finally found him in the foetid alleys of Tarra-Ghum, standing over a pile of refuse buzzing with flies.

He jerked up as Ishrafeli approached. The putrid core of him

319

was already bursting through into his flesh till it shone with a strange iridescence like gangrene. He was among those walking and living dead, racked with disease, skins blotched, ulcerated, their bodies exhausted with fever and flux, lurching towards a merciful oblivion.

Indeg stared at him with exploding rage as if he had long known he would come, and had waited for him in ever increasing hatred.

'Well?' he demanded, his voice high and shrill with accusation. 'What do you want, then?' He flung his arm out, gesturing obscenely at the ruin around them, and the stench arising from disease and death.

'I want to be clean,' Ishrafeli said wearily. It was a cry from the heart. He ached for relief from the filth and heat and abrasion of the moment, and for the depth of freedom from the anger and despair, the self-deceit, and the cruelty of the soul.

Indeg started to laugh, a wild, braying sound. Then he stopped abruptly. 'Here?' he said incredulously. 'They've got plague! Can't you see that? Haven't you got eyes? Can't you smell them? They're rotting where they lie!'

Ishrafeli hurt as if his very soul were bruised. 'I know. I can't help them. It's too late. But I can help you.'

Indeg's face was dark with contempt. He did not need to find words for his derision.

'I can free the best of you from the worst,' Ishrafeli went on. 'As I shall do for all of you. At Mount Sorah the earth will break open your prisons.' He wished passionately that he could force Indeg to go. He was exhausted with having to argue and persuade. But again there was the struggle, the self-disgust, the knowledge in Indeg of his own lies which made him think evil of everyone else. He argued and cursed while Ishrafeli repeated over and over again, like a chant, words to comfort himself because he needed to believe for his spirit to survive.

'Why should you?' Indeg demanded shrilly. 'What do you care whether I have a chance or not? You despise me! Don't lie . . . you hypocrite! Stand there and tell me you don't hate me, you wouldn't get pleasure from seeing me damned!'

'God help me,' Ishrafeli replied. 'I look at you and see the cruelty and the filth and it frightens me. I feel as if I shall never be clean again.' The challenge not to lie cut deep like a razor. 'But I get no pleasure from seeing anyone damned. Though if I did . . . it would be you!' he added.

A leer of triumph lit Indeg's frightened face, as if he had won some moral victory.

Ishrafeli turned away and moved a few steps. He stared at the horizon. The sky was clear high above them, pure enamel blue

320

spread with the faint patina of gold from the fading sun.

Beneath it the whole passionate, subtle and beautiful world was stained with a fatal disease.

He turned back to Indeg. 'Judgement is coming,' he said, staring at him as if he would crawl inside the tumult of minds in his head. 'It will be soon now, and it will be final for those of us who had a chance. If the least foul in you would be free of the most, go to the ravine below Mount Sorah. If not, then it really doesn't matter where you are . . .'

Then he saw with a flash like a spark of fire, that Indeg believed. 'I can't!' he shouted. 'I carry the plague!' It was terror and triumph in him at once, rage and hope boiling inside him, making his skin bulge and tear. 'Say it doesn't matter!' He brayed with laughter. 'It doesn't matter! It doesn't matter!'

'I'll take you by sea!' Ishrafeli shouted back at him. 'Stop that noise! I can sail! I'll find a small boat and take you by sea.'

Indeg was astounded. 'You'll come with me? You'll take us?'

Ishrafeli swallowed his revulsion, feeling his stomach twist. It was all he could do to stop retching. He had to wait several minutes before he could move again and make himself lead the way towards the harbour, hearing Indeg's shuffling, squelching footsteps behind him.

He found a boat and with Indeg's help, lifted the dead bodies of the owners out of it and laid them under one of the sails on the quayside. Then with what clean water Ishrafeli could find, and a bag of diced dates, he ordered Indeg to sit still, and unaided he lifted the sails and set out to sea.

It was the worst voyage of his life. It was only a matter of days, but it seemed like weeks. Indeg did not need to eat, but for himself Ishrafeli caught fish. He did not dare sleep properly, only doze in the stern of the ship, always aware of the creature who sat only feet away, alternately moaning and cursing as one part within him became dominant, then another.

He set Indeg ashore within sight of Mount Sorah, and then put to sea again to go on eastward to the other barbarian army and seek Balour.

He followed a trail of mineheads and craters where the earth had been flung aside and mounds of acid chemical waste lay spread wide, its poison staining the water, the land, even the air. Nothing lived, and the reek of fumes stung his throat and made his eyes water.

After the pale, stinking hills and valleys he moved on to the grasslands which had once teemed with life, and here he found the few remnants of armies still alive, both Peran and barbarian occasionally fighting each other, even now driven by reflex of hate.

321

There, screaming abuse at men who refused to dig or to labour any more, he found Balour. He looked smaller, thinner, and even more ratlike than in the City. The dead and dying lay around him, and he fed on their misery as others grasped at food.

Ishrafeli thought he was prepared for the horror he would see when he looked within Balour, but he was not. Each sin and its misery was different, catching him in an unguarded place, showing him new pain. He was bruised and weary with it, because it had no end. His strength was bleeding away even as he stood in the withered land and argued with the wretched creatures in Balour promising release, trying to make them see the final blessing of one more chance to choose. The weight of cowardice, of apathy of the spirit, was suffocating. He had not known such will to death existed and the touch of it nearly paralysed him. It was strong enough to eat away all life.

But if he once let Balour see his vulnerability, he would fasten on to it, and the rodent in his soul would never loose hold. So he kept his eyes level and prayed for the power to sustain him through all the arguments again, and offer the hope.

When at last he left, Balour was trotting in his strange, jerking gait towards the west and Mount Sorah on the horizon. Now there was only Accolon to find.

Ishrafeli went eastward again, his spirit poured out to exhaustion, driven only by will. And in the slaughter of the last battlefield where the ground was dark with the murdered bodies of the dead, Peran, Shinabari and barbarian alike, where carrion birds tore out eyes and pulled the flesh off faces, he found Accolon, leading the robbers of the fallen.

He stood up suddenly from behind a heap of the dead. His face was haggard, his eyes bloodshot, his long white hands grimed with dirt.

Ishrafeli let out an involuntary cry of horror and stumbled backwards.

He scrambled to his hands and knees, gasping for air, then looked up to see Accolon grinning, great white teeth sharp and square, like those of a horse.

Ishrafeli had no weapons but his faith and the strength of his mind. He dared not think of Tathea, but the words of the Book came slowly to his heart and a peace shone inside him again. It spread until he could catch his breath and stop shaking. God asked of no man more than he could accomplish. There was no pain or terror or grief He did not know and share. Above all He loved, with passion and courage and wisdom beyond mortal dreams to imagine. There was nothing secret from Him, and still He loved.

Ishrafeli focused his vision and stared into the eyes of Accolon.

He saw in them pride and the lust for praise, the need to be adored for any and every reason. He saw the vanity that will not learn, and the crowding guilt that will never dare look inward for dread of what it will find. He saw endless self-justification, argument, anger. He searched, and he did not find one unselfish act or one offence forgiven.

He spoke to Accolon as he had to them all. 'I can tell you where to find freedom from each other . . .'

The same argument back and forth ensued, the same dregs of bitterness to be drained to the last drop, before Accolon grasped at hope and, trailed by that filthy thing with its long hands and horse-teeth, Ishrafeli set out on his own final terrible journey to Mount Sorah.

They passed scenes of hideous defilement, the ground smashed and broken, the crushed bones of animals picked clean by men or carrion bird. Time after time Ishrafeli swung round on Accolon, burning with rage to lash back at him for what he had done, longing to break him as he had broken the earth. And each time he saw the pathetic face and was brushed, slight as a butterfly wing, with pity. Then he saw the leering eyes and his anger returned.

They floundered in dust, soft as mud. Ishrafeli found himself weeping with frustration, close to despair.

Only the words in the Book, repeated over and over, enabled him to dredge up the strength to fight his way out. As if it were a voice within himself, he heard Asmodeus speak: 'What of man then in the day of my power, when his work has crashed about his ears and there is death and despair on every side?'

He turned and reached out his hand to the obscene thing drowning behind him, and hauled it out.

And the answer of God came like the birth of light in darkness: 'In tribulation he will find his greatest strength and his utmost nobility. There will be those in flight from a monstrous foe, who will still return to the very jaws of destruction to rescue the weaker and the slower, though they know Him not, who will comfort the terrified and the grieving without thought of self. Where there is starvation there will be those who will give their last morsel to feed the stranger, or nurse the dying, though the plague afflict them also.'

On and on they struggled, fell and rose again, until at last ahead of them the harsh outline of Mount Sorah stood stark against the sky. Then finally Accolon slithered down to the other Lords of the Undead, and Ishrafeli looked from the cliff edge into the ravine and saw them all standing on the rock, staring up at him, waiting.

He could deliver them only this far. Now it rested with them, and with God. He was too weary to think.

He fell to his knees. 'Father, I have brought them here, as You asked me. Do with them according to Thy will, but please . . . please give the earth a beginning of peace! Let her rest . . .'

He had barely finished speaking when there was a roar in the distance, a trembling deep in the core of the mountain and in the ground under his knees. If he had had any energy, even any coherent thought, he should have been terrified, desperate for any way to escape it. But it filled him with a strange, sweet sense of peace, as if the being of the earth had spoken to him.

The shuddering of the ground grew fiercer and the noise was almost deafening. On the far side of the ravine huge boulders crashed down the cliff edge and shattered like glass.

Mount Sorah seemed to shimmer in the air and move against the purple and sulphur-yellow blaze of the sky, caused by the wind in the clouds, an illusion of the light.

Another roar split the silence, a screaming, tearing like the fabric of the earth being ripped apart. Halfway up towards the peak, a gout of flame shot a thousand feet high, staining the arch of heaven with streamers of black smoke.

The noise came again, and was followed by molten rock, white-hot magma from the core of the world spewing into the air and raining down on to newly gouged valleys. It poured into the old ravine, hissing and roaring until the rocks exploded, shooting into the air, cannonfire of the breaking and rending of worlds. Lava crashed against the walls till the ground screamed and juddered, gaping open in crevasses a thousand feet deep, and more steam and rocks shot into the air.

The Lords of the Undead stared around, stunned and amazed, even as they were swallowed beneath seas of boiling rock, consumed for ever. But as Ishrafeli watched, clinging to the ground, almost choked with heat and fumes, he saw the dark shadows of their souls fly upwards, free at last for one final choice, one spark of the light to seize . . . or to let go.

He must leave. Sulphur was thick in the air. He could not ask to be preserved much longer. His mission was not over yet. A voice spoke in his heart and in the thunder of the earth. He must return to Lantrif and face the Silver Lords, the last betrayal, and the freedom for his beloved earth to yield its mortal life into the hands of God.

Chapter Twenty-One

Tathea was still in Camassia, leading what was left of the resistance as it re-formed a government after the shambles of Cassiodorus' death and Balour's flight to the battlefront in Pera, when she heard the news of Sardriel's death. It was Gallimir, one of the Knights of the Western Shore, who brought it to her. Ythiel had heard it from a Lost Lands mariner, and sent word immediately.

Gallimir was waiting for her as she left the Hall of Justice, and they stood together in the sun where it splashed over the ancient pavements patterned in the warm colours of sand and rose. He told the story simply but his words were so vivid she could see it as if she were there, and feel both the glory, and the grief. And with it came the certainty that time was very short.

But she had known that before Ishrafeli went to seek the Lords of the Undead. Those last few days together had been a final gift, a golden evening before the night of battle which was already on the horizon.

Now she looked at Gallimir's face and saw in his eyes that he had more yet to tell.

'What is it?' she asked.

Gallimir looked at her steadily and his sadness frightened her.

'The old evils have arisen again in Lantrif,' he answered. 'We send embassies there regularly, and they come back as soft as a silken web, too subtle to tell the lies from the truth.'

She should not have been surprised. In the end the masks would be stripped from all. The Book had promised from the beginning that there was no middle ground: everyone was either for God, or for Asmodeus.

'What do you know of it, for certain?' she asked.

'That the Silver Lords no longer hide their power,' he answered, his face grim. 'They have uncovered their ancient arts again that would climb the stairs by magic, not by labour. They would aspire to the omnipotence of God by their own skill, without the humility to love the universe or keep its laws.'

She saw him shiver in the sun, and felt the coldness touch her as

325

if the light had gone, though it was still as bright, but empty now, a brittleness to it.

'Legend says it was so on other worlds,' he continued softly, 'before God washed them clean of the sins which cannot be forgotten, once the knowledge is in the heart. It is folly to destruction to steal the arts we have not the wisdom of the soul to use. The Silver Lords did that in the beginning, and now they have dug them up again out of their secret places, and are using sorcery to prepare for the last battle. We knew it from the old allies we had who have disappeared from office, and from the nature of the men who have replaced them, and word has come of ancient creatures of darkness that have been seen again – the Lamia, the hell-kites over the River, stripping the flesh off dead men's bones.'

Tathea drew in her breath to speak.

Gallimir smiled. 'At first we too thought it was superstition, but it is not.' He reached out and touched her arm gently, and his hand was warm. 'It had to come. Is not reward without labour the heart of Asmodeus' greatest lie?'

'Yes . . . of course it is,' she answered. She faced at last the thought which she had been evading all these months. 'Is that where we will find Asmodeus?'

'It would seem so,' Gallimir agreed.

She knew also that if Ishrafeli returned from Pera it was he who would go and face the Silver Lords, because the men of Lantrif, good and evil, were his people.

If she went first, perhaps she could share the burden, even ease it. Whatever happened, she would not leave him to face it alone. The end must find them together, in heart and deed.

'Thank you,' she said sincerely. 'I shall return with you. We shall leave as soon as you are rested.'

That evening she wrote letters, and packed a few belongings – just the necessities of travel and the staff. In the morning they left the City in the Centre of the World for the last time, and took ship westwards. She stood on the deck and watched its glory and its corruption slip away, gold in the evening light, and fall below the horizon.

She left Gallimir in Tyrn Vawr, and began the long ride across the golden summer. She knew the shores were again ravaged by pirates, raiders from the Sea Isles, and in places even old feuds reawakened. War had touched the Island, as it had to. But here in the Heartlands the fields still shimmered green and the great trees rested on them like billowing clouds. Wild roses starred the hedges, sending their mingled perfume into the air. The purple spires of foxgloves crowded thick. Meadows were vivid with streaks of buttercups blazing in a gold carpet, and red sorrel splashed between. The beauty of it was almost a burden because she knew it could not last.

Already to the northeast Irria-Kand had fallen. To the south Shinabar and Pera were in the throes of the final slaughter. In the centre Camassia was still starving after the barbarian wars, and too much of the land was polluted for it ever to recover.

In the west Tirilis, long prey to the evils of indifference and greed, was now torn by internal strife. And due north Caeva was only scattered settlements in the forests that stretched to the lands of ice.

She rode westward through the summer glory, continuing long into the evening. The sky was fired in amber and burning pink, and the soft air hung hazy over the distance, like a gauze scarf. She knew that perhaps she would never see it quite like this again.

Lantrif was harsher than the Heartlands, a country of steep crags clothed with forests of slender trees, often mist-shrouded by sudden rains and then illuminated with brilliant shafts of light. It was silvers and blues and greens. The wild flowers lay in sheets, pale and delicate.

The pathways through the valleys echoed the sound of birdsong. Tathea saw the white lace of rapids, the dappled bark of trees in a hundred different patterns. Streams rattled over the shallows into pools with lichened stones, cool surfaces dimpled in sunlight.

In the high passes clouds flew like banners from the crags, and above her the thin ribbons of water bounded downwards.

By noon of the second day she came to the first small town that straddled the River with arching bridges. By late afternoon she was where the stream was wide enough to carry the elegant, shallow-drifted, silver-decked barges with their ornamental masts and slender oars which the men of the west had built since the dawn of their race. From here they went down to the city and beyond to the sea.

Tathea left her horse at a hostelry, with sufficient money for its keep, and paid the river master for passage down river on the next barge.

Later she stood on the deck watching the soft wraiths of the mist crawl up off the water's face and feeling the boat move under her like a living thing. Fear tightened inside her as she thought of Lantrif; Ishrafeli had called it by the old name, the City of Fallen Kings. It was walled around and filled with crooked streets and a myriad steps; slender, fluted and corbelled towers. He had told her its people were silent-footed, smiling, beautiful of voice; and yet always secret hearted. He had grown up among them, and still he knew them little.

She could hear his voice in her head saying that there had always been mysteries – not overt, not as simple as locked doors or sealed books, but elusive as a scent in the air. The words were easy, but there was too often another meaning in the eyes. She watched, knowing she should tear the image of his face from her mind, and winding yet deeper into the core of her. She saw the shadow of the trees rising blurred and ephemeral above the water, as if they floated and had no roots in the winding, cool-mounded banks. The moonlight made a silver breath of the vapour and spread sudden, luminous pools across the current.

She was aware of another traveller standing beside her, watching, as she was.

'I have not seen you on the River before,' he remarked. 'Nor did you bring goods with you when you boarded.'

She turned to look at him. He was grey-headed, of the old race of the west, with a delicate, subtle face, and he wore a silver cord around his neck. From it was suspended a sphere of perfect clarity, encircled by a chain, each link carefully wrought.

'I do not trade,' she answered him. 'I carry words only, and beliefs.'

He drew in a long, slow breath, and let it out in a sigh. He was studying her face, reading it with intense thought, as one does a complicated page. Very slowly he smiled. 'I see.' He moved his head in acquiescence. 'Yes,' he said again. 'I see.' And pulling his cloak a little tighter around him against the damp of the night, he gave a very slight bow, and walked silently into the shadows in front of the cabin on the deck, and was no longer visible.

She stood alone with the host of possibilities crowding her mind as to what lay ahead: which emissary of Asmodeus would be waiting for her, and for Ishrafeli – or would it be the Great Enemy himself?

She remembered with startling suddenness the day of Sadokhar's birth, and how Asmodeus had mocked her then, and held up the black keys of the world. The power she had felt from him was as real now, as sharp and all-pervading.

There was no sound but the steady drip of oars and the whisper of the water as it slid past. The whorls of the wake drifted away astern, forming goblin faces beneath the surface, masks of indescribable deformity. Someone in this ancient, ensorcelled land had been weaving the slow, careful snares of long-withheld arts, secrets that men were never meant to know as long as their human weakness darkened their dreams.

Tathea stared up at the sky, now shredded over with flakes of cloud. The stream was broader. The trees on the banks were spectral, boughs silver-mounded in the moonlight as if heaped with blossom. She did not hear the footfall on the deck. She turned suddenly and saw the woman only yards away, slender, her eyes blue-green, the gossamer light on her face, as pale as milk.

'Do you travel to the City of the Fallen Kings?' the woman asked quietly. 'Or beyond? To the sea, perhaps?'

'To the City,' Tathea replied. 'And you?'

'That depends upon the Brotherhood,' the woman answered softly. Then, as Tathea seemed not to understand, she continued, glancing over her shoulder towards the cabin, then back again. Her voice was like the sigh of water eddying around the tree roots at the shore. 'The Brotherhood of the Chain. No one outside knows who they are, but they know each other. They have signs.' Again the woman glanced at the cabin. She was so pale in the moonlight she seemed almost bloodless.

'Does someone threaten you?' Tathea said urgently.

'The Brotherhood threatens all people who are not of it!' She held her fingers to her lips. 'And you are not of it . . . are you?'

'No.'

'I thought not. But they will seek you . . .' She laughed; it was a faint, rippling, eerie sound in the darkness.

Tathea shivered. The woman was so close now that she could have put out her hand and touched her. The soft breath of wind between them might have drifted off ice, rather than the white gauze of moonlight.

'Who are you?' Tathea said with sudden urgency.

The woman smiled, showing a gleam of pearl-like teeth. 'My name is Eris.' Then she swung round and stared, wide-eyed, at the cabin. From it was moving a cloaked and hooded figure. It came towards them, the heavy drapes of the wool masking even the outline of his head, making him terrifying, grossly anonymous.

Eris gave a wild despairing cry and hurled herself at Tathea, clinging to her as if to life itself.

Still the figure advanced. Where his face should have been was a nameless, impenetrable hole. He raised his arms.

Eris was frozen for a hideous moment, then she lunged backwards, drawing Tathea with her. For a wild, teetering instant Tathea felt the deck pitch and fall, and saw the sky pale as whey, swinging in an arc above her. Then the River caught her in its cold embrace, clinging, drowning, consuming her into itself.

The shock robbed her of breath. Water closed over her face. She flailed her arms to be free, but Eris was beside her, her robes imprisoning them both, her body close and cold as the River itself. Her hands were fasted on Tathea, strong as iron.

Tathea fought to the surface and filled her lungs, shouting for help. Her voice was shrill, echoing across the mirror face of the water. Then the mists writhed in, coiling and clinging. And she was pulled downwards. Eris was wrapped around her like a drowning weed. Her hair was around Tathea's neck, tightening, strangling her throat.

Terror of more than death rippled through her body, darkening her soul. A thing namelessly dreadful caught at her feet, sucking her down. Her lungs were bursting. She would be entombed here in this freezing, sightless water, binding her in hair, shrouding her in liquid ice.

Then there was a violence in the weeds, a turbulence. The water seemed for a moment to fragment into shards. She heard no sound, but she was free again. There was a darkness looming, a presence whose vast tentacles grasped towards them. Eris's dragging arms fell away and Tathea found air, sweet, blessed air on her face. The River was washing around her, with spume-white foam and broken tentacles of stems, and yards from her there was the high shadow of the boat swinging round, turning.

A cry echoed back from the wall of trees and the hollowed-under, hungry banks. 'Where are you?'

She recognised the voice of the man she had spoken to on the deck earlier. 'Here!' she shouted back, kicking away the last clinging threads, panic still crawling in her limbs.

The boat loomed above her, an oar came down and she gripped it, heaving herself up. A hand reached out warm with life and held on to her. He was close in the shivering moonlight.

'You are fortunate to be alive, my friend!'

'What about the . . . the woman?' she gasped. She was struggling to keep standing upright, even though the man supported her with surprising strength. 'What happened to her? Why did she let go of me?' She was still shaking with the memory of it and of that older, nameless thing that had come out of the gloom.

'Eris?' he said softly, pushing back his hood so she saw his face again. 'She is not mortal. She is of the River: a Lamia – half-woman, half-fish, who sucks men's blood, and then their souls, when the moon is sickle-sharp. But even she is afraid of the Kraken.'

'Kraken?' she said in amazement.

'Oh, it was not real,' he replied with a faint, wary smile. 'The sign of the Brotherhood has the power to make people see what they fear the most. Even the Lamia is not immune. It takes great courage to pierce the vision, and she is a thing of cowardice, a creation of sorcery risen again.' There was sadness in him. 'But surely you do know this? Is it not why you are here?'

Tathea felt the shudder pass through her and leave her faint. It was only his grasp which kept her from buckling and falling over.

She knew in that instant that none of this was chance. The anonymity she had imagined she had was an illusion, and she was dangerously stupid to have assumed it.

'Yes.' The courage was not in her answer as she had intended. 'Who are you?'

'Parminiar,' he replied. He held up his thin, beautiful hand, sheltered by the folds of his cloak, and she saw that he touched the tip of his forefinger to his thumb, making a circle, like the link of a chain.

There was no time for the games of safety. 'You are of the Brotherhood,' she said, uncertain whether it was hope inside her or only another fear.

His smile was hollow. 'I am the Master of the Brotherhood,' he agreed. 'We expected Kor-Assh to return, but he has sent you, Tathea. Perhaps it is your power that is needed now. The evil is old and very high and the people turn to it because they know we are close to the end. Destruction walks the earth, and who else will fight the Great Enemy for them? Who else has the art, except the Silver Lords, who have been since the beginning, and know the secrets which are as old as the earth, or perhaps older?'

She searched his face, gaunt in the spectral light, and saw something of the age and the wisdom in it, and a profound sorrow.

'You know the answer to that,' she said urgently, willing him to understand it and accept. 'God can defeat any evil, if we will allow Him to use us to the last degree of all we have, all that we are.'

Something flickered in Parminiar's eyes. 'Do you really believe that? Not just when you are standing here willing me to fight beside you, but when you are alone in the darkness of the night, when you have time to think, to weigh good against evil and count the cost?' There was a passionate gentleness in his thin face. 'Do you ever allow yourself to imagine you might fail, even to acknowledge that you could? Do you measure the power of evil and look at it truly? Or do you know the danger of it, and keep your eyes averted?'

'I know the danger of it.' She shuddered as she spoke. 'And I look. I have seen Asmodeus face to face, and he has promised me pain beyond anything I could dream of.'

Parminiar's eyes widened with a new grasp of horror. 'Yes . . .' he said with an indrawn breath. 'You have!' It was an exclamation of understanding. 'Then perhaps the Silver Lords will not take you so much by surprise.' There was still doubt in him, and grief. He only half believed what he said. They had touched him with a fear no words could ease.

'And will I take them by surprise?' she asked with irony. And yet perhaps if they were expecting Ishrafeli . . .

'No,' he said without hesitation. 'They have woken again the forbidden arts of sorcery, learned in the beginning, when men aspired to heaven by the hidden path, not knowing God had closed the door.'

'There is no door,' she answered. 'The hidden pathway seems to go upward, but its end is in another place. When you pick up the Enemy's weapons, it makes no difference who you would use them against, it is you who sustains the wound. The weapon has become part of you and you of it. You have already changed what you are.'

He looked downward. 'I know.' His voice was little more than a sigh. 'I believed once that if the end were good enough, it could cleanse the means and justify it. I know better now.'

She did not ask how. She thanked him for his help, and bade him good night until the morning.

At midday the sun was soft in a mackerel-flaked sky when she stepped ashore with Parminiar beside her. They stood on the quay with the towers of the City of Fallen Kings above them in curious, ornate shapes – some round as globes, some corbelled, some spiral with silver turrets. The highest of all was the ancient seven-sided tower of the first Lords of the River, as old as the black basalt palace from the dawn of Shinabar. The roofs plunged at a score of angles, reflecting the light in unnumbered shades of grey. The streets and alleys between were a maze of steps.

'Are you still determined to speak with the Silver Lords?' Parminiar asked her.

'Of course,' she replied. If she were to take any of the burden from Ishrafeli there was no alternative now. And they probably already knew she was here anyway. To leave now would signal cowardice.

Parminiar sighed. 'Then come, I will take you to Timon, the High Seneschal. He will admit me, and it will save you much waiting. But I warn you, he is no friend to me, or any of the Brotherhood.' He began to walk up the quay and to climb the steps to the street. The grey houses rose on either side with their windows winking in the light, and layered storeys, the steep-pitched and many sloping roofs. The slates were mottled in the shadows and pale as doves' breasts in the polished light.

She waited for his explanation, keeping pace with him.

'The Silver Lords created the Brotherhood in the beginning,' he said at last, 'seven hundred years ago now, as warriors to withstand the Camassian Empire when they invaded the Island.' He smiled bitterly. 'The Silver Lords are thinkers and rulers. They would not risk their own lives, or stain their hands with blood. The Chain symbolises strength, secrecy, equality. Each link is as important as another. Each stands or breaks on the honour of them all, and each is bound only to his neighbours. And yet in times past the whole has been strong enough to bind even the most dreadful power.' He did not look at her, but at the winding street ahead of him and the soaring flight of steps that led upward to an arch across the street. 'I fear it is no longer so. We grew proud, and defied the men who created us. And they became afraid of the power of destruction that is loosed on the world now, and have turned to the old arts to battle against it. There is no longer trust between us.'

'But Timon will admit us?' she urged.

A smile flitted across Parminiar's mouth. 'Oh, yes. He will be curious, if no more. He will already know who you are.' At last he turned to look at her. His face was haggard in the sunlight, his eyes hollowed out with weariness of a long battle whose victory he did not expect to see. 'Be careful, Ta-Thea,' he whispered. 'For all your wisdom, there is much you do not know. These arts are older than you are. In spirit they are sons of Tiyo-Mah. They weave a net that will snare us all in the end. And it is nearly closed.'

For an instant cold poured through her, and she felt alien and alone in this strange silver-grey street with its towers rising against a luminous sky. Despair wrapped her in a darkness like a shadow of the night in which there is no dawn.

She willed herself to remember the power of God in all things, and that He had promised never to leave her alone. She must believe it, know it every moment, waking and sleeping.

'The Silver Lords devour the will,' Parminiar warned. His hand was gentle on her arm, and his thin fingers held surprising warmth. 'They suck the freedom from the soul. When at last the end comes, it creeps like a velvet noose, a silken hand – the shadow so gossamer soft the ignorant skin welcomes its first beginnings.' His lips tightened. 'I know them. And I have felt the breath of the Great Enemy as he comes closer, just as they have. But by the time they realise it is the one art wielded by the left hand and the right hand of the same demon, it will be too late.'

'Not yet,' she said, shaking her head, refusing to look at anything but hope. 'Take me to Timon. Persuade him to see me.'

It proved as easy as Parminiar had said. They waited only a matter of an hour in a hall where curtains hid doors, and windows looked out on to narrow courtyards shafted with light, serried ranks of roofs at hectic angles sliding down to the far, silver light on the River. They were cared for with exquisite hospitality of sparkling wine and honey cakes, until Timon himself received them in his chamber high in the seven-sided tower, with wide windows in every wall.

He was a huge man, powerful of body, but it was his face which fascinated Tathea. His features were strong, with broad nose and full lips, but wreathed in such folds of skin as to give his visage a unique strength, as if there were always a reserve beyond anything visible to the eye. Memory stirred inside her of peace and a great protection from all conflict. He was clothed in long robes of colour so subtle it was impossible to tell if it were blue or violet or some shade of wine, and it seemed to catch an echo of starlight in it, as if it were more than a woven fabric.

He greeted the visitors with guarded courtesy and made no pretence at friendship with Parminiar. He introduced to them his lieutenant, a slender man named Armerio, with a dark and subtle face, who bowed once and then stood back.

Timon looked at Tathea. 'So you have returned at last from Camassia, now that ruin has spread over the centre of the world, and grows even closer to us,' he observed, his voice dark and beautiful, like that of so many in Lantrif. She remembered its richness also, but she could not place it. The emotions it carried were of almost transcending power, sheet lightning of the heart. She was too stunned by it to reply before he continued.

'What is it you wish of me?' he asked her. 'If you come to warn us, it is unnecessary. We have known for years that the evil was waiting. Perhaps now we see it more clearly than you do.'

She forced herself to concentrate. She must speak with intelligence and honesty to this master of sorcery. They desired the same end; she must persuade him to cast aside the weapons which prevented any alliance between them.

'I know you need no warning of armies of men, nor of the intention of Asmodeus to ruin the earth,' she answered him, trying to measure her words. 'But I have seen his weapons and I know something of what may be used against them.'

He smiled very slightly, as if from a bitter amusement. 'You have been listening to Parminiar. The Brotherhood of the Chain have cast aside the powers of the mind in favour of those of the sword. If they are willing to ally with you, I wish fortune to both of you, although I do not believe you will succeed.' His eyes were bright and unreadable. 'The evil you face is beyond the nature of this world and needs higher arts to combat it. It surprises me you do not know that.'

'Of course I know it!' she said a little too tartly, stung by his condescension. 'Men cannot bind Asmodeus, whatever our arts or our knowledge. He will turn the tools of sorcery against us and bring our defeat more swiftly than if we leave him alone.'

Timon's eyebrows rose but his voice held only the ghost of sarcasm – no more was needed. 'You have presided over the desolation of half the world, and more, and you can come here to Lantrif and tell me how to save my people?'

Tathea brought only news of failure with her, and she was surrounded here by a wall of their beliefs like steel, yet she knew she spoke the truth. It rang in her reply with the passion of a victor, not a woman alone, shorn of kingdom, followers or a single disciple to support her faith.

'The war is bigger than this world, and older,' she answered him. 'At the last, when we are face to face with the end, the only weapon of any use is the love of God. Trust in Him, no matter how thick the darkness or how hard the way. When you are stripped of all your own weapons, your strength is gone, then ask of God, and listen to His answer and obey it. Seeing doesn't matter any more. Only faith and love will be enough.'

'Beautiful,' Timon answered, laughter in his eyes wreathed with the heavy folds of his skin. 'But naïve.'

Parminiar opened his mouth to defend her, but Timon silenced him with a gesture of his arm. His voice was iron hard. 'The Silver Lords yield their will to no one. We have always been our own masters, since the dawn of time. We will not abandon the skills which have served us all our existence. You trust God to rescue you if you wish. We shall do battle with the Great Enemy with the weapons of knowledge and power in our hands.'

Tathea struggled to find some argument to sway him. There was a darkness moving in her mind, knowledge of a small thing forever growing, gathering strength and coming closer with every passing second. Memory came at last like the descending night. She saw a great amphitheatre at sunset, Ishrafeli with a harp in his hand, and a young poet choosing the passion and the grief of life rather than the closed womb of Eden. It was Timon then, under his old name, Ikthari who had promised her the ashes of death.

Timon was staring at her now, here in Lantrif. She was as conscious of him as if he held her in an embrace. She heard Parminiar's voice in the distance, indistinct, muffled. She was so cold she could barely feel her hands or feet.

Then the moment broke, and Timon was speaking again.

'A terrible and final evil has followed you here to the City of the Fallen Kings,' he said softly. 'It is in Lantrif already, and is growing closer, even as we stand here. It is an emissary of the Great Enemy himself.'

Followed her here! So he was not here already. Or was it someone else who had come – Ulciber, perhaps? Surely Asmodeus would gather all his forces for the final confrontation?

'I knew there was a body of men,' Timon was continuing, 'armed and on the River, but I had not until this moment understood who they brought with them.' He glanced at Parminiar. 'The Brotherhood knows this also, surely?'

Parminiar nodded. 'We know of their coming. Now I too understand who is with them. I feel the chill of it on my soul. We must ride against them. They have come for Ta-Thea.' He moved a step closer to her, as if he would protect her even more. 'She is the first cause of their enmity because it was she who brought the Book into the world with the Word of God in it, and told us who we are, and who we may become. She still knows in her heart more than any of us. But we ride as sons of God, and we carry only the swords and lances of earthly make.'

Timon drew in his breath, then let it out in a sigh. There was a strange authority in Parminiar, gaunt as he was – little more than sinew and bone under his cloak – but the strength of his spirit filled the room.

'We will not stand against you nor bar your way,' Timon promised. 'We will wait here, to celebrate with you should you succeed, or to defend the City and its people, should you fail.'

Chapter Twenty-Two

Little more than two score men rode out with Parminiar at their head, and Tathea with them. They would meet the enemy on the open road where they could fight unhampered by the narrow streets of the City of Fallen Kings, and without endangering the ordinary men and women who lived there. And they wanted above all a battle clean from the arts of the Silver Lords, whose aid, in whatever cause, was still a tool of Asmodeus.

Word reached them of the enemy troops approaching. They came on the only road that led to the City, westwards, inland from the River, coiled through the valleys and past the towns that nestled by the water. It climbed the steep slopes of the hills and down again. They came willingly, with courage high, knowing who Tathea was, and had always been. Their hearts were set to defend her with their lives if necessary, but they wore only the armour wrought by ordinary hands, and the belief in their cause. They expected victory, but they knew it might very well also be death, and not one flinched from it.

They saw the riders coming towards them as still only a dark patch crowding the road over two miles away, in the green distance of the valley. Without the need for command, the Brotherhood drew into closer order, ready for battle, and increased pace a little, so they would reach a place of advantage when they met the enemy and could ride downhill to the charge. There was no sound but the clip of hoofs on the road and the jingle of harnesses and armour, which was not bronze like the Camassians', nor copper like the ghosts of the Shinabari in Tathea's mind, but silver. Their banners were white and decorated with the single device of a linked chain.

The scouts and outriders watched for a surprise attack. Everyone else faced forward, as if there were nothing and nobody else on earth but the two columns closing on each other, lances high, swords still sheathed.

The awareness of evil was so heavy inside Tathea that she was surprised that it did not muffle sound. She could still breathe, and the air should have choked in her throat. She was sweating, though the day was not hot.

337

She had ridden armed like this before, but if it was Ulciber who led the foe, outrider and herald for Asmodeus, then perhaps this was the last time she would hold a sword in her hand. She wanted to be on her own feet to wield it in the old way as Alexius had taught her.

But there was no choice. They were increasing pace already and their advance would end in a charge. At least it was good to have a fine animal under her, as good as a desert horse. It felt almost like the beginning, over five hundred years ago, when she had ridden away from Thoth-Moara and begun the search for the knowledge of good and evil.

Perhaps that search would end here on this road in Lantrif as she came face to face again with Asmodeus. How trivial that after all it should be a battle with such human things as swords!

The other force rode proudly. They held silver banners aloft like a guard of honour, but they also had their lances lifted and as they came closer they too increased their speed.

The leader of the guard called out a challenge, or perhaps it was a command. It was in the ancient language of the River and she did not understand it.

Parminiar raised his hand to halt them, but the captain of the first twenty ignored it, spurring his horse forward, and with a great cry they all broke into a gallop. Battle was joined with a crash of lances, splinters flying high, then the clang of sword on sword. Tathea was lost in the mêlée, wheeling and striking, backing, lunging again like all the others.

The struggle was short and savage, fought with passion, courage and ruthlessness. It was over as suddenly as it had begun, with the knights of the Brotherhood victorious. The captain of the twenty who had given the command to charge stood with his sword point at the throat of the enemy leader.

Parminiar stared down at him. 'Why do you ride against your own people?' he demanded in a choking voice. 'What manner of evil is it you conceive that you can do this? You poison the air you breathe!'

'We don't attack our own!' the enemy leader retaliated furiously, ignoring the sword. 'We ride only as an escort of honour to our lord!' He gestured wildly. Tathea turned to follow it as did all the others.

Dusty, his face smeared with blood, Ishrafeli staggered to his feet, half supporting a wounded man in his arms.

Tathea's heart soared on wings like an ascending bird. She dropped the reins and slid from her horse, but before she had taken the first step towards him, the captain of twenty behind her called out again.

338

'Stop her! Protect her . . . above all!'

She swung back to protest, to explain, and saw his face directly for the first time. Fear drenched her, dagger-bright with foreknowledge of pain. He was Timon's lieutenant, Armerio. He was one of the Silver Lords who had infiltrated himself into the Brotherhood to betray them. She turned to Ishrafeli. He was looking at her, his eyes wide.

Armerio spoke again, his voice silencing them all. 'She is Ta-Thea, the bringer of the Book to the world. We must protect her – at any cost.' He pointed to Ishrafeli, now risen to his feet. 'He is a servant of the Great Enemy who would destroy her. His hatred for her will never die, because she carries the Word of God. It was the shadow of his coming that touched us with darkness.'

It was an exquisite weaving of truth and lies, the sorcerer's art to deceive with reality.

The men of the Brotherhood moved towards Ishrafeli with swords drawn, and it would have been death for him to resist.

'He is not!' Tathea shouted, flinging herself free from the hands that restrained her. 'He is Ishrafeli, my husband!' She twisted round to face the men she had ridden with and fought beside. 'You know him!' she shouted. 'He is Kor-Assh, your own lord! In the name of God . . . look at him!'

'He only looks like Kor-Assh!' Armerio's voice drowned hers. 'Sorcerers can look like anyone.' He stared at his men, his face beseeching. 'Can't you feel the evil? Trust your hearts, not your eyes! No one can deceive what you know in your heart.'

'He's not!' Tathea cried desperately, struggling now not to be dragged backwards away from Ishrafeli. She swung round to Parminiar. 'He's not! He's my husband! He would never harm me!'

But Parminiar was nowhere in sight, and the others did not hear her. Strong arms held her. Armerio offered her his own flask and it was pressed to her lips. She gasped and drank from it and its fire filled her throat before she caught the sweet, hazy taste of drugs.

Dimly she saw Ishrafeli forced to stand while his hands were bound behind his back and he was lifted on to his horse, the bridle held by another.

She faced Armerio, tears running down her cheeks. She drew in her breath to plead with him, and the words died inside her. The sight she saw was terrible beyond her imagining. He stood cold and still, his skin white, his eyes void as the pits of hell, and she felt herself drawn in as if she were moving physically towards him, closer, suffocating, endlessly down.

She heard in the distance someone charging Ishrafeli with the highest crime left on earth: that of attempting to bring about the death of the Lady Ta-Thea, the last hope of the world against the

339

Great Enemy. He would be taken back to the City of the Fallen Kings for trial.

Her head whirled. Heat like fire scorched her skin. She was falling. Armerio's eyes were huge, consuming her, burning with red flame, and beyond the flames, vast, endless, hideous slime. All the strength drained out of her and she pitched forward. Harsh, wild laughter banged and whipped her ears, then there was darkness at last.

The trial was held in the Great Hall in the Seven-Sided Tower, and representatives of all the people of Lantrif were there. It was a grey and silver day with the sun slanting through the tall windows on to the polished stone floor and picking out the carving on the high-backed ceremonial seats of the judges and the jury.

Ishrafeli was unbound, but he was kept apart by the ornate rails of a boxed-in space reserved for the accused. Tathea was similarly restrained, although her gaolers were termed a guard of honour. She was the most important woman in the world, the Bringer of the Book, and the prime target of the Great Enemy who would destroy all mankind. For the sake of the world she must be kept safe by all the powers and the arts of Lantrif, at the cost of their own lives, if necessary. No argument, no pleading she could offer made the slightest difference. She was as helpless to prevent any of this farce as was Ishrafeli himself.

She stood between her guards, white-faced and in agony of heart. The silver inlaid doors to the chamber opened wide, and the exquisitely robed judge came through and climbed the steps to his seat. Only when he turned and faced the court did she recognise him, the beauty of his countenance untouched by aeons of time: Ulciber, the Lord of Corruption, here all the time in the City of Fallen Kings.

He looked at her levelly for several seconds. Then, his blue-grey eyes wide and bright, he turned to Ishrafeli and his smile was slow and sickly sweet with triumph. At that moment Tathea knew there would be no escape, no rescue. It was like the closing of an inner door, final and complete.

The proceedings began. Witnesses were called to tell of Tathea's arrival in Lantrif. Parminiar, hollow-eyed and in a voice like that of despair, told how the Lamia, creature of sorcery, knowing who Tathea was, had tried to drown her.

Ulciber leaned forward. 'And yet you were there, and had power to rescue her?' he said softly.

Parminiar lifted his head. 'Good always has power over evil!' he said fiercely.

'How did you know to be on deck at that precise moment?'

Ulciber enquired, his voice clear and light, carrying to every corner of the court. 'Did you have some presentiment? Is that part of the power of good to protect this woman who is at the heart of the ultimate war?' He glanced at Ishrafeli and away again.

'Of course!' Parminiar's words stung with their anger and their certainty. 'Would not the powers of good give us the weapons we need?'

A shadow crossed Ulciber's face, fear and victory at the same instant.

Tathea looked at Ishrafeli and met his eyes. She saw a terrible understanding of the betrayal vanish and be replaced by love alone.

Ulciber was still speaking. 'So the power of good warned you, and you were in the right place, at the exact moment the Lamia struck?' he said to Parminiar.

'Yes.'

'Because it is a true principle that the servants of good will be warned so that the right may be served, no matter what power of evil is sent against them?'

Too late Parminiar saw the trap. He had already committed himself. There was only one answer he could give. The word was hoarse as if dragged from his throat. 'Yes.'

'Thank you,' Ulciber said gently. 'You are excused.'

Timon was called, and the respect for him was palpable. He took his place and told how messengers had come to him saying there was an armed force entering Lantrif from the east, and at their head was a great protagonist in the spiritual war. The shadow of conflict was already over them. The danger to the forces of good was so intense it was impossible to think of anything else.

Heads craned round to look at Tathea with reverence, and then at Ishrafeli with a terror controlled only by the majesty of Ulciber in the judge's seat, and the long knowledge of the arts of Timon and the other Silver Lords. It seemed as they had promised: they had proved themselves stronger than all the plans of the enemy. Victory was within sight, whatever the danger had been.

Tathea was desperate. All control had slipped from her. There were only minutes left.

Of course Timon was warned of evil! Of course it was here; the malign passion of it could be felt like a suffocating in the heart now, this moment. How could she show them it was Ulciber, Timon, the Silver Lords – not Ishrafeli!

'Of course you've been betrayed!' she shouted. 'But not by Kor-Assh! You knew him! Think of—' Before she could say more her guards pulled her back, and Timon's voice drowned out everything else, commanding all attention. He told the court how he had felt the power of destruction drawing even closer, and had agreed that Parminiar should lead the Brotherhood out to meet it, even though he knew they were powerless. So he had sent Armerio, while he and the other Silver Lords remained in the City and gathered their strength so they might fight the last action here. They knew the arts of evil better than ordinary men, and could call on equal powers to combat them.

Tathea stood leaning forward over the ebony rails of her protected space, her body clenched tight, every muscle aching as if she were poised for a physical attack.

Timon hesitated, then pointed at Ishrafeli. 'Our own Lord Kor-Assh is the betrayer, the servant of Asmodeus sent to destroy Tathea. Who better? In the purity of her heart, she trusted him.' He inclined his head towards her and smiled. 'Only we were warned,' he went on. 'Tathea herself knew of the evil to come, and she had the courage she has always had, the same fire that drove her in the beginning to dare the conflicts of eternity, and bring back the Word of God for us. She rode to meet him, as she has always done battle with the Enemy . . . face to face.' He stopped.

The irony was overwhelming.

She must speak now or it would be too late. 'The power of evil is the use of Asmodeus' weapons!' she cried out suddenly. 'Whatever we intend or imagine.'

Every face in the room turned towards her.

There was murmured agreement all round, not a word of contention anywhere. However, there was no shadow of understanding of what she meant, except in the eyes of Ulciber, who knew his own control of the court, and of Ishrafeli, who was even more helpless than Tathea to alter the tide which swept over them.

She tried again. 'The evil we felt was not Kor-Assh!' she said passionately. 'He has stood side by side with me against the Great Enemy since the days of heaven before the war began, and fought every battle as hard as I, and sustained as many injuries, and as deep!'

There was not a flicker in any of them. They stared at her with reverence, and total blindness.

She felt the panic rise inside her and knew her whole body was shaking as she plunged on. 'Of course the evil was felt, but it was the power of sorcery, the presence of the enemy trying to delude us all!' Everything she said only supported their beliefs. They were in thrall to the Silver Lords, and saw only what the power of their own sorcery had created.

She went on arguing that the use of magic was not the gaining of power but the yielding of it to forces beyond their control. But even as she pleaded with them she knew it was useless. All around her like a sea was the art of the Silver Lords, and above all the mastery

342

of Ulciber. That they should believe Ishrafeli to be corrupted was his final revenge, and it shone in his eyes and curved his lips into a perfect smile.

The verdict was delivered in a swift, shattering word. 'Guilty.'

It was preposterous. Ishrafeli of all creatures on earth would never have harmed her, and he was to be put to death for the supreme crime of planning her murder. It was the ultimate betrayal. The sentence was that he be burned. Tathea heard it with a horror that scorched through her as if the fires consumed her own flesh.

She begged to be allowed a last moment with him. It was denied.

'We cannot permit it,' Timon said with oozing sorrow. He shook his great head and his shoulders lifted very slightly. 'For your own protection, you understand.'

'He wouldn't hurt me!' she protested with despair.

'It is the voice of your goodness speaking,' he answered, smiling at her. 'You judge from your own heart, and you do not see the evil that is in another's.'

'I see it very well . . .' she began fiercely, but he was not listening. Nothing she said would make any difference. She might as well shout at the stones, except that by allowing him to see her pain she gave him a certain satisfaction. As suddenly as she had begun, she ceased to argue. 'But I am not afraid of it!' she finished, meeting his eyes and seeing blindness and arrogance and spiritual death staring back at her.

'You have no need to be,' he answered smoothly, his eyes and his lips denying each other. 'We shall protect you, my lady. We shall never allow the Enemy to touch you again.'

His words could have meant anything. Whose enemy? There was no purpose in speech. She turned and walked away, hiding her face from him, but keeping her back straight and her head high.

The execution was immediate. Ishrafeli was taken from the prison as soon as the wood had been gathered for the fires. He had known as he rode toward Lantrif that he would not return to Tyrn Vawr ever again. Only for a moment had he been surprised to find Tathea already there, then he realised why she had come, and how she had unwittingly played into the hands of the Silver Lords, who had then betrayed them both.

Ulciber had corrupted the City of the Fallen Kings, Ishrafeli's own people. He had used Tathea herself and their knowledge of who she was to bring about this very moment. It was part of Asmodeus' plan, but above all it was Ulciber's own revenge for being denied a mortal body, that prize he had wanted above all, and which for a brief, soaring instant he had believed Ishrafeli could give him.

Ishrafeli climbed the steps to the heart of the wood and they

343

lashed him to the stake. He saw them pile more brushwood around the bottom. He watched through the blackening smoke the exultation in Ulciber's face, the moment of his supreme triumph. This was the revenge he had sworn in the dust of the road in Pera. Now it shone bright like a radiance inside him.

Ishrafeli turned to Tathea. She was standing in front of the crowd, her body rigid with inner pain, and so close the heat must scorch her skin and the dark smuts flying upward catch in her hair. He wanted her face to be the last thing he saw – in the end the only thing.

The fire was catching hold. The heat of it was sickening pain, filling his whole existence. His lungs were bursting. He concentrated all his strength on not crying out, not screaming. He could see nothing clearly any more, a red light, and then darkness and an agony beyond imagination. It lasted a moment, then rose and exploded, and became nothing. Radiance stretched to infinity with a sweetness that was the breath of God.

Tathea saw him slump forward and her heart knew the moment of his release and her own unutterable loss.

Was it her new and terrible aloneness, or did the air really shudder and a gasp go up from the earth as if it too were bereaved of its heart?

'Why?' The cry rose inside her, but even before it reached her lips, it faded away. There was no anger in her soul. This was unjust, it seemed the triumph of evil, and yet something spoke peace to her that was stronger than damnation. A voice whispered that all was well, all was still in the hand of God.

Dazed and scorched with the heat herself, empty to the core of her, she turned towards Ulciber, and saw with shattering unbelief that the skin on his hands was withering. It was like crepe, a hundred thin lines on it, fragile as paper.

He was looking at her, the triumph brilliant in his eyes. It was a moment lifted above and beyond time. She knew with perfect clarity, and he did not yet, but he would, soon: Ulciber the immortal was dissolving into oblivion. The flesh on his body was shrivelling even as she watched.

He saw something in her face. His look of triumph froze. They stared at each other through the smoke-filled air, past the Silver Lords as if they did not exist. Slowly Ulciber lowered his eyes to look at his hands, which were now ghastly as claws, the veins standing out like blue ropes, the nails buckled. The bones of his wrists protruded where the skin hung empty, splashed with dark blotches.

With horror of disbelief he felt his bowels perish and his belly cave in. His robes settled lower around the sharp edges of his shoulders. He opened his mouth and uttered a high, thin scream that tore the air and splintered glass in the high windows of the towers. Birds scattered in the air. In a language unknown to man, older than the spirits of the earth, he cursed Asmodeus who had deceived him from the time of the war in heaven.

In Erebus Asmodeus knew it. For an instant he savoured the exquisiteness of Tathea's loss. Then the darkness around him grew troubled and the foundations shivered and cracked. It was not the headlong plunge of Ulciber from youth through senility to dissolution, it was the terrible, irreversible knowledge that the earth itself was dying. That was nothing to do with Ulciber, or the sorcery of the Silver Lords. It was not even anything to do with Tathea. It was Ishrafeli's death which had freed it to lay down its burden of the ages and allow its spirit at last to give up the struggle against those who afflicted it, polluted its face and tortured its creatures.

For an instant Asmodeus was brushed by an overpowering fear. Victory or loss for ever were days away, perhaps hours! It was only just beyond his grasp, his hand could almost close on it, but one mistake, one chance not taken, and he could still lose!

And all the Lords of Sin were gone except Yaltabaoth. Even a year ago that had been inconceivable. But surely now, if ever since the daybreak of creation, this was a time when despair could walk the earth? This was the age of Yaltabaoth. How could any creature entertain hope of anything? The earth itself was beginning to taste death!

'Yaltabaoth!' He called only once; there was no need to repeat that dreadful name.

The stars dimmed, as if a shadow had fallen across them.

Yaltabaoth stood in front of Asmodeus, his face bone-white beneath his flying hair, his black cloak ragged as a feathered wing. He did not speak. He too had heard Ulciber's fearful cry as eternity took hold of him, and he needed no man nor spirit to tell him what was wanted.

Asmodeus looked at his face and fear touched with a black hand that chilled the heart. 'Destroy everything that is left,' he ordered. 'Kill it all. Leave me nothing but the woman. I want Tathea.'

Yaltabaoth smiled, and it was like living death.

Asmodeus shuddered and turned away. He did not even see Yaltabaoth leave to begin his last walk upon the earth.

Chapter Twenty-Three

Armies had swayed and clashed across the ruin of empires and finally obliterated themselves, making the earth one vast charnel house. Only the Island at the Edge of the World was left, one small pool of light in an ever-growing darkness.

Alone and dazed with grief, Tathea went on foot from Lantrif of the River, and made her long way back through the rich fields of the Heartlands towards Tyrn Vawr. The golden Book of God was there, the only thing Asmodeus could not touch. The night was closing in, and she had one more meeting to keep.

On the plague-stricken battlefields there was no one left alive. The desert sand was dark with blood and a hundred million bones bleached in the sun, stripped bare and white. Now even the carrion birds starved.

In the cities that had once teemed with the great civilisations of men, the wind blew down deserted streets and the glories of the past sank into a slow decay. Here and there smoke darkened the horizon and the stench of burning soiled the air.

On the Shinabari battlefield Sadokhar knew there was nothing more he could do here in this vast charnel house. Everywhere it was the same. Scorching air blew out of the south as from a furnace, carrying torrents of whirlwinds of sand as if they had lifted the desert floor and spewed it into the sky. Valleys were scoured out and new mountains built. It blew for days and nights with a screaming that never ceased. Oases were buried. Cities vanished as if they had never been.

Sadokhar and Tornagrain travelled north on horseback, hoping to reach the sea, and eventually the Island. Their bodies bent forward, both they and their animals bound with cloths over head and face, covering all but their eyes. They carried water and dried fruit, and prayed for more as a man prays for life. They kept company with God in their thoughts, reciting, in the howling solitude of the storms around them, the pages of the Book committed to heart.

There was nothing to say, and no breath with which to say it. Both knew what must be done and were bent as with a single mind upon accomplishing it. In the destruction of the world there was still one last battle to be fought, and it would be on the Island at the Edge of the World, as Iszamber had foretold. With the protection of God to guide and keep them, they would be there.

In the north, near the sea in the shambles of what was once Tarra-Ghum, they came across fugitives fled from Irria-Kand, south through Pera, and were now driven into Shinabar. Around the campfire at night they cooked what little food remained, and told stories of wind and fire storms that had swept over the plains of their land. Lightning had blazed across the skies and forked to earth, igniting the dry grass until the flames, driven by hurricane winds, had devoured everything for hundreds of miles at a time, leaving a blackened earth behind and the charred bones of what had once been life.

Sadokhar and Tornagrain left in the morning, taking one of the abandoned ships lying in the harbour. They set out towards Tirilis. Clouds darkened the sky and sudden squalls drove them through white water. They were hurled forward at break-neck speed, battered and half-drowned with the force of waves thundering around them.

Three days and nights later they were washed up on the shore, exhausted, gasping for breath, their ship wrecked and floating half-submerged beyond the line of the breakers.

They dragged themselves up the sand and slept, too weary to care whether or not they were safe from roaming men or beasts.

By nightfall they were dry and awake enough to continue, always moving west towards the further coast that looked on the sea that bounded the world, and beyond which lay the Island, and the last battlefield.

Tirilis was devastated by disease. Rotting corpses lay in the streets, pustulant and terrible. No one was left alive, but there was more than sufficient fruit on the trees to sustain Sadokhar and Tornagrain as they walked. There were no beasts left to ride.

As they moved north towards the borders of Caeva, it grew steadily colder. When they crossed into the great forests a hard north wind blew almost unceasingly and the edge of it was like a knife on the skin.

Further north, travelling was even more difficult. They saw the devastation left by ice storms which had killed everything in their path, freezing plants and animals where they stood.

They stood side by side on a bitter ridge, the wind keening in their ears, and gazed around them at a world blinded by snow before and behind. It was piled high on the mountains to every side, valleys shrouded in white like the preparation for some great burial of the world.

Sadokhar was shaking with cold. He turned to Tornagrain beside him, his face grey, body huddled into his clothes. 'Come on, we've got to keep moving!' he urged. 'We'll die if we stop.'

Tornagrain shot him a glance wry with black humour, and set off down the slope without replying.

By the time they reached the next rise it had begun to thaw a little, and three miles on again on the crest of a pass they turned as the entire side of the mountain behind them caved in and crashed down three thousand feet in a roaring, suffocating avalanche of snow. It obliterated the forest that had stood there minutes before and changed the face of the land until it was unrecognisable.

When at last it was still, a crushing silence filled the air. They stood side by side, appalled by the power of destruction and the terrible beauty of it. It was Tornagrain who turned first.

'It can happen again,' he said quietly. 'We'd better move.'

Sadokhar bit his lip, beginning to shiver. 'It could just as well happen ahead as behind,' he pointed out.

Tornagrain raised his eyebrows. 'You want to go back?' he asked sarcastically.

Sadokhar slapped him on the shoulder, and they set off down the slope. The wind was behind them, the temperatures dropping sharply, the sky heavy and dark.

They moved on steadily towards the shore, conscious of the ever-advancing rivers of ice behind them, the broken forests and the drowning snow.

When they came to the last thicket of woods and emerged from it onto the cliff edge, they saw a sight that staggered the imagination. The entire shoreline was gone, as if the ocean had risen out of its bed and inundated the sand hills and the sea walls, the harbour and the town beyond. Everything was broken, spread out and half submerged in mud. It was impossible to conceive of the force which must have devastated it to leave such a wreckage behind.

'God in Heaven!' Tornagrain breathed, lifting his face to the sky. 'What happened? What could have done this?' He turned to Sadokhar. 'Is there anyone alive on earth, except us?'

Sadokhar had no idea. He could only hope, and keep in his heart memories of the beliefs Tathea had taught him in their days in the forest of Hirioth, before he had had the least conception of what evil truly was. She had tried so hard to give him the armour against it, but its magnitude was beyond even her words to tell.

'Yes,' he said with certainty, 'Tathea is still alive. I would know if she were not.' They were brave words, and surely they were true? He would know – wouldn't he?

'What happened?' Tornagrain repeated, looking at the waste before them. 'How could the sea do this?'

'I don't know,' Sadokhar admitted. 'It must have been a wave bigger than anything we've imagined or seen before.'

'More than a hundred feet high to do this!' Tornagrain marvelled.

'Perhaps it was.' Sadokhar started to move forward down the jagged path set in the cliff face, picking his way with care. 'We must find what wood we can and make a boat. We shall have many miles to go before we reach the Island, but we can do it in one day once we have a craft of some sort.'

Tornagrain followed him. 'Maybe we could find a wreck and patch it up?' he suggested. 'It looks as if there used to be a shipyard here once. You'd better pray there isn't another wave!'

'So had you!' Sadokhar said tartly. 'It plays no favourites.'

Tornagrain thumped him gently and continued on down.

They reached the bottom and for the first time realised that the thick mud around them must hide the bodies of a thousand men, women and children who had once lived here. Now there was nothing left but sticks poking out of the desolation, the chimney tops of buried houses, and the bones of an arm raised above the sand like that of a drowning man.

Tornagrain let out an exclamation of horror, and increased his pace, leaving heavy footprints across the expanse. He ran a little, as if he could escape the pity of it.

Sadokhar followed after, the slurp of the tide loud in his ears, reminding him of the ever-present sea like a beast crouching for its prey.

After a full day digging in the mud, hauling planks out of its sucking, choking grip before they could find enough timber to build a boat, they stood exhausted and filthy, staring at their pile of waterlogged planks. It seemed little treasure for so much dangerous and backbreaking labour.

'It's waterlogged,' Tornagrain said in disgust. He lifted his gaze and stared at the horizon in every direction. Everything was smashed and laid waste. There were no houses, no trees, only the dark oozing of mud, and behind them the cliff face. 'And we've nothing to work with,' he added. 'We could dig for eternity and never find tools in this!'

'Anything iron or steel will have sunk anyway,' Sadokhar agreed. 'But there's rope . . .'

'What?'

'There's rope,' Sadokhar repeated with a sour smile. 'We'll have to bind the heaviest planks together and make a raft. And don't make a face like that – unless you can think of something better!'

Tornagrain shrugged. 'At least we won't run into anyone we know!' he said ironically. 'Come on then! Don't stand there!'

It took them another day to build it, and then a day and a night of hard rowing before they landed on the Eastern Shore of the Island. They were north of where they had once lived with Aelfrith in what seemed now like another life in a different, simpler age. The darkness of its memories were washed away. They trusted each other with a fierce passion more innocent men could not have known.

Now in silence they walked up the pale dunes to the sea grasses, nothing but the sound of the waves in their ears where once there had been gulls. The wind drove white clouds high above over the land, shadowing the far rim of the forest.

They met no one. The few farms and cottages seemed deserted, and only now and again did they see a burned shell of what had once been inhabited. No pollution poisoned the land. Wild flowers made the grasses bright and small animals seemed unafraid of the two men.

Sadokhar was deep in thought. The beauty of this after the desolation he had seen was dreamlike, and it crossed his mind more than once to wonder if it was some illusion of the enemy's, built to delude. The great trees resting like green clouds on the swell of the earth could have been drawn from his memory. Even the scent of growing, the whisper of the grass and the brilliance of the air were part of him like the beating of his blood. Iszamber had told Tathea that the Island would stand, even when darkness and havoc covered the rest of the earth, but he had not said it would escape the last destruction.

Sadokhar understood that it had to be, and yet looking at it now, its loss cut too deeply into him and he ached to hold it a day, even an hour longer. All the wisdom and the faith of years could not take the hurt from losing even one flower or tree, let alone the whole glory of it all.

They found horses and rode south and inland, reaching Tyrn Vawr two days later. The stones of the city were still bathed in soft light, as if at any moment a watchman would call and welcome. But the tide of war had washed right to the walls, and there was no one left but the Knights of the Western Shore, scarred, wounded and alone.

Ythiel had ruled in justice, but he could not, nor would he have kept from the people knowledge of the carnage and the desolation that covered the rest of the world. They had fought rebels and invaders on the shores, in the fields and villages, even in Tyrn Vawr itself, and they had won. Now they had completed their part, and lay at peace in the earth. Only the Knights awaited the end.

Sadokhar and Tornagrain rode in together, staring at the silent streets, the signs of work half done, shops untended, doors closed for a last time as both men and women went out to face the enemy.

They did not speak; there was nothing for either to say.

In the centre courtyard Tornagrain took the horses and left Sadokhar to go in alone.

Sadokhar found Tathea in the same room in which she had first shown him the Book, and he had for a moment seen the dark keys of Asmodeus resting on it.

Quietly, in bare and simple words she told him of Ishrafeli's death.

They stood together, clinging to each other, holding close with an aching gentleness. The Book sat uncovered on the table, open since Ishrafeli had loosed the hasp, its blue Lost Lands cloak in rippling silk beside it. She had been reading it again when he had come.

She pulled away from him at last. 'And the Silver Lords are gone also,' she said quietly. 'They tried to use sorcery against the Great Enemy, and he turned it back upon them.' She gave an infinitesimal shrug of her shoulders. 'It is his creation! As all who dare the forbidden paths, they drank madness in the end, and destroyed each other, and everyone who crossed their way. The whole of Lantrif is fallen.'

'Where shall we face Asmodeus?' he asked her.

'We have yet to confront Yaltabaoth,' she answered. 'The earth is dying . . .' She saw sorrow in his face. 'No . . . don't grieve for it,' she said softly. 'It must be. The ability to be born and to die is part of our pathway home – the earth's as well as ours. That was Ishrafeli's greatest gift, the release from travail for the world. Now we must face the last battle. It has to be here, on the Island. Yaltabaoth must fight us because we are all who are left. We will find him where we first met, in the Wastelands when everything seemed lost.' She smiled. 'How little that was, in reality – and perhaps our one small world is little compared with the creations of God.' She looked away from him suddenly, her eyes filled with tears. 'But how infinitely precious!'

She took the Book with her, wrapped in the blue cloak and bound behind her saddle, and her staff in her hand. She, Sadokhar and Tornagrain rode together with Ythiel, Gallimir and the other Knights of the Western Shore. They came dressed proudly in the helmets and breastplates of their ancestors who had first fought against Yaltabaoth, and won. The scarlet cloaks were ragged now, and the armour polished bright showed the scars of old battles, but the plumes were still high and they tossed with the movement of travel like a defiance of grief.

The Knights passed by the forest of Hirioth, and Tathea looked at Sadokhar and smiled. The past was sweet with uncountable small and beautiful things, laughter and friendship, and a love whose depth was truly understood only now.

They climbed the steppes of Celidon, its grasses heavy and deep with summer, and passed on to the wild spaces of the Wastelands. Here the dark hills rose like the bones of the earth, mist-shrouded on the skyline, the heather already purple before the bracken should gild the valleys in the year's waning – except that this summer was the last, even for the Island at the Edge of the World.

They were joined briefly by a fantastic figure, who came on foot, treading softly so the herbs smelled sweet in his path. He wore a parti-coloured jerkin of purple and gold, and breeches the same. On his feet were ridiculous shoes, one of each colour, with long toes that curled over and had tiny bells attached to them, so they tinkled with every step.

He smiled at them and spoke only a few words, then he walked beside Tathea, loping easily as if he never tired. They stopped to make camp for the night a little distance from one of the hundred reed-speared tarns, loud with the call of wild birds.

In high summer as far north as they were, the sun barely dropped below the horizon. The clear sky echoed the light across the arch of heaven and lay mirrored in the shining water.

Tathea stood alone in the vast stillness of it, breathing the clean, wind-scented air. Menath-Dur appeared beside her; his thin, curious face was filled with peace. He gazed at the sky and the hills and for a long time neither of them spoke. When at last he did, it was what he had always said to her, from the beginning.

'Hope . . . remember, always hope. Though heaven and earth fall away, and tomorrow you meet despair, trust in God and hope.' He smiled, then moved among them all, speaking a word to each man, ending with Sadokhar. He looked again at Tathea. Then, as if some emotion filled him almost more than he could control, he turned and moved away so rapidly it was only moments before the gathering shadows engulfed him, and even the bells on his shoes could no longer be heard.

In the morning they rose early. No one had been able to sleep. This day they must be prepared to face Yaltabaoth.

They stood together in a circle for the last prayer, asking only that the Spirit of God be with them. Then they mounted to ride out, Tathea with the Book and the staff, as always.

By late morning, when the aching blue of the sky was a towering arch above them, they heard the thin, terrible cry of Yaltabaoth like death on the wind. They turned as one man to face him, lances high, ready for the charge.

He came out of the east, at first only a dark figure on the slope of the hill, but moving swiftly. In moments Tathea could see there were over a score of riders with their black cloaks flying, helmets gleaming in the sun, black lances raised ready, and beyond them, darkening the hills, uncounted numbers more.

Head high, Sadokhar gave the order and they closed ranks.

The air was heavy with silence. Not even a horse moved. Slowly the hoof-beats of Yaltabaoth's men trembled through the ground, then the sound of them was heard and felt in the blood. The vast mass held back, waiting. The first score drove forward, hollow-eyed, skin burned dark by the wind and rain, mouths wide as if drinking the air. Their armour was black, without gleam or polish, and their helmets were plumed in feathers.

The war cry came again, high and piercing like needles of ice, the wail of lost souls who see the fire and the light of eternity and know it is lost to them for ever.

Sadokhar looked at Tornagrain, then at Tathea, then he faced forward. 'Charge!' he shouted, raising his lance high. Then, levelling it, he spurred his horse forward over the grass.

The two forces met at full gallop with a crash like breaking seas, and immediately the fallen were trampled as animals wheeled and turned, reared and plunged. Swords slashed left and right. The noise was deafening: the clang of metal on metal, swords against shields, against armour, the scream as they met flesh, and all the time the rising wind and the war cry above it all.

Tathea fought with all her skills she remembered from the long past. And as they had then, her comrades shielded her, took blows meant for her, and fell at her feet. The scarlet of blood mingled with the scarlet of cloaks and crests.

She had no idea where Sadokhar or Tornagrain were. Each man fought for himself, and for those beside him. She was battered, bruised and bleeding, her whole body ached, her thigh was torn by the splinters of a lance, but there was no time to heed wounds, only to fight on. The words of Menath-Dur beat in her head and drove her forward, giving strength to her arm and guiding her sword.

There was slaughter all around her. The grass was mounded dark with the bodies of the dead, the black and the scarlet together. Still she had not crossed swords with Yaltabaoth himself, and when she stumbled over a corpse and scrambled to her feet one last, desperate time, she gazed around her and saw only three other figures left standing among the dead. Sadokhar was twenty feet away from her to the left, and her heart soared to see him. Fifty feet away stood Tornagrain, leaning forward a little, the hilt of his sword in his hand, the blade sheared away. Beyond him was the fearful figure of Yaltabaoth, whose black hair was streaming from his head, his mouth wide, eyes deep in the sockets of his skull gleaming with the passion of the final hatred.

He looked past Tornagrain to Sadokhar, and to Tathea and he smiled. He took a step forward.

His vast unused army waited, a mile away, watching.

Tornagrain moved between them.

'Stand aside!' Yaltabaoth commanded. 'Or I will destroy your soul! I will make you taste the ashes of despair until you pray for oblivion, and it does not come!'

Slowly a wondrous joy spread across Tornagrain's face and he lifted both his hands high in the air.

'I am Tornagrain, the Redeemed of God!' he cried. 'And Despair cannot touch me!' And he hurled himself upon Yaltabaoth. The two of them locked together in a clasp that crushed the flesh and broke the bones, and still they did not let go. They swayed back and forth, buckled at the knees and fell, writhing on the ground, and still neither let go.

Sadokhar and Tathea both ran forward, but they could only watch in helplessness as Yaltabaoth thrashed and kicked and gouged and tore, until, still locked in Tornagrain's arms, their blood mingled together. Tornagrain yielded up his spirit and Yaltabaoth gasped, drew in an agonising breath, and reached out to loose Tornagrain's arms from around him.

But he could not. All the strength of his rage and his hatred was not enough. In death Tornagrain's arms tightened. Yaltabaoth gasped, choked and very slowly first his limbs then his body dissolved into a black, viscous slime and was swallowed into the earth.

Tathea and Sadokhar watched in horror as even his skull caved in and seemed to crush beneath its own weight, and the sockets of his eyes gleamed putrescent.

In minutes there was nothing left. Tornagrain lay alone. His hands eased their grip upon emptiness and a radiance shone around him as of a great and perfect peace.

Tathea looked at Sadokhar and saw tears on his face. She knew they were grief only in part; there was also gratitude in them, for Tornagrain, and perhaps for himself also because he could mourn without shadow a friendship that had found honour and compassion and a wholeness of heart.

A mile away the numberless army dissolved into a mist and existed no more.

Tathea was hardly aware of the air growing colder, and the shadows closing in from the horizon on all sides, even though it was little beyond noon and the sun was high and golden in the blue above them.

She knew the earth had at last been released from its labour, so the silence of no bees or birds was not strange to her, nor even the absence of all beasts in the grass.

Sadokhar bent slowly to Tornagrain's body and touched his face.

He bade him farewell in the old way of the warriors of the Eastern Shore, as he had done to Aelfrith years before.

'Safe harbour,' he whispered gently. 'Soft seas on the morning tide.'

It was Tathea who saw the gaunt figure coming towards them through the grass, staggering a little like a wounded bird, her neck forward. The wan light gleamed on her head, bald now but for a few wisps of black hair fluttering like broken feathers. But there was nothing ludicrous about her. She was filled with hate. It was naked in every jerky movement of her, the thrusting angle of her head, the wild scything of her arms as she waded through the heather towards Sadokhar with startling swiftness.

The darkness was growing. The horizon was almost invisible, as if great clouds of dust had covered all the earth but here, and the chill on the wind woke memory of the land of eternal snows.

Tiyo-Mah was only yards away; her ancient face, with its curved nose and cruel mouth, was alight with rage. Her body was so emaciated it could only be passion of will which kept her from collapsing.

Tathea expected to be the victim of her centuries of hate. Their enmity stretched back beyond the beginning of the history of the Book, which was still wrapped in the blue robe beside her on the grass, with the staff. It had begun the day Tathea had arrived as a new bride in Thoth-Moara, and Tiyo-Mah had ceased to be the power behind the Isarch.

Perhaps it was older even than that? Now in this fading light of the world, Tathea remembered clearly the terrible face of the Oligarch Tallagisto who had ordered her death in Sardonaris, where she had overheard the great Council of Heaven, and chosen to take the Book. It was his burning eyes which now looked out of Tiyo-Mah's face, and she realised now that it always had been.

But Tiyo-Mah ignored her, lurching through the heather towards Sadokhar instead, her eyes fixed on him as if she saw nothing and no one else.

Then with a flash like a light in the mind, blazing in clarity, Tathea understood that she had followed him all the way from Shinabar, through the slaughter of the battlefields, across the sea, over the freezing mountains and snow-drowned forests of Caeva, past the deserted city of Tyrn Vawr, driven by the lust to kill.

It was Sadokhar who had provoked Tiyo-Mah to begin Armageddon before Asmodeus was ready, and she, and the Lords of Sin had yielded to the temptation. Now they were all destroyed, even Yaltabaoth, and the earth lay shattered around them. Unless she redeemed herself in his eyes, Asmodeus' vengeance upon her for her disobedience would be terrible and endless. Perhaps killing

Sadokhar would do that, but whether it did or not, before the end she would repay Sadokhar for his part.

Screeching far back in her throat like an animal, she flew at him, fingers tearing at his face like claws, teeth bared and reaching for his throat.

He flung her off easily and turned away, revolted, even now seeing only an old woman beyond her senses with hate. He turned to walk away, back to Tathea, thinking to protect her.

Tiyo-Mah screamed at him in a language older than any he knew, older even than Shinabar; and the earth in front of him crumbled and fell inward, as if it were hollow beneath. He had to scramble to avoid pitching into the hole.

Tathea ran towards him, trying to place herself between him and Tiyo-Mah, but Tiyo-Mah flung her arms sideways, crying again in her high-pitched screech. The earth was gouged out and Tathea found herself falling, sliding, bruised and battered with stones, landing hard at the bottom of a gaping pit.

She clambered to her feet, desperate, crying out her own commands, ordering the soil and clay to part for her. How dare it obey the voice of evil?

But the spirit of the earth had already fled and it was dead matter, driven by the power of hell which moved it, eluding her grasp, crumbling, reforming in front of her. She barely reached the tip of the crater, nails torn and skin bleeding, in time to see Tiyo-Mah trip Sadokhar in the long stems of the heather and leap on his fallen body. She snatched his sword from his side and raising it high in both hands, brought it down with all her strength to slash his throat.

With crippling horror Tathea saw the blood pour in a scarlet tide. She fell to her knees on the grass. Was this how it would end, herself and Tiyo-Mah, locked together, fighting with nothing left to win or lose?

Tiyo-Mah climbed off the corpse of Sadokhar awkwardly, and lurched towards Tathea, the dripping sword still in her hand.

Tathea had no weapon close enough to reach. She had already fought a long and desperate battle and her strength was gone.

Tiyo-Mah laughed, a completely human sound, and raised the sword. Then her face froze and her fingers let the blade slip uselessly to the earth.

Tathea swung around slowly to see Asmodeus walking with his peculiar grace up the sward, a figure of terrifying defiance against the glare of the light. The horizon was lurid, burning yellow with sulphur, and there was a stench on the wind like nothing the world held.

He stopped in front of Tiyo-Mah, and Tathea saw naked terror in the old woman, and the fear of hell in her eyes.

'You disobeyed me.' Asmodeus said it softly, but his words shivered through the air and nothing else on earth or sky moved or made a sound. 'Sadokhar was mine! And you would have taken Ta-Thea from me too! For that I have come to collect payment.'

Tiyo-Mah stood motionless. She had denied God and there was nowhere to turn.

Asmodeus lifted his hands, gently, as if he were to play an instrument of music, but what came from them was more terrible than death, it was the claim of damnation.

In front of Tathea's vision, Tiyo-Mah shrivelled up and her empty robes slid to the ground, clothing nothing but a tiny heap of black powder. The wind gusted with a smell foul enough to make the stomach retch, and the powder blew away. As it did so a shadow arose, and Tiyo-Mah's spirit was carried up into the darkness of the moiling clouds above, and disappeared.

Tathea ran across the grass and picked up the Book, holding it in her arms, and threw herself on to the earth.

She heard Asmodeus' voice close to her, every word sharp as daggers of ice.

'See your world, Tathea,' he said softly. 'See what you have done to it! Look at the City in the Centre of it all!'

And before her closed eyes, burning into the vision of her soul she saw the City desolate, the bodies of its dead like an abattoir. And as she watched, the great cisterns exploded and poured water and filth and acid, engulfing the streets and spewing death till it covered everything in a vast stinking tide.

'See Shinabar!' Asmodeus went on. 'See the civilisation that man created out of the desert!'

And into her mind intruded the endless wastes of sand, howling, scorching, devouring all life.

Then he showed her the places closest to her heart, the wild beauty of the Eastern Shore slimed over and drowned in the mud of waves scoured from the depths of the sea and hurled with violence of primordial force to smash and obliterate even the very rocks of the land.

Then he showed her Tyrn Vawr, forcing his will into her heart so she could not blind herself. The city she and Sadokhar had built crumbled on the ground. Thunder ripped around the horizon and gouts of scarlet flame shot into the air; building after building shattered. The land reeled and erupted fire. The earth shook, tearing itself apart. The sound was like a physical beating on the skin. Boulders flew thousands of feet into the air and columns of ash spewed across the sky.

Lastly he showed her Hirioth, its trees burned and withered,

358

branches like limbs in agony, its creatures mangled and broken, frozen in their last terror.

'Behold your kingdom, Ta-Thea!' he said softly. 'It's all yours now. Taste it! Hold it! See what you have done!'

She looked. In every direction there was convulsion and ruin, and thick darkness covered the face of the earth, and all life had perished. The sun was blotted out and the stars disappeared. There was neither day nor night.

The cold became intense, and she huddled to the ground, clinging to the Book, insensible of time or space, only the chaos around her and the endless, everlasting death. She could see nothing, feel nothing, hear nothing in the blinding impenetrable darkness. Even Asmodeus was silent.

The he was beside her again, his hand stretched out to touch her arm. She felt the hard keys of the world in his fingers.

'Think what I could have done,' he whispered, his breath in her ear. 'I would have saved them all! Not to glory, not to Godhood, but to safety: sweet, eternal safety! I told you in the beginning they were not worth your blood or your tears.' His voice went on, probing, hurting. 'I told you they were ugly and shallow, and in the end they would betray all your dreams. But you wouldn't listen. You wanted power and glory and the dominion of God! Well, this is what you have . . . desolation! You are Empress of nothing!'

She lifted her face and peered towards where he must be in the darkness beside her. 'I didn't want dominion!' she said with a passion of contempt. 'I never wanted to rule! I wanted them to have the freedom to fulfil the measure of all they could be, everything they had the courage and the love to reach!'

'Liar!' he hissed. 'You wanted power . . . like everyone! You are the same as I am . . . cut from the same cloth! You wanted to be the one who saved the earth – well, look at it! Look at it, Tathea! This is your earth, your kingdom!'

She heard his laughter in the dark, and it sliced through to the core of her. Could he be right? Was this the end of it all? Was this the eternal night from which there was no dawn, and she had brought it upon the earth?

'Look at your dominion and your glory, Tathea!' he said again. 'Even God Himself has abandoned you. He's gone . . . left it all . . . and you!'

In the agony of her soul she thought of love, and remembered it, remembered Ishrafeli, and Sadokhar and a hundred others, then all the passionate, yearning millions of humanity.

She knew it with an absolute conviction. 'They were not worthless!' she shouted at him in the dark. 'They were good! They were brave and honest and generous of heart. They were wise and funny and kind! It was worth it! And I am not like you! I love . . .' She faced the emptiness of the void around her, the crumbling ruin of the earth. 'It has to be loved, all the aching, terrible, soul-rending beauty of it, all the courage and pity and life. If God will not love it, then I will! I will love it for Him!'

She felt the keys of the world slither from his hand beside her and fall to the ground. Frantically she bent and scrambled in the dark to find them, the Book under her other arm. There was nothing there, only ash and stones. She moved more widely, fingers clutching. Then she closed over them and lifted them up.

'I will love the earth! Even like this!' she promised, all the passion of her life in the cry.

On the far horizon a pinpoint of light appeared, and as she watched, it grew wider like the first rays of a tremendous daybreak whose shafts fell on the keys in her hand. Even as she looked in wonder, they lost their shape, shimmered and wavered in the brilliance, and became a crystal.

The light spread across the arch of the horizon, pure and unblemished and then blazed over the sky in shining splendour. And in the crystal was reflected the endless majesty of the creation of God.

Beside her Asmodeus threw back his head. A paroxysm of agony shook his body, gnashing, grinding his teeth. He screamed in a high, thin wail like all hope lost for eternity, and his body dissolved into a thing of mist and darkness. His feet lifted off the ground. He tried desperately to keep hold of it, flailing, grasping with his fingers, but it fell away and he was flung high into the air. His voice grew faint as he flew ever upward into the void, and the shadows beyond the light, until at last he ceased to be anything at all.

Tathea stared at the earth before her, and saw in it a glory beyond dreaming, never to be lost again. It was filled with the trees and the grasses and the beasts which had made it beautiful, and the wild oceans that had given it breath. And she saw the faces of all she had loved from the beginning, restored to an everlasting life. They shone with a radiance of joy: Sadokhar, Sardriel and Elessar, Ardesir, Tornagrain and others from centuries gone, Sanobiel, Tugomir, Alexius, Eleni. And Maximian was there too, and Immerith of the Flamens. Not one was missing.

Among them was a youth with dark, shining eyes and features so like her own it tore at her memory with a wrenching familiarity, wakening old love and old pain.

Happiness lit inside her as he smiled back at her with the same dancing, burning recognition. Then she knew him! Habi! Her son whole and living again, restored unblemished of heart.

But before them all was Ishrafeli, holding a small, black and white cat with a pointed face.

But it was not yet to him she turned, it was to the One Who stepped forward and held out His hands towards her, and in His face was that everlasting love which she had sought from the beginning, the holiness which lights eternity.

He smiled at her. 'Tathea . . .'

'Father!' she whispered.

He took her hands in His, holding them gently over the Golden Book. 'You have walked the long path, and been willing to pick up My burden and bear it,' He said softly. 'Welcome home, my Daughter, welcome home.'

The Book

Child of God, if your hands have unloosed the hasp of this Book, then the intent of your heart is at last unmarred by cloud of vanity or deceit.

Know this, that in the beginning, through the dark reaches of infinity, was the law by which every intelligence has its being and fulfils the measure of its creation.

When God was yet a man like yourself, with all your frailties, your needs and your ignorance, walking a perilous land as you do, even then was the law irrevocable.

By obedience you may overcome all things, even the darkness within, which is the Great Enemy. The heart may be softened by pain and by yearning until love turns towards all creatures and nothing is cast away, nothing defiled by cruelty or indifference. The mind may be enlightened by understanding gained little by little through trial and labour, and much hunger, to perform great works. Courage will lift the fallen, make bearable the ache of many wounds, and guide your feet on the path when your eyes no longer see the light.

When your spirit is harrowed by despair and all else fails you, compassion will magnify your soul until no glory is impossible.

By such a path did God ascend unto holiness.

But the law is unalterable, and unto all, though the tears of heaven wash away the fixed and the moving stars for you, though God has shed His blood to lave you clean; each act without love, each indifference, each betrayal robs you of that which you might have been. Eternity looks on while you climb the ladder towards the light, but neither God nor devil takes you a step up or down, only your own act.

If it were not so, where would be your greatness at the last? Would God rob you of your soul's joy? Of that day when you stand before Him in eternal life and say not as a stranger but as a citizen, 'I have walked the long path. I have conquered all things. Thou has opened the door for me and I have come home.'

The conversation between Man of Holiness and Asmodeus, the Great Enemy:

363

Asmodeus: I have seen the plan and it will fail because your commandments are impossible. You ask perfection, and it is beyond man even to dream of it. The void echoes with laughter that you mock him, and his arrogance that he could believe you. He cannot do it. From the beginning he will fail. He is blind, and his journey is futile.

Man of Holiness: To be perfect is to do your best, without shadow of deceit or cowardice, without self-justification or dissembling. It is to strive with an honest mind and a pure heart, and an eye single to the love of good. It is not to climb without falling, but each time you fall, to rise again and continue the journey, no matter how hard it may be, discounting the bruises and the pain, the grief and the hope deferred. It is to face the light with courage, and never to deny it. It requires all that a man has, to the height and breadth and depth of his soul, but it does not require more. I give no commandments, except I make a way that they may be accomplished.

Asmodeus: Man will not believe that! He is short-sighted and full of fears. He will drown in the enormity of it. If you were just, you would ask for less. You would make the path easier.

Man of Holiness: Then he would not grow to the measure of his fullness, but be stunted and forever less than his spirit's dream, a bird without wings, a song unsung. I know the joy and the pain of every step, as I know the scars of My own feet. He can do it, if he will.

Asmodeus: That you did it is to him a sound without meaning, a burnt paper in the wind. That journey is not for him. He will burn his soul in the fire of it and then wander lost in the dark.

Man of Holiness: He is My child. Where I have gone, he can follow, and My glory may become his. It is My purpose and My joy that in time beyond thought he may become even as I am, and together we shall walk the stars, and there shall be no end.

Asmodeus: He is weak, and will despair at the first discouragement. But if you were to set lanterns to his path of rewards and punishments, then he would see the good from the evil, and his choices would be just.

Man of Holiness: They would also be without virtue because he would do good for the reward it would bring him, not for the love of good, and eschew evil because it would hurt him, not because he understood its ugliness and his soul was sickened by it. The path of life would divide only the foolish from the clever, not the righteous from the wicked. At the end, when judgement dawns white in the everlasting day, we would see what a man has done, but not what he is. And before I give him his place in the houses of eternity it is not his acts in the noonday, nor in the secrecy of the night, that I must prove, but the desires of his soul, because that is what he will fulfil when he holds My power in his hands to create worlds and dominions and peoples without end.

Asmodeus: He will never do that! The dream is a travesty! Give him knowledge, a sure path. He will never be god, but he will be saved from the darkness within him.

Man of Holiness: If I save him from the darkness, then I also make the light impossible. An unknown path will test his faith. If he will begin, I shall be a guide to his feet. My arm will protect him and My spirit will go before him. As he seeks, I will give him a gift, a portion at a time. I shall bless him and cause miracles in the bright wake of his belief in My word.

Asmodeus: After! Cause them before, and you will create his belief!

Man of Holiness: Miracles to the unbelieving create awe, and sometimes obedience, for a little space, then they are forgotten. They are reasoned away and man forgets Me, or else he becomes superstitious and seeks after signs to prove and to test Me. That is not faith, nor is it honour, nor yet love. It is not the courage to walk the untrodden path and face the terrors of the night, because his heart has heard My voice and will follow it for ever. If he will show that trust in Me, and live by every word of My mouth, then nothing within the law of heaven is impossible. No lovely or joyous thing is beyond My power or will to give him.

Asmodeus: And beyond the laws of heaven? What then is outside your gift?

Man of Holiness: Man of Holiness is My name. I am the Beginning and the End. I am God, not for My power or dominion, but because I have walked the long path and I have kept the law, which is from everlasting to everlasting. Were I to break it, creation would rise up in anger and dismay, and I should cease to be God. You think it is power. You have walked and talked with Me, watched My work, seen My face, as I have seen yours, and still you do not understand. It is love . . . it has always been love.

365

I will not rob man of his agency to choose for himself, as I have chosen in eternities past, what he will do and who he will become. Wickedness can never be joy. Even I cannot make it so.

Asmodeus: He will not understand that, and if you tell him, he will not believe it. He is frail, selfish, racked with terrors and delusion, easily discouraged, deceived, and diverted by the moment. He cannot see further than a few days, a few years. He will always sacrifice the future for the present, the bliss of eternity for a little pleasure today. He is brief of remembrance and fragile of understanding. The weaknesses of the flesh afflict him, disease and weariness, appetites that ruin and make dark.

You have given him a body in your own image, but he will defile it! If you give him no hunger, then he will wither and die. Give him desire and he will indulge it until it governs him. It will consume all other good in him. That which should sustain his life or heal his ills will become his master. He will coarsen and become gross, devouring for sensation, consuming without need. He will misuse herbs to give himself illusion so that he may escape the realities you have put there to teach him patience, endurance, and compassion. He will use them to deny the pain you have put in his path so that he may learn truth and understanding.

Man of Holiness: It is part of the soul of man to hunger, as it is the greatest of his lessons to master himself. If he would become as I am, and know My joy, which has no boundary in time or space, then the first and greatest step on that journey is to harness the passions within himself and use their force for good. Without that he has no life but only a semblance of it, a fire-shadow in the darkness.

Asmodeus: Life? The power to beget life he will abuse above all the other powers you give him. He will make of that desire a dark and twisted thing to ruin and torture, to feed his hunger of the flesh and the lust for dominion which corrodes his mind. He will corrupt and pervert, distort its very nature until it grows hideous. He will call dependence, pity, even the exercise of tyranny, by the name of love. Torture of mind and body, destruction and despotism will be justified by that one word alone. More abominations will be committed in your name than in any other.

Man of Holiness: I know it, and My soul weeps. But it must be. The more sublime the good, the deeper the evil that is possible from its debasement. The corruption of love will lose more souls than any other force, and the realisation of it will redeem more, even that which had seemed lost into darkness beyond recall.

Asmodeus: It will not be. Man is riddled with doubt and ingratitude. In his ignorance and impatience he destroys what he holds. Despair walks beside him and whispers to him in the hollows of the night.

Man of Holiness: I give him weakness that he might learn humility, and out of his own failures might find gentleness and pity for others who also stumble. And in that pity he will help, and find a greater love. In his frailties, if he will look to Me, I will make him a giant, and My grace shall be sufficient for all things. I shall consecrate his griefs and his trials to him, that at the last he will know even the depth of the abyss and the heights of heaven which have no end. He will love all the workmanship of My hands because he has walked beside it, laboured with it, laughed and wept with it, and he will cherish it, that his joy may be full even as Mine is full.

Asmodeus: But what you give is arbitrary and unjust! You favour one above another. For some there is happiness, health of body, an abundance of treasures; for others only misery, affliction, and the burden of loneliness. How can an unjust God command respect, far less love? I have heard the prayers, even of the righteous, echo unanswered in the empty caverns of the night.

Man of Holiness: No prayers are unanswered, but many answers are unheard, because man's spirit listens only to its own voice and has not learned to hear Mine. And sometimes the answer is 'no' or 'not yet' because what is asked for will not bring the happiness he imagines. I know him better than he knows himself. I give to every soul that which is necessary for it to reach the fullness of its nature, to know the bitter from the sweet, which is the purpose of this separation from Me of his mortal life. It is a brief span for an eternal need, for some too brief for happiness also. But to each is given the opportunity to learn what is needful for that soul, to strengthen what is weak, to hallow and make beautiful that which is ugly, to give time to winnow out the chaff of doubt and impatience, and fire to burn away the dross of selfishness. The chances come in many forms and oft times more than once.

Asmodeus: He will see it as capricious and unfair, that you love one and hate another.

Man of Holiness: Too often he sees but a short space, and cries in the night, because he is a child. He does not see as I see, who understand him, and love him, and know the end from the beginning. It has been decreed from the birth of all things that I cannot and would not withhold any blessing when a man has fitted himself to receive it by obedience to the law upon which it rests. If I give it to him too soon, he will not understand and he will break it, or let it slip from his grasp at the moment of earning, and virtue will be swallowed up in self-interest and the treasure will not bless, but corrupt.

Without waiting, and cost, there would no longer be the sublime gift of sacrifice, which is the greatest love. There would be only payment, the certainty of an even more precious return. It would end not in holiness, but in destitution of heart.

Asmodeus: Will you tell him of this promise? If you do, he may not believe you. If he does, he will still give, in hope of gain. And if you do not tell him, then you lie, by withholding.

Man of Holiness: I will tell him, as I tell him all things pertaining to his joy. Some will believe, and some will not. Some will give with cold hearts, conscious of their own rectitude, and with an eye to reward, and their payment is dust. But some will give because they themselves know need and have felt hunger and what it is to walk alone, and they would spare another. They understand ways of love, and I shall keep them in the hollow of My hands for ever. Their names shall be upon My lips.

And others will not believe that I am, but in love they have walked My path and I have been beside them though they knew Me not. Their deeds have spoken My name, and when they see My face they shall know Me, and I shall bless them with a great blessing.

Asmodeus: You see man as you wish him to be, not as he is. Give him a religion and he will become a fanatic, a rulekeeper, a guardian of his own soul who preserves the letter of the law and waits for the reward with open hands and a closed heart. He will persecute others in the name of the law, understand nothing, and your name will be an excuse for lies and corruption and torture. Hypocrites will whisper it with a smile, and murder faith and hope as they do it.

Man of Holiness: I know. And if they do not repent, and learn to understand what it is they do, and if they will not then change, their path will lead to the last aloneness, where I cannot follow, and the gulf between us will become everlasting. But if there is not the choice to take the downward road, then the road upward has no meaning.

Asmodeus: You know all that he needs better than he knows himself. Why do you compel him to ask you daily?

Man of Holiness: I teach a step at a time because that is how he learns. There is a season for all things. If I gave him the greater knowledge at once he could not grasp it. Like you and like Me, he must hunger for it, and seek it, and learn by experience, in order to understand not only the nature of its beauty, but also its price. What he gains too easily he will not value, and too often he cannot hold. Time and ease seep it away from him, the first bitter wind freezes his fingers, and his treasure is let go and he cannot call it back.

I do not seek gratitude for My sake, but for his. It enlarges his soul who feels it. It is a thing of joy, unclouded by arrogance or triumph. It is a bond between the giver and the given. Its sweetness lingers in the heart long after the gift is forgotten.

Asmodeus: His words are dead leaves in the wind. Gratitude writes nothing in his heart.

Man of Holiness: There are gifts which are laboured for and earned, and those which are given of grace. All men are responsible for the burden to magnify them with wisdom and humility, and to share their fruits with all, both the loved and the unloved.

The greatest gifts of the spirit are the hardest to bear well: the gift of knowledge, of healing, of prophecy, the power to lead others and share the light. Such gifts define the path for him and he must pick them up, or lay them down. There is no middle way. Once offered, there is no choice but to accept, with all the weight he can bear; or to refuse, and close the door on the journey forward, and sit alone in the night, having set aside for ever what he might have been. All knowledge places on him the right and the responsibility of choice. Then he must walk the path to its final step.

Asmodeus: You speak as if knowledge were there for all. It is not! Some have intelligence, keenness of mind and swiftness of understanding. Others are slow and muddled in thought. Some are tormented by unreason. Millions, like the sands of the sea, labour all their days merely to survive. Philosophy is not in their world. Again you are unjust, a respecter of persons.

Man of Holiness: Each man takes with him into life what he has chosen and laboured for here, in the creation before life. Some have already learned much and need only take the flesh upon them and stay but briefly, even an instant, and return to Me. Some have limitations upon them, disorders of the mortal flesh which dull and confuse the mind. Others call them simple, or deranged. They need no more learning, and they are not answerable for their weakness. They too need no probation, but they live in order to test the patience and the compassion of others. But it is each man's choice whether he will grow or wither, take up My burden, or pass it by.

He will teach others, but before he teaches he must learn. If he lives worthily and seeks My way, I will give him words for the questioner and answers for those who seek. He will tell in response more than he knows, even hidden things, and both will be touched by the light.

Asmodeus: You place an intolerable burden upon those to whom you answer with truth! What if it is too great for them and they cannot bear it? What if they turn aside and seek a softer path?

Man of Holiness: Those who have sought My face and to whom I have spoken as one man speaks to another, and have then turned from Me, will follow their road to its end, which is the eternal darkness, because it is where they wish to be. My heart yearns within Me, My soul grieves, the angels water heaven with their tears, but it is not in My gift to change it, even as I cannot change you. If I were to, I should cease to be God, and chaos would consume the stars. It would be the end of all things.

Asmodeus: Then when you spoke of mercy and love, it was mockery, a hideous farce of pretended light. You knew before he began that he would fail! Over and over he would fail. Sin and error would flow from him like the rivers of the firmament. You begat him for damnation!

Man of Holiness: I know he will sin and make mistakes. He is yet learning. His life in the flesh is a journey, not an arriving. For this reason has My best beloved offered Himself to face all frailty, all pain, and all darkness and loss, that the creation which surrounds us and has kept its holy estate without strain, may grant Him the wish of His heart, which is the eternal life of all the children of My spirit and the workmanship of My hands. Thus even until the last day of judgement before Me, there may be repentance.

But repentance is more than words and more than sorrow. It is understanding the bitter from the sweet, the light from the darkness, casting aside all sin because it is vile to the soul, and loving the light above cost or price. To repent is to change, no longer to desire that which separates from Me, which injures and cramps and withers the soul. When hunger for that change fills the heart of man, then will I give the grace and the power to accomplish it. And

370

when it is done, I will wash the sin from all remembrance, and it will exist no more.

Asmodeus: Repentance takes time and experience. What of those, countless as the leaves of the forest, who will have no time? What of the legions of those lost in wars and famines and pestilence?

Man of Holiness: For them I have decreed a space between the death of the flesh and the last judgement. In that time will be the teaching and the repentance of the dead. No spirit of man ever conceived shall be without knowledge and time to choose all that he will be.

Asmodeus: You ask man to live in hope and faith in that which he cannot see. You give him nothing but words in the air!

Man of Holiness: I will never leave him alone. The night and the day are filled with the spirits of those who love him, who will speak to him in the language of his friend, and in the voice of the stranger who passes his door, whose hands will bless him and whose arms will bear him up when he is weary and broken. Hope is the gift of angels.

Asmodeus: Another gift! You have promised him all manner of gifts and powers if he obeys. If you then withhold them, you break your word. Yet if you keep it, and give him power to perform miracles, then he himself will remove the need for faith, and for the growth you hold to prize above all. The righteous will walk the earth healing the suffering. They will calm the tumult of the elements, create bread out of the dust, command war to cease, and it will do so. And you will be defeated by your own gifts.

Man of Holiness: I will give power to man only as he learns wisdom to use it, and as he understands the purpose of life. And if he misuses it, I shall take it from him again. There is no swift or easy path. The power to feed the hungry, clothe the naked, heal the sick, even to raise the dead, does not bring one soul a step closer to the fire of courage, the purity of honour or the love which is the light of the universe. If it did, then I would do it myself. Man in his frailty and his hope, his blindness and his compassion, already has all he needs to teach the truth, to heal the heart, and to lead the way upward.

Asmodeus: The seeds of contradiction are in your words. If you do not give him power, he will never learn its use; if you do, then soon he will abuse it because he will forget who gave it to him, and in the imagination of his mind he will think it is his own. He will tyrannise and oppress because it is his nature.

Man of Holiness: Real power is to understand the difference between good and evil, to know who he is, and what he desires to be, and then to have such a passion, a hunger, that he can govern himself until he becomes what he wishes, until he has the courage, the integrity, and the compassion he has glimpsed in vision. When he has strength, and can stay his hand from using it, when he trespasses on no man's agency, when he can let go of an injury and forgive, when he loves Me with a whole heart and there is no division in him, then he has real power. And in suffering oppression he will learn the fragility of freedom, and its cost. He will learn to treasure it for others as deeply as he does for himself, knowing that in the end it is the same thing.

Through pain and knowledge of what it is to sin, he will learn to forgive others, as he himself longs to be forgiven. Love is the beginning of all redemption, and no one can love with the infinite passion and tenderness, the laughter and the patience and joy that is My way unless they first forgive.

Asmodeus: Man may forgive when he is weak and knows his own need for mercy, but he will not see another's offence with the same eyes as he sees his own. Wait until he is strong; then it will be far different. Power is the ultimate corrosion of the soul. It is the worm in the night, grown monstrous on its own blood. In the end it will devour all else. Yet without power, he cannot go where you have gone, nor become as you are.

Man of Holiness: The probation of the flesh has many purposes, but none greater than learning to use power righteously, and none more difficult or more dangerous or beset with as many traps and snares for the soul. He must learn to stay his hand, never to trespass on another's agency to choose, no matter how much wiser he may believe his vision to be or how much greater his own light. He may see the path far ahead, and every precipice that hovers on the lip of the abyss, every morass that would suck a man into its bowels and consume him utterly. He may plead and teach, exhort and implore, yet he must not rob another of his right to choose for himself, good or ill.

Love does not excuse. Even I must watch and wait, because to do otherwise would begin the chain of ruin which would in the end destroy heaven itself. There must be opposition in all things; without the darkness, there is no light.

Asmodeus: Man will never understand that! He will not accept loss! It is beyond his concept of morality with its urgency, its blindness to all but the individual and the moment. His small, finite mind cannot imagine so far! The strong will abuse the weak, most of all when the weak believe they love them. They will protect them unwisely, because they glory in their own strength. They will trust their own wisdom above yours. Their pride will not allow admission of error in themselves or in those of their blood or their race.

They will foster dependence because to be needed is the ultimate dominion. They will demand obedience because in it is the illusion of glory. Thus the weak will lean upon the strong, and both will be damned.

Man of Holiness: It is the test of the strong that they should help the weak for as long as that need exists, that their patience should never tire or grow short. They should nourish the young, the tender, the frightened, and the weak until they too become strong and no longer need them. To love is to desire growth, that every soul may reach the greatness of all its possibilities.

Asmodeus: But what of the impaired of body or mind? What of those who are not whole?

Man of Holiness: The impairment is temporary. The limping step of the cripple is to see if the swift will stay his speed and bend to lift him up – if need be, to forfeit the victory of the racer to carry him who is maimed and weary, to guide him who is lost and bear his burden for him. To all I will visit some weakness, in the full tide of life or in the limitations of age. I will test his humility to accept the help of others with grace, and without anger or envy, self-pity or despair.

Asmodeus: He will rail against you when his strength fails him. Man is born to ingratitude. He will let nothing go, except you force him. You will break his fingers before he will lose his grip on what he deludes himself is his. Allow him authority over another and then take it from him, and he will hate his successor. He will hate you also for his pride's sake. He will imagine that to magnify another diminishes him, and that service is a lesser call.

Man of Holiness: I give him earthly power not to exercise dominion, but to minister to his fellows, and in ministering to learn those skills which he does not yet possess, each in its turn, until he has them all. And as he gains each, he must step back and with the patience of love and his greater skill, sustain his fellow while he too learns, and forgive him his errors.

Asmodeus: And is the earth also to forgive? Man in his arrogance will imagine himself its master. He will defile it, corrupt it in his greed and his stupidity, desecrate its beauty for his petty gain, pollute its very life, murder and torture its creatures. Is that too merely experience?

Man of Holiness: The creatures of the earth are Mine also, the workmanship of My hands. In beauty have I formed them, in infinite complexity, each perfect in its sphere, and their innocence is blameless before the judgement of eternity. They have kept their order and have no sin for which to answer, and on the last day it will be well with them. Every bird that flies, every fish that inhabits the oceans and creature that runs or creeps upon the land, every flower and herb or tree of the forest from the smallest to the greatest, whether the span of its life be an hour or a millennium, not one of them is hurt without My knowledge and My grief. I know all things, and they shall not perish from My sight.

For a space the earth is lent to man to be under his stewardship, not in his possession, and he will answer to Me for every stick and stone of it, every leaf, every living thing upon its face, for good or ill. Just as there are those who will ruin and destroy, so there are those who will cherish and make beautiful, those who will love and who will heal, those who will praise and see My hand in all things.

All gifts, all wealth, whether it be of goods or of talents, of health or of intelligence, of wit or laughter or the art to create or to build, or of time itself, are a trust, to see whether they be used with generosity of heart or with meanness, with love or without it, with joy and gratitude and humility, that he return it to Me, rich with the harvest of sharing. And I will magnify it to him into time and eternity without end.

Asmodeus: Then you have to command him in all things, because he will do nothing that does not repay his own need. He thinks only of the day, or the hour.

Man of Holiness: Man who loves, whether he seeks My face or not, will do much without command. He will always be engaged in searching for good. The joy of others will become as dear to him as his own. He will not look upon any man's sorrow without seeking to heal it. I will instruct him in the first thing, and he will find the hundredth for himself. He will rejoice with those who win, and his heart will ache with those who lose and who mourn. Every man will be his brother.

Asmodeus: As long as all is well for him, why should he do otherwise? But what when the earth fails him? What of his care for the weak then, the burdensome, the profitless mouth when there is famine, the sick when there is plague? And there will be, because you have not removed either their foolishness or their greed from them, nor their ability to destroy. Neither have you taken my power from the world. I can still spread rumour with my word and my breath. I can sow hatred and whisper lies, and I can reap the last grain of destruction. I can cover the face of the earth with war until the armies of humanity have drowned the soil with blood, or with disease and deformity in the noonday and madness in the night, until a man knows not the face of his brother and the flesh rots from his bones. I can corrupt nations in the light of the sun, and lead them open-eyed to the grave. And I will! My promise is as sure as yours!

Man of Holiness: I have known you from the birth of time. You too are My son, and I will not take the right to choose even from you. You will be what you wish to be, and the everlasting recompense for that will be yours, as it will be all men's, and has been from the beginning.

Asmodeus: You have not answered me! What of man then, in the day of my power, when his world has crashed about his ears and there is death and despair on every side?

Man of Holiness: In tribulation he will find his greatest strength and his utmost nobility. When he is persecuted, there will be those who will bear it with patience and without hatred, self-pity, or vengeance. There will be those in flight from a monstrous foe who will still return to the very jaws of destruction to rescue the weaker and the slower, though they know him not, who will comfort the terrified and the grieving without thought of self. When there is starvation there will be those who will give their last morsel to feed the stranger, or nurse the dying, though the plague afflicts them also. Where there is tyranny and war there will be those who will offer their own lives for their fellows, and who will look even upon your face rather than deny the good they believe. They will sacrifice all they possess for love of the light they have seen. And those are they who in eternity I shall take to My heart, and all things shall be theirs, even My glory. They shall see the light of the worlds like the risen sun on the dew of the grass. The heavens shall be before them, and they shall understand and be filled with that shining peace which has no end and that joy which is the everlasting laughter of the stars.

Asmodeus: And what of the others, those lost millions who do not seek the heights of courage and sacrifice? Have you no pity, no love for them?

Man of Holiness: For each one there shall be the glory he can abide, the kingdom and the dominion whose laws he is able and wills to keep. In any more, or less, he would find no peace. It can be no other way. When a man leaves his tabernacle of clay for a space, and then at the last is made complete again with a perfect flesh, never more to be divided, he carries with him nothing but the wisdom he has gained, and the nature and desires of his heart. Experience shall make him whole, for good or ill, and that is his treasure, the sum of what he is, which shall never be taken from him.

Asmodeus: Where is the proof for him? You have left in the world no evidence that cannot be disputed a hundred ways. You ask him to walk an unknown path with belief rooted in no more than hunger and hope, a shred of meaning, the cry in the night of a watchman on a tower he cannot see. No echo is left from the time before the veil was drawn over his soul. He will not do it.

Man of Holiness: No man can give to another his faith. It is learned little by little, by accepting the small things, putting to the test one principle at a time. Nourish it with courage and hope, and it will grow until it has the power to divide oceans, or create bread out of ashes, or any other thing that is wisdom in Me. I shall never fall short nor give less, until faith shall become knowledge.

But more blessed is he who trusts Me when he has not yet seen but walks by faith, and with courage. From the first stumbling beginning until that day when he walks upright beside Me and needs no command because he sees all things, I shall ask of him nothing whatsoever, except it be for his eternal good. But he must have the white fire of courage, which defies even the darkness of the pit. It is that virtue without which all others, even love itself, may in the end be lost.

Asmodeus: So much is wasted in your economy. Man is proud, rebellious, and full of doubts, like shadows in the wind, and disobedient to the core. Everywhere he will see waste and pain, futile effort, hope destroyed and trust betrayed. Weariness and disillusion is the common path. Your prize is for the few. Mine would have been for all!

You are bound by the very laws which make you God to allow man his choice! Then let him choose between my plan and yours!

See if he will not take mine, with the lesser reward – and the lesser risk! Not one will perish or lose that which should be his. And the hosts which follow me shall be mine for ever!

Man of Holiness: No good or lovely thing will be lost to those who keep My law and who have loved Me with a whole heart. To no one is My glory impossible. Every man is My child, with My image graven upon his soul. But many will not choose Me, and if they choose you, then they are yours to have and to hold for ever. The morning that he was born of My spirit, I gave him his freedom.

Asmodeus: That was your first and great mistake. On that rests all the others. He is a flawed creature and will never be what you want him to be. He will always betray you in the end.

Man of Holiness: He is My child, even as you are, and I have taken all into reckoning. My purpose cannot be frustrated. I am God, and from the beginning have I known the end.

Asmodeus: The end will be war, and the abomination of destruction! Ruin will cover the face of the earth as the waters cover the sea. When that time comes there will be no more middle ground, no safety for the heart or mind or body, and in terror and despair man will choose me!

Man of Holiness: There never was middle ground, only for a space of sunlight was there the illusion of it, while the thunder of guns was far away. But out of that desolation I will create a new earth, and those who have chosen Me I will welcome home, and they shall be before My face for ever. They shall never again taste fear nor stand alone, and they shall know Me as a man knows his father, and together we shall dance to the music of eternity.

Asmodeus: But why? Why all these aeons of labour and pain, all this waiting and yearning, the making and toiling of worlds, the hope and the failure, the disappointment and the agony of pity, all for a creature who is worthy of nothing? A firefly on the winds of darkness.

Man of Holiness: You do not understand. It is because I love him.

Asmodeus: Is that all?

Man of Holiness: That is all. It is the light which cannot fade, the life which is endless. I am God, and Love is the name of My soul.